MORTAL DILEMMA

A MATT ROYAL MYSTERY

H. TERRELL GRIFFIN

Oceanview Publishing
Longboat Key, Florida

ISBN 978-1-60809-174-4

Published in the United States of America by Oceanview Publishing
Longboat Key, Florida
www.oceanviewpub.com

10 9 8 7 6 5 4 3 2 1

PRINTED IN THE UNITED STATES OF AMERICA

In memory of my friend
Jeanie R. Austin
A Woman of Distinction
1933-2000

ACKNOWLEDGMENTS

Writing, I have come to conclude, requires both passion and dedication. Perhaps, in the absence of passion, there would be no dedication, and the author's story would never be told. I am lucky to have had the passion for writing since I was old enough to begin to understand that there was a person, a writer, behind the stories I so enjoyed. But, alas, I lacked the dedication that is necessary for the storyteller to translate the ramblings of his imagination into the written word.

The reason? I suppose it was my other passion, the law, and that passion was indeed a jealous mistress, demanding all of my time and energy. I still love the law, if not the way it's practiced today, but when I retired from the profession, I found that I had time to engage my earlier passion, writing. With the encouragement of my wife Jean, who'd seen me through college and law school and the many years of trying lawsuits, I embarked on what I term the icing on the cake of my life—writing mysteries.

So now, I offer you, the reader, the tenth book in the Matt Royal series. I hope you will find it acceptable, because you, my friends, are perhaps the most important part of the process. If you didn't read my books, I'm afraid I'd lose interest in writing them.

I am backstopped by friends who read chunks of the manuscript as they come out of the printer. They edit it, make suggestions, give me ideas, and encourage me to soldier on. Peggy Kendall, David Beals, Lloyd Deming, Chris Griffin, and Jean Griffin are my long-suffering teammates whose input always makes my books better. This particular work is in essence the brainchild of Lloyd Deming who suggested the theme of this story. Without Lloyd's input, this book would not have been written.

I am privileged to be one of the many writers in the Oceanview Publishing stable. Bob and Patricia Gussin, the company's founders, lead by example. They are hardworking, talented, and dedicated to publishing mysteries and thrillers. They manage to keep so many balls in the air at one time that it makes me tired just to contemplate it all.

Emily Baar, David Ivester, and Lee Randall find time in their busy schedules to talk to their authors, soothe our frazzled nerves, encourage us, pump up our egos, and lend a hand to any task with which we might need assistance. I miss Frank Troncale who retired last year, but I'm happy to report that his can-do spirit thrives even in his absence.

And while I am these days engaged in my oldest dream, writing, I would be remiss not to mention the passion that underlies it all, my family. My wife Jean, our sons Greg, Mike, and Chris, our daughter-in-law Judy, and our grandchildren Kyle and Sarah are the most precious gifts that any man could have bestowed upon him. They are the collective sun around which my life revolves.

The blood-dimmed tide is loosed, and everywhere
The ceremony of innocence is drowned.

—William Butler Yeats

MORTAL DILEMMA

PROLOGUE

On the first day of November, in a little bar tucked away in the corner of a small shopping center on the north end of Longboat Key, I met the meanest man I'd ever known. Four days later, I killed him.

CHAPTER ONE

THURSDAY, OCTOBER 30

AUTUMN WAS SETTLING over the Florida peninsula, washing away the heat and humidity of the summer. I was chugging along the beach, pounding out my daily four-mile jog as the sun rose over the mainland. The surf was higher than usual, hitting the shore with an energy that was rare for our normally placid Gulf of Mexico. Far out at sea, dark clouds streaked by lightning hung low on the horizon. There was a storm out there somewhere, and the wind it generated was sending the surf rushing our way. If the storm moved onshore, we'd have a nasty day of rain and wind, but for now the sun shone brightly on the beach and the onshore breeze permeated with the smell of the sea tickled my senses. The air was soft and sweet and cool and my mind was full of images of my girl, the wondrous J. D. Duncan. She had been off-island for three days, working a murder case in the little panhandle town of Apalachicola. It seemed longer.

She would be coming home today, starting the six-hour drive right after she and the local law had finished comparing notes. She had not wrapped up the case, but she thought she had made some progress. She said that all she could see were shadows, fuzzy images that she could not quite bring into focus. She had found no clue as to who the bad guys were and she had not come up with a motive for the murder, except that it seemed tied directly to a Longboat Key cold case that she had been looking into, an unsolved murder that had taken place three years before. It was that connection that had drawn her north.

My name is Matt Royal. I served in the U.S. Army, saw some combat, earned a law degree and practiced law in Orlando for a number of years. I tired of the rat race the law practice had become, lost my wife to divorce, sold everything I owned, and dropped out. I moved to Longboat Key, a small island that is ten miles long and half a mile wide at its broadest point. It lies just off the Southwest Florida coast between the small cities of Bradenton and Sarasota, south of Tampa Bay, about halfway down the peninsula. I had accumulated enough money to last the rest of my life if I were careful.

In the fall, which comes late to Florida, the somnolence of our summers gradually gives way to the frenetic energy brought about by the annual seasonal migration of the snowbirds, our friends from the north who winter with us each year. The island population grows exponentially by the week until the end of February when the key groans under the staggering weight of people, signaling the beginning of the height of the season. At Easter, they begin to leave, and by mid-May, when the heat and humidity of the long summer wraps the island like a hot, damp blanket, they're gone, and our key becomes a less interesting place.

But on this late October day, the snowbirds were slipping onto the island, the early arrivals fleeing the snow that was already clogging the roads back home. Every day brought more people into the bars and restaurants and out to the beaches. It was a time to renew the old friendships that waxed and waned with the seasons.

Jennifer Diane Duncan, the woman I love, is the Longboat Key police department's only detective. She had arrived on our island a couple of years before when her mother died and she inherited a condo on Longboat. She'd been a detective on the Miami-Dade police force for twelve years and risen to assistant homicide commander before she decided to give up the fast lane that was Miami-Dade County and move to the relative quiet of Longboat Key. Our chief of police, Bill Lester, had jumped at the chance to hire her. She wormed her way into my affections over the first year she was on the key and we became lovers. She says that's not quite the case, but in reality she felt sorry for me and took me in as anybody with a heart would take in a stray puppy. To be frank, her version is probably closer to the truth.

The murder of a young man in North Florida was the first light to be shed on a three-year-old murder case that had no leads, no suspects, no motive, and not much chance of being solved. Four days before, on a Sunday, she had gotten a call, routed through the Longboat Key police switchboard, from the Franklin County sheriff's office. A twenty-five-year-old man named Jeremy Smithson had been shot the evening before and left to die beside a county road that snaked through Tate's Hell State Forest. A Franklin County deputy patrolling the desolate area found him at sun-up, but by the time Smithson arrived at the hospital, he was near death. He knew he was dying and asked to talk to the deputy who had found him. He didn't know who shot him, but he thought it might have to do with a murder he'd committed on Longboat Key three years before.

A man had offered to pay him ten thousand dollars to kill a woman who was living temporarily on Longboat. He'd get five thousand when he killed her and another five grand at the end of three years if he kept quiet and stayed out of trouble with the law. He took the job, snuck onto the key, shot the woman through the head with a pistol he'd been provided by the man who hired him, and left. He'd spent maybe thirty minutes on the island, tossed the pistol off the Longboat Pass Bridge on his way out, and left no trace that he'd ever been there.

Smithson did not know the name of the man who'd hired him, but he gave the deputy a good description. He'd only seen him once, when he was given the money and the pistol and was told that if he didn't get the job done within the next week, he would be killed.

The dying man asked for a preacher, and told the deputy he was sorry about killing the woman. He knew it was wrong, but he thought Jesus might forgive him and take him into heaven since he confessed his sin, even though it was to a deputy sheriff and not to a man of God. Maybe the deputy could ask the preacher to hurry. He smiled, closed his eyes, and died.

Jeremy Smithson had lived in Franklin County most of his life, and the sheriff knew his family. The boy had been in trouble since his early teens, nothing too serious, but a steady stream of small-time crimes that had once landed him in a juvenile facility and later, when he was no longer a minor, a one-year stint in the county jail. Then he disappeared. The sheriff heard that Jeremy had moved out of state and was trying to turn his life around.

When the sheriff talked to Jeremy's parents about their son's murder, they told him that Jeremy had come up with five thousand dollars about three years before. He told them he'd won it in a scratch-off card game sponsored by the Florida State Lottery. The next day he left home. They heard from him occasionally, but had not seen him since he left. He told them he had been living in Birmingham, Alabama, and working in a bar in a less-than-desirable part of town. He asked that they keep his whereabouts a secret.

He showed up at their door the day before his death, late in the afternoon, and said he'd come for a visit, but that he had to see a man who owed him some money. He'd be back later in the evening. He never showed up.

The sheriff called the Longboat Key police department to inquire about any murders on the island about the time that the young man said he killed the woman. He talked to J.D. who remembered the case. It had happened shortly before she went to work for the Longboat

Key PD and replaced the retiring detective who had investigated the murder.

After she joined the LBKPD, she would occasionally review the file, hoping to find something that the other detective had missed. She had gotten nowhere with the investigation, and it haunted her.

The victim was a forty-year-old woman from Atlanta named Rachel Fortson who was visiting her brother's Gulf-side house on the north end of Longboat Key. She was alone, and had only been in residence for two days when she was killed. The forensic technicians had gone over the crime scene with meticulous care. They found nothing, and searched again, disappointed and puzzled at the total lack of evidence.

J.D. left for Franklin County the morning after the phone call from the sheriff.

CHAPTER TWO

THURSDAY, OCTOBER 30

I REACHED MY turnaround point, a beachfront condo two miles from where I started. I reversed course, slowed my pace, and churned north, my mind racing ahead to my best friend, Jock Algren, who was ensconced in my cottage, drinking himself into oblivion. He'd been there for five days, seemingly intent on exhausting the supply of bourbon I'd stocked when he called me from Beirut, Lebanon.

"Podna," he'd said when I answered the phone. "I'm on my way to the key. It's bad. Very bad. The worst it's ever been. Get the booze laid in. I might be there awhile."

"You okay, Jock?"

"No."

"Jock?"

"I'll see you tomorrow." He hung up.

I'd met Jock Algren on the first day of the seventh grade. I was the new kid in the little town in the middle of the Florida peninsula and I guess he felt it was his duty to challenge me. My family had just moved down from Georgia, and I didn't know anybody in the school. Jock was the most popular kid there and that knowledge gave a kind of swagger to his gait that I, at first, took to be a small birth defect. His popularity seemed to imbue him with certain obligations to the pre-teen society that so admired his athletic prowess and his good looks. Apparently, his duties included intimidation of the new guy.

"Where're you from?" he asked me on that first day of school.

"Georgia."

"Georgia? Nothing but a bunch of fools in Georgia. Why did you move here?"

"My daddy says that when people move from Georgia to Florida, it improves the intellectual level of both states."

That comment would have gone over the head of most twelve-year-old bullies, but Jock's mind was among the best I'd ever met. He immediately understood the insult. "Now I'm going to have to kick your ass," he said.

He swung at me, his fist catching me in the middle of the chest. I staggered backward, regained my footing, and charged, taking him to the ground. I got two strikes into his abdominal area before a teacher pulled me off him.

"What the hell do you think you're doing, Matthew?" the teacher asked, his voice restrained, his anger controlled.

"Nothing," I said.

"Nothing? You just beat up Jock and you say you were doing nothing? You report to detention at the end of class."

"Yes, sir," I said, and walked toward the aging schoolhouse.

When the bell rang to signal the end of detention, I walked into the hallway to find Jock leaning against the wall. He stuck out his hand and said, "You're a stand-up guy. You didn't rat me out."

I shook his outstretched hand. "Didn't need to," I said. "I'd already kicked your ass."

He grinned. "That you did."

And that was the day we formed a friendship that had lasted until now, and would continue until one of us shuffled off this mortal coil we call life. It turned out that we were both the sons of truck drivers who spent way too much of their time lost in a haze of cheap whiskey.

We were both poor and lived in houses that many of the other kids would never deign to enter. I think it was the adversity of our teen years, that hormone-wracked period when young men struggle with coming-of-age issues, that turned us into brothers. It was a time when we clung to our friendship in order to survive personal worlds that were becoming meaner and more restrictive each year. That time of travail and teenage angst cemented a bond that was stronger than blood.

It turned out that Jock wasn't a bully. He was just a guy showing off for a girl on the day he accosted me. He took his defeat at my hands with good nature and never bragged that he could have taken me. Privately, he always told me he was about to roll me off him and give me a good ass-whipping.

Jock used his brilliance to win scholarships to college and upon graduation joined the most secretive agency of the U.S. government, an intelligence group that was so buried in the bureaucracy that it didn't have a name. He became a top agent, a gatherer of information, and when the situation demanded, an assassin.

Jock always kept in touch, but sometimes he would disappear from our lives for weeks at a time. When whatever mission had pulled him away was completed, he would come to Longboat Key to decompress. For a few days, he, J.D., and I would hang out on the beach or the boat and in the bars and restaurants where we were sure to see our friends. He and I would fish and talk and reminisce, and he and my island friend Logan Hamilton would play golf and embarrass themselves with their ineptness. I finally decided that they didn't know enough about the game to be embarrassed, so they were happy as duffers.

On occasion, Jock was called on to do things for the protection of his country that disgusted him, and once in a while, when he did things that were so terrible, so deeply wrenching that he sickened of the death and destruction that he wreaked in the name of national security, he needed what he called *the healing time*. It was those times, when he was almost overwhelmed by remorse, that he would come to my house and drink himself into oblivion. He'd tell me about his latest mission and what he'd done that had seared his soul, and on the fifth day, he'd start sobering up, running the beach, sweating the alcohol out of his system, eating great fatty meals, and visiting with his other friends on the island. By the eighth day, he'd hug J.D. and me, wave good-bye, and head back to his home in Houston to await the summons to the next battle in the terrorist war that had no end.

This time, it was different. We were in our seventh day, and Jock had cracked open another bottle of Maker's Mark before I left for my morning jog. So far, he'd refused to talk about what had sent him into his special hell. This was the worst I'd ever seen him.

Every time I asked if he were ready to talk, he'd say, "Not yet. But soon. I promise." And he would disappear into another bottle of good bourbon. I was concerned, but not yet worried. He'd always pulled out of it before, but I had long harbored the fear that there would come a time when he could not walk back from the abyss. Maybe we were approaching that time, but I had decided to give him another day or two before calling his boss at the agency.

J.D. understood Jock's need to find some solace, and my need to help him maintain, or possibly regain, his sanity, to be the friend who stood close, listened to the horror he had experienced, and let him know that at least someone understood his pain and did not judge him for his actions. J.D. would leave us to work through the healing time, and she, in turn, stood nearby to prop me up as I slogged through the miasma of Jock's life.

I was nearing the North Shore Drive crossover that spanned the dunes, hoping that Jock would be a little better when I got home. I had slowed to a walk when my phone rang.

"Good morning, studmuffin," J.D. said.

"Wow. 'Studmuffin?' Are you a bit randy?"

"Not at the moment, but I'll be thinking about you all the way home. Might help."

"We'll see," I said, my voice surely dripping with hope. "Are you on your way?"

"As soon as I finish up with the sheriff. It'll probably be close to noon. I'll grab a Big Mac and eat in the car. I should be home by six. What are you doing?"

"Just finishing my run. I'm going to check on Jock and then go to The Pub for a grouper sandwich and a beer."

"How's Jock doing?"

"About the same. I'm a little worried about him. He's usually coming out of it by now."

"Has he told you what's bothering him?"

"Not yet, but he keeps telling me we'll talk soon."

"Hang in there. I'll be home by dark."

"Drive safe."

"Bye, sweetie. I love you." She was gone.

CHAPTER THREE

THURSDAY, OCTOBER 30

THE RUN DOWN from Carrabelle in Florida's panhandle had been rough. The sea was unseasonably agitated, large swells rolling off the starboard quarter, the boat yawing, her bow dipping into the waves as she tried to climb the walls of water the stiff wind flung at her. She was constantly pushed toward the shallows that guarded the big bend area of Florida, that desolate part of the state that the tourists and snowbirds never see. The captain had furled his sails early in the trip, and relied on his sturdy little Yanmar diesel engine to push him through the Gulf of Mexico.

The man was a seasoned sailor, knew his boat and trusted her. Still, there were moments during the trip to Cortez when he'd questioned his sanity in heading out into a sea that was so uninviting. But he was under orders, orders that superseded his wants or even his safety. So he sailed on.

On Wednesday morning, just at daybreak, he'd received a phone call from his principal, a shady private investigator from Tallahassee, telling him to go to Cortez and tie up at the Seafood Shack. He would be contacted and given further instructions in the next day or two. He knew the trip involved killing somebody, because that's what he did for a living. He killed people. The name of the doomed person would be part of his instructions. That was it, a milk run, easy as pie, and a lot of money for his effort. The man from Tallahassee had hinted that he would be killing a police officer, a detective on the Longboat Key police department. He would be paid a premium for killing a cop. The sailor knew that a detective from Longboat, a woman, had been in Franklin County investigating a murder and was trying to tie it to a murder that had occurred on Longboat Key three years before. His source in the Franklin County sheriff's office told him she would be finishing up and returning home on Thursday.

He had set sail immediately from Carrabelle, running into the teeth of the storm moving northeast across the Gulf from southern Mexico, beating his way south through Wednesday and Wednesday night. He stayed well offshore, fighting the vicious sea, intent on not being observed. When his GPS system told him he was off Longboat Pass, he turned eastward, hoisted the Mexican courtesy flag, and sailed into the sunrise and under the Longboat Pass Bridge. His boat bore the evidence of a rough crossing, and the flag would indicate that he'd come from Mexico, not the panhandle.

Early Thursday morning, he moored at the Seafood Shack Marina at the mainland end of the Cortez Bridge about two miles north of Longboat Pass. He checked in with the dockmaster, set his alarm clock for three hours, and fell exhausted into the bunk in the boat's bow. He'd rest up and stay ready to complete his mission. He'd been told that he would be there no more than a couple of days, three at the most. Easy money. Make the kill and get out. No sweat.

CHAPTER FOUR

THURSDAY, OCTOBER 30

I WALKED OVER the dunes and up Broadway to my home. Jock was in his bedroom, asleep and snoring. I didn't know if he was sleeping it off, or just catching his breath before digging into the next bottle. I found the one he'd been sipping from when I left for my run, sitting on the kitchen counter. It was three-quarters full. I thought that was a good sign.

I spent the rest of the morning tidying up my cottage, getting rid of the detritus accumulated by a week of bachelor living. J.D. and I did not live together. She had her own condo a mile or so from my house, but we spent more nights together than apart, and I tried diligently to hide from her the fact that I was an inveterate slob.

When I finished with the house, I washed my boat. She was a twenty-eight foot Grady-White named *Recess*, and was waiting patiently at her dock behind my house. I wiped her down, showered and changed, checked on Jock, and walked the two blocks to the old restaurant squatting on one of the choicest pieces of real estate on the key.

It was nearing one o'clock when I walked into the Mar Vista, known to the locals as The Pub. The place was empty except for Anthony, the manager, standing behind the bar, and my buddy Cracker Dix on his usual stool. The tables on the outside deck were full, diners finishing lunch and lingering over their drinks, enjoying the pleasant weather and the view of the bay.

"Hey, Matt," Anthony and Cracker said simultaneously.

"Hey, guys," I said. "Did you get demoted to bartender, Anthony?"

He laughed. "Not yet. Deke called in sick. Sheila should be in soon. You want a drink?"

"Got a Miller Lite and a grouper sandwich?"

"On its way," he said, and disappeared into the kitchen.

"Somebody was just here looking for you," Cracker said.

"Who?"

"Don't know. He just asked if I knew Matt Royal. I told him I did, and he asked where you lived. I didn't tell him."

"You didn't get a name?"

"No. I asked, but he didn't answer. He didn't have much of a personality and what I saw was plain nasty."

"How so?"

"Hard to say, but you wouldn't call him friendly."

"Can you describe him?"

"About six foot two or three, rangy, ropey muscles, gray scraggly beard, deep water tan, wearing one of those sleeveless t-shirts, the kind they call wife-beaters, very dirty jeans, and boat shoes that were falling apart. The t-shirt had the logo of a bar in Panama City on the back."

"You're very observant," I said.

"It's early yet, and I think Anthony is watering down the wine."

Cracker was an expatriate Englishman who'd lived in Longbeach Village on the north end of the key for thirty years. The locals knew the area simply as "the village," and it was the neighborhood that included my home and Mar Vista. Cracker was in his late fifties and, because of his vast network of friends, he knew everything that happened on our island. He was an extremely intelligent man who'd never lost his distinctive English accent, and often regaled us with outrageous stories of his youthful travels around the world seeking hippie nirvana.

"I always get a little nervous when somebody I don't know is looking for me," I said. "He didn't give you any indication as to why he wanted to know where I live?"

"Nope. But it's no big secret, you know. If he asks around enough, somebody's going to point him in the right direction."

Anthony brought out my lunch and the three of us talked about things of little consequence, whiling away the afternoon and drinking a little beer. I was concerned about a stranger looking for my home, but it was probably nothing. I thought briefly about going back to the house to check on Jock, but if anybody was intent on harming me, they'd be very surprised to run into Jock, who is more dangerous drunk than most men are sober.

CHAPTER FIVE

THURSDAY, OCTOBER 30

J.D. DROVE SOUTH on Highway 98, turned east on Highway 27, and stayed on it until it intersected with Interstate 75. She turned south and headed for home. There were shorter routes, but the Interstate was the quickest. It saved her fighting the traffic as she neared Clearwater and St. Petersburg.

She was passing through Gainesville on I-75 when she noticed a low-slung black Chevrolet Camaro following close behind her. She was in the right lane, her cruise control set to seventy miles per hour, the limit on this stretch of road. She kept her eye on the car, waiting for it to pass.

As she got south of Gainesville and was driving on the causeway that crossed Paynes Prairie, the Camaro made its move, crossing into the middle lane of the three southbound lanes, moving up on her very slowly. He seemed to be hanging back in her blind spot. She looked over her shoulder and saw that the car had darkly tinted windows, much darker than the law allowed.

She checked her rearview mirror. Another car, a minivan with New York plates on the front, had slipped in behind her, taking the place of the Camaro, keeping closer to her bumper than was prudent.

The Camaro started to speed up and the right passenger window slid down. She saw a shotgun barrel poke out of the opening. Instinct took over and she slammed hard on the brakes. She heard the squeal of tires behind her. The minivan. The Camaro shot ahead and braked. The shotgun fired, the slug passing over her hood. In the same second J.D. hit the gas and accelerated into the middle lane, winding up the Interceptor engine in her unmarked police car. She was going to ram the Camaro, but the driver must have seen her move into his lane. He accelerated.

J.D. pulled her pistol from the equipment belt on the front passenger seat. She didn't know what was going on, but she was pissed. She would take her shot if she had a chance. She was closing on the Camaro's rear bumper when she felt a hard impact on her right rear quarter panel. The rear of her car was pushed to the left. She steered in the same direction, trying to regain control, but she was hit again in the right rear.

She straightened out the front wheels and found herself headed directly into the low land of the prairie. She slammed on the brakes and fought to bring her car under control. She saw the minivan in her peripheral vision. Its front end had sustained severe damage and it had crossed the berm. It was out of control and was starting to roll over as it continued down the steep slope that defined the edge of the highway.

J.D. had regained some control and turned the front wheels slightly to the left, trying to stay on the shoulder. The brakes were gaining traction on the grass berm when her car seemed to teeter on the decline that sloped down to the prairie. It slid right and began to roll. It turned all the way over and came to rest on its wheels, finally coming to a stop. J.D. took stock of herself. Nothing broken. No pain. She'd have a bruise on her left shoulder where the seat belt strap had dug into her flesh as the centrifugal forces tried to throw her out of the vehicle. The device had done its job and held her in the cruiser.

J.D. let herself out of the car, pushing the crumpled door with her feet. She was still holding her pistol as she ran back toward the van.

The Camaro was nowhere in sight. The van was upside down laying just off the road's shoulder, several feet down onto the prairie. Was the driver part of the attempt to kill her? Was he working with the people in the Camaro? She didn't know, but she had visions of a family trapped in the vehicle. She approached at a run, her pistol still in her hand. As she neared, she saw a man crawling out of the driver's side door.

"Are you all right?" she called to him. "Anybody else in the car?"

The man was beginning to stand upright. She was about thirty feet from him when she saw the pistol he was holding. Her brain automatically assessed the situation. The pistol was a semiautomatic, a nine-millimeter perhaps, or a forty-five. Very dangerous, either way. The man was raising the pistol in her direction. Her brain was telling her to react, raise her weapon, defend herself.

The man took his first shot as J.D. was moving to her left and dropping to the ground, aiming at the man. "Police officer," she said. "Freeze." The man shot again, the bullet kicking up dust a foot to the left of J.D.'s head. She shot him. Twice. In the middle of the chest. In less than a second. He fell and she got to her feet and ran to the man, now lying on his back, his gun still grasped in his right hand. She picked up the pistol by its barrel and placed it on the ground out of reach of the shooter. She checked his pulse. Nothing. He was dead.

She looked into the van. Nobody was there. The dead man had been driving alone. Was he part of the group in the Camaro? No way to tell. She needed the local law to figure all that out.

J.D. pulled out her phone and dialed 911. "This is Detective J. D. Duncan of Longboat Key PD. I've been involved in an incident on I-75 in the southbound lanes near the north end of Paynes Prairie. I shot and killed the driver of one of the cars involved. Please send the highway patrol and sheriff's detectives. The other car involved was a new Camaro, black, very dark tinted windows, Florida license plate.

I didn't get the number. The men in the Camaro are armed and dangerous. It was headed south at high speed about five minutes ago." She hung up before the operator could start asking a bunch of useless questions.

Cars were pulling to the side of the road and several people were walking toward the wrecked van. J.D. held up her badge and called out, "Police. Please back away. This is a crime scene. The highway patrol will be here shortly." They complied.

Her next call was to Chief Bill Lester at the Longboat Key police station. She told him what had happened and assured him that she was okay.

"Did you get an ID on the guy who took the shot at you?"

"No. I didn't search him. I'll let the detectives do that. I don't want to corrupt the scene."

"Good thinking. Are you sure you're okay?"

"Yes, Bill, I'm sure."

"I'll call Matt. You need somebody with you."

"Don't do that, Bill. You know how he is. He'll be on his way up here to take care of me. I don't want that. I'll call him when I have a better handle on what's going on."

Lester chuckled. "Okay, but make it soon. I don't want him to think I'm holding out on him."

"I will. I'm afraid the cruiser is a wreck. I'll rent a car and drive home as soon as I can get away."

"I can send one of our guys up to get you."

"No. Just pay for the rental."

"The department will take care of it. Be very careful, J.D. Somebody's trying to kill you."

"Yeah, I got that," J.D. said, and closed the connection.

CHAPTER SIX

THURSDAY, OCTOBER 30

I GOT BACK to my house at three, carrying a large juicy hamburger and fries from Mar Vista. I heard the shower running when I entered the cottage. Jock was up. A few minutes later he plodded into the kitchen. He'd shaved, but not well. He'd nicked himself several times, and little bits of tissue were affixed to his face in an attempt to staunch the blood flow. His eyes were bloodshot, little ribbons of red running through the whites. "How're you feeling?" I asked.

"About like I look, podna."

"Your eyes are so bloodshot you look like you'll bleed to death if you open them too wide. Here. I brought you some food."

"Thanks." He dug in, ripping big bites off the burger, going at it like a starving man.

"Slow down, Jock. You're going to choke yourself."

He nodded and took a smaller bite. I'd put a glass of water on the table, and he gulped it down. I refilled the glass. "I'm sorry to be such a piece of shit," he said.

I waved the apology away. "You want to talk about it?"

"The thing I value most in this world is your friendship and your opinion of me. Next in line is J.D.'s. I can't lose that."

"You're family, Jock. There's nothing you can do or say that will ever change that."

"But J.D.'s become part of that family," Jock said. "You love her. She loves you, and she's the best thing that ever happened to you. She hasn't lived through what you and I have. I'm not sure she understands our relationship, or how we depend on each other. She may think the whole thing a little odd. And I know she doesn't approve of what I do for a living. I don't think our relationship, hers and mine, will survive this one."

"You know I won't tell her anything you don't want me to."

He shook his head. "She has to know what you know. If you, or we, start hiding things from her, all the relationships start to fray. I won't be a party to anything that causes a rift between the two of you."

"You've been called on to do some terrible things, Jock, and you did them for all the right reasons." And he certainly had. J.D. had shied away from that at first, but she'd come to understand that there's a jungle out there where laws and rules and ethics mean nothing. She came to realize that without men like Jock, the ones who took out the predators, the jungle and the people who thrive there would overtake us all, and thousands of years of civilization would disappear.

"Maybe so, but nobody can condone what I've done."

"Tell me about it."

"Not yet, podna. Maybe tomorrow."

The phone rang. J.D. "Matt, about an hour ago somebody tried to kill me." Her voice had a jittery quality, the sound of great stress.

That hit me like a punch to the chest. "Are you okay?"

"I think so. I killed the guy. The one who tried to shoot me." She told me what had happened on I-75. "I just finished with the statements and the paperwork. I'll be home in a couple of hours."

"Where are you? I'll come get you."

"I'm in a car with an Alachua County deputy. He's bringing me home. My cruiser isn't drivable. We should be there in a couple of hours. I'll come to your house. Is Jock okay?"

"Better."

"See you soon."

"J.D.?" I said, not wanting to hang up.

"Yes?"

"I love you."

"I know. I'll see you in a couple of hours."

I told Jock what had happened. "She's pretty stressed out," I said.

"I'm not surprised. Killing takes a lot out of you. I think a little part of your soul dies with every one."

Jock's tone had a self-pitying element that I'd never heard before. "Are you all right, buddy?"

"Not yet, but I will be. It gets better every day. Time to stop the boozing."

I was relieved. That was always the sign that he was better, that whatever had caused his pain was receding into the recesses of his memory. "Glad to hear it."

"You got another problem headed your way. J.D.'s going to need all of your attention for a few days. She's not as tough as she wants everybody to believe."

I laughed. "I know, but I'd never let her know that I know. She'd chew me up and spit me out."

"Hold her close, podna. She's the best part of you."

We talked for another hour or so, reminiscing about our high school days and the girls we'd loved, or maybe just lusted after. We talked about J.D., and Jock tried to allay my fears about what her near-death experience would do to her. We did not mention his recent experience, whatever it was.

Finally, as the sun lowered itself toward the Gulf's surface and the clock neared six, I heard a car pull into my driveway and saw an Alachua County sheriff's cruiser come to a stop. "J.D.'s here," I said.

"I'm going back to bed," Jock said. "You take care of your woman."

"She'll want to see you."

"Not right now. She'll need you to herself. You take good care of her or I'll have to kick your ass again." He was grinning. A good sign.

"Again?"

"Yeah. You know, like that time in the seventh grade."

I laughed. "You're still drunk. I'll wake you for dinner."

"Nah. The hamburger did the trick. Let me sleep."

CHAPTER SEVEN

Thursday, October 30

I was standing at the front door as J.D. got out of the cruiser and walked toward me. She half-turned and waved at the deputy as he backed out onto the street. She looked a little deflated, somehow diminished, not quite the J.D. I saw every day. There was an absence of the confidence she always exuded.

I backed into the room and held out my arms. She came quickly to me and I enfolded her. She kicked the door closed and began to cry, sobs wracking her body. I said nothing, just held her quietly, letting the pain and fear leach out of her. I knew she'd been holding it all in, intent on not showing weakness to her law enforcement colleagues. She was tough, but like most of us, a soft core lurked beneath the armor.

Minutes passed. "Let's sit," she said, and I led her to the sofa and held her some more. The sobs stopped and then the tears, and she slowly came out of the darkness. "Sorry," she said. "I didn't expect that."

"You're home now. Safe. Want to talk about it?"

"There's not much to talk about." She gave me more detail on the crash and the shooting. "I was so scared when that bastard pulled his gun. I thought I was dead. He missed with the first two shots and I killed him before he had time to fire again."

"You did good."

"Yes, but I killed a man."

"A man who was trying to kill you."

"Still, he was a human being."

"Barely. Did you find out anything about him?"

"Alachua County is still investigating, but the fingerprints identified the guy. He was released from prison in Georgia two weeks ago after serving twenty years on a murder charge."

"This wasn't his first rodeo," I said.

She laughed. "I guess not. But it turned out to be his last."

"You'll be all right."

"I know. This isn't the first time I've killed a bad guy, but it never gets easier."

"It's not supposed to."

"I don't know how Jock does it," she said.

"Every kill takes something out of him. He may be finished. I've never seen him like this."

"Where is he?"

"In his room. Sleeping. He was still drinking this morning, but he says he's done with the booze. We'll see."

"What happened to him this time?"

"I don't know. He won't tell me. He said he was afraid it was so bad that you and I wouldn't be able to accept it. He's afraid he'll lose us."

"That won't happen."

"I told him that, but I'm not sure he believes me. He said he might tell me about it tomorrow. Are you hungry?"

"Famished. But I don't want to go out."

"Pizza?"

"Sounds just right."

"I'll call Oma's."

* * *

We ate the pizza and talked some more. J.D. seemed to revive a bit, maybe from the conversation, but more likely from the food and a glass or two of her favorite white wine. "Feeling better?" I asked.

"Lots. I need a hot shower and a little snuggling and I'll be good as new."

I grinned at her, trying for a leer. "Snuggling? Anything else?"

"Maybe. Let's see what comes up." She leered back at me. Really.

CHAPTER EIGHT

FRIDAY, OCTOBER 31

I WOKE AS the light of the false dawn seeped into our bedroom. A new day, Halloween, All Hallows' Eve, a time for pint-sized ghosts and goblins to roam the neighborhood seeking treats in return for not trashing your property. I'd laid in a supply of candy to keep the urchins at bay. It was one of my favorite evenings of the year.

J.D. was balled into a fetal position on her side of the bed, her back to me. I slipped out of bed, dressed in a pair of sweatpants and an old t-shirt, and tiptoed into the kitchen. An envelope addressed to me was propped against an empty coffee cup on the counter. The handwriting was Jock's.

I opened it and pulled out a note that read:

> *Got to go, Matt. J.D. needs you and I'm doing fine. I'm off the booze and ready to get back to the wars. I'll check in with you in a couple of days. Take care of our girl.*
>
> *Jock*

I checked his bedroom. Empty, the bed made, toilet articles gone. Most of his clothes were in the closet, but those were the ones that permanently hung there awaiting his visits. His rental car was missing from its usual parking space. Jock had left the island.

I was worried that he'd left too soon, gone before he'd healed. I suspected that his reasons for leaving had a lot more to do with J.D.'s need to spend a few days recovering than with his complete rejuvenation.

I called his cell. It went straight to voice mail. I left a message. "Jock, call me."

I made coffee, scrambled some eggs, put bacon in the pan, and popped bread into the toaster. The aroma of frying bacon would bring J.D. out of her slumber. I wanted to talk to her about Jock.

It didn't take long. I heard her stirring in the bedroom and a few minutes later she came into the kitchen and kissed me on the lips. She tasted of toothpaste and sleep. She pulled back and looked at me. "I feel so much better. Last night was just what I needed."

"Glad I could help."

She grinned. "I was talking about the shower."

"Oh."

She hugged me again and whispered into my ear. "You helped, too, sugar. Is Jock up?"

"Jock's gone."

She pulled back. "Gone? Where?"

I handed her the note. She read it. "Did he leave because of me?"

"Not entirely. He's pretty screwed up about his last mission. I don't know what happened, but it must have been terrible."

"Is he ready to go back to work?"

I shook my head. "I doubt it."

"Did you call him?"

"Yes. Went straight to voice mail. I left a message to call me."

"I don't like this. Should we call his boss?"

"Not yet. Let's give it a day." Jock's boss, Dave Kendall, was the director of the agency with no name. He'd recruited Jock into the group and had been his friend and mentor. As Dave rose in the ranks, he had heaped more and more responsibility on Jock. When he became the director, he gave Jock direct access to the president of the United States, the only agent with that privilege.

Kendall also understood that J.D. and I were Jock's only family, and after a lot of bureaucratic rigmarole, had cleared us both to know anything Jock cared to tell us about his job and his missions. He also knew about the cleansing times and what they entailed. It wasn't needed often, and when it was, a week or so was all it took to get Jock ready again for the wars he fought all over the world.

"Will Dave tell us what happened on Jock's last mission?" J.D. asked.

"No. Our deal was that Jock could tell us whatever he wanted, but Dave would keep everything confidential. I think he wanted to give Jock complete discretion about what we're told and what we're not."

"I guess that makes sense. What do we do now?"

"We wait to hear from Jock. Let's eat."

* * *

Bill Lester, the Longboat Key chief of police, called a little before eight. "How's my detective?"

"She's fine, Bill. Getting dressed for work."

"Is she ready?"

"I tried to talk her out of it, but you know J.D."

"I do indeed. Tell her to take the day off. She's going to be on administrative leave for a few days until the Alachua sheriff sorts out the shooting yesterday."

"I think I'll let you tell her. Can't you put her on desk duty or something?"

"I could, but I don't think I'll be able to keep her there."

"I think she needs to be busy. Can't she work the panhandle cold case from her desk?"

"I don't see why not, Matt. Let's give it a try. I'll talk to her when she gets in."

"Bill, keep an eye on her. She's pretty fragile right now, but she's not about to admit it."

"I'm not surprised. I'll call you if anything starts to go sideways."

CHAPTER NINE

FRIDAY, OCTOBER 31

THE GRIZZLED SAILOR sat in the cockpit of his boat reading the morning's edition of the Sarasota newspaper. The front-page story was about the murder attempt on the Longboat Key detective. He was pissed. What was going on? Who was trying to kill the bitch? Why? He didn't understand and couldn't figure out who was pulling the strings. Oh, well, he thought. Not his problem. He had a mission and he was determined to complete it. His life depended on it.

He re-read the article, searching for some clue. There was nothing. Just the bare bones story, the kind the new breed of reporters write, bereft of important facts and proper English. He knew the papers were in financial distress, but thought that maybe if they hired competent reporters they'd sell more newspapers.

He folded the paper and dropped it in a trash can next to the patio at the Seafood Shack. He walked on, crossed Cortez Road, and slipped into a booth in a waterside café. Time for breakfast.

* * *

J.D. walked into the usual morning bustle of shift change at the police station at mid-key. Activity stopped and many of the officers crowded around, offering support, making sure she was okay. Most just stood silently, letting J.D. know they cared about her. She nodded, thanked them for their concern, and made her way to the chief's office.

Bill Lester looked up from the document he was perusing. "Hey, J.D. You doing okay?"

"I'm fine, Chief."

"Glad to hear it. You know I've got to put you on desk duty until the Alachua sheriff clears the shoot."

"I was hoping that wouldn't be necessary, given the circumstances."

The chief waved his hand. "You know how it goes."

"I do. What do you want me to do?"

"I want you to sit at your desk and work on the Rachel Fortson case. See if you can tie the kid up in the panhandle to somebody who wanted her dead, somebody desperate enough to pay that idiot five grand to kill her."

"What if I need to do some legwork?"

"If you can't do it from your desk, get Steve Carey to help you."

"Okay. How long do you think this is going to take?"

"A week, maybe. Hopefully less."

"I'll talk to Steve," J.D. said as she left the office.

She spent most of the morning on paperwork. She had to bring the Fortson file up to date on her activities in the panhandle and fill out more forms about the shooting. She emailed them to the Alachua County sheriff's office to supplement what she'd told them the day before.

J.D. dialed dispatch and asked where Steve Carey could be found. He was a young patrolman with whom she had worked in the past. He was a good-natured guy with a quick mind and an intuitive sense of how to solve a mystery. He'd be a detective someday, probably on a bigger force than the Longboat Key Police Department.

He called her a few minutes later and said he'd come to her office as soon as he finished a meeting with an elderly lady who had called to complain about hearing people in her attic. It was a call that one or another patrolman answered every few weeks. The big problem was that the lady didn't have an attic, but every time the call came in, a cop responded and assured the woman that she was safe. She was always happy and a little less lonely when the officer left. It was the island way.

When Steve arrived at her office, J.D. handed him the Fortson file. "I'm going to be stuck at this desk for the next few days because of the shooting. The chief said I could use you for legwork on this case. You up for it?"

"Sure," he said with a grin. "I get to work with the world's greatest detective and learn some of her secrets of deductive reasoning."

J.D. smiled. "I deduce that you think flattery will work on me. You're right. It always does."

"Good. We're on the same page. What do you need first?"

"Right now, I'd like you to familiarize yourself with the file, see if I'm missing anything. I interviewed everybody I could up in the panhandle, but some of them wouldn't talk to me. When the chief cuts me loose, I'll probably head back up there."

"Do you think the shooting yesterday was connected to this case?"

"Probably. I can't think of any other reason for somebody to try to kill me. You might see what you can turn up on the dead guy. Alachua County is looking into him, but it won't hurt to have a second set of eyes on him." She gave him another file with all the information she had on the attempt on her life.

"Are you okay, J.D.?"

"I'm fine." Her voice was a little tight, like she was tired of hearing the question.

"Sorry."

J.D. softened. "Thanks for asking, Steve. I'm glad people care enough to ask about me, but I'm doing okay. And I'll be better tomorrow. This isn't the first time I've killed somebody."

"They say it never gets easier. Anything I can do, you just holler."

She smiled. "Thanks, Steve."

CHAPTER TEN

FRIDAY, OCTOBER 31

AFTER J.D. LEFT for work, I puttered around the house for an hour and then went for my morning run. I was concerned about J.D. going back to work so soon, but maybe it was best to keep her mind busy on her cases. I was hopeful that the mandatory investigation of the shooting would be completed within a couple of days and she could become engaged fully in her work. The horror of her near-death experience and the fact that she'd taken another human being's life would begin to fade, and soon, I'd have my girl back.

As I was nearing the end of my run, my phone rang. The caller ID was blocked. I answered.

"Matt, Dave Kendall."

"This can't be good news."

"Bad news? I don't think so. Is Jock with you?"

"No," I said. "He left this morning."

"Headed home?"

"He didn't say. I don't know where he was going, but I don't think it's Houston. He just took off without saying anything. He left a note."

"What time did he leave?"

"J.D. and I went to bed about nine o'clock, I guess. He was here then, and gone when I got up about six this morning."

"Shit. He's not answering his phone. Goes straight to voice mail."

"Same thing happened to me," I said. "Don't y'all have one of those tracking devices on his phone that'll tell you exactly where he is?"

"Yeah, but he knows how to disable it. When he didn't answer his cell, I got the printouts on his phone. The last time it pinged us was about midnight. He was at the Tampa airport."

"He must have left here shortly after we went to bed. Do you have the license plate number on his rental?"

"Yes. According to what we've found out, he turned the car in to the rental company about the time he disabled the tracking device. I was calling you in hopes that something had gone wrong with the electronics and he was still hanging out with you."

"Not likely."

"No, but before I loosed the dogs I wanted to make sure he'd truly gone. What kind of shape was he in last night?"

"Better than in the last week. He said he was finished with the booze and would be back at work in a few days. I didn't really believe him, though. Whatever he was involved in put him lower than I've ever seen him. Can you tell me what happened?"

"Sorry, Matt. I can't. He'll have to be the one to tell you."

"What are you going to do about finding him?"

"I just got a list of all the flights leaving Tampa after midnight. We'll check the passenger manifests against Jock's aliases, but if he's trying to hide from us, he'll use one we don't know anything about."

"What else?"

"We'll hack into the airport security cameras and see if we can spot him. He'll know about those, so he might be able to figure out a way to dodge them."

"Will you keep me posted, Dave?"

"I will. I'll get back to you within the hour with what we find."

I cut the connection and called J.D. "I just got off the phone with

Dave Kendall. If you can come by for lunch, I'll have it ready and fill you in on what Dave had to say."

"I'll see you at noon. You've got half an hour to get it ready. It better be good. I'm bringing a guest."

"Who?"

"Your buddy. He stopped by to see how I was doing. He's talking to the chief right now about fishing."

"Logan doesn't know anything about fishing."

"A lack of knowledge never stopped Logan from talking about any subject."

"Right." I hung up, jogged home, and after a quick shower drove the two miles down the key to Harry's Deli and bought our lunch. I had not told her I'd make the lunch, just that I'd have it ready.

* * *

Logan Hamilton, my best friend on the island, was a financial services executive who'd made a lot of money and retired early. He once said that the reason for his early financial success was the karmic need for someone to show up on Longboat Key and take care of Matt Royal.

Logan and Jock had become close over the years, and when Jock was going through one of his cleansing times, Logan stayed away until Jock was ready for some carousing. Logan was of the opinion that he was a better carouser than I, and would therefore be of more use to Jock after the cleansing had been completed. Logan was at least half right. He could carouse better than anyone I'd ever met.

Over lunch, I brought J.D. and Logan current on Jock's disappearance.

"Have you checked to see what flights were leaving at that time of night?" Logan asked.

"No," I said. "Jock's boss, Dave Kendall has that and is checking to see if Jock took any of them. He will know what aliases Jock has access to, so it'll be easier to figure out where he was headed. But Dave told me that Jock probably had an alias that the agency wouldn't know about."

"What do you think he's up to?" J.D. asked.

"I'm afraid to think about it," I said.

J.D. reached across the table and took my hand. "You have to think about it, Matt. You know him best. He's in trouble. He's never been this depressed before, and I don't think he just left for the heck of it. He cut off communication with you and his agency. We need to find him."

"I know," I said. "I know. I'm afraid he's going off somewhere to die."

"That's a pretty radical thought," Logan said.

"I've been worried about this for years. I've always been afraid that the day will come when he can't escape the specter of self-loathing that haunts him, and whatever draws him closer and closer to the edge will finally consume him. That'll be the end for Jock. He'll slink off like an elderly pet who somehow knows it's time to die and wants to find a secluded place to wait for the end."

"Do you think that's what Jock's doing?" J.D. asked.

"I hope not. Maybe he's just giving us the space he thinks we need."

"Then, why the secrecy?" Logan asked. "And why cut off communication with Kendall?"

"There's that," I said. "And that's what worries me."

CHAPTER ELEVEN

FRIDAY, OCTOBER 31

J.D. WAS ON her way back to the station when Steve Carey called. "Peter Fortson, the brother of our victim, is on the key if you want to talk to him."

"Good detecting. How did you find that out?"

"I called his house and he answered the phone."

"You'll go far in this business. What reason did you give him for calling?"

"I told him we'd reopened the case and would like to stop by and discuss it with him. He said to come anytime. I thought now might be a good time."

"I'm less than a mile from his house. I'll meet you there. Don't mention this to the chief. I'm supposed to be on desk duty."

"I doubt that he believes you'll stay in your office."

"Nevertheless."

"Yeah. Got it."

* * *

The house was large, with an expansive view of the Gulf. It was set back from Gulf of Mexico Drive and separated from the road by a small jungle of native plants. The house had been built before the rules requiring certain setbacks from the beach had been implemented, so it abutted the sand, with only enough room for a small swimming pool between the house and the low dunes.

J.D. parked in the driveway and waited for Carey. He pulled up in a cruiser within minutes and they approached the house together.

A middle-aged man wearing shorts, t-shirt, and flip-flops answered the door. "Come in," he said. "I'm excited that you're reopening this case."

J.D. introduced herself and Officer Carey. "Actually, it's never been closed. We just haven't had any leads in the past three years. Not until now."

Fortson led them into the living room. The three of them took seats and J.D. told him what she'd learned in the panhandle.

"So," Fortson said, "you know who killed my sister."

"We do," J.D. said, "but he's dead. I don't think he just up and decided to drive to Longboat and kill a woman he didn't know. Somebody paid him five thousand dollars to do it, and I want to know who that was."

"How can I help?"

"I want to go over a number of things that you've already given us. Back when the murder first happened. I've read the transcripts and the reports, but I'd like to start from the beginning and see if what you know might bring this new information into sharper focus."

"I don't think I understand."

"I'm working with a lot more information than the detective who interviewed you three years ago had. I'm hoping that something you can tell me might add to what I know now. The other side of that coin is that the new information I gathered from the sheriff in Franklin County might help me think of questions that weren't asked before."

"Okay. Fire away. Some of what I have to say might be a little fuzzy. May I see the transcript of my earlier interview?"

"I'm sorry. I don't have that with me. Can we proceed?"

Fortson shrugged.

"Do you still live in Orlando?" J.D. asked.

"Yes. Windermere."

"What do you do for a living?"

"I dabble."

"In what?"

"Real estate, stocks, bonds, that sort of thing."

"How long have you been doing that?"

"All my adult life."

"What is your age?"

"Forty-six."

"So you were about three years older than Rachel."

"Almost to the day."

"Do you have any other siblings?"

"No. It was just the two of us."

"Any other family?"

"No, my parents are dead. There are some distant cousins whom I really don't know."

"Windermere's pretty pricey real estate. So is a Gulf-front house on Longboat Key. You must do pretty well with your dabbling."

"Pretty well, but you probably know that I've got a substantial trust fund."

"Tell me about it."

"My grandfather made a lot of money in Orlando real estate. He left it all to his only child, my dad, in a trust that was divided between my sister and me at my father's death."

"Do you have any idea why someone would want your sister dead?"

"No. She was a sweet woman."

"Did she live in Orlando?"

"No. She lived in a condo in the Buckhead section of Atlanta."

"Did she work?"

"She didn't have a job, if that's what you mean. She volunteered for several charities, served on their boards, gave them lots of money, that kind of thing."

"Why was she here in Longboat when she was killed?"

"She'd been through a rough time. She was ending a ten-year marriage and the legal process had drained her. Did you know that in Georgia divorces are tried before a jury? It was brutal, but the jury didn't give her husband anything and the judge restored her maiden name. The divorce was final and she was a basket case. I suggested she come down here and lay on the beach for a couple of weeks."

"Do you think her ex-husband had anything to do with her murder?"

"I doubt it."

"Why? He'd seem to be a reasonable suspect."

"Two reasons. He's a quiet type, an academic, a college professor. I just can't see him as the murderer. Secondly, he couldn't get his hands on five thousand dollars to pay a hit man if his life depended on it."

"Do you know if he's still in Atlanta?"

"As far as I know. I haven't seen him since Rachel's funeral."

"Ever talked to him?"

"No."

"I gather that Rachel didn't have children."

"Right. Neither she nor her husband wanted them."

"What happened to her marriage?"

Fortson scoffed. "Coed-itis."

J.D. smiled. "He started fooling around with his students."

"Yeah. Rachel put up with it for a while, but finally gave him an ultimatum. Quit screwing around or get a divorce."

"He didn't stop."

"No. I don't think he could. It was an addiction. I thought it had to do with power. He could cajole the twenty-year-old students into his bed. He was a good-looking guy and the girls thought he was some kind of genius. He also controlled their grades, so they were easy pickings."

"What did he teach?"

"Humanities."

"But you don't think he had anything to do with Rachel's death."

"No."

"What about the coeds?" J.D. asked.

"What about them?"

"Could one of them have been involved in Rachel's murder? The scorned lover? Jealousy?"

"I guess it's possible, but I doubt it. None of those romances lasted beyond the semester. He taught at a community college and every girl that Rachel told me about was finishing her second year. She'd be moving on to a university or into the job market. I doubt that he ever saw them after they left. He'd lost his control over them and there were always classes full of coeds coming along."

"What happened to Rachel's trust when she died?"

"The trust was set up so that each of us benefitted equally. It also funded a life insurance policy on each of us. We were the beneficiaries of the each other's policy, so when Rachel died, I got the proceeds from her policy. I also became the sole beneficiary of the trust."

"Do you have any children?"

"No. And I'm not likely to have any. I'm gay."

"So, what happens to the trust when you die?"

"It all goes to charity."

"What was the face amount of the policy?"

"Five million dollars, and my income from the trust doubled. I think I know where you're going with this. All that money must seem like a motive, but I assure you I didn't need any more money than I already had. I think the detective who was originally assigned to this case looked into that issue quite thoroughly."

"Enough to satisfy me," J.D. said. "His report is very detailed."

"Glad to hear it. The insurance company ran me through the wringer looking for an excuse to deny the claim."

"They always do that." J.D. looked at Steve. "Do you have anything, Steve?"

"No. I think you covered it."

She turned back toward Fortson. "Thank you for your time, Mr. Fortson. By all reports, your sister was a wonderful woman. I hope we can find the person who set this up. I'll keep you posted."

CHAPTER TWELVE

FRIDAY, OCTOBER 31

DAVE KENDALL CALLED as I was cleaning up the kitchen. Logan had left shortly after J.D.

"This is kind of strange," Dave said. "Jock left Tampa on a flight to Miami. He was traveling under his own name, and to make sure we didn't miss something, when he got to his gate, he held a piece of paper up for the security camera that had 'Miami' written on it. He was grinning and looked sober as a judge."

"Did he actually take the plane to Miami?"

"We looked at the security camera tapes from the Miami airport. We saw him leaving the jetway at a little after one o'clock this morning."

"Any rental cars, credit card use, that sort of thing?"

"Nothing. At least not under any of the aliases we know about. He's disappeared completely."

"Thanks for the update, Dave. I don't know what he's up to, but it can't be good."

"Let me know if you hear from him."

I finished in the kitchen, chewing on what Dave had told me. I couldn't come up with any reason for Jock to go to Miami. I was concerned that he'd used that as a transit point. He would have complete identification documents, including a passport, in a name nobody knew about. He could have used those to go anywhere in the world. For the first time that I could remember, I had no way to contact Jock, and no idea where he was.

I spent an hour sitting on my patio overlooking the bay, trying to puzzle out where Jock might have gone. Something on his last mission had affected him more than anything else he had experienced in a twenty-year career. If it was bad enough that he wouldn't even tell me, then it was really terrible. Jock had always teetered on the edge of a crisis of conscience. He was called on to do things that disturbed values that were important to him, but they were things that had to be done to protect the nation he loved. It was these things that built up to the cleansing times that came every couple of years. But this was worse than anything that had come before. This one might be the one to take him out. I couldn't let that happen. But I had no idea what to do.

My phone rang, snapping me out of my reverie. The caller ID was blocked. Probably Dave. I answered.

"Is this Mr. Matt Royal?" A female voice.

"Yes."

"Mr. Royal, my name is Tina Rudek. I'm a social worker at the Lower Keys Medical Center in Key West. Do you know a man named Mark Bailey?"

"Afraid not. What's this about?"

"Mr. Bailey is in our emergency room. He's unconscious and he has a card in his wallet that says that we are to call you in case of an emergency."

That struck me as odd. Jock wouldn't be carrying around a card that told anybody who came across it to call me. That was the quickest way to lead right back to Jock and his real identity. On the other hand, if he wasn't going to be anyplace where he was in danger, he might have carried such a card in case he decided to kill himself. He'd want me to know. "Can you describe Mr. Bailey?"

"He's about six feet tall, probably one hundred seventy pounds, male pattern baldness, dark hair, early to mid-forties."

It was Jock. What the hell was he doing in a hospital in Key West? "I know him. Why is he in the ER?"

"Sorry. I can't go into all that, but I can tell you that his condition is not life threatening."

"Is he drunk?"

She was quiet for a moment and then, almost in a whisper, said, "Very."

"Is he hurt?"

"Not bad."

"An assault?"

"Probably."

There was almost nobody in the world who could take Jock in a fight, even if Jock was as drunk as a gutter alcoholic. It'd be very hard to even shoot him, but that could be done in an ambush. "Gunshot?" I asked.

"Not bad."

"Where?"

"Left shoulder."

"From the back?"

"Yes."

"Have you called the police?"

"We're required to do that under the circumstances."

"I understand. Which agency?"

"Key West PD."

"Are they there yet?"

"On the way. They should be here in a few minutes."

"Okay. You'll be hearing from a Monroe County sheriff's detective named Paul Galis in a few minutes. Would you ask the Key West officers to check with the detective before they do anything? I think it'd be prudent to put a guard on your patient so that nobody slips in and kills him."

"My goodness. Are you serious?"

"Ms. Rudek, this is a national security matter. I'm as serious as I can be. I'll be on my way to Key West as soon as possible."

"I'll need some insurance information on Mr. Bailey."

"Don't worry about it. I'll clear it up when I get there."

"But the hospital needs—"

"Thank you, Ms. Rudek. I'll see you soon and clear all this up." I cut the connection, found a number in my phone's directory, and dialed it.

"Detective Paul Galis." The voice still had the traces of a West Virginia twang.

"Paul, Matt Royal. I need your help."

"Name it."

"Jock Algren is in the Lower Keys Medical Center under the name Mark Bailey. Somebody shot him. I think he's in pretty good condition, but he's dead drunk and he needs a guard on him. Key West PD has been notified and officers are on their way to the hospital. Can you get over there and take charge? I'm on my way down."

"I'll be there in five minutes. You bringing J.D.?"

"Yes."

"Good. See you when you get here."

"Paul, don't blow his cover. I don't know what's going on."

"Got it."

I called my friend Russ Coit. "Jock's in the hospital in Key West. Can Coit Airways fly J.D. and me down there?"

"We've got a plane leaving at your convenience."

"Are you on the island?"

"No. I'm at Misty Creek. Twelfth hole."

"Sorry to interrupt you, but I've got to go immediately."

"Not a problem. Is Jock okay?"

"I think so."

"The plane will be ready when you get to the airport."

Russ was a retired Delta Airlines pilot and owned a six-seat single engine plane that he referred to as Coit Airways. The eight-hour drive to Key West would be reduced to a one-hour flight. I called J.D.

CHAPTER THIRTEEN

FRIDAY, OCTOBER 31

"I THOUGHT THE report on the financial part of this case was very thorough," Steve Carey said, "but I would've thought we needed to backtrack and check all that out again."

He and J.D. were sitting in J.D.'s office twenty minutes after leaving the Fortson home. She smiled. "I plan to do exactly that."

"He'll probably find out that you're replowing that ground. You're going to need subpoenas and that means that whatever financial institution is involved will let Fortson know you're looking at him."

"Exactly. I want him to be a little nervous. If he thinks he's under suspicion, he'll get nervous. If he's nervous, he might make a mistake."

"But you just as much as told him that he's not under suspicion."

"Right. And when he finds out that he is, and that I lied to him, he'll get even more nervous. If he's guilty, his mistakes might open a door wide enough for us to walk through and arrest him."

"Isn't it difficult to get subpoenas in Orlando for a murder on Longboat?"

"It is for a local cop. But it'll be a snap for the feds. They like investigating financial institutions."

"You're going to get the feds involved? How?"

"I'm not sure, yet. I'll think of something."

"Okay," Steve said. "Fortson had plenty of money to hire a hit man, so that gives him the means. His sister was here on the key alone, so that gave him, or his hit man, the opportunity. But I don't see any motive. He had plenty of money, so why would he need the five mil from Rachel's life insurance policy?"

"That's what we need to find out. Maybe he wasn't as rich as we think and he needed the money. Maybe his sister knew some bad stuff on him, maybe they hated each other—lots of possibilities. Money, revenge, and jealousy are the most common reasons for murder. I'm betting the money had something to do with this one. Let's start with the financials."

"Okay, boss. What now?"

"You might as well hit the street. Surely somebody out there is speeding."

Steve laughed. "Yeah. I need to get back to the mean streets and do some real police work."

"I didn't know we had mean streets."

"Think about Gulf of Mexico Drive at the height of season."

"I see your point," J.D. said. "Steve?"

"Yes."

"I'm glad you're helping out on this one. You've got a good head for this stuff. I'll keep you in the loop."

"Thanks, J.D. See you later."

J.D. sat in the silence, thinking about Fortson and the man who tried to kill her not twenty-four hours ago. Was the attempt on her life connected to Rachel Fortson's murder? Had she disturbed a hornet's nest when she was in Franklin County? She picked up the phone and called the Alachua County sheriff. She got right through.

"How're you doing, Detective?"

"I'm fine," J.D. said. "Deskbound for a few days until you get finished with your investigation into the shooting."

"We're moving this as quickly as we can. There's no question that it was a good shoot. Self-defense. We've just got to check all the bureaucratic boxes."

"Thanks, Sheriff. I appreciate your jumping on it. What can you tell me about the shooter?"

"His name was Mabry Jackson. He served twenty years on a second-degree murder charge up in Georgia. Got out about two weeks ago. He had a cell phone in his pocket, but it was a burner bought last week at a Walmart in Sanford, just north of Orlando. The only calls were to a pay phone in a rooming house about two blocks from the Walmart."

"I didn't know they still had those."

"Rooming houses?"

"Pay phones."

"I think there're a few left. I asked the Seminole sheriff's office to check the place out. A detective named Glenn Howell called me back. It seems that the late Mr. Mabry rented a room there. Howell tossed it and found a bank deposit slip. It showed that Mabry had deposited five grand when he opened the account on Monday. The bank officer who opened the account remembered that the initial deposit was cash. Fifty one-hundred-dollar bills. No way to trace it."

"What about the minivan he was driving when he tried to kill me?"

"Stolen from a hotel in Ocala about three hours before the shooting."

"And the Camaro?"

"Nothing. They got clean away."

J.D. was quiet for a moment. "Sheriff, I was coming from Apalachicola on Highways 98 and 27. I got onto I-75 just north of Gainesville. How would anybody have known that?"

"I hate to tell you this, but you were definitely the target. We found a GPS tracker device attached to your car. Whoever was after you must have put it there. We found a thumbprint on it that belongs to a civilian employee of the Franklin County sheriff's office. He works in the equipment room, so we're thinking he probably handled it."

"He could have handled it when he was putting it on my car."

"I thought of that. I've got the sheriff up there looking into it. He's a career lawman and a buddy of mine. He's pretty pissed that one of his people might be involved in the attempt on a cop's life."

"What does the civilian employee have to say about any of this?"

"Don't know. He's out of pocket. Apparently he's on a fishing trip. Left yesterday and is due back on Monday. The sheriff will be on him as soon as he gets back."

"I keep wondering about something. If they knew where I was, I would think a secondary highway like 98 or 27 would have been a better place for an ambush."

"Maybe they thought the Interstate would make for a cleaner getaway."

"Probably. At least now I know it wasn't mistaken identity."

"Are you working on anything that could get you killed?" the sheriff asked.

"Maybe. I've got a three-year-old murder case that's heating up. That's what I was doing in Franklin County. Maybe I got too close to somebody."

"Have you got protection?"

"Yeah. A nine-millimeter semiautomatic."

"I don't want to suggest that you can't take care of yourself, but if you were one of my deputies, male or female, I'd have a full-time guard on you."

"Yeah. My boss is going to want the same thing as soon as he hears about the GPS tracker."

"Take care. I'll try to push this report through by the end of the day tomorrow. Get you out of police purgatory."

"Thanks, Sheriff. I'll be talking to you."

J.D. hung up and Googled the Seminole County sheriff's office's phone number. She called, identified herself, and asked to speak to Detective Howell. She was placed on hold for only a few seconds.

"This is Detective Howell."

"Good afternoon, Detective. This is Detective J. D. Duncan in Longboat Key, Florida."

"How's Matt?"

That took her by surprise. "What did you say?"

"I asked about Matt Royal."

"I'm sorry. Do I know you?"

The voice on the phone was polite, a bit playful. "No, but we have a mutual friend. Manatee County Detective David Sims. He and I were fraternity brothers in college."

"Oh?"

"When the Alachua County sheriff's dctective asked me to look into the late Mr. Mabry, I was told it had to do with the attempted murder of a Longboat Key police detective. He gave me your name. I called David to see if he could tell me anything about you. I got an earful." Howell laughed. "All good. He did say that you and your boyfriend Matt Royal and some kind of shady government figure named Jock had dragged him into some interesting situations."

J.D. had to laugh. "It's a small world sometimes."

"It is. Needless to say, if there is anything I can do on this end, all you have to do is ask."

"I appreciate that, Detective. May I call you Glenn?"

"Please do. Any friend of Sims', etcetera."

"Were you asked to follow up on Mabry?"

"Nothing more than what I've done. I guess the Alachua sheriff filled you in on that. The bank account and all."

"He did. I think the attempt on my life might be tied to a

three-year-old murder case here on Longboat Key. A woman named Rachel Fortson was shot to death in her brother's house on the beach. The crime scene was absolutely clean and we had no leads. The case has just taken up space in a filing cabinet until last weekend when a man up in Franklin County gave a deathbed confession to a sheriff's deputy that he was the killer and had been paid five thousand dollars to do the deed. I spent three days up there talking to people and was on my way home when the bad guys tried to kill me."

"I didn't know that. Is there anything else I can do here?"

"Does the name Peter Fortson mean anything to you?"

"Afraid not."

"He was the brother of the murder victim. He owns the house where she was killed. He's a rich guy, a trust-fund baby who lives in Windermere. I thought he might have made the newspapers for something or other."

"Windermere's full of very rich people. Are you familiar with it?"

"It's an Orlando suburb. On the south side. That's all I know."

"You think Fortson was involved in the murder of his sister?"

"It's possible," J.D. said. "He got five million dollars from a life insurance policy and his sister's share of what appears to be a very large trust fund."

"If he had a big trust fund, I wouldn't think he'd have to murder his sister for money."

"He probably didn't. The detective who worked this case when it happened did a pretty in-depth investigation of that angle, but he didn't actually get into the bank accounts or books of the trust. He didn't have a reason to dig that deeply and it might not have been possible anyway."

"You'd like to see those books."

"I sure would, but I don't have any way to get to them."

"If you do figure out a way, Fortson would probably find out that you're looking at him."

"That's not a problem. I want him to think I'm looking at him as a suspect. It might concern him enough that he makes a mistake."

"Do you think he set up the hit on you?"

"I don't know. I thought it was a bit too coincidental for Mabry to have gotten the same amount of cash that the guy in the panhandle got for the hit on Rachel Fortson."

"Is there a bank involved as a trustee?"

"Yes. The Third National in Orlando."

"Some years back, I had a case that required me to get a look at some bank records. I talked the U.S. attorney into issuing an investigative subpoena for the records. I think it goes easier if the U.S. attorney, rather than the state attorney, goes after a nationally charted bank. If you talk to the U.S. attorney in Orlando, he may be able to help you out."

"Thanks, Glenn. That's a good idea. I know him. I'll talk to him about the records. One of our guys is working with me on this, so if you hear from Steve Carey, he's legit."

"Okay. Tell Matt hello for me."

J.D. laughed and hung up. She looked up a number on her cell phone directory and dialed it.

"David Parrish," the mellifluous voice of the U.S. attorney for the Middle District of Florida answered. His speech carried the light accents of his native Georgia, a honeyed quality that J.D. always found soothing. Probably because it reminded her of her late father, who'd spent his career as an Atlanta cop. "How's my favorite detective and why are you still hanging out with Matt Royal?"

J.D. laughed. "I'm fine and I'm trying to find a new man, but it's difficult. Too bad you're married. I'm calling to see if you can help me on a case."

"You know I will if I can. What's up?"

She explained the Fortson case and told him about her need to see the bank's books on the two trusts, particularly those that cover the time of Rachel's death. "I'd also like to see what his trust was doing for a year or two before her death and how he's handled the money since."

"Since it's a murder case, and possibly involves fraud on a federally insured financial institution, I think we can legitimately issue an investigative subpoena without going before a judge for a search warrant. How soon do you need it?"

"Yesterday."

He laughed. "It's too late to do anything today. Banks keep banker's hours, you know. How would first thing Monday morning work?"

"That'd be great. Thanks."

"Tell Matt hello."

She clicked the off button and was putting the phone back in her pocket when it rang. Matt. "We're going to Key West. Leaving on Coit Airways as soon as you get home and throw some stuff in a suitcase. Jock's in the hospital down there. I'll tell you about it on the way. I need you here as soon as possible."

"Leaving now. Pick me up at my condo."

CHAPTER FOURTEEN

FRIDAY, OCTOBER 31

IT WAS NEARING seven o'clock as we started our final approach to Key West International Airport. The sun was sinking into the Gulf and the lights in town were winking on, providing the festive air that defined this little town at the end of the continent. A cruise ship, aglow with colored lights that painted the sea in bright colors, glided out of the port. The small island was alive, day and night, the energy palpable. I could almost feel it as we slipped low over Duval Street on our way to the airport.

Russ' wife Patti had joined us for the flight. J.D. sat in the right seat next to Russ, and Patti and I took the seats right behind them. After we had reached cruising altitude, I leaned over the seatbacks in front of me and told them what I knew of Jock's condition. I told them that the only other thing I knew was that the Key West police were at the hospital and so was a friend of mine who was a Monroe County detective.

Russ greased the plane onto the runway and taxied to a fixed base operator's private ramp. "We can stay if you need us," Patti said.

"We'll be fine," J.D. said. "We've got reservations at the Pier House and there's a rental car waiting for us here."

We thanked them for the ride and watched as the little plane took off and disappeared into the darkness. The ride to the hospital was short, less than three miles. The emergency room looked pretty much like every one I'd ever been in. It was full of people waiting to be seen, most of them shabby looking, their clothes unwashed and hair unkempt. Children sat in their moms' laps, some sleeping, some crying. A television, tuned to a twenty-four hour cable news channel, was bolted to the wall in a corner of the waiting room, its volume turned low enough that nobody could understand what was being said, but loud enough to be annoying.

A surly woman sitting at the reception desk glared at me as I approached. "I'm Matt Royal. Would you tell Ms. Rudek I'm here?"

"What's this in reference to?"

"She'll know."

She glared some more, trying, I think, to determine if I was some deranged maniac who went around to hospitals and killed social workers. "Have a seat," she said.

I stood there until she picked up the phone and said, "A gentleman named Royal is here to see you." She stressed the word "gentleman," like she didn't think for a minute that it fit me. I smiled at her and took a chair next to J.D.

In a minute or two, an attractive woman came from the back of the department and introduced herself to me as Tina Rudek. I introduced her to J.D. "Come on back," she said. "Mr. Bailey is resting easy and Detective Galis is with him."

She led us to a treatment room where I found a Key West patrolman sitting by the door. "Mr. Royal?" he asked.

"I am, and this is Detective J. D. Duncan, Longboat Key PD." J.D. flashed her badge.

The cop nodded and opened the door, "Detective Galis is waiting for you."

Paul Galis and I had met each other a few years back when I was visiting Key West. Jock had been with me and he and Galis had become friends. A year or so later, Jock saved Paul's life when a dicey situation that also involved J.D. turned murderous. Galis shook my hand and hugged J.D. "How is he?" I asked.

"Drunk and shot," Galis said. "The gunshot is superficial, the drunk took some work."

"Do you have any idea what happened?"

Galis looked at the social worker. "Tina, would you excuse us?"

She nodded and walked out the door.

"Key West PD is investigating, but they don't have a lot to go on. Jock was in a bar on Duval Street, and, according to the bartender, had been there since they opened at nine this morning. The bartender said he was flying low when he got there. He must have been drinking for some time. He didn't eat anything all day, didn't talk to anybody, just sat in a corner and sipped scotch. Around three o'clock this afternoon, he fell off his chair and the manager cut him off and told him to leave."

"We know he flew from Tampa to Miami last night," J.D. said. "He got to Miami about one this morning. I wonder how he got from Miami to Key West."

"He could have driven it in three hours or so at that time of the night," Galis said. "Or he could have chartered a plane. Our airport's open all night."

"I'm betting on the plane," I said. "He would have been here easily by three o'clock. That'd have given him six hours to drink before he got to the bar on Duval."

"But where would he have gone to drink?" J.D. asked.

"There are a lot of places that don't pay too much attention to our liquor laws," Galis said. "Who's he running from?"

"Himself."

"What's going on, Matt?"

"He's in bad shape. His last mission must have been rough. He can't seem to pull out of it. He's been with me on Longboat for the past week trying to sort things out. He disappeared last night and his boss tracked him to Miami."

"Have you told his boss he's here?" Galis asked.

"No. I wanted to make sure it was really Jock before I made the call. How did he end up in the hospital?"

"We're not sure. We think someone saw him lying on the sidewalk and called a taxi to come get him and take him home. Jock woke up enough to tell the driver to bring him here, then passed out again. The driver didn't know he was shot. Just thought he was another drunk."

"What time was that?"

"He got here about three this afternoon and passed out in the reception area. They brought him back here and discovered the gunshot wound. When they went through his wallet, they found your name and number."

"Jock would never have taken that information with him on a mission. He must have been planning to disappear, but wanted me to know if he ended up dead. I take it the gunshot wound wasn't serious."

"Grazed his left shoulder. Barely a flesh wound."

"Doesn't it seem a little bizarre that he got shot in broad daylight on a busy street and there are no witnesses?" J.D. asked.

"Bizarre as hell," Galis said. "I'm guessing whoever shot him must have used a silencer. Nobody in the area complained about hearing a gunshot."

"What about witnesses?" J.D. asked. "Did the police canvass the neighborhood where he was picked up by the cab?"

"We had a cruise ship in port," Galis said. "Those things dump a couple thousand people on us every other day or so. They arrive from Miami or Lauderdale or Canaveral early in the morning and leave at dusk. If any of them saw anything, I doubt they'd speak up. They wouldn't want to miss their sailing.

"Then there's Fantasy Fest. This is the biggest gathering we have all year. People come from all over to get drunk and hang out in outrageous stages of undress. I had to call in some favors to get you two a room at the Pier House."

"Could it have been a routine mugging?" I asked.

"We don't think so," Galis said. "He had several hundred dollars in his wallet and a passport in the name of Mark Bailey. Plus some credit cards in that name. None of that was taken."

"The silencer would indicate something more than a random shooting," J.D. said. "Most muggers who carry guns don't have silencers. Sounds professional."

"I agree," Galis said.

"He's going to have one hell of a hangover," I said.

Galis chuckled. "That he is, my friend. Have you two had dinner?"

"No," I said, "but I need to be here when he wakes up. If he decides to leave, nobody will be able to stop him. If he knows I'm here, he'll be okay."

"I can order a pizza," Paul said.

When Paul had gone, I said, "Too bad we're stuck here. This is the night of the Fantasy Fest parade. We could get naked and walk down Duval Street."

"Hush your mouth. I'd never do that. Again."

"Again?"

She flashed a familiar smile, the one that is so enigmatic that I normally just shut up. Not this time. "You walked totally naked down Duval Street?"

"I wasn't totally naked."

"Glad to hear it. Makes me feel better about your judgment."

Again the smile. "I wore a Halloween mask and flip-flops."

"That's all?"

"You don't want to know."

"But I do."

"Sorry. I didn't mean to stir up your prurient interests."

"Well, you did."

"You have prurient interests?"

"Yeah. They mostly deal with you."

"Only 'mostly'?"

"I meant to say 'only.'"

She smiled again. "I knew that."

"Are you going to tell me about your sashay down Duval?"

"I didn't sashay, thank you. I just walked. Normally."

"Tell me about it."

"Maybe later." Again, the smile. "We can let our fantasies run wild."

"Fantasies?"

"Yes. You don't really think I'd walk naked down Duval Street, do you?"

"You wouldn't?"

"Only in your fantasies."

"My fantasies?"

"Our fantasies. I'll tell you all about it later." And she blasted me again with that smile that was so full of mystery and promise that I almost forgot about the pizza.

CHAPTER FIFTEEN

FRIDAY, OCTOBER 31

THE SAILOR WAS on Longboat Key, sitting at the far end of Tiny's bar listening to the local gossip. He didn't know the people there, but they all seemed to know each other. "Russ flew Matt and J.D. down to Key West for some reason," the one they called Logan said.

"Why Key West?" the bartender named Susie asked.

"Maybe just to get J.D. away for a few days," said the man named Steve. "She's wound pretty tight after somebody tried to kill her yesterday. She got a call from Matt, told the chief she was going to Key West for a few days, and left."

"The chief was all right with that?" Susie asked.

"Yeah," Steve said. "She was supposed to be on administrative leave anyway because of the shooting. I'm kind of filling in for her."

Shit, the sailor thought. Steve's a cop and the bitch is in Key West. He'd already heard that she was doing the guy named Matt Royal, but he hadn't been able to find him. Now he knew. Royal was in Key West with the bitch. He paid his tab and left.

* * *

Jock was waking up. I watched his eyelids move a bit, as if he was rolling his eyeballs behind them. Then his eyes popped open and he saw me. He grinned. "Whatcha doing, podna?"

"Just waiting for my dumbass buddy to wake up."

"Where are we?"

"The emergency room at the Key West hospital."

"Is it still Friday?"

I nodded.

"What time is it?"

"A little after seven in the evening."

"How long have I been here?"

"Since about three this afternoon."

"Why are we here and what's wrong with my arm?"

"Somebody shot you."

"How did you get here?"

"Coit Airways. A social worker found the card in your wallet with my contact information and called me."

"Is Russ here?"

"No. He and Patti flew back to Longboat. J.D. is out in the waiting room with Paul Galis waiting for the pizza delivery guy."

"You eat too much pizza."

"What happened?" I asked.

"I'm not sure. I was doing some serious drinking in a bar when they asked me to leave." He was quiet for a moment, thinking. "That's the last thing I remember. Who shot me?"

"Nobody knows. Yet."

"It doesn't hurt too bad."

"Flesh wound. Whoever tried to take you out wasn't a very good shot."

"And if he didn't mean to take me out, he was a great shot."

"There's that."

"Any witnesses?" Jock asked.

"Not yet. The guy who shot you might have used a silencer."

"How did I get here?"

"Taxi. Jock, what the hell is going on?"

"It looks like somebody's gunning for me."

"Gunning for you?" I laughed. "What? You think this is Dodge City?

"Well, you know what I mean."

"Who's after you?"

"Could be any number of people. I made a lot of enemies over the years, podna. Most of them are really bad people."

"How would somebody like that even know who you are, much less how to find you?"

"I don't know."

"What made you leave Longboat? And why the secrecy?"

"I'd been there long enough and I wasn't getting any better. J.D. needs all your attention right now." He grinned. "If I'd told you I was leaving, you'd have pitched a fuss and I would've had to kick your ass again."

"But you made a point of letting Dave know where you were going when you left Tampa."

"Only to Miami. I'd called ahead and had a charter pilot fly me down here. I didn't think the agency would be able to track me to Key West. At least not for a few days. By then, I'd probably be gone."

"Where'd you get the alias you're using? Mark Bailey. Dave Kendall didn't know about this one."

"Mark's a guy I met hiking in the Pyrenees last summer. I always have an alias or two the agency doesn't have anything to do with. Just being cautious. Mark doesn't stay in one place too long, so his ID was a good one for me to use for a few days if I ever needed it. I put it together when I got back from Spain."

"Talk to me, Jock."

"I may have put you and J.D. in danger."

"How?"

"By just being your houseguest, maybe. More likely, somebody may have figured out that you're my family. Killing you and J.D. would be their revenge for what I've been involved in."

"How would anybody have figured that out?"

"I don't know, but the world is getting more dangerous. We ferreted out a mole in our operation a year or so ago. Maybe we missed one."

"And you didn't tell J.D. and me that we might be in danger?"

"I just figured it out. Sitting in a bar all day. I think the shooting up in Alachua County may have been connected to me. I was going to call you, but apparently I got too drunk to do anything but get shot."

"Somebody tried to kill you."

"I don't think so. A pro would have gotten me. I'm thinking he meant to barely wound me. That would get you and J.D. here."

"How would he have known that you carried the card with my name to call in case of an emergency?"

"I've never had such a card, Matt. Somebody put that information in my wallet after I went down this afternoon. Somebody who knew you'd be here as soon as you heard I was in the hospital. Somebody who wants you here. I may be like the staked goat. Just the bait to get you and J.D. to the killing ground."

CHAPTER SIXTEEN

FRIDAY, OCTOBER 31

"YOU'RE AWAKE," J.D. said, leaning in to plant a kiss on Jock's forehead. "How're you feeling?"

"Hung over, but I'll survive."

"Glad you're alive," Galis said.

"Paul. It's always good to see an old friend. How are you?"

"I'm fine, Jock. What can you tell me about what happened?"

Jock told them what he'd told me.

"And you don't know who's after you," Galis said.

Jock shook his head. "I'm not sure, but my best guess is that it's some very bad terrorists. I've pissed a lot of them off over the years."

"What makes you think whoever is after you is here in Key West?"

"I spotted a guy in the Tampa airport whom I thought might be following me. I wasn't sure, and he didn't get on the flight to Miami, so I didn't think much about it. Nobody caught my attention when I got off the plane in Miami, but when I started thinking about it this morning, I remembered a young couple at the gate who didn't seem to be paying much attention to anybody but each other. I don't think they were waiting for anybody and there were no other planes coming in or leaving at that time of the morning. Maybe they followed me to the charter outfit and found out I was headed for Key West and passed the information on to somebody here."

"I don't understand why anybody would lure us to Key West," J.D. said. "Wouldn't it be easier to take us out on Longboat?"

"Maybe not," Galis said. "There's a better chance for them to get lost in the crowd here, particularly during Fantasy Fest and when a cruise ship is in port."

"There's also the fact that Cuba is only a couple of hours away in a fast boat," Jock said. "And if you were killed because you came here to take care of me, there'd be no question in my mind that I was the cause of your death. Maybe they'd planned to do it on Longboat, but when I left suddenly, they made it up on the fly."

"I'm not sure any of this makes a lot of sense," I said, "but we better take precautions."

"Matt," Galis said, "I don't like the idea of you staying at the Pier House. Too public. I've got a guest room that'll fit you and J.D. just fine. I live up on Lower Sugarloaf Key, well away from the crowds."

I thought about that for a moment. J.D. nodded at me. "We'll accept your hospitality," I said. "What about the Pier House reservation?"

"I'll take care of it," Galis said. "They won't have any trouble renting that room tonight."

"What are we going to do about this lump?" I was looking at Jock.

"He's welcome to the sofa. I'd like to keep you guys close until we get this sorted out. Do you have weapons?"

Jock nodded. "I checked my bag at the airport. There's a nine mil in it."

"Where's your bag?" I asked.

"I left it with the desk clerk at the private terminal where the charter pilot let me off."

"I'll have someone retrieve it for you and bring it to my house," Galis said. "Matt?"

"Yeah. A nine-millimeter Kel-Tec."

"I've got a Glock 17 in my purse," J.D. said.

"Jock, what time did you get to Key West this morning?" Galis asked.

"About three, three thirty."

"Where were you from then until nine when the bars open?"

"Bars are always open if you know where to look. Or find the right cabbie."

"Stock Island?" Galis asked.

Jock grinned. "You're one hell of a detective."

Tina Rudek, the social worker, came through the door. "I'm sorry to bother you, Mr. Bailey, but there is the matter of insurance."

"Send the bill to me at the sheriff's office," Galis said. "We'll get it taken care of."

She smiled in apparent relief. "Thank you, Detective."

When she'd left, J.D. said, "Hospitals always have their priorities straight. You made her a very happy young woman, Paul."

CHAPTER SEVENTEEN

FRIDAY, OCTOBER 31

PAUL GALIS' WIFE had despaired of life in the Keys some years before and returned to Minnesota. "Said she missed the snow," Paul said. "I was going to use that as evidence when I sued for divorce on the grounds of insanity. Fortunately, she was happy to get rid of me, so there was no contest. She signed the papers and left."

The house had been redecorated in what might be described as Lower Keys Bachelor Pad. The walls were covered with photographs of the flora and fauna of the Keys that Paul had taken over the years. Some of them were surprisingly good. It was a very orderly home and reminded me of my old boating buddy, Bucky Buckmaster's, mantra, "A tidy ship is a happy ship." If that applied to houses, Paul lived in a very happy home.

It was close to nine o'clock when we settled into the living room with drinks in hand. J.D. was sipping from a glass of wine, Paul and I were drinking beer, and Jock had a large glass of ice water. We'd gotten him a Big Mac with cheese and fries on the way to Galis' house and he had dived into them like a ravenous dog. By the time we got to Paul's, there was nothing left but crumbs.

"How's the hangover?" I asked.

Jock shook his head. "Better by the minute."

"The arm?"

"Nothing to it. A little sore, but I'll live."

Paul finished his beer and stood. "I'm off to bed. Jock, you and Matt can flip for the sofa. Loser has to sleep with J.D." He grinned and was gone.

"Probably be easier if I took the sofa," J.D. said.

"Hush," I said.

"I couldn't take the excitement," Jock said. "Headache, you know."

"If you two are finished," J.D. said, "we need to call Dave Kendall."

"Not yet," Jock said.

"When?" I asked.

"Soon. But not yet."

"Talk to me, Jock," I said. "Why are we in Key West?"

"I couldn't think of anyplace better to go, and the next plane leaving Tampa when I got there was headed to Miami. I wanted an island and Key West is an island and it has a lot of bars that'll serve you all night. It seemed like a good idea at the time."

"Why don't we call Dave? You're going to have to do it soon."

"I don't think I'm going back."

"Back where?"

"To the agency."

"What's up, Jock?" J.D. asked. "Please tell us what's going on. I'll leave you two alone if that'll help."

"No. You need to be part of this, to understand what kind of person you're dealing with."

"I already know that, Jock."

"I think you might change your mind when you hear it all."

"Tell us. Get it out in the open."

"I'm done with the killing. No more."

"You can leave the field, Jock," I said. "Become an analyst or something that keeps you in an office."

"I'd still be involved in the killing, even if I wasn't the one pulling the trigger."

"You only kill bad guys," I said.

"Right. But what if the bad guy is also a good guy?"

"What do you mean?" J.D. asked.

"Even the foulest murderers have mothers."

"That's pretty obvious," I said.

"Sometimes they have wives and children and hold down day jobs," Jock said. "They get up and go to work just like regular folks. Our own clandestine services are full of people just like that. And sometimes, mistakes are made."

He was right, of course, but there was a very distinct difference. "Our people don't cut off the heads of innocents, send suicide bombers to kill children, or execute people just because they follow a different faith."

"That's what separates us from them," Jock said. "But sometimes when I kill a bad guy, I deprive his wife and children of their husband and father, maybe their livelihood. How do I square that?"

"Maybe you can't," said J.D. "Any more than the soldier who kills the enemy in combat, the enemy soldier who has a family back home and is just doing his duty to his own country, can square the whole thing. You just kill the enemy to protect the lives of your own people. It took me a long time to understand what you do and why you do it, but I've come to terms with the necessity of it. You're a good man, Jock Algren, maybe the second best man I ever met." She smiled. "And there are days when I'm pretty sure you're the first best."

Jock laughed. "Those are the days when Matt's in the doghouse."

She pointed a cocked finger at him. "Bingo."

"Still," he said. "I'm done. I've thought about this a lot over the last week. If somebody wants to kill me, they can do it. I probably deserve it, and there'll be a certain kind of symmetry to being killed by someone whom I've brought grief to in the past."

"What are you going to do?" I asked.

"I thought I might stay here for a week or two and then maybe find another island somewhere."

"Not much of a plan," I said.

"I really haven't thought it out. I realized earlier today that I've put you two in danger, and the more I thought about it, the more it made sense."

"How so?"

"If I killed somebody's loved one, and the survivor wants to hurt me, how better to do it than to kill my loved ones? Tit for tat. Death is quick. Grief can last forever."

"That sounds like a bumper sticker."

"Maybe. But it's true. When I was drinking in that bar this morning, it started to make sense that somebody might be after you two."

"Why?" J.D. asked. "What happened on this last mission to make you think like this?"

"I can't talk about it. Not yet. It's too raw. But it was very bad. And it gave me reason to think about your safety. If I'd put it together before I left Longboat, I wouldn't have left. Now we're here, and I don't know what to do. I'm scared."

That was the revelation that hit me in the gut. Jock was the toughest man I'd ever known. He always met challenges head-on. That was part of what made him a top agent. He had always seemed fearless to me, and while I knew that not to be absolutely true, I had always thought of him as the least fearful man among us. Now he was telling us that he was scared. "Scared of what?" I asked.

"Life."

"That doesn't even make sense."

"My nerves are shot, podna. I don't think I could even pick up a weapon, must less shoot somebody. Not even to protect you and J.D. Or myself, for that matter. I've got this black cloud hanging over me, surrounding me. I can't see through it or past it. I feel like

I'm already dead, an empty husk just waiting for the undertaker to show up."

"You packed your gun," J.D. said.

"I brought it just so I could throw it into the ocean. A symbolic act. I was thinking about maybe following it, saying the hell with it all. If I were gone, there'd be no reason for anybody to come after you."

I'd never seen him this way. I wondered if the soldiers and Marines and SEALS who developed post-traumatic stress disorder in Iraq and Afghanistan displayed the same symptoms. Maybe Jock had reached his breaking point and simply could go no further.

"Shut the fuck up," I said, my voice pitched low. "When did you turn into such a pussy? If there's a threat out there, we don't kill ourselves. We face it. We kill the threat. It's that simple."

"Matt," J.D. said quietly, putting her hand on my arm.

"No, goddamnit. He needs to hear this." I turned to Jock. "I've known you most of our lives. You've never even understood the word 'quit.' Why now? What the hell happened to you? What did you do?"

"I killed a family and created a monster."

CHAPTER EIGHTEEN

FRIDAY, OCTOBER 31

THE STORY WAS as old as the Greek tragedies, a story of duty and remorse and revenge. A man named Abdullah al Bashar, a banker who lived in Aleppo, Syria, was suspected of funding one of the most vicious terror groups operating in the Middle East. "They were cutting off heads before it became fashionable," Jock said, wryly. "They'd video the murders and send the tapes to media outlets all over the world. Most of them never aired the execution videos, but the intelligence agencies took them apart pixel by pixel."

"Al Bashar had studied in London and had a good command of the English language. He was well respected internationally in his profession, and over the years, had made a number of speeches to international gatherings of bankers. The CIA had long suspected that he might be a funding source for terrorists, but didn't have proof. About fifteen years ago, after one of the videos of a beheading was released, one that featured the murderer giving a little speech before he cut an American hostage's head off with a knife, some bright analyst finally got around to using some speech comparison software, or something like that, and came to the conclusion that al Bashar was the killer."

"What about the money?" J.D. asked.

"There was no follow-up on that. It didn't matter. Al Bashar had very publicly and brutally murdered an American citizen. I was sent to kill him."

"Did you?" J.D. asked.

"Yes. But first I went to Aleppo and spent some time setting it up. I figured out his routines, knew where he lived, decided on the best time to kill him and make my exit from the country. Al Bashar had a wife and two young sons and they lived in a house in an upper-class neighborhood. His servants were given one night a week off to visit their families. Friday. The Muslim holy day. I was surprised to find that both al Bashar and his wife were pretty secular. She didn't wear the hijab, the headscarf worn by Muslim women, and the family didn't frequent the local mosque. Al Bashar spent a lot of time with his family. The children, who were six and eight, were being taught English by a tutor who came to their house five days a week. They didn't seem much different from an upper-middle-class family anywhere in America."

"Except that dad was a murderer," J.D. said.

"Right. The two faces of evil. One pointed toward civility and the other toward chaos and death."

"What happened?" I asked.

"I picked my time to go after him. He seldom left home at night and was surrounded by people at his bank during the day. I went in on a Friday, when the servants were gone. It was late, but I found the family gathered around a TV watching an American sitcom dubbed into Arabic. I had my pistol out and surprised them. I told the wife to take the children and leave the room. She refused, told me to get out, and when I shook my head, she said, and I'll never forget the words, 'If you're going to kill us, we'll die together.'

"I told her I was only going to kill her husband, and she said something to the effect that I'd have to do it in front of his family."

"What did al Bashar have to say?"

"Nothing, really. He seemed resigned to his fate. It was like he'd been expecting me. He did tell his wife to take the boys and leave. She refused."

"Bad scene," I said. "That must have been gut wrenching."

"The worst moments of my life, up until that time. It got even worse when the smaller boy said, 'Please don't kill my father.' Both boys began to cry. I shot their dad though the head and left. I went straight to Longboat Key and got drunk for a week."

"I remember that," I said. "I was still practicing law in Orlando. I took the week off and we just hung out. That was the first cleansing time. You never told me what had happened."

"In a way, that killing precipitated the next cleansing, about two years later."

"I remember that one, too. How were they connected?"

"There was another public beheading that took place a few weeks after the one al Bashar took part in. There was another voice analysis done. It turns out the murderer was al Bashar. Again."

"You didn't kill him," J.D. said.

"No. I did. He was definitely dead. I was grilled about that at some length at the time, and I think I convinced the CIA folks that it couldn't have been al Bashar who conducted the second execution. At least my boss believed me, and I think he finally convinced the CIA folks."

"Who was the second killer?" J.D. asked.

"It sure as hell wasn't al Bashar. That was all I knew for about a year. Then word came from Israel's intelligence agency, the Mossad. The second killing had been a Mossad agent, and they finally ran down the thug who'd murdered him. They interrogated the bastard and got irrefutable proof that not only had he killed their agent, but he was the one who killed the American that al Bashar was accused of murdering."

"You killed the wrong man," J.D. said.

"Yes. After the CIA found out that they'd screwed up, they went back to the money trail, trying to tie al Bashar to the funding of the terrorists. They found absolutely no evidence implicating him in any way. He was an innocent man."

"That's a terrible thing for you to carry around," J.D. said. "But it wasn't your fault. You were just doing your job."

"Yeah, but I began to think about what a dirty job it was."

"Why didn't you just quit?"

"By the time I found out that al Bashar was innocent, 9/11 had happened and three thousand innocent Americans were dead. The terrorist threat had grown and was continuing to get bigger. I was in a position to help do something about that, so I stayed on, tried to put it behind me, convince myself that al Bashar was just another innocent casualty of war, not unlike the good people who died in the fire bombings of Dresden or Tokyo during World War II."

"Did it work?" J.D. asked.

Jock laughed bitterly. "I still see those little boys in my dreams, the ones who begged me not to kill their dad, and then watched me do it."

"That was a long time ago," I said. "Why is all this coming to a head now?"

"Because I saw the little boys a couple of weeks ago. Not in a dream. In what's left of Aleppo. Only they're not little boys anymore."

CHAPTER NINETEEN

Three Weeks Before

Aleppo. What had once been a bustling city, the largest in Syria and perhaps the oldest continuously inhabited town in the world, was now a city of the dead, the blasted hulks of buildings the only tombstones for the fallen.

Jock Algren picked his way carefully through the desolation that had been a city of culture and learning. Its historical buildings, many dating to the Middle Ages, lay in ruins, brought down by the relentless struggle between the many factions fighting for supremacy. The only thing for certain was that no matter who won, it would not be good for America.

Jock's sun-darkened skin and his fluency in Arabic allowed him to pass as a local as he searched for the terrorist he'd been sent to kill. It was ironic, he thought, that the one city in the world that generated most of his nightmares was now in ruins, devastated by the very people who lived in his angry dreams, those crazies who fought each other for the supremacy of their own brand of the same religion. He'd never understood them or their reasons for killing each other, but he appreciated the danger they posed to the Western world.

A young man whose *nom de guerre* was Abu Bakr was a bomb-making genius. He'd been responsible for the deaths of hundreds of people and he was getting more and more sophisticated. The people in

Washington who knew about these things were afraid that he'd find the holy grail of bomb makers, the bomb that could not be detected by any means yet known. Then we'd start seeing airliners fall out of the sky and the public would panic. No one knew what this would do to the world economy, but all the assessments were bleak. Jock had been sent to find Abu Bakr and kill him.

He'd been on the bomber's trail for several days and was homing in on him. His latest intelligence was that he was holed up in a ruined building in a neighborhood near the center of the city. Jock had an address, but it was difficult to find his way through the rubble. There was nothing to guide him, to give him a sense of perspective. He thought this part of Aleppo must look like Berlin did in 1945.

He had a picture of Abu Bakr that had been taken by a Mossad agent two years before. It had been taken from a long way off with a telephoto lens that could not quite compensate for the distance. The photo was a bit blurry, but it was good enough that Jock would recognize the man if he saw him.

Jock moved farther along the street between the broken buildings. He glanced at the pre-war map he carried, trying to get some perspective, some way to determine where he was. His best guess was that he had another block or two to go. A shot rang out and the bullet ricocheted off a large piece of rubble laying in the road a couple of feet from where he stood.

Jock dove head first, seeking the safety of a big piece of concrete next to the one hit by the bullet. Another shot rang out and another bullet hit the far side of his cover. A rifle. It had the sound of a Kalashnikov, the one known to the world as the AK-47.

"Hey," Jock shouted in colloquial Arabic. "Why are you shooting at me?"

"Why are you here?" the man with the rifle shouted back.

"I'm hungry," Jock said. "I'm looking for food. There used to be a bakery around here. I thought there might be something left."

"Not around here. You need to leave."

"Will you shoot me if I leave?"

"Maybe."

"Why? I haven't done anything to you."

"And if I shoot you, you never will."

Jock pulled his pistol from the folds of the loose Arabic robe he wore. He would try to draw the shooter out into the open and deal with him. He found a small crevice that gave him a tight view in front of the rock without having to show his head. He watched quietly for a few minutes, saw nothing. Then there was movement from the area from which Jock surmised the rifle shot had come.

"Are you still there?" the man shouted.

Jock stayed quiet, tried not to move. He watched. Another shout. "Hello, friend. Come on out. I mean you no harm."

More minutes went by. The man moved out from his cover. He was walking slowly toward the spot where Jock was hiding. He was well within pistol range, but Jock held his fire and sat quietly, watching the man walk toward him. A pistol shot would alert whoever was inside the building to the fact that an armed man was outside shooting at their guard. Jock was now convinced that the only reason a man with an assault rifle would be standing guard outside a ruined building was if someone important was inside. He pulled a large knife, a K-BAR, from the scabbard attached to the belt he wore under the robe. And he waited.

The man with the rifle walked slowly in Jock's direction. He was alert, suspicious that there might be danger lurking in the rubble. "Hey, friend," he called. "Where are you? Come on out. We have food inside the building."

Jock crept to the edge of his rock hideout. He couldn't see the man with the rifle, but he could hear him as his boots disturbed the mess that had once been a part of one of the nearby buildings. And he could smell him. The rancid odor of a body unwashed for days mixed with what could be described as terminal halitosis. He was close, coming slowly now. He stopped. Tried once more. "Friend? Don't you trust me?"

It was the moment Jock was waiting for. The man's concentration would be a little less acute, not much less, but maybe just enough to give Jock the edge. He sprang from his hiding place, knife held high. He had seen that the man carried the rifle in his right hand. He saw Jock and in the nanosecond it took him to appreciate the danger, Jock was on him, his left had reaching out and grabbing the muzzle of the rifle, his right hand thrusting the knife into the man's throat, severing his vocal chords and his jugular in the first thrust. The man could not make a sound, and he bled to death in less than a minute.

Jock picked up the rifle, checked the magazine. It had the full complement of thirty rounds, less the two fired at him. He put his pistol back in its holster and the knife in its scabbard. He worked his way cautiously toward the opening in the building that had once been a front door. He didn't think there were any more guards. If there had been, at least one of them would have helped his buddy ferret out the intruder. But he wasn't sure, so he took his time working his way to the door.

As he approached the entrance, he heard subdued voices inside. He couldn't make out the conversation, but it sounded like two men talking. Were there only two in there? Not likely, if they had a guard. But on the other hand, they might just be two semi-important people, important enough to justify one guard, but not valuable enough to warrant more. Or it could just be that nobody really expected any danger in this devastated neighborhood.

Jock crept on into the building. He stopped for a moment to let his eyes adjust to the dimness. The voices were louder, but Jock still couldn't make out the words. They sounded friendly, like two guys having a discussion over a couple of beers.

He crept closer and began to sense light coming from a room off the main corridor. He was within a few feet of the doorway when he stepped on a loose rock that skittered away. "That you, Ahmed?" asked one of the men in the room, speaking in Arabic.

Jock mumbled something unintelligible, just loud enough for the men to hear him, to put them at ease. At the same time he lurched forward into the room, the AK held in front of him in the firing position. His very first fleeting thought was that he'd found Abu Bakr, the man in the fuzzy picture he'd gotten from the Mossad. He was sitting at a small table across from another man who bore a family resemblance to Abu Bakr. Jock recognized the odds and ends on the table as the makings of a bomb.

"Keep your hands on the table where I can see them," Jock said in Arabic.

The men looked at Jock, their faces showing shock, and distress, and something else. Recognition? Jock wasn't sure, but he knew he'd never seen these men before. "Abu Baker," he said in Arabic. "I've been looking for you."

"You scumbag," Abu Bakr said in English. "I know you."

"I don't think so."

"I see you every night in my dreams."

"How is that?"

"I watched you kill my father."

Jock saw it then. The child had grown into manhood, but there was still a shadow of the small boy somewhere around his eyes, maybe in the way he cocked his head, something. "You're al Bashar."

"Yes."

"And this is your little brother."

"Yes," said the other young man. "My brother Youssef. Are you here to kill us?"

"I'm here to kill Abu Bakr." He looked directly at the older brother. "You've killed hundreds of innocent people with your bombs. That does not go unpunished."

"And what about you?" Abu Bakr asked. "Were you punished for killing an innocent man, one who had nothing to do with the cause?"

"No," Jock said. "Not in any conventional way. But I've lived with that mistake. It was the worst thing that ever happened to me."

"I am so sorry for you," Abu Bakr said sarcastically. "Do you know what happened to my mother?"

"No."

"She hanged herself. A few months after you murdered our father. Youssef and I found her when we came home from school. She left a note apologizing to us and telling us that she could not live without our father. We went to live with an uncle."

"I'm sorry."

Abu Bakr used his feet to push his chair back and over. As he fell to the floor he pulled a pistol from the loose-fitting trousers he wore. He was raising it to a firing position when Jock pulled the AK-47's trigger and shot him through the head.

"You son of a bitch," Youssef said. "You better kill me now or I'll come after you. You won't be safe anywhere in the world. I'll take out your family first and then I'll make sure that you die horribly, begging for mercy."

Jock pointed the rifle at him. "Those are strong words for an unarmed man to make when I'm holding a loaded rifle."

"Shoot me, you asshole. You've killed my whole family. Go ahead. Pull the trigger. I dare you."

Jock put the rifle's muzzle to Youssef's forehead. "I'll see you in hell, kid."

CHAPTER TWENTY

Friday, October 31

J.D. and I sat in stunned silence when Jock finished. Then J.D. got out of her chair and sat next to Jock on the sofa. She wrapped her arms around him and said, "I'm so sorry, Jock."

We sat some more, letting the silence wrap around us. I could hear the ticking of a grandfather clock in the foyer, the occasional firecracker in the distance, probably set off by some kid dressed as a pirate, or a devil. More minutes went by, and finally I said, "If they're all dead, who do you think is coming after us? Or you?"

"I didn't kill Youssef."

"Why not?"

"I created him, him and his brother. And I killed his entire family in the process. It's no wonder the boys turned into murderous radicals."

"Why didn't you kill him, anyway? He told you he was coming after you. Did you think he was incapable of doing that?"

"No. I knew Abu Bakr's brother was the leader of a squad of terrorists. I just didn't know they were the al Bashar brothers. The agency had decided not to kill Youssef. At least, not yet."

"Why?"

"He wasn't that effective, and we figured if we took him out, he might be replaced with someone who could do more harm."

"But once he threatened you?"

"I've already told you. I created him. And now I'd killed the last remaining member of his family. Don't get me wrong. The older one had to die, if for no other reason than to save the lives of the innocents he would kill with his bombs. Besides, how in the world would he ever find me? My identity is well protected. I'm a ghost to those people."

"But you think they've found you," J.D. said.

"Maybe."

"So what are you going to do?" I asked.

"I'll stay here for a few days, if Paul will let me. Then I'll slip out to Miami and find myself an island somewhere."

"And if they follow you to whatever island you land on?"

"Then it'll be the end. I'm done with killing. If they get me, they get me." He smiled. "Karma, don't you know?" He yawned.

"You need to get some sleep, Jock," J.D. said. "You've had a long day. Let me look at your wound site and we'll call it a night."

J.D., like all the cops on Longboat Key, was a trained emergency medical technician. She examined the wound, gave Jock her smile of approval, then spread sheets and a blanket over the sofa. She kissed him on the cheek and followed me into the bedroom.

"What now?" she asked.

"I'm going hunting," I said.

"Hunting?"

"If somebody's after Jock or you and me, we have to stop them. Might as well do it now."

"You're pretty good in a fight, sweetie, but you're not a hunter. That's Jock's job."

"He's not going to do it. He's given up."

"That'll last for about as long as it takes him to completely sober up."

"I don't know, J.D. I've never seen him like this. He reeks of defeat.

His whole demeanor, his 'affect' as the shrinks say, is one of surrender. It's like he's crossed into some strange land where he's gone to await death."

"And atonement?"

"Maybe, but not in the religious sense. He's probably thought it out and figures that the universe will fall a little more into balance if he's killed by the same people he's spent his career fighting and killing. He'll atone for the deaths he's responsible for by giving up his life."

"You read all that into the way he looks?"

"I've known him most of his life. I think I pick up on clues that, without context, would be meaningless, but because I know him so well, I can, by extrapolation, deduce what he's thinking."

She scoffed. "You're awfully full of crap sometimes, Royal."

I laughed. "Probably, but something tells me I'm right about this."

"Your famous gut reaction?"

"Yeah. It works more than it doesn't."

"I know, baby, and I'm worried about him, too. But that doesn't mean I want you to go after these guys. They're a nasty bunch."

"I owe Jock," I said.

"I know. We'll talk about it in the morning."

But we didn't.

CHAPTER TWENTY-ONE

SATURDAY, NOVEMBER 1

I WAS AWAKENED at three o'clock in the morning by the harsh ring of J.D.'s cell phone. This couldn't be good. She reached over me and took the phone from the bedside table, checked the caller ID, put it on the speaker, and answered, "This better be good, Steve." My girl and I were on the same wavelength.

"Sorry to wake you up, J.D., but we need you."

"What's going on?"

"Peter Fortson's been murdered."

"Tell me about it."

"Tom Jones found the body a couple of hours ago."

"Tom Jones, the singer?"

"No. Tom Jones, the builder. Lives over in the Orlando area."

"Little joke there, Steve. Tom's a friend of mine and Matt's."

"Oh. Okay. You know where Tom's beach condo is?"

"Yes," J.D. said. "It's just a couple of doors down from Fortson's place."

"Right. Well, Tom and his wife Linda were out walking on the beach."

"At one in the morning?"

"Yeah. Tom said he couldn't sleep and thought a little walk might relax him. Linda came along."

"Where was the body?"

"On the beach about halfway between Tom and Linda's condo and Fortson's house."

"In the water?"

"No. Between the high tide line and the dunes. Whoever murdered him wasn't concerned about hiding the body."

"How was he killed?"

"His throat was cut. Almost took his head off. Looks like somebody knew what he was doing."

"Do you know the time of death yet?"

"The medical examiner's guy says it probably happened around midnight. They'll know more when they get him to the morgue."

"Is the body still there?"

"Yeah. Kevin, our crime scene tech, is still nosing around. He's got the county lab people on their way to help out."

"It's about an eight-hour drive back to Longboat. I'll get started within the hour."

"Chief Lester prevailed on his buddy the sheriff to send one of his choppers for you. It's winding up at the airport now. They ought to be in Key West in a couple of hours."

"Okay, Steve. Can you get to the pilot and ask him to call me? Tell me where he wants me to meet him. I assume the fixed base operator's private terminal at the Key West airport, but I'd like to be sure."

"No problem, J.D. See you soon."

She shut down the phone and looked at me. "Duty calls."

"I wonder if this is connected to his sister's death."

"Seems reasonable."

"Why would somebody kill the brother now? She's been dead for three years."

"Good question. Maybe it's not connected. I guess we'll start digging and see if anything turns up."

"J.D., I want you to ask the chopper pilot if he can get clearance to land at the Naval Air Station on Boca Chica. I don't want you going to the airport. The bad guys might have it staked out, and I don't want you to end up dead."

"That might not be a bad idea. I'll talk to the pilot when he calls."

She dressed quickly, took the call from the chopper pilot and was ready to leave. "The helicopter is already airborne. The pilot said he'll be at Boca Chica in about an hour. The gate guards will be expecting us. How far is the base from here?"

"Not far. It'll only take fifteen minutes or so. We probably should get moving in case he's early."

The drive to the base was quiet, each of us immersed in our own thoughts. I wasn't happy about J.D. going back to Longboat where I couldn't protect her, but I knew better than to mention that to her. She thinks the last thing she needs from me is protection. She's probably right, but old ideas, like the one about the strong man protecting the little lady, are hard to get over, especially when the little lady is the center of your very existence.

She would be better protected on Longboat than she would be in Key West. The cops there would take care of one of their own. Still, I was going to call the chief as soon as she got out of the car and bring him up to date on the situation with Jock.

I needed to stay in the Keys. It was time to start hunting. I didn't have a clue as to where to begin, except for the bar where Jock had been drinking the day before. Maybe he had enough memory of the day that he could at least point me to the place he'd gone in the morning. According to what the bar manager had told the police, Jock showed up at opening time and stayed until he was kicked out.

We navigated our way through the main gate security, and one of the gate guards directed us to the ramp where the sheriff's chopper was scheduled to land. We checked in with the sailor who manned the desk in the small office adjacent to the helicopter landing area. He examined our IDs again and told us the aircraft was inbound and should be on the pad in about twenty minutes.

A half hour later I watched the lights of the sheriff's helicopter disappear in the distance, heading due north for Longboat Key. I pulled out my phone and called Chief Bill Lester.

CHAPTER TWENTY-TWO

SATURDAY, NOVEMBER 1

THE PILOT WAS descending toward Longboat Key when J.D. called Steve Carey and asked that he send a car to pick her up at Bayfront Park near mid-key. The Little League ball field there was the only place on the island with enough open space for a helicopter to land. It was a little before six and astronomical twilight was supplanting the night sky, the sun still hidden below the eastern horizon.

The chopper touched down and J.D. thanked the pilot and walked to the waiting patrol car. She was at the murder scene five minutes later. Steve Carey was waiting for her beside Gulf of Mexico Drive, standing beside a line of vehicles, including police cars and vans from the crime scene section and the medical examiner's office. Steve led her to the beach where the body lay sprawled on the sand. It was dressed in a polo shirt and shorts, no shoes. Police tape was strung in a square twenty feet to a side, guarding the area where the body was found. A police all-terrain vehicle, one they used for beach patrols, had pulled three large light trailers into the area and the beach was brightly illuminated. The crime scene techs were there, milling about outside the protected area, waiting for daylight to finish their examination of the scene.

"Anything new?" J.D. asked Carey.

"No. The techs are waiting for daybreak. They've done all they can in the artificial light, but they don't really expect to find much more. The scene is clean as a whistle."

"That points to a professional job."

"It does," Steve said. "Maybe we got pointed in the wrong direction. Maybe the brother didn't have anything to do with his sister's murder."

"Maybe, but I don't want to abandon that line of investigation. Maybe Fortson's murder isn't connected to his sister's, but let's not jump to conclusions."

"That'd be a pretty big coincidence if there was no connection."

"Yeah."

"I guess Matt wasn't too happy about me pulling you away from your vacation," Steve said.

"Oh, he'll live. He's got friends down there. And there are a lot of bars."

Steve grinned. "Lots of women, too."

J.D. shook her head. "I'm pretty sure he doesn't have a death wish."

"I hear you, Detective." Steve was still grinning.

"I saw the Manatee County crime scene van parked on the road. Who's in charge of the techs?"

"Kevin's running the show."

"I need to talk to Kevin, then. I'd like to know the details of what they've found."

Kevin Mimbs was in charge of Longboat Key PD's crime scene investigations, but he was a one-man department. The Town of Longboat Key is divided at mid-key by the county line between Manatee and Sarasota Counties. It's a bit confusing at times, and it might be better if the town were located wholly in one county, but neither county wanted to give up its share of the tax revenue generated by the island. When something big happened on the key, like a murder, either the Sarasota County or Manatee County crime scene investigators were brought in to assist, depending on where the crime occurred. But, Kevin was in charge, and the techs from either county reported to him.

J.D. found Kevin sitting on a tarpaulin spread on the sand, a Styrofoam cup half-full of coffee in his hand. "About time you showed up," he said. "I heard you and Matt were down in the Keys playing hooky."

She laughed. "Yeah. I try to get away from you people and you drag me back, kicking and screaming. What've you got?"

"Not much, J.D. It's a very clean crime scene and the beach isn't the best place for evidence. The tide washes it away or sand gets kicked over it. I'm thinking a professional hit, but that's just a guess. No evidence of it."

"Give me the reasons you think it's professional. I've always trusted your gut reactions."

"First of all, the cut to the victim's throat was clean. We'll know more when Doc Hawkins does the autopsy, but it looked like the killer got the vocal chords, the carotid artery and the jugular vein with one swipe of the knife. That's something they teach the special operations troops. Getting the vocal chords makes sure there's no noise. It's a quiet death."

"And quick."

"Yeah. He'd have bled out in less than a minute."

"Anything else? Footprints, maybe?"

"There were a lot of footprints, some barefoot and others with all kinds of shoes. Typical beach environment. There's no way we could track the killer's route. He could have come from anywhere and gone anywhere."

"Does it look like Fortson was taken by surprise?"

"Yeah. Another thing that makes me think a pro did it. The victim's on an open beach, no cover close to him, yet the killer snuck up and took him from behind."

"Maybe," J.D. said, "Fortson knew the killer and they were just out for a stroll."

"I hadn't thought about that. I guess it's possible."

"Was there any identification on the body?"

"No. He didn't have anything in his pockets. Tom and Linda Jones recognized him, but the medical examiner will run prints just to be sure."

"Could you tell if he'd been drinking?"

"No way to tell yet," Kevin said. "They'll run tox screens when they get him to the morgue. We'll know soon enough."

"I take it that there's been no canvass of the neighbors."

"Not yet. We're waiting until people start waking up. The chief didn't want to roll them out of bed in the middle of the night. He was afraid it would cause a panic. Dead neighbor on the beach in the wee hours."

"Do you know where the chief is?"

"He had to go back to the station for something. Here he comes now."

Chief Bill Lester was picking his way through the low dunes that bordered the beach. J.D. walked to meet him. "You sure know how to interrupt a vacation, Chief."

"Welcome back, J.D. Did you enjoy Key West?"

"You mean all seven hours of it?"

The chief smiled. "Sorry to drag you back, but I figured you might have some walking around knowledge about the victim's sister's murder that would help us here. Something that didn't get into the paperwork."

"No sweat, Bill. I don't know what this is all about, but I think the sister's murder is the place to start. I've already got somebody in the Orlando area trying to dig up some financial information on Mr. Fortson."

"You suspect him for the murder of his sister?"

"That may be too strong, but I certainly want to dig a little deeper on him. He got a lot of money as the result of Rachel's death."

"Who gets the money now that Fortson's dead?"

"Good question, Bill. I'll have to wait until Monday to start digging into that."

"You've got your work cut out for you. What about Matt?"

"I left him in Key West. Am I still suspended?"

"No. The Alachua County sheriff gave me verbal clearance to get you back to work. Said it was a good shoot and he'll be filing the paperwork on Monday. You're good to go."

"Thanks, Chief. All things considered, I'd just as soon still be on suspension and lying on a beach in Key West."

"There are no good beaches down there."

"Well, there's that."

CHAPTER TWENTY-THREE

Saturday, November 1

It was a little before six. I was sitting on Paul Galis' deck reading the morning paper and sipping a large coffee that I'd bought at an all-night convenience store on the way back from Boca Chica. "Anything interesting in the news?" Jock asked. He'd slipped quietly outside and gave me a start. It must have shown. "A little jumpy, podna?"

"Jeez, Jock. You've got to start making more noise. You scared the hell out of me."

"What's on the agenda today?" he asked.

"We need to talk, old buddy. There's a coffee maker in the kitchen. Already loaded. Just turn it on."

He returned a few minutes later with a steaming cup. "J.D. still in bed?"

"She's probably in Longboat by now."

"Lover's spat?"

"Bill Lester called her back for a murder that happened on the beach a few hours ago. I took her out to Boca Chica, and a sheriff's helicopter picked her up."

"I slept through all that?"

"We tried to keep quiet," I said. "I never want to interrupt a man and his hangover. How're you feeling this morning?"

"Like a man who survived a hell of a drunk. I'm done with the drinking for a while."

"What about your plans for finding an island and going to ground?"

"That's still my plan. I was dead serious last night. I'm done."

"I have a favor to ask. A big one. Maybe bigger than anything I've ever asked before."

"Whatever you need, podna. You know that."

"I want you to agree to stay here at Paul's for a few days. Give me a chance to sort things out. Figure out who's trying to kill you."

"I'll be putting you all in danger."

"Think about it for a minute. Nobody knows you're here. The bad guys wouldn't know that you and Paul have a history, or for that matter that Paul and I do. J.D.'s on Longboat surrounded by cops. Bill Lester knows what's going on, so he's going to be extra vigilant."

Jock chuckled. "I can't see J.D. sitting still for that."

"She won't know."

"Okay. What about you?"

"I'll be fine. I'm not just some retired lawyer lying in the sun."

"Matt, I know that better than anyone. I've watched you work. We've been in scrapes together, and of all the people I know, including some of the best trained agents in the world, you're the one I'd always pick to be on my side in a fight. But these guys, if they're who I think they are, are the most brutal bastards in the world. They'd think nothing of taking out a building full of women and children if their target was there. Killing is what they do. They're like wolves. They run in packs. You take out one and there're several more waiting in the shadows. They won't stop until they're all dead. Or we are."

"I know that."

"Then, leave it alone."

"You haven't been thinking too straight, Jock. If you disappear, the threat to J.D. and me remains. The fact that they can't find you won't stop them from trying to kill us."

"You've got a point," Jock said.

"And what if they do find you and kill you?"

"Then I'm dead."

"And what about J.D. and me?"

"What do you mean?"

"You're worried that the bad guys want to kill us to ruin your life. What do you think your death will do to us?"

He sat quietly, mulling over a thought that apparently had not occurred to him. "I haven't thought that through very well, have I? What are you thinking about doing?"

"How many people are in Youssef's group?"

"About ten, we think."

"Do you have names, pictures?"

"Yes."

"I think you need to call Dave Kendall and let him know what's going on. We need the information on Youssef and his people."

"Okay. What else?"

"We need to figure out how they know who you are and how they found out about J.D. and me. How do they know where you are?"

"I've been thinking about that," Jock said. "There has to be a leak in our agency."

"What about other intelligence agencies you've worked with in the past? Could the leak be coming from there?"

"Possibly."

"We need to find out."

"I'll call Dave this morning. Bring him up to date and get him to send the pictures and names of Youssef's men."

"Jock, call Dave now. Roll him out of bed if necessary, but I want to be at the bar you were in yesterday when they open this morning. I'd like to have those pictures to show around. You never know. Maybe somebody saw the one who shot you. Have Dave send the photos to my phone."

CHAPTER TWENTY-FOUR

SATURDAY, NOVEMBER 1

I FOLLOWED PAUL Galis to a small café perched on the side of U.S. 1, just before the bridge leading to the next key. It was a little after seven and I was craving breakfast. I was wearing my running shoes, a pair of chinos, a baseball cap bearing the logo of the Tampa Bay Bucs, and a golf shirt that hung over the Walther PPK/S twenty-two-caliber pistol that was tucked into my pants at the small of my back. Jock had given me the weapon, saying that it was untraceable. I parked the rental next to Paul's unmarked cruiser and walked into the air-conditioned restaurant.

A server brought us menus and coffee, and we settled into a booth overlooking the sound. "They've got the best waffles south of Miami," Paul said. "And real maple syrup they get directly from Vermont."

"Sounds just right." I nodded at the waitress.

When she'd gone, I said, "Can you put up with Jock for a few days?"

"Sure. What's going on?"

"I think he needs to keep out of sight. I want to see if I can find the people who're trying to kill him."

"How're you going to do that? We don't have any clues, nowhere to start."

"Paul, you know what Jock does."

"Sort of. I don't know much beyond the fact that he works for a secretive government agency and has lots of pull."

"That's about all anyone needs to know. But, I know a lot more and have some information that I can't share with you. National security and all that crap. I've at least got a starting point, and Jock's agency will give me more help as I need it."

"What can I do, other than babysit Jock?"

"I'm going to start turning over rocks and there may be some very bad people crawling out from under them. They're not going to be cooperative. How close are you to the sheriff?"

"Like brothers. We started with the department on the same day and were partners on patrol for a couple of years. I took a leave of absence and ran his campaign six years ago when he was first elected. Why?"

"I need him to make me a special deputy, give me some law enforcement credentials."

"I'm pretty sure you have to go through a police academy to get deputized."

"You're right," I said. "I looked it up. But the sheriff is a constitutional officer in Florida and he has the power to appoint a special deputy. One who has no enforcement powers. He can't arrest anybody or enforce the law in any way. He's just honorary, but he gets a badge. If the sheriff will appoint me, nobody has to know that I'm toothless as a cop. I just need a badge to flash."

"Doesn't the badge say 'honorary' or something like that on it?"

"It does. But mistakes happen, and I could inadvertently be given a real badge. Given the people I'll be dealing with, I don't think it'll ever come back on the sheriff."

"Let's go to the station and I'll run it by him."

* * *

I followed Paul as he crossed the bridge to Stock Island, turned north, passed the Key West Golf Club and the animal shelter and pulled into a reserved parking space in front of the modern building that housed the sheriff's headquarters. I parked a few places down from him in what seemed to be general parking. We bypassed security with a nod from Paul, took the elevator to the second floor and a secretary escorted us into a spacious office overlooking a lot of green water.

Galis introduced me to the sheriff and explained a bit about Jock's background and why I was trying to ferret out the bad guys and what I needed. He might have led the sheriff to believe I was an agent of the same shadowy organization to which Jock belonged. I didn't say anything. If it came to that, Dave Kendall would back up the story that I was one of his.

The sheriff called his secretary and asked her to dig up a badge that hadn't been assigned to anyone. When she brought it in, he swore me in as an honorary deputy and handed me the badge. It was real, not an honorary one. "You'll need to go down to the ID section and get Matt a picture identity card to go with the badge. I'll have Carla call down and tell them the ID needs to be real, not honorary."

"Would it be too much to ask that we give me a fictitious name?" I asked.

"I guess not," the sheriff said. "In for a penny, in for a pound. What name do you want on the identification card?"

"Don Monk," I said.

"Okay. If this comes back to bite me, I'll just blame Carla," the sheriff said. He laughed. "Damn if I'm not turning into a real politician."

When we finished at the ID section, I was a bona fide Monroe County deputy sheriff, at least as far as the idiots I'd be dealing with would know. I left Paul at the elevator and made my way back to my rental. It was only a little after eight and the bar I was headed for wouldn't open until nine. Paul had given me the name and phone number of the cab driver who'd taken Jock to the hospital. His name was Tariq Gajani, a Pakistani national who was a legal resident of the U.S. That information was like a big red arrow pointing to Gajani as a bad guy. But then I was probably letting my darker side slip out. The fact that he was Pakistani, and presumably a Muslim, did not make him a terrorist. Still, it didn't hurt to keep my guard up.

According to the background check run by the sheriff's detective working on the case, Gajani had come to America a couple of years before and was working for his brother-in-law who was a shift manager for the cab company. He had no criminal record.

I called him. I didn't want to give him my real name in case he was somehow involved in the whole thing. I was pretty sure my ID would pass even a close inspection. "Mr. Gajani, this is Detective Don Monk. I'm with the sheriff's department and I'd like to talk to you about the guy you took to the hospital yesterday afternoon."

"Okay. I don't know what I can tell you, though." He spoke heavily accented English. "I just took him to the hospital. He wasn't saying much at all."

"Just routine," I assured him. "Trying to get the paperwork in order. Where can I meet you?"

"We can't do this on the phone?"

"Afraid not. It shouldn't take but a few minutes."

"Can you meet me at the Starbucks at the corner of Duval and Fleming?"

"I can be there in ten minutes," I said.

"I'm wearing a Florida Marlins ball cap."

"I'll find you."

Just as I touched the off button on my phone, it chimed, indicating an incoming text. It was from Dave Kendall and contained ten photos of dark-skinned men caught in candid shots. I assumed they had been taken with a long lens. Some of them appeared to be low resolution and were a bit blurry.

* * *

Gajani was a small dark man with a mustache and smartly trimmed beard. He was neatly dressed and appeared to be in his late twenties or early thirties. He was sitting at a table next to a window overlooking Duval Street. He stood when I approached and we shook hands. "Can I get you a coffee?" I asked.

"Thank you. I'll have three shots of espresso in a small cup."

Ugh. I'd be climbing the walls. I ordered my standby, a skinny vanilla latte. It's never too early to start watching your weight. I brought the drinks back to the table and took a seat. "Mr. Gajani, I appreciate your meeting me. I only have a few questions. Just trying to tie up all the loose ends."

He nodded.

"First of all, can you tell me how you happen to be in this country?"

"I graduated from University in Pakistan as an electrical engineer. I came to this country on a work visa, but the company in New York that hired me to work as an engineer lost a big contract a few months after I started there and they didn't need me. I also needed to work on my English, so my brother-in-law got me a job with the taxi company he works for."

"How long have you been in Key West?"

"A little over a year."

"You like it?"

He smiled. "What is not to like?"

"Let's talk about yesterday afternoon."

"Okay."

"Were you dispatched to pick up the wounded man?"

"No. I was driving by."

"What made you think to stop?"

"He was pretty drunk."

"How could you tell?" I asked.

"He was staggering, and seemed about to pass out."

"Did you see any blood on his shoulder or arm?"

"Not at first."

The timbre of his voice changed when we started talking about his picking up Jock and there was a little tightening around his eyes, a subtle change of expression. It's hard to describe, but experienced trial lawyers learn to read small signs that tell them when a witness is lying. We call it our bullshit meter, and it seldom fails. When the meter pegs into the red zone, the lawyer's mind moves into cross-examination mode. I had to be careful here.

"When did you first notice the blood?" I asked.

"When he got into the back seat."

"Did he tell you where he was going?"

"No. He mumbled something, but I did not understand him. When I saw the blood, I drove him to the hospital."

"I guess you see lots of drunks in Key West. Especially during Fantasy Fest."

"Yeah, but you see that most every night."

"So, you must pick up a lot of drunks. How many per day, would you say?"

He hesitated, unsure of what his answer should be. Did he sense the trap? "Not so many."

"Why not? There are a lot of them on the streets."

"I'm pretty busy with sober customers."

"Where would you have taken your passenger yesterday if you hadn't noticed the blood?"

"Wherever he wanted to go." He was taking quick sips of his espresso before he answered each of my questions. Trying to give himself time to think. As soon as he answered, I threw another question at him. I wanted to keep up the momentum, keep him off balance.

"You just told me he was almost passed out when you first saw him. What would have happened if he had gotten into your car and passed out without giving you his destination?"

He took another sip of espresso, then faltered. He started to rise from the table. "I have to get back to work."

"Sit down, Tariq," I said. "Now."

"I am leaving."

"If you don't take your seat, I'm going to arrest you."

He sat. "I'll call my brother-in-law, and he can have a lawyer meet us at the jail."

I pulled my pistol and held it close to my chest at table height. I wanted him to see it, but didn't want to spook the other customers. His eyes widened as he caught sight of the weapon. "Tariq," I said, "I want you to listen to me very carefully. I am not going to take you to jail. I am going to find a nice deserted place and tie you to a tree and see how many questions you can answer before I put a bullet in your head."

He blinked several times, took a final swallow of his espresso, and spoke very quietly. "If I talk to you, they will kill me."

"Who'll kill you?"

"The jihadist."

"Here in Key West?"

"Yes."

"Tariq, you're in what we call a lose-lose situation. If you talk to me, some very bad guys will kill you. If you don't talk to me, I'll kill you. The jihadists can't protect you from the law, but I can protect you from the jihadists. Think about it. Your best bet is to talk to me."

"Are you really a police officer?"

I showed him my brand-new badge and ID card, pulling it back quickly so that he didn't have time to look too closely at it in case there was some flaw that I'd missed. "Yes."

"And you would shoot me?"

"In a New York minute."

"I do not believe you."

"The man you took to the hospital is my brother. Somebody's trying to kill him, as well as my girlfriend and me. I'm not going to let that happen. Now tell me how you ended up picking up my brother yesterday, or so help me God, I'll shoot you."

I raised the gun again, keeping it below the table, but in a position so that Tariq could see it. I pointed it directly at him, a determined scowl on my face, and he gave it up. I could see it in his eyes before he opened his mouth.

"I was parked on Duval Street waiting for a call for a fare yesterday morning. A man walked up and got into my cab. He spoke to me in Arabic. I told him in English that I didn't understand. He asked me in English where I was from and I told him. He asked if I was a good Muslim. I told him I was. Then he said it didn't matter where I came from, he had a job for me. He told me he wanted me to pick up a man who would have been shot, put something in the man's wallet, and take him to the hospital."

"What were you supposed to put in his wallet?"

"It was about the size of a business card, but I don't think it was. The card was folded so that I could not see what was on it."

"You agreed to do this?"

"No. I told him I wouldn't. He put a pistol to my head and told me I didn't have a choice. If I didn't do it, he'd kill me."

"How did it work?"

"I had to stay near Mugsy's Bar where the man was drinking and wait for a call from the jihadist. He'd let me know when I was to drive the block to the bar and pick up the man. I would put the card in his wallet and take him to the hospital. That was all."

"What were you to do if the man didn't pass out? How would you get the card in his wallet?"

"I asked the jihadist that. He said for me not to worry. The man would definitely pass out as soon as he got in the car."

"Did you ever look at the card?"

"No. I was very afraid."

"Did the jihadist give you his name?"

"No."

"Did you get a good look at him?"

"Yes. I was facing him as we talked."

I pulled my phone from my pocket and scrolled to the pictures Dave Kendall had sent me. I showed them to Tariq. "Do you recognize any of these men?"

At the sixth picture, he said, "That's him."

"Do you recognize any of the others?"

He took his time, scrolling slowly through the pictures. He stopped again at the last photo. "I'm pretty sure this man was with the one who got into my cab. I saw the other one standing on the sidewalk watching us."

I took the phone back and checked the pictures against a list of names Kendall had sent along with the photos. Picture number six was Akeem Said, and number ten, the man on the sidewalk, was Youssef al Bashar.

"Tariq, I can provide protection for you."

"I think I'll be okay as long as you don't tell anybody about this conversation."

"There are some people I'm going to have to tell about this, but I promise you they won't leak anything to anybody that would pose a danger to you. You've got my cell number in your phone from my call this morning. Get in touch with me if you have any reason to think you're in danger."

He smiled ruefully, rose, and walked out the door.

CHAPTER TWENTY-FIVE

SATURDAY, NOVEMBER 1

MUGSY'S BAR HUGGED the sidewalk in the middle of a block on Duval Street within easy walking distance from where the cruise ships docked. It was flanked by a t-shirt store advertising a two-for-one deal and a cheap souvenir shop. The door to the bar was propped open and at a few minutes after nine the place was half-full of tourists. A few of them were wearing shirts with the logo of a well-known cruise line whose ship had docked at the local pier an hour before. I went to the bartender, flashed my badge, and asked to speak to the manager.

In a few minutes, a man wearing shorts, a Hawaiian shirt, and flip-flops came from the back of the bar. "I'm Mugsy O'Brien, Detective. How can I help you on this glorious morning?" He had a friendly Black Irish face, his dark hair hanging just below his ears, his face broken by a big grin.

"I'm investigating the incident you had in here yesterday," I said. I was about to say more, but he interrupted.

"What incident would that be, Detective?" he asked, grin still in place.

"How many did you have?"

"None."

"I was thinking about the one where the guy got shot and had to be taken to the hospital by a taxi. Ring any bells?"

His face lost some of its friendliness, the grin becoming a mere smile. "That happened after the gentleman left my premises."

"After you kicked him out?"

"Yes. After he fell face first into the table he was sitting at, knocked over his drink and almost fell out of his chair."

"Are you suggesting you might have over-served him?"

"He's over twenty-one."

"Are you aware that the law requires you to stop serving someone who's obviously drunk?"

Now his face was dead serious. "And how the hell am I supposed to determine when someone is, quote, obviously drunk? What do you need, Detective?"

"I want to see your security tapes for yesterday."

He brightened a little, the grin returning. "Sure. Just give me a copy of your warrant."

"Warrant? Today's Saturday. I won't be able to get one before Monday, if then."

"Then you can come back on Monday."

I looked around the bar. "Got a pretty good crowd here already. Cruise ship came in this morning, I guess."

"Yep." The grin was back. "And another ship will be docking before noon. On top of that, most of the Fantasy Fest people are still here. They drink a lot."

"Good for you. I'll have some uniformed deputies here in about half an hour."

"What the hell for?" His face hardened.

"Crowd control. And the two Department of Alcoholic Beverage agents I brought down from Miami last night are going to be here as soon as they finish their breakfast. Seems they need to do some kind of audit. Anonymous complaint. Probably keep you from selling any booze for the next several days. They're very persnickety, you know."

"You can't do this. You don't even have jurisdiction here. This is a city case."

"Ah, Mugsy. How can one man be so wrong on so many issues? My jurisdiction runs county wide, and the beverage agents have statewide authority."

"I'm calling my lawyer."

"Good thinking. He can always get to court on Monday and maybe a judge will feel sorry for you. He might even take on the state attorney general, whose office will argue the case for the state Department of Alcoholic Beverages and Tobacco. With any luck, you could be back in business by next Thursday or Friday. Well, unless the state files an appeal."

"The video is in the office. It's on a hard drive of my main computer. You want a flash drive copy?"

"That'd be very nice, Mugsy, but I also want to watch your original on the hard drive."

* * *

The bar's office was small and crowded. A metal desk sat in one corner and held a computer monitor and keyboard. Wires attached them to a computer sitting on the floor next to the desk. Stacked boxes of booze took up most of the rest of the space.

"I'll pull up the security video for yesterday." O'Brien said. "There are four cameras and you can watch each of the videos separately, or see all four at once on a split screen." He showed me how to set it up and gave me a thumb drive to make a copy of anything I needed. "I think all you're going to find is that I run an honest business here." He walked out.

After fiddling with the videos for a few minutes, I got the hang of zooming, pausing, fast-forwarding, split screen and all the other marvels of modern technology. One of the cameras was set high above the bar and gave a view of the entire place. Another, next to the first one, was angled so that the bar took up most of the screen. I could clearly see the bartender pouring drinks and depositing money in the register. It didn't look like Mugsy trusted his bartender.

Another camera was placed in a corner and gave me a view of about half the entire place. The final camera was in the opposite corner and covered the other half. I put the split screen up so that I was looking at all four scenes. I saw Jock walk in a few minutes after the videos started. There were already several people at tables and others were coming in. Drinking never stops in Key West, and those who do get a little sleep begin again at nine when the bars open.

I focused on Jock for a few minutes. He took a seat, ordered a drink, and sat quietly, staring at nothing. Minutes went by and he didn't move, except to raise his glass to his lips, take a swallow, and return the glass to the table.

I knew I had a limited amount of time with Mugsy's computer. Sooner or later, he was going to figure out that I was probably lying to him about the deputies and the beverage agents. I didn't want the city police busting in and arresting me for impersonating a law enforcement officer.

I scrolled through the video until I came to noon. The time stamp told me I was at a few minutes after twelve. I focused on the one that included Jock's table and watched closely. He was still drinking steadily, but he didn't seem to be off balance. He sat straight in his chair and handled his glass of booze with no hand tremors that I could see. I fast-forwarded the video, using a slow speed. About every twenty minutes, a waitress would bring him a full cocktail glass and take the used one away. Jock was drinking about three drinks per hour. A lot of booze over the course of the day, but not more than I'd seen him drink in the past.

The time stamp told me it was 2:48 when I saw Jock's head drop to the table, his upper body following. He was sitting in the chair, bent over with his head and chest on the tabletop, his glass overturned and the booze dripping onto the floor. I watched as Mugsy came to the table, bent down, and said something. He stood back up and waved someone over. Two men wearing muscle shirts with the logo of the bar on the front came and took Jock under his arms, stood him up and dragged him out of the video frame.

I backed the video to 2:35 and ran it forward at a speed somewhat faster than real time. I watched the waitress come to the table with a drink. Jock said something to her and smiled. She smiled back and left. He took a drink, put the glass down, took another slug, put the glass down and two minutes later passed out and fell across the table.

I quickly copied that whole scene onto the thumb drive and went back to the video from the camera that kept tabs on the bartender. I fiddled with the screen until I had the video with the time stamp of 2:40, eight minutes before Jock passed out. I saw the bartender talking to a customer at the end of the bar. I couldn't get a good look at the man, but watched as he handed something to the bartender. I stopped and zoomed in. The video wasn't very high resolution and it began to pixelate as I zoomed tighter on the hand-off. I got as close as I could without completely losing the picture. It appeared to be a standard number ten envelope that the man was slipping to the bartender. It was fairly fat, as if it contained several sheets of paper, and there was a bulge at one end.

I pulled back on the zoom and tried to get a look at the customer at the end of the bar. The angle wasn't good, but when the man turned leave, I got a pretty good shot of his face. Unfortunately, it was not good enough to identify him.

I watched the bartender as he opened the envelope and took a small vial out of it. He put the envelope in his pocket, pulled a cocktail glass from the shelf, and emptied the vial into the glass. He put a few cubes of ice in the glass and poured a generous dollop of bourbon over it. A minute later the waitress appeared, picked up the drink, and took it to Jock's table.

I copied it all onto the thumb drive, shut down the computer, and left the office. I found O'Brien at the bar talking to a customer. He saw me and came over. "Got everything you need?" he asked.

"I think so. Who was bartending yesterday after lunch?"

"Jimmy Stripling. He works from noon to eight at night."

"And the waitress who was serving the guy who got shot?"

"That'd be Wanda."

"Are either of them working today?"

"Wanda's here. Jimmy comes in at noon."

"Which one is Wanda?" I asked.

He pointed to a willowy blond standing at the service bar waiting for a drink order to be prepared. I recognized her from the video.

"I'd like to talk to both of them," I said.

"About what?"

"Just their general sense of things. There were a couple of guys at the bar that I'd like to talk to the bartender about. Maybe Wanda can tell me something about the state of mind of the man I'm looking into. Nothing serious. Just some background."

"Hey. What's the big deal with the guy who passed out? Is he some kind of celebrity or something?"

"He's a very big deal, or the sheriff wouldn't have me out working on Saturday trying to figure out what happened to him."

"Who is he?"

"Can't tell you. But the next guys who come looking into this may be some very tightly wound feds. I'm doing you a favor by getting ahead of them."

"Shit," he said. "I don't need the hassle."

"Tell you what. Tell Wanda to take a break and meet me in your office. This won't take but a couple of minutes."

I watched as Mugsy pointed me out to the waitress and she walked toward the office. I joined her. "Wanda," I said when we were seated, she on the desk chair and I on a carton of Jim Beam bourbon, "I'm Detective Don Monk with the Monroe County sheriff's office. Do you remember serving a man yesterday who was here right at opening and passed out in midafternoon?"

"I sure do. Nice guy. He held his whiskey better than most. I was surprised when he passed out. He didn't seem all that drunk."

"Did you have any conversation with him during the day?"

"No, other than the usual. He'd order his drink and he always thanked me when I delivered it."

"How did he pay for the drinks?"

"He gave me a credit card when he got the first one and told me to run a tab."

"I watched the surveillance video. It appeared that you served him about three drinks an hour. Does that seem about right?"

"Yes, but we can check to be sure. His tab will still be at the register."

"Can you get it for me?"

"Sure."

I followed her out to the bar. She told Mugsy she needed to see the tab from the passed-out man. She looked closely at the register tape and said, "This looks about right. I served him his first drink at nine twenty and then two more before ten. There were three more drinks before eleven. Then a grouper sandwich. The next drink was keyed into the register at eleven forty-five."

"He ate something? May I see the tape?" I'd missed his meal on the video, but I was fast-forwarding through the morning and didn't really start watching closely until around noon. I looked at the tape again and noticed something peculiar. "Wanda, when does happy hour start in Mugsy's?"

"We don't actually have a happy hour, if you mean a time when drinks are two-for-one or something like that."

"Then why does this tape show that you were charging your customer half price for the drinks he had after he ate lunch?"

She laughed. "He had put away a lot of bourbon by the time he had the sandwich. I decided to water down his drinks. He was only getting half the whiskey he normally would for the rest of the time he was here."

"Do you do that often?"

"No, but he was a nice man and he seemed to be brooding about something. And he was alone and drinking way too much."

"He didn't notice that you were watering his drink?"

"If he did, he didn't say anything."

"And you charged him half price?"

"Yes. The drinks were half-sized."

"And Mugsy was all right with that?"

"I didn't ask him. I just told the bartenders to charge half price."

"Did he appear drunk when you served him that last drink before he passed out?"

"Oh, yeah. He was drunk, but not drunk enough to pass out. That's what surprised me so much when he went down."

"Did it occur to you that the bartender might have doctored the drink?"

"No. I just thought I misjudged how drunk he was."

"I noticed on the tape that when you served him that last drink he said something to you. Do you remember what that was?"

"I told him that I was getting off at three and I needed to check out and would he mind paying his bill. I'd start a new tab for the girl taking my place."

"His response?"

"He said he was happy to do it and that he appreciated my taking care of him and that I should add a 50 percent tip to his bill."

I looked at the credit card receipt. The card was in Mark Bailey's name. "There's no tip on this."

"No. He passed out before I could bring it back to him. I didn't think it was right to add the tip under the circumstances."

The tab came to almost a hundred dollars. I pulled a fifty-dollar bill from my wallet and gave it to her. "Don't worry. He's a friend of mine. He'll pay me back. Thanks for taking care of him yesterday. You could have taken advantage, you know."

"Not my thing," she said and went back to work.

I turned to Mugsy. "Give me Stripling's address and I'll talk to him before his shift starts. Won't have to bother your customers while he's working."

"Let me get it for you."

"Mugsy?"

"Yes."

"Don't tell him I'm coming. If I find out that you did, I'll just go fishing and let the feds take this thing over."

"Got it. Be right back."

CHAPTER TWENTY-SIX

SATURDAY, NOVEMBER 1

OVER THE YEARS, Key West had become an island of wealthy people. The funky outcasts who had made this southernmost outpost of the continental United States home as late as the 1980s had been run out because of the continually rising cost of housing. In that sense it wasn't so different from Longboat Key, but at least Longboat was only a couple of bridges from the mainland. Key West just hung there at the end of a string of little islands connected by the asphalt and bridges of the overseas highway, U.S. 1, one hundred twenty-six miles from the southern tip of the Florida peninsula.

But there is always a pocket, a small piece of a town that hasn't yet fallen to the developer who sells a lifestyle to harried executives in New York or Chicago or some other places where winters are frigid. The whole town has not yet become completely gentrified, and it was in such a pocket of old Key West where Jimmy Stripling hung his hat.

The man who answered the door of the well-kept little house was about my height and probably outweighed me by thirty pounds of flab, most of it surrounding his waist. He was wearing a t-shirt, running shorts, and flip-flops. He was the same man I'd seen on the video tending bar at Mugsy's the day before. "Jimmy Stripling?" I asked as I flashed my badge.

"Yes. What can I do for you?"

"We need to talk. May I come in?"

"Sure." He stepped back and swung the door open.

I walked in. Just as I got past Jimmy, I felt an arm snake around my throat and begin to apply pressure. Old training kicked in. I jabbed backward with my left elbow, putting all the power I could behind it. It caught him in the soft spot just in front of his left ribs. At the same time, I raised my right leg and brought the heel of my shoe down hard on his virtually bare foot. It was a jackhammer blow, and I felt the crack of some of the small bones just under the skin of his instep. I reached around to my back with my right hand, and as he pulled backward from the elbow strike to his gut, I grabbed a handful of testicles and jerked downward, squeezing with all the strength I could muster.

The net result was old Jimmy screaming and falling forward onto his knees, holding his nuts with one hand and his stomach with the other. I pushed the idiot to the floor, put a knee in his back, and stuck my pistol's barrel in his ear. "Can you hear me, shithead?"

"I want a lawyer."

"That option just went out the door."

"I know my rights." He was moaning as he talked.

"You waived those rights the minute you attacked me. You ready to die?"

"No. Please. I didn't know you were a cop."

"You're even dumber than you look. You saw my badge and you wanted to tell me all about your rights. Who'd you think I was? The neighborhood drug dealer? Let's talk."

"You almost ripped my dick off. What do you want?"

"How much money did you get for slipping that mickey into the guy's drink yesterday afternoon?"

"I don't know what you're talking about."

"Don't move a muscle," I said. I stood and kicked him in the side. He screamed. "Lie to me again and I'm just going to give up and leave.

I'll call the cops and tell them your body is here so it doesn't stink up the neighborhood."

"A thousand dollars."

"You gave a man you didn't know a mickey for a measly thousand bucks? If he'd died, you'd be charged with murder."

"It wasn't anything that would hurt him. Just some kind of knock-out drug."

"That's what the guy told you?"

"Yeah."

"And you believed him?"

"Yeah."

"What was his name?"

"He didn't give it to me."

"Had you ever seen him before?"

"No."

"So this guy you don't know just walks into your bar, gives you a vial of something, you don't know what, and a thousand bucks and tells you to drug a customer's drink."

"He told me it was a mild sedative."

"You believed him."

"That's about it."

"And you'd never seen the man before, didn't know his name, and you still committed a crime for him."

"Well, yeah, and for the thousand bucks."

"I'm going to show you some pictures and I want you to pick out the one who gave you the money."

"If I do that, will you let me go?"

"Yes, but I'll know if you're lying and I'll shoot you."

He sat up, his face showing the pain that was coursing through his rotund body. I showed him several of the pictures on my phone. He peered closely at each one and then pointed to the one of Akeem Said. I wasn't surprised.

"Good job," I said. "Now, where is the money?"

"What money?"

"The grand you got in the envelope yesterday."

"Why?"

"It's my money now."

"Shit."

"Yep."

"It's in the bedroom."

"Take me to it."

He stood and limped toward the bedroom, favoring the foot I'd stomped. I followed, gun in hand. He bent over a bedside table and pulled out a drawer. "If I see anything other than an envelope coming out of that drawer, I'll shoot you," I said.

He handed me the money. Ten one-hundred-dollar bills. "See you around," I said, and turned to leave.

"You going to give me a receipt?"

"I'll mail it to you."

"You're not really a cop, are you?"

I laughed. "Don't fret over that, but hear me on this. If I find out that you've gone to the law about our meeting today, and I will find out, I'll come back and kill you. In fact, if you tell anybody about this, you'll be dead within twenty-four hours. We clear?"

"Yes."

I walked out, leaving him standing in the bedroom massaging his balls. As I was nearing the front door, I heard several hard raps. A visitor. I went back to the bedroom. "Somebody's at the door," I said. "Answer it, but if I hear you say a word about me being here, I'll shoot both you and your guest. Got it?"

"Yeah, it's probably old Mrs. Harper from next door. She checks in with me most mornings."

I stood behind the door between the bedroom and living room, peeking through the crack between the door and the jamb. I watched

Stripling waddle across the room and open the door. A swarthy man pushed his way into the room, shoved the door shut with his foot, raised a silenced pistol, and shot Stripling in the chest.

I was moving by the time the shot was fired, my pistol in hand, taking a bead on the shooter. He was concentrating on Stripling's body lying on the floor. He must have heard me, or caught sight of me in his peripheral vision, or maybe perceived danger from some feral instinct that lies deep in the reptilian part of the human brain. He was moving the muzzle of his pistol in my direction when I shot him in the face.

He dropped like a bag of rocks, landing on his back. I saw a neat hole, the entrance wound, just to the right of his nose. I shot him again. Right in the middle of his forehead. You can't be too sure in these situations. "Sayonara, Akeem," I said.

I'd recognized the man when he first pushed his way into the house. Akeem Said, the man who'd paid Stripling to put the mickey in Jock's drink. I had not expected him to shoot the pudgy bartender, but I can't say I was surprised. The best way to ensure silence from a co-conspirator is to kill him.

I felt no remorse about my actions in taking Akeem out. He would have killed me, or much worse, J.D., without any more thought than stepping on a bug. He was a predator and the world was better off without him.

One down and nine to go, I thought. Assuming Youssef had brought his entire group to America. I needed to find out about that. I couldn't protect myself, or J.D., or Jock, if I didn't know the dimensions of the threat. How many were after us?

I had parked the rental two blocks from Stripling's house, a precaution on which I now congratulated myself. I drew the blinds in the living room and walked through the kitchen and out the back door. I wasn't too concerned about the sounds of the gunshots. Akeem had used a silencer and my little pistol didn't make much noise. The day was warm, and most of the neighbors were locked in their hermitically sealed houses with the air conditioning running on high.

I had walked about a block when I spotted a car parked on the side of the road, the driver's side next to the sidewalk, a man behind the wheel. He was looking down, perhaps fiddling with the radio. He didn't see me. I stepped behind a big gumbo-limbo tree that stood next to the sidewalk, its low limbs hiding me from the man in the car.

I could tell that the car's engine was not running. The front side windows were rolled down, an attempt to catch the little breeze that blew across the island. I couldn't imagine why anyone would be sitting in a parked car in the heat, unless he was waiting for a passenger.

I peered around the tree trunk, pulling my head back quickly. The driver was dark skinned, his eyes steely, searching the street. He wore a white short-sleeved dress shirt, the collar unbuttoned. I pulled my phone out and went through the photos Dave Kendall had sent me. The man in the car matched one of the pictures. Mohammed al Tafari.

I pulled my ball cap low over my face, stepped out from behind the tree, and walked nonchalantly toward the car. I wanted it to appear to the bad guy that I was coming from the house that shared the lot with the gumbo-limbo tree.

The man behind the steering wheel watched me as I approached the car, but showed no concern. I was just a neighborhood guy out for a walk. I hoped. When I was even with the driver's side front door, I moved quickly, sidestepping to the car, pulling my pistol, and sticking it in his face before he could react. He flinched, and I said, "Don't move and put your hands in your lap."

The surprise on his face was morphing into anger. I wasn't sure if he was going to follow my orders. If not, I was prepared to shoot him, and I told him as much. The look of anger dissipated and was replaced with one of resignation.

"I'm a cop," I said. "Do you understand?"

He shook his head.

"Do you speak English?"

Again, the head shake.

"Okay, I'll just have to shoot you." I pushed the muzzle of the pistol into his temple.

"No. I speak English."

"Do you know who I am?"

"Yes. I've seen your picture. You're Matt Royal."

So much for my cop disguise. "Ah," I said. "That's better. We can have a conversation. Where's Youssef?"

His English was heavily accented, but I could understand him, and he could obviously understand me. Apparently, martyrdom in the hot sun of a Key West autumn didn't appeal to him.

"I do not know."

"I don't want to play games with you. The reason you're here alone is that I just killed Akeem in the house where he went to kill Stripling. I'll kill you the next time you lie to me. Do we understand each other?"

"Yes."

"Good. Let's try again. Where's Youssef?"

"He's here. In Key West."

"Where?"

"I do not know. He is like a ghost. He moves around all the time and then calls us with orders."

"Who's us?"

"Our team."

"How many of you are there?"

"Five."

"Where are the others from your group or cell or whatever you call it?"

"They are fighting in Syria."

"Why did you only bring five?"

"We only had five passports."

"Fake ones?"

"Yes."

"How did you get to the U.S.?"

"We flew to London and then to Miami."

"For what purpose?"

"We were to go to Longboat Key and kill you and the woman."

"Why?"

"I do not know. Youssef said it was revenge for the one you call Jock Algren killing his family."

"How did you know we were friends with Mr. Algren?"

"I do not know. Youssef did not tell us anything about that. He is our leader. We go where he says to go and do what he says to do."

That had the ring of truth. "How did Youssef even know who Jock was?"

"I don't know that, either."

"What did he tell you about Jock?"

"Just that he had found out the man's name and that he was visiting his friends in Longboat Key. He said that you and the woman were his only family and that you had to die."

"Did he give you a reason?"

"I do not think he actually told us a reason, but we all knew it was revenge for the killing of his family."

"If you were going to Longboat Key, how did you end up in Key West?"

"Youssef called me yesterday and told me to go to Key West and meet Akeem."

"Did he say why you were to come to Key West?"

"No."

"You didn't ask?"

"I follow orders. I do not ask questions."

"How long were you in Miami?"

"Two days."

"How did you get to Key West?"

"I stole this car in Miami and drove here."

"How did you hook up with Akeem?"

"I met him and Youssef at a small hotel on the last island before Key West."

"Stock Island?"

"Yes. I think that is what it is called."

"Were you with them yesterday when they found Jock?"

"Yes."

"How did you know where he was?"

"Youssef knew."

I pushed the pistol up under his chin. "What do you know? Lie to me and you'll find your martyrdom."

"Okay, okay. Youssef got a call from a man who works with us. He said that the man called Jock was flying to Miami. I was staying at a hotel in the airport terminal. I went down to the security area and saw him leaving the concourse. I followed him to a charter service office on the other side of the airport."

"Who was the man who called Youssef?"

"I do not know, but he followed Jock from Longboat Key to the Tampa airport."

"How did Jock get to the charter service office?"

"In a taxi. I followed him in another taxi and went into the office. I heard Jock ask about a charter to Key West. I called Youssef and told him what I had found out."

"How did you know what bar Jock was in when you got the cabbie to slip him a mickey?"

"A mickey? I do not understand."

"Knockout drops. Something to make him pass out."

"I did not arrive in Key West until about noon. I called Youssef and he told me where to meet him and Akeem. I went there and stayed in the car while they met with the taxi driver. That's all I know. I swear."

"What's your name?"

"Mohammed al Tafari."

"What was the name on the passport you used to enter the U.S.?"

"Amal Bargoon."

"And the names on the other passports?"

"I do not know. I never saw the passports."

"I need their real names."

He hesitated and I shoved the gun a little deeper into his throat. "Okay," he said and gave me two more names. They matched names on the pictures Kendall had sent me.

"What's the name of the motel where you're staying?"

He gave it to me. "But I checked out this morning."

"Why? Are you planning on leaving?"

"No, but we were instructed to only spend one night in a place, check out early, and then move to another late in the evening."

"How does Youssef call you? Cell phone?"

"Yes."

"Let me have your phone. Where is it?"

"It's in my shirt pocket."

And that's when I made a fatal mistake. As I reached for it with my left hand he grabbed my wrist with his left hand and jerked my arm down toward his lap. At the same time, he was beginning to move his right fist toward my face. The force of his grip and the jerking motion on my left arm pulled me toward him and my right hand, the one with the gun, was forced down from his neck. I had no time to react. I simply pulled the trigger. The pistol was pointed down toward his left chest. He died immediately, probably shot through the heart.

I pulled his phone from his shirt pocket and looked around to see if anybody had observed what had happened. The sound of the shot had been muffled because the barrel was buried in his chest and was inside the car. I didn't see anybody, but somebody could have been looking out a window. I straightened up the body so that a passerby might think he was sleeping. The blood that had appeared at the point where the bullet entered his chest couldn't be seen from the street. I reached into the car as if I were shaking hands with the corpse, waved good-bye and walked around the corner to my car.

As soon as I was out of the neighborhood, I called Paul Galis and told him what happened. "So," he said, "you left two bodies in a house and one in a car on a public street, two of them terrorists, all in the Key West police department's jurisdiction and you want me to take care of things."

"I'd be forever grateful."

Paul made a grunting sound. Maybe he was reaching for a chuckle.

"The dead man told me he was staying in a small hotel on Stock Island," I said, "in case you want to check it out. He left this morning." I gave him the name of the hotel.

"I'll have a team get over there and see what they can find. I've got a drinking buddy who's a detective on the Key West force. I think I can get him involved and give you about two days before we have to start moving paperwork on the dead guys. Can I blame this on Jock?"

"Jock?"

"Yeah. If I put Jock in your place, nobody at Key West PD is going to do anything about it. Jock's boss can make a phone call or two and that'll be the end of it."

"Sounds like a plan," I said.

"This all has to be worked out between the agency and the local law. Let's have Dave Kendall call the sheriff and the Key West police chief and tell them that an unnamed agent killed them because they were terrorists who were here on a mission to blow something up. The agency was on to them but had not determined their target. What about the gun you used to shoot those guys?"

"The gun belongs to Jock and it's untraceable, but I wouldn't want either of us to be picked up with that pistol in our possession."

"I understand. Ditch the pistol."

"I'm going to throw it off a bridge. I'll have to find another weapon."

"I've got a couple of untraceable ones at the house," Galis said. "You can take your pick. Are you going to do any more hunting on my island?"

"Depends."

"On what?"

"I know the group's leader, Youssef, is on the island. Or at least he was yesterday when Akeem threatened the taxi driver. And the one I just killed said Youssef was in Key West but didn't know where. If I find him, I'll take him out. Cut off the head of the snake."

Galis let out a sigh. "Shit. I wish you'd take your fight somewhere else. Let me know if I can help you get the bastard."

"Thanks, Paul. There is one thing. I've got the dead man's cell phone. It's probably a burner, but he told me he got his orders from Youssef by phone. It might be worth checking out the phone and the numbers that called him. Can your people handle that?"

"Not a problem, but if they're all using burners, it won't give us much."

"Yeah. When the cops get to Stripling's house, they might want to check the dead Arab for a phone. I didn't think about that when I was leaving."

"I'll call my buddy at Key West PD."

I drove to Duval Street and found a parking place near St. Paul's Episcopal church. There was a poor box attached to a wall near the altar, with a sign that said something about helping those who had little. I deposited the ten bills I'd gotten from Stripling and stood quietly for a few minutes, mulling over the two deaths I'd been responsible for that morning. I'd killed men before, and in some manner I'd regretted each one. But I couldn't find any contrition in my heart over the deaths of the two terrorists.

I wondered how many innocents they'd killed, and I knew the world was better off with them out of it. Besides, they wanted to take away my most precious gift, J.D., to wipe her off the face of the earth. I could not imagine a world without her. I shrugged, and walked out into the sunlight.

CHAPTER TWENTY-SEVEN

SATURDAY, NOVEMBER 1

THE SUN SLIPPED above the eastern horizon, bathing the beach in a soft light. The crime scene techs were on their knees scouring the sand, looking for any piece of evidence, no matter how small. One of the ME's assistants knelt over Fortson's body, closely examining it, looking for any anomaly other than the obviously slashed throat.

J.D. stood nearby, watching the assistant work. After a couple of minutes he looked up at her and said, "We'll know more when we get his clothes off, but I doubt we'll find anything other than the gash in his throat."

"Okay. Bag him and let's get him out of here before folks start looking out their windows. We don't want a corpse to ruin their very expensive views."

J.D. pulled out her cell phone and called Tom Jones. "Did I wake you up?" she asked when he answered.

"Not a chance, sweetheart. Neither of us has been able to sleep after seeing a dead man on the beach. Have you caught the killer yet?"

"You're my number one suspect."

"Ha. I don't have it in me to hurt anybody. You might want to take a look at Linda, though."

J.D. laughed. "You're a piece of work, T.J. Ratting out your own wife. I would like to talk to you guys. I gather no one took a formal statement from you last night."

"No. It was kind of confusing. Are you down on the beach?"

"I am."

"I heard the chief was dragging you back from Key West. I bet Matt liked that."

"He'll get over it."

"Come on up. I'll put some coffee on."

"Would you and Linda mind coming down to the beach? I'd like to talk to you at the scene. Maybe you can point out something you might have noticed. Being there might jog your memory."

"We'll see you in a few minutes. Want me to bring coffee?"

"I'd kill for a cup. Black."

"On the way."

J.D. walked over to the chief. "Bill, Tom and Linda Jones are coming down to give a statement. You want to sit in?"

"Might as well. Maybe they can put some context to this mess. Can you see any connection to Fortson's murder and your case on his sister?"

"Not yet, but if it's there, we'll find it."

"How's Steve Carey working out?"

"He's a big help. He's going to make a good investigator. He's got the instincts."

"Let's get him over to talk with the Joneses. Maybe the three of us can come up with some intelligent questions."

* * *

Tom and Linda were showing J.D. about where they were standing when they noticed Fortson's body on the sand. "We almost stumbled over him," Linda said. "It was pitch dark out here. It'd been overcast late in the afternoon, so I suppose we still had cloud cover. No moon at all. And no stars."

"Was anybody with you?" Carey asked.

"No," Tom said. "We'd just come back from dinner with Tom and Nancy Stout and Sammy and Courtney."

"Ole Sammy," Steve said. "Who's Courtney? His girl du jour?"

Linda laughed. "Hardly. She's way too smart for that. She's the bartender at the Lazy Lobster. She and Sammy are just buddies."

"Did you know Fortson?" J.D. asked.

"Just to see him on the beach sometimes," Linda said. "He always seemed pleasant. I heard stories about his sister being killed in his house a few years back."

"He invited me up on his porch once," Tom said. "We put away a bottle of wine and enjoyed the sunset. He told me his home was in Orlando and that he made his living as an investor."

"Anything else?" Lester asked. "Had you ever met him in Orlando?"

"No. We'd never met until we bought the place here. That afternoon we mostly just chatted about the island, gossiped a little. You know, drank wine and talked about nothing important."

J.D. asked, "Did either of you see anybody else on the beach just before or after you found the body?"

Tom looked at Linda. "What about the guy from next door we saw going into the building?"

"Yeah, but I think he was just one of our neighbors out for a walk. Like we were."

"Did you recognize him?" J.D. asked.

"No," Linda said. "It was real dark."

"What made you think he was your neighbor?"

"Well," Linda said, "I guess because he was going into the condo building next door to ours."

"Did you speak to him?" J.D. asked.

"No," Tom said. "He was already past us before we got close enough to say anything."

"Can you describe him?"

"No," Tom said, "I didn't get a good enough look."

"He was white," Linda said, "and I think he had a white beard. He was wearing a ball cap."

"Anything else?" J.D. asked.

"No. I just got a quick glimpse when he walked by the security light at the condo beach access. You know how they have to shield those things because of the turtle nestlings. They don't give out much light, so it was real quick."

"You're sure the beard was white?"

"I can't be sure. It looked white in the light, but it could have been gray. Or even red, for that matter."

"Did you actually see him go into the building, or just walk toward it?"

Linda shook her head. "I just saw him walk into the garage that takes up the ground floor. I can't say whether he got on the elevator."

J.D. looked at Tom. "Me neither," he said.

"Thanks," J.D. said. "That at least gives us some information."

"You think he was the killer?" Tom asked.

"I don't know," J.D. said. "He might have been a resident or guest in one of the condos. Looks like there're only about six units there. As soon as the people start waking up, we'll talk to them and see if there's anybody there with a beard. We should be able to figure that out pretty quickly. If nobody there has a beard, it might mean that the man you saw was the killer. On the other hand, it might just mean that he was trespassing on the property. Cutting through to the street. We'll have to follow up on it, though."

* * *

J.D., Steve Carey, and Kevin Combs, the crime scene technician, were standing in the late Peter Fortson's living room, the vast expanse of the Gulf of Mexico visible through the large windows that took up the west wall of the house. The sun had crawled higher in the sky as midmorning approached, and the glare off the water was strong. "Are we looking for anything specific?" Kevin asked.

"Yeah," J.D. said, and yawned. "I want you and the Manatee crime scene people to take this place apart. Treat it like you would a murder scene. But specifically, I'd like to see any financial records you can come up with, or any documents that might lead me to bank accounts. That sort of thing."

"I'll get the people and get on it. Where are you going to be?"

"I'm going to look around, see if anything pops up. Like maybe a computer. After that, I'll be on my cell. If I find a computer, I'll probably be at the office with the department's geek."

"J.D.," Carey said. "Are you thinking about a computer like that laptop sitting on the table in the dining room?"

She laughed. "You're going to make one darn fine detective, Officer Carey."

J.D. sat at the table and booted up the computer. It was password protected, but she tried several times using name combinations. Finally, she ran out of tries and the computer shut down. "Got to take this to the geek," she said, and left the house.

* * *

People expected the department geek, who described himself as a "computer nerd," to be a small man with rimless spectacles and longish hair wearing a t-shirt and jeans, maybe flip-flops. In reality the geek stood six feet three inches tall and had the build of a man who worked out regularly. He had grown up across the bay in Bradenton, earned a football scholarship to Florida State University, was red-shirted his freshman year and started at outside linebacker in every game for the next four years.

At the end of his fifth year in college, he graduated with a master's degree in computer science and was drafted in the first round by the Tampa Bay Buccaneers. He signed a four-year contract worth about twenty million dollars, played out the contract, got tired of being beat up by big offensive linemen, retired, and moved to Longboat Key. He'd offered his services to Bill Lester for a nominal salary and came to work every day just like he needed the money. His name was Reuben Carlson.

Twenty minutes after J.D. had turned the laptop over to him, Carlson called her on the office intercom and said, "I'm in. Are you looking for anything in particular?"

"Financial records, Reuben. Anything you can find. I'm going home for a short nap. Steve rolled me out of bed at three this morning and I'm beat. I'll call you when I wake up, probably around noon."

"If I find them, I'll print them out for you. Anything else?"

"Go through it with a fine-tooth comb. You know the drill. I want his Internet history, his emails for the last couple of months, the names of everybody he's corresponded with by email for as far back as you can go, anything that looks the least bit interesting."

"I'm on it, J.D."

CHAPTER TWENTY-EIGHT

SATURDAY, NOVEMBER 1

J.D. STRIPPED AND stepped into her shower. She let the hot water run over her body, rejuvenating her a bit. She'd had little sleep, a long helicopter flight, and hours of standing around on the beach. She was gritty with sand and exhausted by the stress that a murder investigation always brought. She soaped herself, rinsed, and turned off the water. She dried herself with the large beach towel, hung it on the hook on the back of the door and fell into bed. She was asleep almost instantly.

She awoke when she heard a noise from the front door of her condo. A key in the lock. Her bedside clock told her she'd slept for almost two hours.

She got out of bed, realized she was naked, and grabbed another beach towel from a nearby chair. She wrapped the towel around her and pulled the service pistol from its holster laying atop the pile of dirty clothes she'd discarded as she'd headed for the shower.

She was sure she'd engaged the dead bolt when she came into her condo. She ran it through her mind and couldn't specifically remember doing it. It was force of habit, though, and she thought she could rely on the routine. The dead bolt was a security measure ensuring that no key could unlock the door from the outside. She heard the key in the lock turn again, then again, and then a hard bang, as if someone was hitting the door in frustration. Then, silence.

J.D. walked to the door, listened carefully, and heard nothing. She turned the dead bolt and pulled the door open, her gun in her hand and pointed outward. Sunlight flooded into her condo, a cool breeze ruffling the palms that grew from the ground past her second floor and on up to the building's third story. An open walkway ran the length of the building, with the individual doors to each of the units opening onto it. "Who's there?"

Nothing. Then she heard a moan. It came from her left, from the area of the alcove that held the elevator landing. She walked outside, pistol ready, holding her towel tightly around her. She saw a man sitting on the walkway and leaning against the railing. He was holding his head, shaking it a little as if trying to clear his mind. She recognized him. The condo's maintenance manager. She rushed to him, knelt beside him. "Larry, what happened?"

He looked at her. "Hi, J.D. I don't know. Somebody came out of the elevator and knocked me in the back of the head."

"Did you get a look at him?"

"No. I was unlocking the door to the storage room and had my back to him."

"Did he get your keys?"

Larry looked down at his waist where he kept his keys attached to his belt. He felt around to his back, shook his head. "Looks like he did."

"You've got a master key that lets you into any unit here, right?"

"Yeah. It's gone, too."

"Will that key open a door if the dead bolt is engaged?"

"No."

"Isn't that a bit unusual?"

"Yeah, but when the developer built this building, he was planning for it to be mostly rentals. He installed locks that work like the ones they put in hotels. As long as you've got the dead bolt engaged, nobody can get in."

"Okay. Stay right here, Larry. I'm going to get my phone and call for the paramedics. I'll be back in two seconds."

"Thanks, J.D. I'm feeling a little nauseous."

When J.D. returned, she was on the phone to the fire department and paramedics were being dispatched. She relayed that information to Larry, and then called the police dispatcher. "Iva, this is J.D. Somebody attacked the maintenance man at my condo and stole his keys. Whoever it was tried to get into my place with the master key, but I had the door dead-bolted. I'm okay and the paramedics are on the way to check Larry out. I need the crime scene people to come over and see if they can find anything that would tell us who was after me."

"Martin Sharkey's parked around the corner from you at Cannons talking to David Miller. He'll be there in two minutes."

"Thanks, Iva."

A minute after J.D. hung up, an unmarked police car rushed into the parking lot and stopped. Deputy Chief of Police Martin Sharkey jumped out and in another minute was leaving the elevator. J.D. was still kneeling beside Larry. The ambulance siren was getting louder. The paramedics would arrive shortly.

"You all right, J.D.?" Sharkey asked.

"I'm fine, Martin." She told him what had happened.

"That towel looks good on you, but I think you'd better go put on some clothes. I'll stay with Larry."

J.D. had forgotten about her state of dishabille. She went to her condo, dressed quickly in shorts, a pullover top, and flip-flops. When she got back to Larry, the paramedics were arriving in the elevator. She explained what had happened to Larry while they examined him. They decided they needed to have him checked over by a doctor at Blake Hospital. Larry didn't resist. He climbed onto a stretcher, and the little group headed for the ambulance in the parking lot.

"Matt's going to be really pissed," Sharkey said.

"About what?" J.D. asked.

"We were supposed to keep an eye on you."

"Who's we?"

"Us. The department. Cops."

"What are you talking about?"

"Matt called the chief early this morning just after you left Key West. He told Bill you might be in danger and he was worried. Matt asked him to make sure you were protected."

"Crap. I hate that. I know he's just looking out for me, but I can't stand to be babied."

"He told Bill about Jock's thoughts that some very bad people want to kill you."

"That may be so, but I can take care of myself."

Sharkey held up his hands in a sign of surrender. "I know you can. That's why I didn't have one of our guys guarding you, even though the chief told me to do just that. I didn't think you needed it, and I knew it would embarrass you. I'm sorry, J.D. I could have gotten you killed."

"Martin, if that guy, whoever he was, had come through my door, I'd have blown him away. I don't need protection."

"Be careful, J.D. Somebody tried to kill you in Gainesville a couple of days ago, and Jock thinks some crazy Arabs are after you. If he's right, you've got lots of people trying to kill you, and we don't know why."

"I know why the terrorists want me dead. What I can't figure out is who those people in Gainesville were. Could they be connected to the mess Jock is talking about?"

"What is Jock saying? Why do some terrorists want to kill you?"

"I'm sorry, Martin. I can't talk about that. But I trust Jock and I trust his instincts."

"Did you get a look at whoever was at your door?"

"No, but he probably ran down the stairs at the end of the building. He could have gotten out the door and into that empty lot next door. It's pretty wooded and would have given him some cover."

"What about Larry?"

"He didn't see anything. When the elevator door opened, Larry was standing in that little alcove unlocking the door to the storage room. The bad guy hit him in the back of the head before Larry could react."

"Hit him with what?"

"I don't know. I'm assuming the butt of a pistol."

"Did you see a pistol?"

"No. But I'm pretty sure if someone was after me, they would've brought one."

"You're probably right. I've got to call Matt, you know."

"Yeah, I know. Tell him to call me when you two finish plotting my security. And Martin, thanks for your confidence in me. For understanding that I really don't need a babysitter."

"You're welcome. But Matt's still going to kill me."

CHAPTER TWENTY-NINE

SATURDAY, NOVEMBER 1

I DROVE TO Lower Sugarloaf Key to bring Jock up to date on what I'd found. He was sitting in the living room watching Fox News with the sound turned off. He looked up when I walked in and returned to the TV without saying anything. I'd stopped at a small store on Stock Island just over the bridge from Key West and picked up some sandwiches and soda. "You hungry?" I asked.

"Sure."

"You want to hear about my morning?"

"Maybe after lunch." He was still staring at the TV.

"You okay, buddy?"

"Fit as a fiddle."

I opened the bags of food and handed him a sandwich on a plate I found in a cabinet over the sink. I was getting my sandwich out of the bag when my phone rang. The caller ID told me it was Martin Sharkey.

"Jock," I said, "I'll take this outside."

I answered as I walked out the door. "What's up, Martin?"

First, he assured me that J.D. was fine and then told me what had happened at her condo. He admitted that he'd ratted me out on my request for protection for her, but assured me that she didn't appear too mad about it. I figured I hadn't heard the end of this one.

J.D. is serious about her ability to take care of herself in a job that has traditionally been for men only. She had the respect of every cop she'd ever worked with and was feared by every criminal she'd ever sent to prison. The problem was that she didn't know that, or at least, she didn't believe it, or understand it. This all led to a lot of sensitivity over my overly protective nature. It wasn't that I didn't have confidence in her ability to protect herself, but rather that my greatest fear was the possibility of losing her. I was the nervous Nellie, not she.

I called J.D. as soon as Sharkey hung up. "Are you okay?" I asked when she answered.

"No worse for wear, Matt. What're you up to?"

"Tell me what happened this morning."

"I'm sure Martin filled you in."

"He did, but I want to hear it from you."

She gave me the whole story, and then said, "If he'd come through the door, I'd have shot him dead. I'm not in danger."

"I know you can take care of yourself, sweetie, but be very careful."

"I will. Now tell me what's going on with you."

"I've had a busy morning. I can't talk about it on the phone. I'll tell you about it when I get home."

"When's that going to be?"

"Tonight. I'm at Paul's house. I'll get my stuff and start for Longboat. It'll take me seven or eight hours."

"Can't you get a flight?"

"I don't want to take a chance on one of the terrorists seeing me if they're watching the airport. The less they know of my whereabouts, the safer I'll feel."

"What about Coit Airways picking you up at the Naval Air Station where the sheriff's chopper picked me up this morning?"

"The Navy isn't going to let a private aircraft land there."

"Then I guess you're driving. Are you coming home to take care of me?"

"No. I'm coming to let you take care of me. You'll understand when I tell you about my day."

"Bad?"

"Bad enough."

"What about Jock? Are you bringing him?"

"I think I'll leave him with Paul. He's pretty well hidden down here and I don't think he feels any need to leave. It's like he's moved into some sort of different dimension. He's in the house watching a news program on Fox with the sound turned off. He didn't say anything to me when I walked in and he wasn't interested in what I'd been doing since I left him early this morning. I'm worried about him, but I've got to keep him alive until things settle down and we can get him some treatment."

"I'm sure his agency has shrinks who take care of this kind of problem. Maybe they can help."

"Good idea," I said. "I've got to call Dave Kendall about what's going on. I'll ask about the shrinks."

I went back inside and asked Jock if I could use his encrypted cell phone to call Dave Kendall. "Help yourself," he said. "It's on the counter in the kitchen."

"Do you want to talk to Dave while I've got him on the phone?"

"Nah. I'll talk to him later."

I stepped back outside and called Kendall. I told him about my morning and about the state that Jock seemed to be in. I gave him the names of the two men I'd killed and the other three the man in the car had identified.

"Good work," Dave said. "We at least have the names of the five that are in the country."

"If Mohammed was telling the truth."

"Maybe I can help find out if he was lying to you."

"How?"

"We've got people on the ground in Aleppo. I think this little group has become dangerous enough to be put on a kill list. I should have something in a couple of days. That'll only leave you two more to run down, plus Youssef."

"Thanks a lot, Dave. Based on what Mohammed said before he died, it sounds to me as if someone is tracking Jock. Could that be one of your people, a mole?"

"If it is, he's well hidden. We're trying to track him down. If we find him, he's finished."

"You're not talking about firing him."

Dave laughed once, more of a "hah," some bitterness leaking out. "Not exactly. We'll wring him dry and then he'll meet with a fatal accident."

"Well deserved."

"Matt, do you need some help? I can send an agent down."

"Let me think about it. I'd just as soon not have any of your people know about the state Jock's in these days. I hope he'll get better if we can get rid of the terrorists."

"I can also send one of the shrinks to Key West."

"I think it's too early for that. Let's see if we can get this mess cleaned up and bring Jock back to Longboat. That might be the right time to get the shrink involved."

I hung up and called Paul Galis at his office. I told him about J.D.'s problem in Longboat. "I need to get back up there. Do you mind keeping an eye on Jock for a few days until I can get this mess settled?"

"Not at all. How're you getting home? The flights out of here aren't all that good, unless you're going to Miami."

"I'm going to drive. I'll get moving as soon as I get my stuff together."

"Can't you get your buddy to fly down and pick you up? Be a lot quicker."

"I want the bad guys to think I'm still in Key West. They seem to have a lot of eyes, and somebody might be watching the airport."

"Not if you use Lower Sugarloaf International."

"What's that?"

"It's our less-than-famous airport on Lower Sugarloaf Key."

"You're kidding."

"Nope. Have you noticed the sign on the highway advertising Sky Dive Key West?"

"Yes."

"Well, right down that road, there's an old airstrip. It was just dirt for years, but recently they paved it. There're no lights, so it's only good for use during the day. Nothing out there but the little building the sky divers use and two or three planes."

"Can anybody land there?"

"Sure, but I think they have to check in with the Navy people at Boca Chica. I'm pretty sure you can't get in there without air traffic controllers at the base helping you out. They don't want to bend one of their jets on some yahoo trying to land on that strip."

"I'll call Russ. He'll know about all that. Or he can figure it out."

"Okay. Let me know what you decide. I'll keep an eye on Jock."

I called Russ to see if Coit Airways was operating. He assured me it was.

"Did you know anything about an airstrip on Lower Sugarloaf Key?"

"Hold on."

He was back in a couple of minutes. "I've got all the FAA airport information on my iPad. That little strip on Lower Sugarloaf is big enough for me to land on. When do you want me to pick you up?"

"There're no lights on this strip. Can you get here around dusk and still have time to take off before it's too dark to see?"

"If I'm in and out by six this evening, we're in good shape."

"Suppose I meet you at the strip at six. Will that work?"

"See you then."

CHAPTER THIRTY

Saturday, November 1

I called J.D. again to tell her Russ would pick me up and I'd be on Longboat by seven-thirty or so. She was back in the police station putting together what little evidence they had on what the locals were calling murder on the beach. "Sounds like a good name for a drink," I said.

"Yeah, or a mystery book store."

"Have you found anything that points you to the murderer?"

"Not really. The killer left nothing at the scene. The best evidence we have is the description Linda Jones gave us."

"Not much to go on," I said. "What about your situation?"

"The crime scene techs didn't find anything. They think the guy was wearing gloves, so no fingerprints. They found Larry's keys on a step in the north-end stairwell and some shoe prints in the dirt in that hedge that separates our property from the lot next door."

"What about the shoe prints? Anything that'll help?"

"Too early to tell. The techs are going to run them and see if they can identify the shoe's manufacturer, but they think it's hopeless. The prints look like the kind you see on millions of athletic shoes. They may not even belong to the guy who was at my door."

"And nobody saw anything?"

"Maybe. Marylou Webster and Susan Mink were in the hot tub down on that end of the property and they saw somebody running through the hedge. They didn't get a good look at him, but both of them thought the guy had a white or gray beard. That sounds like the man the Joneses saw leaving the beach where they found the body."

"That sounds like too much of a coincidence," I said.

"Yeah, but it probably won't mean anything. Doc Hawkins puts Fortson's time of death at eleven p.m., give or take an hour. The Joneses saw the bearded man at about one a.m. I'm pretty sure the killer wouldn't have stayed around for an hour or more after he murdered somebody."

"Has Hawkins finished the autopsy?"

"He's going to do it on Monday. We know the cause of death, so there's no big hurry. I didn't want to ruin his weekend."

We hung up and I sat and thought about a plan that I had been mulling over. I was pretty sure that Tariq Gajani, the cab driver, wasn't as innocent as he would have me believe. He could very well be part of Youssef's group, maybe a sleeper who'd been inserted into South Florida to be activated when needed. Or, he might have been completely intimidated by Youssef and dragged into the operation. Whatever the situation, if my suspicions were correct, I thought I might be able to use Tariq.

I made another call to the cabbie. "Mr. Gajani, this is Detective Monk. I need to meet with you again."

"I do not think so."

"It's important. I've just got a few details to iron out."

"And I have my life to think about."

"Tariq, I've done a little digging. Your status here in America might not be as clear as you led me to believe. I'm not the border patrol and I really don't care about your status, but if you don't meet with me, you may have some problems you don't want to deal with." I was taking a shot in the dark, but it landed.

A long sigh. "Okay. Where do I meet you?"

"Are you working?"

"Yes."

"Can you take your cab out of service for a half hour?"

"Yes."

"Okay. Meet me at the marina in the Garrison Bight. Turn off Roosevelt Boulevard onto Palm Avenue and there's a parking lot on your immediate left, right at the beginning of Charter Boat Row. You know it?"

"Yes."

"I'll meet you there in an hour."

"Okay."

* * *

I wasn't sure what to expect. Maybe I had Tariq figured all wrong. Maybe he was an electrical engineer from Pakistan temporarily driving a cab. Or maybe he was a terrorist, a jihadist. Something had bothered me when we met at Starbucks. I couldn't put my finger on it, but I thought he'd been less than honest with me. My bullshit meter was pinging in the red. But that meter wasn't always right. Maybe I'd know more after another conversation. Just in case, I had one of Paul Galis' untraceable pistols in my pocket. It was a thirty-eight-caliber revolver, not much good at a distance, but I reasoned that if I needed to shoot Tariq, it'd be from up close.

A half hour after I hung up with Tariq, I pulled into the parking lot right behind the boats moored stern-to along the bulkhead known as Charter Boat Row. I parked the rental at the far end of the lot. I wanted to be early and inconspicuous. I wanted to see whether Tariq arrived alone or brought reinforcements. I walked back along Charter Boat Row. As I neared the end closest to Roosevelt Boulevard, I saw four men standing on the sidewalk at the stern of a forty-five foot sportfish boat, a beautiful assembly of gleaming fiberglass, teak, and stainless steel. I had dressed in something more akin to what the tourists wore, a Hawaiian shirt, shorts and athletic shoes, a ball cap pulled low on my forehead. The pistol was tucked in the short's waistband, hidden by the overhanging shirt.

"Beautiful boat," I said, as I walked up to the little knot of men.

"You in the market for a charter?" one of them asked.

"I wish. I couldn't afford the tariff. What do you guys usually fish for?"

They were happy to tell me about their experiences. We were into a conversation not unlike those of idle men everywhere. I kept my eye on the parking lot, waiting for Tariq. He pulled up in his cab within a few minutes. He, too, was early and he had a passenger sitting in the front seat. He stopped on the road and a swarthy man got out. Tariq drove on down Palm Avenue, circling the marina and disappearing from sight.

The passenger walked down the pier jutting out from the seawall on the other side of the road. The pier was flanked on either side by permanently moored houseboats, most of them large, some with second stories, structures that floated but had never been meant to move. People lived on those boats.

The man was carrying a long package covered in brown wrapping paper. A rifle? Fishing rod? I couldn't tell, but I felt the first flush of an adrenalin rush. My system was telling me that I needed to be alert.

I watched as the man with the package walked up the little gangway to the third boat in the row, the first one with a second story. He knocked on the door, waited, got no answer. He bent to the door and used either a key or a pick to unlock it. He disappeared inside.

I had continued my conversation with the fishermen as I watched the swarthy man. I told them that I enjoyed talking to them and made my exit. I walked toward the houseboats, keeping my head down, the bill of my cap shielding my face. I stepped onto the gangway of the boat the swarthy man had entered. I was counting on the fact that if he were watching the pier, he would not pay any attention to me, thinking I was just another resident or visitor to the houseboats.

The boat was large enough that it didn't move as it took my weight. I tried the door handle. The man hadn't relocked it. I pulled my pistol, eased the door open, and slipped inside. I stood quietly for a moment, getting my bearings. I was in the living room, which seemed to take up most of the first floor. There was a staircase at the back of the room leading to the second story. I could see a small kitchen and dinette near the stern. I was going to be one very embarrassed interloper if it turned out that the man was an innocent citizen bringing a new fishing rod to his own home.

I started up the stairs, putting my weight on the outer edges of the steps where a squeaky step would be less likely to give me away. As my head rose even with the second floor, I could see that it was one big room, a bedroom with windows overlooking the marina on one side and the parking lot on the other. The man I was following was standing at an open window, a rifle with an attached scope in his hands. He was staring at the parking lot, waiting, probably for me. My instincts were right. Tariq was one of them.

I took two more steps up, high enough that I could train my pistol on the rifleman, but still low enough to give myself some protection. "Drop the rifle," I said, "or I'll shoot you dead."

The man turned his head and looked squarely at me. I saw a look of recognition cross his face. He knew me, and he was hunting me. But what he didn't know was that I'd been hunting him, too. I recognized him immediately. He was one of the men in the array of pictures Dave Kendall had sent me. He started to turn his body toward me, the rifle coming around. "Drop the weapon," I said, loudly. He was bringing the weapon up into firing position when I shot him in the chest. Twice. Two quick shots, each one finding its mark.

CHAPTER THIRTY-ONE

Saturday, November 1

Midafternoon, Reuben Carlson walked into J.D.'s office. "Got a minute?" he asked.

"Sure. What you got?"

"I've gone through all the emails on Fortson's computer. I don't think he ever deleted anything. There were more than a thousand of them, so I didn't actually read them all. I read enough of them to get a sense of what was going on and then used a search function to find names or words that I thought might be pertinent. That tends to weed out the garbage."

"Did you find anything of interest?"

"Some things. He had a fair amount of correspondence with a lawyer in Orlando named D. Wesley Gilbert. Does that name mean anything to you?"

"No," J.D. said. "I never heard of him."

"I Googled him. It seems that he's a big deal in Central Florida. I think he's the head honcho in the city's biggest law firm, and they have branches in several states. The firm is called Gilbert and Deming and is named for the two guys who founded it about a hundred years ago. D. Wesley is the grandson of the original Gilbert."

"Matt will know him. He practiced law in Orlando for a long time. I guess I'm not surprised that Peter Fortson was dealing with the top legal people. The trust was huge."

"That's the problem," Reuben said. "I don't think Gilbert was actually representing Fortson or the trust."

"How about the bank that serves as co-trustee?"

"Nope. The bank uses the same firm, but a different partner represents it."

"Was the connection between Fortson and Gilbert just social?" J.D. asked.

"It could have been, but that's not what piqued my interest in Gilbert. The emails between them seem to be using a rudimentary code. Some of the sentences don't make a whole lot of sense in plain English."

"Don't tell me you were able to break the code."

"I wish. But there were some words and phrases that struck me as an attempt to disguise who they were really talking about. For example, the term Abe's Kids pops up several times in discussions that appear to be about transferring money for charitable deductions, but I could find no reference anywhere to a charity by that name."

"Anything else?" J.D. asked.

"There were several emails dating to a few weeks before Rachel's murder from Gilbert to Fortson that sounded a little intimidating. The lawyer seemed to be warning Peter that somebody named Wally would be upset if he didn't get the money Fortson owed him. A few weeks after Rachel died, there was another email from Gilbert saying that 'everything was hunky dory with Wally.'"

"I wonder who Wally is," J.D. said, "and why Peter owed him money. Gambling debts, maybe?"

"Could be. Maybe we'll know more when we get the financial records."

"If we get them," J.D. said. "Anything else?"

"Think about this. If D. Wesley is the connection between Wally and Fortson, and Wally is some kind of enforcer for gamblers, then we might be able to track them all online and see just what Gilbert is up to and whom he's dealing with."

"You're making my head spin. Do you think Gilbert might be dirty?"

"If Fortson was dirty," Reuben said, "it would stand to reason that the lawyer was, too."

"We'll need to tread very carefully if we try to tie Gilbert into this. He sounds like he's heavy timber in the legal community up there."

"When you talk to the detective who's helping you out in Orlando, can you ask him about Gilbert? See if there's any dirt on him that Matt might not have known about."

"I can. You keep plugging on Fortson's laptop. Maybe we'll strike gold."

CHAPTER THIRTY-TWO

SATURDAY, NOVEMBER 1

I LET MYSELF off the houseboat and walked back up the pier. No one took any notice of me. Enough noise emanates from a working marina that the puny sounds made by the little revolver would have been lost among the ambient racket made by people working on boats, starting engines, and calling to one another.

I stopped at the harbormaster's office at the end of the pier. The man behind the counter wore a blue short-sleeved work shirt with "Cap'n Dave" embroidered above the right pocket. "Cap'n Dave?" I asked.

"That's me. Can I help you?"

I flashed my badge and said, "I hope so. I'm Detective Don Monk. Does anybody live aboard the houseboat in slip three on the first pier?"

"Sure. The Abbotts, but they're off on a Caribbean cruise. Won't be back for another week. Anything I can help you with, Detective? Is there a problem?"

"No, thanks. There's no problem. Somebody told me they thought an old friend of mine had moved aboard that boat, but I didn't get an answer when I knocked."

"Maybe it's another boat. I could check."

"Thanks. His name is Paul Reich."

He checked his computer. "No. Sorry. No Reich here."

"Okay. My friend must have been mistaken. Thanks, anyway."

I walked outside and stood in the shade of the overhang on the harbormaster's little building, watching the parking lot. I thought about the Abbotts, a couple I didn't know and in all probability would never know or even hear about again. But our lives had intersected in a strange fashion, and the Abbotts would never know about it or about me. If the sniper had come while the Abbotts were home, they would surely be dead now. On the other hand, if I'd never come to Key West, they'd be alive, regardless of whether they had gone on the cruise or stayed home on their houseboat. It is often some such random intersections of lives that spell disaster and sometimes, under other circumstances, great happiness. We don't get a choice about those chance junctions, because we cannot see them coming.

It was about time for Tariq to arrive, if he was going to. I was pretty sure that the man on the houseboat was going to plug me as soon as Tariq identified me. On the other hand, maybe he didn't need Tariq to tell him I was the target. I was also curious as to why they would take out a sheriff's detective, unless they knew who I really was.

I called Dave Kendall while I waited. "Dave, I've taken down another of the bad guys, the one named Kadir, but now I've got a body on somebody's houseboat. Any suggestions?"

"Damn, Matt. You'll killing people right and left. What's gotten into you?"

"Survival instincts, I guess. That and the fact that those guys have really pissed me off." I explained what had happened and Tariq's involvement. "The people who live there won't be back for another week. Can you help me get rid of the body?"

"I've got a cleanup team in Miami. I can get them there tonight. Give me the address."

As I was hanging up, I saw Tariq's taxi pull into the parking lot across Palm Avenue. He backed into a space, giving him a view of the entire lot. I crossed the street and came up behind his car. I stayed at an angle so that a chance look in the rearview mirror wouldn't give me away. I moved quietly to the passenger side of the taxi, reached for the handle and snatched the door open. I slipped into the front passenger seat and stuck my pistol in Tariq's side, down low where it wouldn't be seen from the parking lot. "Drive," I said.

He looked at me, looked at the pistol, and cranked the car. "Why are you doing this, Detective?" he asked.

"Why did you set me up to be killed?"

"I don't know what you're talking about."

"Your friend Abdullah Kadir knew."

"Who?"

"The guy with the rifle. You know, the one you let out of your car twenty minutes ago. He's dead, by the way. Now drive or I'll shoot you right here."

"Where are we going?"

"I'll direct you. Just get moving."

* * *

Twenty minutes later, we pulled into Paul Galis' driveway on Lower Sugarloaf Key. It was nearing four o'clock. I wasn't sure what condition Jock would be in, but I was hoping he was up to a little interrogation. "Get out of the car," I told Tariq, "and get in the trunk."

"No."

"Get in the trunk or get shot. It won't make any difference to me."

He got out of the car as I held my gun on him. I pulled the keys out of the ignition and opened the trunk. He crawled in. "I won't be long," I said. I closed the lid and went inside the house.

Jock was still sitting on the sofa drinking a glass of what appeared to be iced tea. He looked up as I walked in. "Hey, podna. You okay?"

"I'm good. How're you?"

"Better. TV's getting a little monotonous."

I was happy to see a little spark of humor. "I need you to talk to a man who tried to kill me today. You up to that?"

"What happened?"

I told him about Tariq, supposedly a Pakistani who was in the country legally, and my suspicions about his involvement with Youssef's group. "He brought a sniper with him and put him in place to kill me. I got the sniper and brought Tariq here. I need you to talk to him. Find out who the hell he is."

"Did you bring the sniper, too?"

"No. He's dead."

"You killed him?"

"Yes."

"One of Youssef's men?"

"Yes."

"Was the killing necessary?"

"Yes. It was him or me."

"Good."

"Suppose it hadn't been self-defense, Jock? What if I had killed him in cold blood?"

"But you didn't."

"Yeah, but I would have if it had come to that."

"Then his death would eat your soul. Eventually."

"Are you up to talking to Tariq?"

"Yes. Where is he?"

"In the trunk of a taxi out in the driveway."

Jock grinned. "Did the driver charge you extra for hauling the guy in the trunk?"

I laughed. Jock was coming around. A little at a time. I went out through the garage to get Tariq. I pulled him out of the trunk and tied his hands behind him with a piece of rope I'd found on a work-table in the garage.

I brought him into the house and sat him down in a chair across from Jock. They stared at each other for a moment or two and then Jock spoke to him in a language I did not understand. Tariq stared at Jock and didn't say a word. Jock spoke to him again and Tariq spoke back, agitated, pleading.

Jock looked at me and said, "Let's go outside for a minute."

We walked to the front door and stood on the stoop. I could watch Tariq through the glass pane set into the door. "He's not Pakistani," Jock said. "He's an Arab."

"How did you figure that out?"

"Urdu is the national language of Pakistan. Almost everybody speaks it, and certainly someone with the education Tariq claims to have would be fluent in it. Since English is also an official language, he would be fluent in that as well. You said his English isn't very good and now we know he doesn't understand a word of Urdu. I told him in Urdu that I was going to cut his nuts off and then ask him some serious questions. He didn't even blink, but when I told him the same thing in Arabic, he about had a heart attack."

"I didn't know you spoke Urdu."

"Not much call for it except at the convenience stores." There was that little spark of humor again.

"Let me call Paul and tell him what's going on. I've got to meet Russ Coit at six, so I need to get everything we can out of Tariq quickly."

* * *

I came back into the living room. Jock and Tariq were sitting and staring at each other. I'd talked with Paul who told me that he was on his way home, but he'd make arrangements to hold Tariq in an isolation cell at the jail for as long as we needed him kept there. He'd just need some paperwork from Dave Kendall justifying the detention on national security grounds. I assured him we'd get that moving.

I sat down in front of Tariq. "You tried to kill me. Why?"

"I'm not saying anything."

"Tariq, I'm not going to let you bleed all over my friend's furniture, but I don't mind taking you out back, tying you to a tree, and slowly cutting off body parts. I'll probably start with your dick."

He stared at me. I pulled my pistol and hit him across the face with the barrel. The sight on the end cut his cheek and blood started to flow. I got up and went into the bathroom and brought back a towel, wrapped it around his neck, and sat back down.

"I told you I didn't want blood on my friend's furniture. The towel will catch it, but I warn you, next time I'm going to cut something off."

Jock got up and walked out of the room. "You okay, Jock?" I asked.

"I can't watch this." He was slipping back into the state he'd been in since he'd arrived in Florida. I didn't know what to do about that, so I concentrated on Tariq.

"You'd better start talking to me, Tariq."

"I know who you are, Mr. Royal."

That surprised me. "Well, that explains it. I thought you were just stupid enough to go around killing cops. How did you know?"

"I knew when I saw you at Starbucks this morning. I'd seen a picture of you."

"Who gave you the picture?"

"My associate."

"Youssef?"

"Yes."

"When did he give you the picture?"

"Yesterday."

"Why?"

"It was a picture of you and a woman. He said I was to kill you if I saw either of you."

"Who are you, Tariq? We know you're an Arab, not a Pakistani. Do I have to send somebody to bring your brother-in-law out here?"

"He's not my brother-in-law."

"Who is he?"

"A Pakistani man with a family."

"Why is he helping you out, pretending to be your brother-in-law?"

"Because I told him I would kill his family if he didn't."

"Your name's not Tariq Gajani, is it?"

"No. I am Shaheed Mustafa."

"Who is Tariq?"

"The taxi manager's brother-in-law. I took his place."

"How did you pull that off?"

"Tariq is dead, but his brother-in-law thinks we're just holding him. I don't go to the taxi company's office or have anything to do with the other drivers. The brother-in-law gave me the cab to use."

"How long has this been going on?"

"I was in Miami where I've been since September. I've been working on a project there."

"Terrorism."

"Holy war."

"Right. I'm sure our people will want to know a bit more about that. What brought you to Key West?"

"I got a call from Youssef early yesterday, shortly after midnight. He told me to go to Key West and wait for orders. I got here at sunup and called Youssef to let him know I had arrived. He told me about the cab driver, Tariq. I was to call for a cab and ask specifically for Tariq. I told the dispatcher that Tariq had brought me from the airport the day before and I liked him and wanted to use him again."

"How did you manage to kill him?"

"I asked him to take me to a house where Youssef was staying. I pulled my pistol and made him go inside. Youssef cut his throat and I took the taxi and waited for further orders."

"Why did you identify Akeem's and Youssef's pictures at Starbucks this morning?"

"I don't know. Youssef told me that if you showed me any pictures of them, I was to identify them. We knew the police wouldn't be able to find them, and we wanted to appear to be cooperating."

"Did Youssef know who I was at that time?"

"No. We thought you were Detective Monk. Until I recognized you."

"But you identified the men to me even though you knew I wasn't the police?"

"I saw your badge. It looked real. I thought you might be working with the police, so I identified them."

"Is Youssef still at the house where you took Tariq?"

"No. The house was empty and Youssef just used it to get the cab. He left with me and I dropped him off on Duval Street."

"Where's Tariq's body?"

"In that house."

I heard a car pull into the driveway. Paul was home. I glanced at my watch. Five thirty. I had to get a move on. Paul came in the door and I told him that the man on his sofa was Shaheed Mustafa and that he was a terrorist and had been responsible for the death of Tariq Gajani. Paul talked with Shaheed for a few minutes, got the address of the house where Tariq's body was located and then turned to me. "I'll get this idiot bedded down in a nice isolated cell. Can you get Kendall to send the paperwork right on?"

"I'll do that," I said. "I need to get to Lower Sugarloaf International. My friend will be landing there in about twenty minutes. And I left my rental car at the Garrison Bight Marina."

"The forensics people can pick up the taxi and get your car back to Avis. I'll drop you off at the airstrip on my way back to the jail with this asshole. Where's Jock?"

"In the guest room, I guess. He walked out when I hit Shaheed with my gun. Your gun."

"Keep it. Let's check on my houseguest."

We walked into the guest room. Jock was on the bed, sound asleep.

CHAPTER THIRTY-THREE

Saturday, November 1

Youssef al Bashar and Saif Jabbar sat on the sand of Smathers Beach in Key West. It was late in the day and the crowd would be gathering at Mallory Square on the other side of the island to watch the street performers and the sunset. Each of the Arabs was wearing shorts, a t-shirt, and boat shoes. It was their attempt to blend in with the local tourist population, and it worked because Key West drew people from all over the world. Even their beards were not out of place in an island city that drew more than its share of latter-day hippies.

"I'm worried," Youssef said. "I haven't heard from any of the others and they don't answer their phones."

"What do you think happened?"

"They've either been taken or they're dead."

"Four men in one day?" Jabbar asked. "How could that happen?"

"I don't know, but Jock Algren is a very dangerous man."

"Is he good enough to take out four good men?"

"Three good men. The cab driver is a planner, not a fighter. But he was the only one we could get at the time. He was already in Miami for some reason. I was told to use him."

"What do we do now, Youssef?"

"We must assume the others are dead. My source tells me the woman called Duncan has gone back to Longboat Key, but that Royal is still here. Abdullah was supposed to have killed him today, but both he and the cab driver have disappeared. Royal may still be alive."

"Do you think he killed Abdullah and the cab driver?"

"No. Royal's a lawyer who likes to fish. He would be no match for our men. It has to be Algren who took them."

"Do we go to Longboat Key?" Jabbar asked.

"Not yet. I want to get Royal and I think he's still here. The woman will not be a problem. There is a man, an American, who is my source on Longboat Key. He will take care of her. I do not trust this man. He is not one of us. He is not a believer. But he will kill her for money, and she won't be expecting a Westerner to come after her."

"Do you think Algren knows we came to kill his friends?"

"Probably. Our source told us that Royal and the woman came to Key West. He also told me that they flew in a private plane. Algren is smart and he probably knows we planted that card in his wallet and the only reason we'd do that is to lure Royal and the woman here."

"How do you know Royal is still in Key West?" Jabbar asked. "He could have left today."

"I know he was here this afternoon because the cab driver called me and I ordered Abdullah to set up an ambush and kill him. The cab driver called me when he let Abdullah off at the Marina and said everything was set. That was the last I heard from him."

"It's a six- or seven-hour drive to Longboat Key. If he's going, maybe he'll fly," Jabbar said.

"Yes. I want you to go to the airport and watch for him at the private terminal. The only scheduled flights out tonight would actually take him longer than driving. If you get the chance, kill him."

"What if he's already gone?"

"Then we'll hear about it when he gets to Longboat Key."

CHAPTER THIRTY-FOUR

SATURDAY, NOVEMBER 1

I STOOD IN the gathering dusk in front of the ramshackle building that served as the sky dive office and operations center. I watched the Coit Airways' flagship, a single engine Beech Bonanza, line up on the runway on final approach. Russ to the rescue.

He was his usual jovial self and didn't ask me anything about Key West. He talked about his days as a young Navy fighter pilot stationed at the Key West Naval Air Station, and the good times to be had on Duval Street before the tourists began to come in swarms. It was the days when an unknown singer named Jimmy Buffet performed in the Chart Room Bar at the Pier House hotel, and an aspiring writer who was called Taco Tom tended bar and grew into the popular mystery writer and spinner of Key West tales, Tom Corcoran. It was a magical time, Russ said, and a place where young men's dreams came true. At least for a while.

When we landed at Sarasota, I called J.D. "Patti's going to meet Russ and me at Tiny's. Want to join us?"

"Sure. When?"

"It'll take us some time to get the plane gassed and cleaned, and drive to Tiny's." I looked at my watch. "Eight o'clock?"

"I'll see you then. How will I recognize you?"

"I'll be the guy whose bones you'll immediately want to jump."

"Other than Russ, you mean."

"Well, yeah. I guess. Of course, I'll probably be too tired to be of much use to you."

She laughed. "We'll see."

* * *

Tiny's was crowded with the usual cocktail-hour folks who were still hanging around. Some would be there until closing time, and some had been there since Susie opened the doors at one in the afternoon. Patti Coit was sitting at a high-top table in the corner. I waved and Russ went to join her. Susie, the owner and bartender, was right behind him with the vodka and cranberry he always drank.

My buddy Logan Hamilton was one of those who came early and stayed late. He was sitting at the bar kibitzing with Cracker Dix and Sam Lastinger, his voice slurred by the scotch he'd been drinking all afternoon.

"Been here long?" I asked him.

"My philosophy is that if you're going to drink all day, you have to start early."

"I think I saw that on a t-shirt in Key West."

"Those bastards. Plagiarism is a sin. You'd think they'd know that."

"Heard you were in the Keys," Sam said, "and J.D. kind of stranded you there." Sam was a bartender at the Haye Loft, an upscale bar on the key. He knew everybody and usually knew everything that was going on in our little slice of paradise. He was the central node on the island's information highway, whose sole purpose was to carry island gossip. Sammy was in his mid-forties, looked younger, and apparently appealed to women of every description.

"Yeah," I said, "I thought she might have been sneaking around with you, so I came back."

"I understand your concern, Matt, but you don't have to worry about J.D. and me. She seems well preserved, but she's what, late thirties? Anybody over twenty-five has already aged out of my dating parameters."

"What's the younger end of that rather short spectrum? Eighteen?"

"Usually," he said, enigmatically, and went back to his drink.

"Matt," Cracker said in a low voice, almost a whisper. "You remember a couple of days ago I told you that some guy was at Mar Vista looking for you?"

"Yeah. Has he been back?"

Cracker pointed to the end of the bar. "That's him."

The word "unkempt" didn't quite do justice to the man I saw on the last of the six stools at the short bar, his back to the wall that ran at right angles to the counter. He was glaring at us, sipping his beer from a bottle. He was wearing a white muscle shirt, and even in the dim recesses of Tiny's, I could see stains of various descriptions. Mustard, ketchup—which I surmised might really be blood, probably from fish, but who knew—engine grease, coffee, and several other smudges that I did not recognize. His denim shorts had been cut from a pair of jeans, one leg shorter than the other, both legs frayed, no hems. His ball cap might have once been green and it sported a generic fish embroidered on the crown. His feet were stuffed into ancient boat shoes. He wore a scraggly, anemic beard, gray and sparse, like a man who was incapable of growing a full beard, or maybe one who had contracted mange from a decrepit dog. Patches of reddened skin showed in random blotches in places where hair didn't grow.

I walked over to him, and was hit by a scent that transcended body odor. He smelled like three-day-old roadkill. I had a sudden vision of buzzards following him around and attacking like the birds that went after Tippi Hedren in Hitchcock's movie, *The Birds*. I was a bit surprised that he wasn't as old as he appeared from a distance. He was a guy who kept in shape. Except for regular baths. I held out my hand, and said, "I'm Matt Royal. I understand you were looking for me."

He grinned, showing big yellow teeth not unlike those of predators that show up in nightmares. He spit in his right hand and held it out to me. I quickly withdrew my hand. "Look," I said, "I used to be a lawyer and I dealt with assholes on a daily basis. You don't even come close to some of the ones I tried cases against. What did you want with me?"

"Go fuck yourself."

"Maybe you could demonstrate that maneuver to me."

"What?"

"I would like for you to show me how to fuck myself. I think it's an anatomical impossibility."

"I heard you were a wiseass."

"Some would call me humorous."

"I'd call you an asshole."

"Yeah," I said. "Some call me that, too. Now what did you want with me?"

He laughed, a guttural sound that was as much growl as anything. "I came to tell you that I'm going to kick your ass and then I'm going to fuck that girl cop you hang out with."

My first instinct was to punch him in the face, to beat him until I got tired, or just pull out my pistol and shoot him, maybe in the balls. I swallowed my anger, reasoning that I couldn't bust up Susie's bar, and if I shot the guy, I'd probably go to jail, no matter the provocation. I said, "That might be harder to do than you think."

"How do you figure that?"

"First of all, I might be a lot harder to whip than you think, and even if you were able to take me, you'd still have to deal with J.D. She'd kick your ass all the way back to whatever swamp you crawled out of."

He laughed again, or growled. "You look like some dandified pussy to me."

I saw it coming, but was almost too slow to stop it. His right hand was wrapped around a beer bottle and it was coming off the bar, headed directly to my precious face. I put up my left arm in a blocking motion and took most of the force with it. At the same time, I punched him on the side of his face with my right fist, driving through and pushing his head into the wall. I followed him in and pushed my forearm into his neck, under his chin, trapping him against the wall. I heard the beer bottle shatter as it hit the floor.

I reached around with my left hand and pulled the pistol Paul Galis had given me out of the waistband at the small of my back. I put it up under his chin. I got close to his face and whispered, "I ought to kill you, you worthless son of a bitch, and I will if I ever see you within a mile of my girl. You got that?"

"Fuck you, lawyer man," he hissed. "You shoot me here and you'll spend the rest of your life in jail. Go ahead. I dare you."

I didn't take my eyes off him. I called out. "Does anybody see a gun around here?"

A chorus of "no's" filled the small space. "Maybe not," I said and brought my knee up forcefully into his crotch.

He slumped to his knees and then began to struggle to stand, his face suffused with anger and pain and what I can only describe as meanness so pure that it sent a shiver of dread through my system.

I was backing off, my gun still pointed at him. The whole action had taken no more than a minute or so. The front entrance was only three or four feet from where I was standing, separated from the bar by a permanently affixed narrow high-top table and four stools. I sensed the front door opening, and then J.D.'s voice, controlled and menacing. "What's going on, Matt?" She'd taken in the scene as she entered, processed it, and was ready to take action if needed.

"Not much," I said. "This man is just leaving, but I want you to take a good look at him. He says he's going to rape you."

"I didn't say 'rape,' asshole. She'll be begging for it."

I had to give it to him. He still had some fight left. J.D. came up beside me, held out her badge and said, "I'm Detective Duncan. Let me see some identification."

"I don't have any on me and I'm not required by the United States Constitution to carry any."

"Then I'll have to arrest you."

Again, the laugh/growl. "On what grounds?"

"Public brawling."

"Look at this situation. I've been hit in the face, choked and kneed in the balls by a man with a gun. How long do you think it'll take my lawyer to get me out and sue the shit out of your department?"

The man did have a point. "Let it go, J.D.," I said. "But next time you see him, plug him. Call it self-defense."

"Get out of here," she said to the man. "Stay off my island."

He grinned. "I'll leave, but you can't make me stay off the island. I'm a United States citizen. I got lots of rights you don't want to fuck with."

I backed up and he walked out, bent a little as he favored his testicles. Just as he pushed open the door to the outside, he said, "We're not done, Royal." He winked at J.D., grinned, said, "Later, babe," and was gone.

"Nobody touch the beer bottle," J.D. said. "I'll be right back." She walked out the door.

"You might have underreacted there, buddy," Logan said. "Probably should have shot him."

"You're probably right," I said. "I get the feeling that I'll have to deal with him again."

"Yeah," Logan said, "and you know what Jock always says: 'Preventive maintenance.'"

Susie was standing behind the bar, pouring me a cold draft. She laughed. "I think you mean 'preemptive strike.'"

"Well, it was something like that."

J.D. returned with an evidence bag and latex gloves from the supply she always kept in her car. She pulled the gloves on, picked up the shards of the bottle, and put them in the bag. "I'll have the techs run his prints first thing in the morning," she said.

"You were very ferocious, Matt," Cracker said, his voice slurring some. He'd been here awhile, too. He and Logan always found a way to spend an otherwise boring afternoon. Cracker maintained that the more he drank, the less boring his day became. A sentiment to which Logan happily subscribed.

J.D. hugged him. "Cracker, you're a hoot, but if you think you saw ferocious just now, you should see Matt when his bacon isn't crisp enough."

"A terrible sight, I'm sure," Cracker said. "Why do you put up with him?"

"Probably the same reason you put up with Logan," she said. "He responds on short notice."

"Logan responds to offers of good whiskey. But you're not talking about scotch, are you?"

J.D. grinned and turned to me. "Are you okay, Matt?"

"Yeah. This has been a pisser of a day. Let's go home and I'll tell you all about it."

CHAPTER THIRTY-FIVE

SATURDAY, NOVEMBER 1

THE DAY WAS winding down. Night was approaching, and twilight enveloped the island. J.D. and I were snuggling on the sofa, the house lights dim. A commercial mullet boat, its running lights glowing in the dusk, ran north on the Intracoastal, headed for Cortez and home. A gibbous moon was poking its head above the eastern horizon, its beams casting a glow on the darkening surface of the bay.

"Do you know a lawyer in Orlando named D. Wesley Gilbert?" J.D. asked.

"Old D. Wesley. I know of him. I've never actually met him. We didn't exactly run in the same circles. Why?"

"What do you think of him?"

"He's a supercilious ass. Why are you asking about that idiot?"

"He's turned up in the Fortson case. Could he be dirty?"

"I've never heard anything like that, but I wouldn't be surprised if he was."

"Why do you say that? That you wouldn't be surprised."

"I never knew D. Wesley's dad or grandfather. They were both dead by the time I began practicing in Orlando. Everything I heard about them was good. They were first-rate lawyers and between them, over a period of fifty years, they built one of the largest firms in Florida. D. Wesley's dad was a decorated infantry officer in Europe during

World War II, and he came home and went to work with his father's firm. D. Wesley was born shortly after the war, went to law school and came back to the firm."

"Sounds like quite a family. Why are you so down on D. Wesley?"

"He's an ass," I said.

"You said that. Give me something more. Why do you think he's an ass?"

"He's one of those guys you meet every now and then who is the apple that fell a long way from the tree. He's pretty much the antithesis of his father and grandfather. He has a place in the firm, but he's just there. They don't let him do any legal work because he doesn't know how. The firm has continued to grow, but that's because of the other partners."

"Doesn't he own the firm?"

"No. The firm grew so much and has so many partners, that no one owns even as much as 1 percent. He inherited a lot of money from his dad, but I doubt he gets paid much by the firm. He has an office there, but I don't think he even shows up much. He's rich and he's lazy, and that's a dangerous combination. I've heard from some of the partners in the firm that they pay him a salary with the stipulation that he stays out of their hair."

"So, what does he do?"

"Plays a lot of golf and marries a new trophy wife every few years. He shows up at big social functions and likes to get his picture in the papers."

"Is he rich on the same level that Fortson was?"

"I doubt it. I've heard rumors a few years ago that he might be headed for financial trouble. The law firm wasn't paying him anywhere near enough to finance his lifestyle. But then the rumors stopped. Maybe he'd come into some money. His grandfather had owned a lot of property in different parts of the country. People figured some of that sold and D. Wesley got the money."

"He probably would have known Fortson," J.D. said.

"Probably. Fortson was old-line Orlando, so more than likely they knew each other."

"You didn't know anything about Peter Fortson?"

"I'd never heard of him. Some of Orlando's richest people, especially those who didn't earn their money, keep a low profile, spend a lot of time in other parts of the world traveling and living in third, or fourth or fifth homes. It's a tough life."

"Enough of that," she said. "You told me you'd had a bad day. Want to talk about it?"

I told her about my day, the killings, the information I'd gleaned from the people I'd talked to, Jock's condition, and the beginning of the confrontation in Tiny's. When I finished, she put her arm around me and pulled my head down to her shoulder. "I'm sorry, Matt."

"Not your fault."

"I know. I'm just sorry you had to go through all that. How do you feel about killing those three?"

"It's funny, J.D. I had to do it. I didn't have a choice. If I hadn't killed them, they would have killed me. But I've been in that situation before, and it always bothered me that I killed somebody. Not this time. I think the fact that all three of the men today were cold-blooded killers who would think nothing of taking out a nursery full of small children if it somehow fit into their worldview had a lot to do with my lack of remorse. Innocents will live because they died. Maybe it's more complicated than that. Maybe I should feel guilt or regret or something. But I don't. How about you and the guy you killed up in Gainesville? How did you square that?"

She sighed and leaned back on the sofa. "I don't know. I've mostly felt guilt at not feeling remorse, if that makes any sense. I think I should feel bad about killing that guy, even though he was trying to kill me, but I don't. And that makes me feel guilty. Not for the killing, but for the lack of emotion."

I shifted on the sofa and drew her close, wrapping my arms around her. She laid her head on my shoulder and said, "Are we losing our humanity, Matt? Are we becoming one of those people who can kill with impunity? If so, we're no better than the bad guys."

"That's not us. Don't even think like that. In our own way, each of us, Jock, you, and me, are part of the thin line that separates us from barbarity, from those who would take us back to the dark ages of Europe. We're in a war for our very survival, and people die in battle. They're fanatics, and we'd probably have to kill every last one of them to win this one. Maybe we'll have to do that in the end. Or maybe this war will never see an end. It's a sobering thought."

She sat up and looked at me. "Boy, you're a real cynic. Let's talk about something else. Tell me about Jock."

"That's a puzzle. You know how he was last night, sort of resigned to his fate, not willing to do anything to protect himself, weird. He wasn't much different this morning when he got up, but when I brought him lunch, it was like he was a different person, detached from the world. It was like he'd gone deeper into a hole since I'd left him a few hours before. But when I brought Tariq, or Shaheed, out to Paul's place, I saw sparks of the old Jock. Then he just sort of collapsed and went in to take a nap."

"Did you tell him about killing those men?"

"Yes and no. I didn't get a chance. At lunch, I asked if he wanted to hear about my morning and he put me off. Went right back to the silent TV. This afternoon, I told him about killing the sniper, and he seemed to be most interested in whether I'd killed the guy in cold blood. He said that would eat my soul. His words. 'Eat my soul.'"

"Did you talk to Jock's boss about an in-house shrink at the agency?"

"I did. He said he'd send one down, but I suggested he wait until we get this mess taken care of and get Jock back to Longboat."

"Do you really think he's safer down there with Paul Galis?"

"Nobody has any reason to suspect he'd be at Paul's place. I don't think Jock's in any danger, but he would be if he were staying here with me. He's such an easy mark for the terrorists. He won't defend himself or even try to avoid his assassins. I think he'd welcome death at their hands. In his mind, it would put the universe back in balance, establish a karmic equilibrium, or something like that."

"What are we going to do?"

I looked at her for a long moment, holding her eyes. "You know I'm going to have to kill Youssef. His buddies, too. In cold blood, if necessary."

She looked down, held it for a beat, and said, "I know." Her voice was infinitely sad.

"Are you okay with that?" I asked.

"No, but I understand why you have to do it. You and Jock are caught in a mortal dilemma. You leave them alone and eventually they'll kill you and a lot of other innocents in the future. You have to kill the terrorists in order to save yourself and their potential victims. It's really a Hobson's choice. You actually only have one option. You have to kill them.

"I've about come to the conclusion," she continued, "that killing those people would be the moral equivalent of stomping on a couple of roaches. But I'm worried more about how it will affect you. Will it?"

"I don't know," I said. "I worry about the same thing. We won't know until it's done. How will my killing those roaches affect you?"

"I'll be okay."

"Are you sure?"

"I think so."

"What about us?"

"Nothing you do will change how much I love you, Matt."

"That works for the Matt Royal you know now, but if I have to execute these bastards, I'll be a different person. I've watched Jock over the years and I know the killing is corrosive. You can't do that and walk away. The killings are like acid. They eat away at you until there's nothing left. I think that's where Jock is right now."

"That hasn't changed your feelings for Jock," she said. "Why do you think it might change my feelings about you?"

"Because, if it did, I wouldn't want to live."

"And if you, or we, don't take them out, they'll get us."

"And what about the justice system? Do we ignore the law and just kill these guys?"

"Matt, I'm coming to the very reluctant conclusion that maybe our legal system isn't geared to take on terrorism."

"You might be right. That's where Jock and people like him come in."

"I worry that we as a society may be sinking into the muck, and that we might never get out."

That cold reflection from my girl, the cop whose life was wrapped up in the law and the system, who believed deeply that justice worked only when left to the judicial system, made me sad. She was beginning to make exceptions to her understanding of the rule of law. It was a bit like watching a beautiful butterfly regress into an ugly caterpillar.

"Let's talk about something else," I said. "Tell me what's going on with the Fortson investigation."

J.D. told me about her day, the frustrations, the dead ends in the investigation, her concern about the man who tried to break into her condo. "I wonder if the man at Tiny's might be the same guy that Sue and Marylou saw running from the property."

"I think I'd treat that as a distinct possibility. Can you connect him to the Fortson murder? Could he be the one that Tom and Linda saw leaving the beach this morning?"

"Maybe. But it doesn't make sense that he'd stick around the scene for that long after the murder. If he did the killing."

"Maybe he came back and was surprised by the Joneses."

"But why would he have come back to a murder scene?" she asked.

"Could he have lost something? Maybe something that would tie him to the murder."

"That's a possibility, I guess. We sure didn't find anything at the scene."

"What about the shoe print you found in the hedge at the edge of your property?"

She shook her head. "I don't think that's going anywhere. The forensics people called this afternoon. They looked into that, and it turns out that the shoe is a Nike, but they've sold millions of them."

"And you didn't find any similar shoe prints on the beach?"

She was silent for a moment, thinking. "Maybe. Manatee County made molds of some of the prints, but those never stand up very well when they're left in the soft beach sand. The Manatee techs probably don't know anything about the prints in our shrubbery. Our department handled that."

"Even if they match," I said, "the only thing it would prove was that the same man who wore the shoes was at both scenes. We can't tie it to the guy in Tiny's."

"Check," she said. "But I'd like to know if it was the same person. I'll call the Manatee lab first thing in the morning."

"Tomorrow's Sunday, you know."

"Yeah. I'll have to muck up somebody's day off."

"What about David Parrish? Anything from him yet?"

"He called this afternoon. Said that he's got the subpoena ready and will serve it on the bank first thing Monday morning. I'm not sure how much good that'll do now that Fortson's dead."

"You may be able to track the money back to whoever put the hit on you."

"Yeah. I'll follow up on it. We'll see. Reuben found a lot of financial stuff on Fortson's computer. I'll get it to a forensic accountant on Monday. See what the data tell us."

"I've got a buddy that can do that for you and have you some answers by tomorrow. Will the department pay him?"

"Sure. Who've you got in mind?"

"Ken Brown. He's a CPA who practices in Orlando. He testified as an expert in several cases I tried over the years. He'll do a good job and get it done quickly."

"Set it up," she said. "I'll have Reuben email him the documents we found on Fortson's computer."

I called Ken and he agreed to look over the documents and be ready to give us some conclusions by Monday.

J.D. called Reuben Carlson and got the documents moving toward Ken Brown. She came back to the sofa and settled in. "You hungry?" I asked.

"As a bear."

"We could go to Moore's. The stone crabs are in."

"Yummy. Let me take a shower first."

"Want some company?" I asked.

"What about the crabs?"

"You've got crabs?"

She laughed. One of those big ones that always sets me back on my heels. "Stone crabs," she said. "Just stone crabs, silly boy."

* * *

We sat at the bar at Moore's and ate stone crab claws as we chatted with the bartenders, Tina and Rebecca. The crabs were pulled from the bay on a daily basis and served fresh. The crabbers detached one claw from each mature crab caught in their traps, and threw the crab back into the sea. It would grow a new and larger claw soon enough.

The bar was crowded with newly arrived snowbirds, and we welcomed a couple of friends, who spent many of their winter evenings in Tiny's, back to the key. It was this time of the year, at the beginning of the season, when the year-rounders, those of us who live on the islands full time, begin to hunker down in our homes, hesitant to venture out lest we become overwhelmed by the traffic on the roads and the waiting lines at the restaurants.

Each year, we'd notice that some of the regulars from the north didn't show up. Soon the island gossip would let us know that one of the couple had died or was too ill to travel. We knew they'd never see the island again, and that always brought us a fleeting sense of loss and a renewed appreciation of the fragility of life, the inevitability of frailty and, eventually, the certainty of death.

Our island demographic is mostly old people. I think the average age is seventy-one, so death is a constant. Logan once said that the loss of friends is part of the tax we pay for enjoying life in our little slice of paradise. As was often the case, I thought he was exactly right.

We finished our crabs, had one more drink, and walked home, holding hands and enjoying the cool evening. Our day had started when J.D.'s phone rang at three o'clock that morning in Lower Sugarloaf Key. It had been very eventful for each of us, and a good night's sleep beckoned.

J.D. was staying over. The house was quiet, and although I hadn't expected anything out of the ordinary, I was relieved not to have to confront any more situations that day. We got ready for bed, turned out the lights and I went to sleep thinking how nice it was to be snug in my own bed, safe and sound.

CHAPTER THIRTY-SIX

SUNDAY, NOVEMBER 2

"HIS NAME IS Charlie Bates," J.D. said, as she walked in the front door of my cottage. She'd gotten up early and met Kevin Combs, the Longboat Key police department's forensics investigator, at the station. He'd run the prints left on the remains of the beer bottle that Bates had used the night before in his attempt to brain me. "Got a heck of a rap sheet."

I looked up from my newspaper. "Bad guy?"

"Bad enough. Most of the stuff is fairly minor, assault, battery, breaking up a bar. But he was charged with murder twice, the last time about four years ago, but neither one of them stuck. Strangely enough, in both cases the witnesses all changed their stories and a couple of them disappeared. Guess where he's from?"

I shrugged.

"Franklin County."

"That's where you were last week."

"Exactly. I called the sheriff up there. He's well aware of Mr. Bates. Says he's like a walking bomb with a defective fuse. Anything can set him off. He lives on a sailboat he keeps in a marina in Carrabelle, and has no visible means of support. Law enforcement thinks he's engaged in illegal activity, but they can't catch him at anything. There've been rumors that he's not above killing for hire."

"Any ideas about what he's doing here?"

"Yeah," she said, "but you're not going to like it."

"Try me."

"The sheriff said Bates fits the description of the man who paid that kid up there to kill Rachel Fortson."

I put the paper down. "You think he killed Peter Fortson?"

"Probably."

"Do you know where he's staying here?"

"I'm guessing he's on his boat. The sheriff checked with the marina where Bates keeps it. It's not there, so I'm assuming he sailed it down here. I've got a description of the boat, and Steve Carey is calling around to see if he can find it."

"You don't have enough evidence of Bates' involvement to get a search warrant."

"I know. If we could have found any bit of evidence at the scene of Peter's death, it might be enough, but there's nothing. Kevin got the shoe prints the county guys took on the beach, and they seem to match the ones found in the hedge at my condo."

"So, Peter's murderer is the same guy who came to your condo yesterday."

"I think so, but the prints aren't of good enough quality to be sure."

"But good enough for you."

"Yeah," she said. "I think it was the same guy. And I think I might be on his list."

"Why?"

"I don't think he was making a social call yesterday."

I grinned. "Maybe not. By why would he want to kill you?"

"If he killed Peter, he might just be cleaning up loose ends on Rachel's murder. This might be connected to the shooting up in Gainesville. Maybe whoever is behind all this thinks I know more than I do about Rachel's murder and that makes me a loose end. If

Peter was involved, he was probably the weak link and needed to be taken out. Ergo, Bates was sent here to kill both Peter and me."

"I'm not law enforcement," I said. "If you find his boat, I can go in, warrants be damned."

"Right. And then when the defense lawyer finds out about your involvement with the search, he'll use the fact that you're my squeeze of the moment, and whatever evidence you find will be thrown out, along with anything we glean from that evidence. Fruit of the poisonous tree."

"Squeeze of the moment? The moment? What the hell are you talking about?"

She laughed. "It means you better stay off Bates' boat."

"What boat?"

"There," she said. "I like it when you're docile."

"Do you have a description of Bates' boat?"

"Yes. It's an older Hunter thirty-three footer with a green hull, named *Wayfarer*. Why?"

"We could take *Recess* out today, cruise through the marinas, go up to Tide Tables for lunch. I don't think either Bates or Youssef will get to us out on the water."

"Sounds like a plan, but I need to call Ken Brown. See if he's made any progress."

"He just got all that stuff late last night," I said. I looked at my watch. "It's not even eleven, yet."

"I need to see anything he's got, even if it's not much. I want him to concentrate on any links between Fortson and Bates. I can't believe there's not something there. If it doesn't involve Bates directly, then somebody Bates reports to or deals with in the panhandle."

"Okay. I need to check on Jock." She left for the bedroom to make her call.

I called Paul Galis. "How's your houseguest doing?" I asked when he picked up.

"He seems okay, but I don't think he's tracking too well."

"How so?"

"He's back in front of the TV with the sound off. I don't think he's really paying much attention to the programming, but he seems glued to the screen."

"Is he drinking?"

"No. I got all the booze out of the house, and he hasn't asked about a drink."

"How's his arm?"

"No problems. I had a paramedic who lives down the street take a look at it yesterday after you left, and he said it's healing nicely. No restrictions in his movements."

"Is Jock talking at all?"

"Not much, but when he does talk, he sounds lucid."

"Paul, I'm sorry to have dropped this on you."

"It's fine, Matt. I owe Jock a lot. My life, probably. I'll do everything I can."

"I appreciate it. Can you put him on the phone?"

I heard Paul in the background telling Jock I wanted to speak with him. "Hey, podna," Jock said, "how're they hanging?"

His voice sounded fine, just like the old Jock. "Loose, Jock. How're you doing?"

"I'm okay. I think spending a little time here with Paul is just what the doctor ordered." His voice had changed quickly, now carrying a hint of resignation. "Are you and J.D. okay?"

"Yes." It was time to tell him. See what kind of reaction I got. "I killed three of Youssef's men yesterday before I left Key West."

"Including the one you told me about yesterday?"

"Yes."

"How many does Youssef have with him? Do you know?" Suddenly, his voice was back to normal, his cadence businesslike, a professional marshaling the facts he needed in order to put a plan into operation.

"Five altogether. Plus Tariq, the one you met yesterday. He's in isolation in the Monroe County jail. That leaves Youssef and one more. I have their names and Dave Kendall is trying to find out what he can about them."

"Have you talked to Dave?"

"Several times," I said. "Have you?"

"Not yet."

"When?"

He sighed. "I'll call him today. I ought to come join you guys in Longboat."

"Jock, promise me you'll stay where you are for now. If you come here, I'll just worry about you, and I don't have time for that."

"I'm better, podna. Maybe I can help up there."

"Are you ready to kill Youssef?"

"No. I don't think I'll ever be ready for that," he said. "I'm done with killing anybody. Ever."

"I'm ready," I said. "I'll take care of it. You stay put until I do."

"What are you doing, Matt?"

"I'm not sure, but I'll let you know when it's over. Do I have your word that you'll stay with Paul until then?"

"Yes, but you be careful. Are you sure you want to do this?"

"I don't have a choice, Jock. If I don't take care of Youssef and his guys, they'll get J.D. or me, and then you. I've got things under control." I hung up thinking I had badly overstated my situation.

CHAPTER THIRTY-SEVEN

SUNDAY, NOVEMBER 2

WE WERE TRAVELING north on the Intracoastal, maintaining an idle speed, enjoying the sun and the lack of humidity. I told J.D. about my conversations with Jock and Paul. "One minute he sounds like the old Jock, and the next minute there's a change. He sounds tentative, not sure of himself, depressed, maybe. He wanted to come up here, but I talked him into staying in the Keys until I can sort things out. I asked him if he was ready to kill Youssef and he said he might never be ready for that."

"As soon as we can get this mess straightened out, we need to get him up here. Maybe get one of Dave Kendall's shrinks to come down and work with him."

"What did Ken say?" I asked.

"He did a lot of work overnight, but the results are a bit confusing. There was one connection that has some interesting possibilities. There were several big checks made payable to Wayfarer, Inc."

"That's the name of Bates' boat."

"Yeah," she said. "But that makes everything a little too neat. I doubt it's related. When we get back to your house, I'll go online and find out what the secretary of state's office can tell us about the corporation."

We were nearing the Tide Tables restaurant on the south side of the mainland end of the Cortez Bridge, across Cortez Road from the Seafood Shack. We decided to go under the bridge and cruise the Shack's marina on the off chance that Bates' boat was moored there.

Just as we cleared the bridge, J.D. said, "It's there. On the first pier."

And there she sat, the hull coated with the residue of salt left from a rough crossing. The boat looked as sloppy as its owner, a pigsty that I thought probably smelled like a couple of hogs had died in there.

We reversed course and motored back under the bridge and tied up at a dock next to the restaurant. We sat on the patio and ate while watching the boats go by on the Intracoastal and the commercial fishing boats as they headed up the channel to sell their catches at the fish houses that lined the shore and still operated on weekends. A twenty-eight foot Coast Guard boat idled by us, coming from the Coast Guard station just up the channel, probably on its way to a safety patrol among the large number of pleasure boats that ply our waters on beautiful Sunday afternoons. It was an idyllic setting in which to enjoy a shrimp po-boy sandwich and a cold beer on a pleasant fall day.

* * *

When we got back to my house, J.D. called the dockmaster at the Seafood Shack and found out that *Wayfarer* had checked in on Thursday morning. The captain said he'd sailed in from Campeche, Mexico on the Yucatan peninsula. "I'm pretty sure he didn't come from Mexico," J.D. told me. "He must have come directly from Carrabelle. How long would that have taken him?"

"Probably close to twenty-four hours. If the weather was bad, maybe longer."

"That means he would have left Carrabelle early Wednesday morning. The dockmaster said the captain was around the marina most of the day. That means he couldn't have had anything to do with my being shot at on Thursday afternoon."

"Sounds right to me."

J.D. booted up my computer and went to the Florida secretary of state's website and looked up Wayfarer, Inc. It was a corporation that had been formed almost four years before and listed the address of its principal place of business in an office building in Tallahassee. It had a three-member board of directors. Their names meant nothing to me. Neither the president's nor the corporate secretary's names rang any bells.

J.D. Googled the names, but none of the board members showed up. That was a very strange result in this day and age when almost everybody in the world can be found on Google. The president was another matter. He was a licensed private detective in Tallahassee, and although he kept a low profile, there was a little information since he had to be registered with the Florida Department of Agriculture and Consumer Services. He was a fifty-year-old man named Wally Delmer who had held a private investigator's license for fifteen years. His office address was the same one listed by the secretary of state for Wayfarer, Inc. She could find nothing on the official website that would tell us whether he, or any other PI, had ever suffered any disciplinary action. Wally himself did not have a website.

"Do you know any Tallahassee cops?" I asked J.D.

"I just happen to know the chief," she said. "Very well."

"Uh-oh."

"Nothing like that. He was my boss when he was the homicide commander at Miami-Dade PD. He left just after I did and took the job as chief of police in Tallahassee."

"Couldn't do without you?"

She grinned. "Very likely."

"Can you get him to dig into our boy Delmer?"

"We can find out. I've got his home phone number."

"It's Sunday," I reminded her.

"Not a problem."

"I need to call Dave Kendall," I said and walked out to the patio.

"Is Jock okay?" Dave asked as he picked up his phone.

"Hard to tell. I talked to him this morning. Paul Galis says he just sits and stares at the TV with the sound off."

"That's not good."

"No, but our conversation was kind of strange. It was like I was talking to two different people, the old Jock and the new Jock. He sounded perfectly okay one minute, and then he'd change. Any news on your end?"

"Yes. We've found the other half of Youssef's bunch. All five of them were holed up in a half-ruined building in Aleppo. Two of them left for some reason early this morning, their time, and one of our people followed and took them out. We've got eyes on the other three, and I'm pretty sure this is their last day on earth."

"Any progress on finding your leak?" I asked.

Dave was silent for a moment, and then said, "Matt, have you noticed anything different about Jock in the last few months? I mean, before he came to Longboat this time."

"How do you mean?"

"I'm not sure. Absent minded, maybe. Not as focused as he usually is."

"He's very tired, Dave, if that's what you mean. Tired of the traveling, tired of the danger, and most of all, tired of the killing. He keeps talking about retiring, leaving the agency and moving to Longboat. I've always thought it was just his way of blowing off steam. But this time, when he came back, he was pretty much at his rope's end. What's this got to do with the leaks?"

"Jock is the leaker," Dave said.

"I don't understand."

"Jock has always been meticulous, a hunter who goes in, does his job, and gets out without leaving a trace. He's a ghost, and the bad guys have always feared him because they never saw him coming.

"This time he made a big mistake," Dave continued. "In Aleppo. It wasn't even a rookie mistake, because no rookie would ever make it. I wonder if he might have done it on purpose."

"What?"

"Have you ever heard the term 'suicide by cop'?"

"Sure. Some yahoo decides he wants to die, but he's too chicken to kill himself. He uses a gun to confront an armed police officer and the cop kills him."

"I think Jock may have done that in this case. Sort of a 'suicide by terrorist.' It probably wasn't even a conscious act on his part, but I know he's always been haunted by the death of Abdullah al Bashar. Then he meets the bomber and finds out that he was one of the little boys who watched Jock execute his innocent father. On top of that, the other little boy, Youssef, is now grown into a terrorist and tells him their mom's dead because Jock killed their dad. That might have been enough to throw Jock into some kind of psychological break. At least that's what our shrinks think."

"I still don't understand what Jock did. What happened, Dave?"

"Our people in Aleppo interrogated the two they caught up with this morning. They both told the same story when they were questioned separately. Jock told Youssef his real name. Jock Algren. We think they followed him to Longboat Key."

I was stunned. "Why would he do that?"

"That's the psychological break our shrinks are talking about. They think it was his way of saying the hell with it. 'I've done such bad things that I need to die.' They think Jock was in so much pain that he couldn't live with himself and he was arranging his own death in hopes that Youssef would find some peace knowing that he would kill the man who'd destroyed his family."

"I don't believe it," I said.

"Jock probably wasn't thinking those things consciously," Dave said. "And the consensus is that he would have no memory of telling Youssef his name. The shrinks also think Jock's reason for going to Longboat Key was to say good-bye. To you and J.D. and a life he dreamed about living. He loved your island and the people on it. He talked about retiring there, starting a new life. After the events in Aleppo, he came to the conclusion that he didn't have a future. So he went straight from Aleppo to Longboat and, in his way, said good-bye. When he'd done that, his plan was to go somewhere and die. Maybe to make himself available to Youssef so that there would be meaning in his death. At least that's the shrink's version."

CHAPTER THIRTY-EIGHT

SUNDAY, NOVEMBER 2

"WALLY DELMER IS a bad guy," J.D. said, joining me when she finished her phone call to the Tallahassee police chief. I hadn't moved from the patio after I'd talked to Dave Kendall. What he said had made some sense, but I wanted to let my mind work through it as I tried to concentrate on my still-unfinished newspaper. I sipped a Diet Coke, enjoying the sun and the cooling breeze that blew from the north, ruffling the bay's surface.

"How so?" I asked.

"The chief says he's a well-known sleazeball. He works in the shadows and nobody seems to know what he does. His income isn't large and he lives frugally. His office is in an old run-down office building in downtown Tallahassee, so his rent isn't very high. The chief said it's a one-room affair."

"Doesn't sound like very grand digs for Wayfarer, Inc. How big were the checks from Peter Fortson to Wayfarer?"

"Ken said they were all six-figure checks. I didn't ask for the exact amount."

"How many checks in all?"

"Five," she said. The first one was written by Peter Fortson a month or so after Rachel's death. The other four were spaced out about six months apart. The last one was fairly recent."

"That's a lot of money going to a corporation that doesn't seem to do anything and shares a one-room office in a run-down building."

"There may be another connection. Reuben found that connection between Fortson and Wally on Fortson's computer. Fortson and D. Wesley Gilbert emailed each other regularly. The lawyer didn't seem to represent Fortson or either of the trusts or anything, but Gilbert told Fortson at one point that Wally wasn't happy with him; Fortson, that is. I'll bet the Wally mentioned in those emails is Wally Delmer."

"That would make sense," I said. "Fortson was sending some big checks to Delmer. It sounds like Gilbert might be some sort of go-between."

"Ken's going to keep digging. Maybe Parrish can move quickly and we can hear something tomorrow. The fact that Peter's dead might make things move more smoothly in Orlando. I'll see if Glenn knows anything about Gilbert. If not, maybe he can dig up some information on him."

"I called Dave Kendall while you were on the phone with the chief." I told her about my conversation and the shrink's thoughts on Jock's actions.

"That can't be true. Jock wouldn't do that. He'd face this thing head-on."

"They think Jock had some sort of psychological break with reality. That would certainly explain his recent actions. The more I think about it, the more I can see the signs leading up to it."

"How so?"

I told her what I'd told Dave about Jock's concerns about his way of life. "And he hasn't been himself since he arrived here almost two weeks ago."

"No. He hasn't. I hope the shrinks are wrong. If Jock truly has a death wish, I'm afraid there's nothing much we can do."

"We've got to try," I said. "I want to get Youssef and his buddies and then start thinking about how to get Jock well."

"There's something I still don't understand. Even if Jock gave Youssef his name, how did they track him? There are over three hundred million Americans. That's a lot of people to sort through to find one man."

"I asked Dave about that. His people are trying to run it down. They think it may have been as simple as following Jock back to Longboat Key. He made his way from Aleppo to Beirut, and took a flight from there to London, another from London to Atlanta, and another one to Tampa. There aren't many airports in the Middle East that have direct flights. It wouldn't have been too big a deal to have each of those airports watched for a man with Jock's description. Once he got on the plane to London, somebody would have called ahead and had that plane met and Jock followed to his next gate and so on. Jock rented a car at the Tampa airport. No big deal to follow him right to my house."

"I can't believe Jock wouldn't have spotted that kind of surveillance. He's been doing it for years."

"The old Jock would have spotted them and taken some action," I said. "But we have to remember that we're dealing with a broken and very fragile Jock right now."

I watched as two men in a center console boat idled up the lagoon on which my cottage sat. One of the men was looking through a pair of binoculars, scanning the shoreline. He swept over us and continued his sweep.

"Let's go inside," I said. "I don't like the looks of the boat coming this way."

J.D. didn't hesitate. We went inside and closed the sliding glass doors. I picked up my own binoculars and trained them on the boat. As it got closer, I saw the fishing gear, two rods and reels stowed in the rod-holders on the gunwales. I recognized the men in the boat. They were locals, a couple of older guys whom I'd see occasionally at one of the restaurants or bars on the key. Just a couple of friends out for a day of fishing.

"It's okay," I said. "They're locals." But I'd been spooked. I didn't like the idea of my island, my little refuge from the world, becoming a place where I had to be on guard all the time.

"Let's go to Orlando tomorrow," I said.

"I've got to work."

"This is work. We can talk to Ken Brown and Glenn Howell, have lunch with my old law partner and maybe get a line on what's going on with D. Wesley these days."

"I think I can swing that."

"I'll call Ken and tell him we'll be at his office in early afternoon. Can you set us up with the detective for midmorning?"

"Sure," J.D. said. "It's almost four o'clock. What do you want to do with the rest of our day?"

I tried for my Groucho Marx imitation, an exaggerated wiggling of my eyebrows, a bit of a leer

"Besides that," she said.

"How about drinks and a light dinner at the Haye Loft? Sammy's working tonight and I'd like to spend a little time talking to him. He always lightens my mood."

* * *

Apparently my Groucho impression worked and we didn't get to the Haye Loft until almost seven. The place was full and both Sammy and Eric Bell, the bartender who'd worked there for thirty years, were busy. Eddie Tobin was at the piano, playing and singing. J.D. and I took two seats at the end of the bar, the only two left.

"They're back," J.D. said.

"Who's back?" I asked.

"The snowbirds. I'm glad. I like the island during the summer when it's so quiet, but by October, I start missing all those Yankees."

"Careful. Your Southern roots are showing."

"Yeah, great-great-grandpa's probably turning in his grave."

"What's up?" Sammy was standing across the bar from us, a Miller Lite beer and a glass of Pinot Grigio in his hands. "Matt, you sure kicked that guy's ass last night in Tiny's."

"A little bit," J.D. said. "If I hadn't shown up, the guy would probably have taken Matt."

Sammy looked at me quizzically. I looked at J.D. and was sucked in by that smile. "What the lady said," I said, grinning.

"Right," Sammy said. "You're just trying to get lucky."

"Or," J.D. said, "maybe he's just being agreeable because he already got lucky."

"My gawd, man," Sammy said in his best Scottish brogue. "Have you been having carnal knowledge of this lass?"

I shrugged and gave him a knowing wink. "What've you been doing, Sam?"

He laughed. "Same thing I usually do. Work, drink on Bridge Street, sleep to noon, have lunch with my girlfriend, get ready for work. It's a full day."

"Which girlfriend?" J.D. asked.

"Whichever one I wake up with."

"You're a true gentleman," she said. "Where do you usually have lunch?"

"My place. I keep hot dogs on hand just in case."

J.D. made a face. "Ugh. Forget what I said about your being a gentleman."

"I was kidding, J.D. As you know, my tastes tend to run to the gourmet."

"Oh yeah. Sorry. I forgot who I was talking to for a minute. You're more of a chicken-wing kind of guy."

"Right. You ready for some more wine?"

The banter and conversation went on like that while we ate our dinner. Eric came over and asked about Jock. I told him Jock was doing better, and we laughed about how many of the Loft's pizzas Jock could eat at one sitting.

We greeted some of the snowbirds, listened to their stories about their summers, talked to our friends Tom and Nancy Stout, sang along with Eddie and his piano, and called it a night.

"My place or yours?" I asked as we walked down the outside stairway.

"Let's spend tonight at my condo. There's only one way into the place and there's a very good dead bolt on that door. It might be safer if there're really some bad guys looking for us."

And that's what we did. All in all, it was a very pleasant evening on our island paradise.

CHAPTER THIRTY-NINE

MONDAY, NOVEMBER 3

THE DRIVE UP I-4 was pleasant. Well, as pleasant as I-4 ever gets. We had a quick breakfast at the Longbeach Café and started our three-hour drive to Sanford, the seat of Seminole County and the home of the Seminole County sheriff's office.

We were getting close to Orlando when J.D.'s phone rang. She answered. "Hold on, David," I heard her say into the phone. "Let me put you on the speaker. Matt's here and I want him to hear what you have to say."

The three of us chatted for a minute or two and then Parrish said, "I've got lots of paper that I don't understand. My people served the subpoena this morning on the bank that oversees the Fortson trust. We got a huge load of documents on a flash drive. I've looked at them but they make no sense to me. I can get one of our people with an accounting background to look at it, but that may take some time. They're buried in a huge fraud case. What do you want me to do with them?"

"It sounds like a lot of stuff," J.D. said. "Can you email it to our department I.T. guy?"

"I don't know. Ours can probably figure it out. I'll call you back if we can't do it."

"I really appreciate this, David." She gave him Reuben's email address and hung up.

"Maybe something good will come out of that," she said. "I'll call Reuben and have him forward the stuff to Ken Brown."

* * *

Detective Glenn Howell was a blond man who stood a couple inches below six feet and spoke with a decided Georgia inflection. He was gracious in the Southern way and offered us a seat and coffee. We accepted both.

"You sound like you're from Georgia," J.D. said.

"I am. Originally. I was born and grew up in Fayette County, just south of Atlanta. I've been here since I graduated from college. You're from up that way, too, I think."

"Born in Atlanta," J.D. said. "My dad was an Atlanta cop for twenty-five years and when he retired, we moved to South Florida. I was about twelve at the time."

"It's good to meet you both," he said "Sims has told me so much about you, I feel like I know you."

"Sims lies, you know," I said.

"I know, but I didn't think that was well known outside the confines of the great state of Georgia."

"It apparently slipped over the border," I said. "Spread like wildfire."

"He only said good things about the two of you."

"He does still have some lucid moments," I said.

J.D. laughed. "You guys stop ragging on poor old Sims."

"Okay," Howell said. "We've got a lead on the people who tried to take J.D. out. A salesman of some sort left his car at one of those privately owned remote parking lots near the Orlando airport last Wednesday. He used his car in his work and kept meticulous notes on the miles he drove for tax purposes. When he got back and picked up his car on Saturday he noticed that several hundred miles had been put on it since he left."

"The Camaro with the shotgun?" J.D. asked.

"It fits the description you gave the Alachua sheriff. The owner of the car called the Orlando PD and a detective came out to see what was going on. The lot is set up so that when a car pulls into a gate, the driver takes a ticket from a dispenser and then is told what row to park on. He's picked up by a shuttle bus and taken to the airport terminal. When he returns, the reverse happens. Nobody at the lot ever gets his keys. But there is a surveillance camera that keeps an eye on the entrance and exit. The detective reviewed the video and saw the car leave the lot within an hour or so of the owner leaving it. It was returned late Thursday afternoon."

"The time frame fits, but what made you think it was the same car?"

"When the forensics people examined the car they didn't find even one fingerprint in the obvious places. The interior had been completely wiped down. Except that there was one print found on the underside of the little lever on the left side of the driver's seat that is used to adjust the seat. They got a hit on it. A young man named Xavier Duhns, who works for the parking company driving one of the shuttle buses. He lives in Seminole County, out near Altamonte Springs. Orlando PD asked us to pick him up. We got him last night and an Orlando detective is due here any minute to talk with him. I thought since you were coming anyway, you might want to sit in."

"I still don't see the connection," J.D. said. "The only thing in common with this car and the one with the people who were after me is the make and color. There must be millions of those cars on the road."

"The mileage fits," Howell said. "That's about it. But if the car had been driven to Gainesville and back, the distance is very close to the mileage on the car. It's probably not your guy, and I wouldn't have asked you to come all the way over here just to sit in on his interview, but since you were on your way, I figured why not."

"It won't hurt to take a look at it," J.D. said. "What can you tell me about Duhns?"

"Not much. He's twenty-two years old, has a record of several minor infractions, never enough to go away for. Always got short probations."

"No car theft in his background?"

"None. But, and this is an interesting factoid, his older brother is serving a ten-year stretch in prison for car theft. I busted him about three years ago. He and a couple of buddies were stealing cars all over the county and shipping them to Miami, where they were put on boats and sent to the Caribbean and Central America. They were pretty professional."

"So maybe big brother taught Xavier how to boost cars," J.D. said.

"Probably."

"That isn't that easy these days. Not with all the technology built into the cars."

Howell's desk phone buzzed. He took the call, said "okay," and hung up. "Detective Vargas from OPD is here."

* * *

Xavier Duhns was sitting at a table in a bare interrogation room, his right arm cuffed and attached to an O-ring in the floor. A video camera in a corner pointed at Duhns, a little red light showing that it was recording. J.D., Glenn Howell, and I were standing in a small anteroom watching through a one-way mirror.

Detective Vargas walked in and took a seat across from Duhns and introduced himself. Duhns nodded. "Do you know why you're here?" the detective asked.

"No."

"Car theft."

"You've got me mixed up with my brother."

"You think he stole a car on Wednesday?"

"He's in prison."

"Yeah. I heard. You're not real smart, are you?"

"Smart enough," Duhns said.

"Smart enough to get out of a beef for attempted murder of a police officer? I hope so, because that could put you in prison for life."

That got Duhns' attention. "What're you talking about?"

"You've got one chance here, Xavier. Did you know that your employer had video cameras at the entrance and exit to the lot?"

"No. So what?"

"We saw you leave in a car that was parked there and we watched you bring it back on Thursday. We also watched you drive the shuttle bus that took the owner of that car to the airport on Wednesday." Vargas was stretching the truth a little, since the angle of the cameras and the dark windows of the Camaro did not give us a clear picture of the driver.

"So?"

"We also found your fingerprints in the Camaro."

"You're lying. That car was clean." Duhns stopped, a look of consternation on his face. He might have just stepped in it.

"Not completely clean, Xavier. You're a big guy. Do you remember adjusting the seat?"

"Maybe."

"We found your prints on the lever that controls the seat's position."

"So?"

"So we've got you on the car theft charge, Xavier. You're going away for a few years, but you'll still be young when you get out. On the other hand, that attempted murder charge will put you away forever."

Duhns leaned into the table, put his forearms on it, and grinned. "Good try, Detective. Okay, you got me on the car beef, but I never tried to kill no cop and you can't prove I did."

Vargas leaned back in his chair, scratched behind his right ear, and sighed. That was the signal. J.D. opened the door and entered the room. "Hello, Mr. Duhns," she said, her voice as pleasant as if she were greeting him at a lawn party. "How nice to see you again."

Duhns looked up at her, a puzzled look on his face. "Have we met?"

"I'm surprised you don't remember. I'm Detective J. D. Duncan. We met last Thursday up on I-75 at Paynes Prairie, just south of Gainesville. You were driving a beautiful black Camaro."

Duhns blanched, stuttered a bit, and finally got it out. "What do you mean?"

J.D. leaned on the table, her palms planted flat on its surface, her face twisted into a grimace and inches from Duhns'. Her voice dropped a register, her words flat and clipped. "I mean when you drove that Camaro next to my car and some asshole pushed a shotgun out the window and tried to kill me." J.D. was using a bit of profanity, words that almost never escaped her mouth. She was really stressed out about her near-death experience and more pissed off than I'd ever seen her.

"You couldn't possibly have seen who was driving," Duhns said.

"Whether I did or not isn't relative to this conversation," J.D. said, her voice like steel. "The question is, who do you think a jury will believe? You or me?"

Duhns chewed on that for a moment, then turned to Vargas. "What do you want to know?"

"How many were in the car with you when you took the shot at Detective Duncan?"

"I didn't take the shot."

"How many?"

"Just me and Skeeter."

"Who's Skeeter?"

"That's all I know. Never heard his last name."

"How do you know him?"

"I don't, really."

"You just picked up a guy with a shotgun and drove him to Gainesville?"

"He was a friend of my brother's down at the Glades Correctional Unit."

"A car thief?"

"No. He doesn't know how to steal a car."

"But you did?"

"Yes."

"What did he tell you he wanted with a car?"

"He said he needed me to get the car and then drive to Gainesville. He didn't say anything about killing a cop."

"You just thought he brought the shotgun along as a companion?"

"No. I didn't know what it was for."

"He didn't tell you why he wanted you to steal a car and drive him to Gainesville?"

"Not until we got there."

"Tell me what he said." An edge had slipped into Vargas' voice. He was tired of playing word games with this idiot. "You've got one chance here. You tell me what you know and when you knew it and you might have a chance to dodge the attempted murder charge. No more playing dumb. You lie to me and we're done. You're on your way to a life sentence. You got me?"

"Yes. He told me on the way up that he'd been hired to kill somebody. We were going to do it out on the highway. I-75. I'd pull up to the car and he'd shoot and we'd be on our way back to Orlando. He had an iPad and he kept checking on something, so he knew exactly where the car we were looking for was located."

"What made you get involved?"

"Skeeter paid me two grand."

"How do I find Skeeter?" Vargas asked.

"I don't know. I promise. I'd tell you if I knew. I didn't know he was trying to kill a cop. I wouldn't have gone with him if I had known."

"I don't have anything else. Detective Duncan?"

"Who was the guy in the van?" J.D. asked.

"What van?"

"The one that was behind me on I-75 when you passed me. The one that was your backup."

"I don't know what you're talking about. Honestly."

J.D. stared at him, her face impassive, giving him a look I'd seen only once before. It was hard and scary enough to frighten a dead man. "You listen to me, you little bastard. You tried to kill me. I had to shoot your buddy in the van. You come clean or there's no deal. You got me?"

"I don't know who he was or where to find him."

"He's in the morgue in Gainesville."

"He's dead?"

"Yes. I killed him."

Duhns was near tears. "If I knew who he was, I'd tell you. Please believe me."

J.D. looked at Vargas. "I don't have any more questions, Detective. Thank you for letting me sit in."

Vargas stared hard at Duhns for a minute or two. Duhns sat still at first, but then began to fidget under the detective's hard gaze. Finally, Duhns said, "Do I need to sign some papers or something?"

"Papers? For what?"

"Our deal."

"There is no deal. You lied to me."

"No, I didn't."

"You told me you didn't take the car."

"Yeah, but then I told you the truth."

"You've got a point, Xavier, but there's still the principle. You lied to a police officer. You'll be with us for a while, I think."

"Life?"

"We'll see."

"When?"

"As soon as I find Skeeter."

CHAPTER FORTY

MONDAY, NOVEMBER 3

"THAT GUY'S AN idiot," Vargas said as we sat in Howell's office.

"Most of them are," J.D. said.

"I guess you don't see much of his type on Longboat Key."

"More than you would expect, but I was in homicide with Miami-Dade PD before I moved to Longboat, so I've seen my share of idiots."

"I bet. What about you, Matt? You've been very quiet today."

"Not a natural state, I assure you," J.D. said. "Matt's a lawyer."

"And I thought he was a nice guy," Vargas said.

"He has his moments. I think it's mostly because he's retired and doesn't think like a lawyer anymore."

"All right," I said. "You guys have your fun."

Howell came through the door. "Okay. I've got Skeeter. I talked to the warden at Glades Correctional. Skeeter's real name is Jerry Evans. He was released about two weeks ago after he completed almost all of a five-year sentence for aggravated assault. I also talked to his parole officer. We'll pick him up today. J.D., you guys are welcome to come back this afternoon. I'll hold the interview until you're ready."

She looked at me and I nodded. "We've got nothing better to do."

* * *

We were in downtown Orlando in time for our one o'clock lunch meeting with my former law partner, Paul Linder. Paul was one of the best lawyers I'd ever met and a font of lawyer gossip in Central Florida. He was a congenial soul who worked hard and spent a lot of time with other lawyers over lunch or drinks after work. His grandfather had settled in the Orlando area in the 1920s and the Linders had lived in the area ever since. I knew he would be able to answer a lot of the questions I had about D. Wesley Gilbert, Esquire.

After we'd chatted a bit about all kinds of things, I said, "Paul, what can you tell me about Wes Gilbert?"

He chuckled. "Why in the world do you want to know anything about that guy?"

J.D. explained Gilbert's possible connection to some pretty bad people and a lot of money and how it might have something to do with a murder case she was working.

"He's a piece of work. Lots of money, no brains," Linder said. "I see him most mornings at the Citrus Club. He's usually there for the free breakfast buffet they put out for the members. He always wears a coat and tie and makes a big production about going to the office or having some major piece of legal work to handle. It's all a load of crap. He hasn't handled a legal matter in decades."

"Have you heard any gossip about his being involved in something shady?"

"Not specifically. A few years back, I heard he was in financial trouble, but he apparently pulled out of it."

"What did you hear?"

"Not much. Just the usual talk down at the University Club. He was way behind on his dues there as well as at the Country Club of Orlando. He wasn't paying the mortgage on that huge pile of bricks he lives in with that new wife. You know how bankers talk when they have a few scotches. But he pulled out of it, caught up on everything, and paid off his house."

"Do you know how he did that?"

"The prevailing wisdom is that he sold some of the property his grandfather accumulated out west. Maybe Montana, Wyoming, one of those places."

"How's he been doing lately?"

"Financially? Fine, I guess. I haven't heard anything to the contrary."

"Is the firm doing well?"

"Seems to be, but I don't think he's making much money out of it. I heard he sold what was left of his interest back to the firm years ago. I know they don't pay him much of a salary. They won't let him practice law."

"What does he do with the firm?"

"Nothing. He has an office there, but I think that's just because he carries one of the founder's names. He doesn't show up most days."

"Could the money he got from selling his interest in the firm been enough to pull him out of his difficulties several years ago?" I asked.

"One of the partners told me they didn't pay him enough to buy a car, so I'm sure that didn't take care of his problem. Besides, I think that buyout happened before he really got into money trouble."

"Do you think he would get himself involved in something illegal to make enough money to climb out from under his debt?"

"I wouldn't put anything past him. If he thought he could get away with something and make a little money in the bargain, he'd do it. All those ex-wives are expensive."

"Even drugs or gambling?"

Linder was quiet for a moment, thinking. "There was a rumor several years ago that old Wes had a gambling problem. That was kept pretty quiet and even the bankers over at the club didn't know anything about it."

"What were the rumors?" J.D. asked.

"Just that he was laying a lot of money off on a bookie, betting on professional sports. I heard he was losing more than he was winning. He might have pissed some bad people off, but I think he'd be sleeping with the fishes, as they say, if he'd done that."

"Or gone to work for them," J.D. said.

"Maybe."

"Do you have any ideas about what happened?" I asked.

"No. The talk just dried up. If he was in trouble because of the gambling, I guess he worked it out. He's still here and still breathing."

"Who would know about the land sale out west?" J.D. asked.

"Lloyd Deming probably. He owns most of that land with D. Wesley. Their grandfathers, the two guys who founded Gilbert and Deming, were partners in all their land deals and Wes and Lloyd inherited it."

"No other heirs?" I asked.

"No. The old men each had only one child, a son, and each of the sons each had one son. So D. Wesley and Lloyd jointly own whatever's left. They're about the same age."

"Is Deming a lawyer?" I asked.

"No. He's a retired airline pilot. I'm surprised you don't know him."

"Never met him. What can you tell us about Lloyd?"

"As I said, he's a retired airline pilot. Before that, he graduated from Florida State with an Air Force ROTC commission. After pilot training, he flew more than three hundred combat missions in Vietnam and later flew C-5As, including a career in the Air Force Reserve. He retired from that as a lieutenant colonel. He lives up in Altamonte Springs."

"J.D.," I said, "that's where Ken Brown's office is. Do you think we have time to meet with Deming if we can set it up?"

"I don't see a problem. Our meeting with Ken is at four. We

could maybe see Mr. Deming at three and still have time to sit in on Skeeter's interrogation. We'll be a little late getting home, but that's not a problem."

"Can you set up a meeting for three, Paul?"

"Sure. If he's not on a trip somewhere on his motorcycle, he'll either be at home or at Starbucks."

* * *

Altamonte Springs is an Orlando suburb, about a twenty-minute drive from downtown. Lloyd Deming was a thin gray-haired man in his late sixties. He introduced himself and invited us in. His wife Gale offered iced tea. We declined and she left the room to, as she said, let us talk business.

"Gale can't stand D. Wesley," Deming said. "Paul Linder said you have some questions about him. He told me Wes might be part of a murder investigation, so, of course, I want to do anything I can to help, but Wes and I've never been close. I don't know how much I can tell you."

"Mr. Deming," J.D. said, "I would appreciate your confidence on this. Mr. Gilbert may be completely innocent of any wrongdoing, but his name came up in the investigation, and I'm obligated to look into him. If he is involved, I wouldn't want him to know we're looking into his activities."

"I'll keep this just between us. How can I help?"

"We understand that you and Mr. Gilbert own land together out west," J.D. said.

"True."

"Have you sold any of it in the past few years?"

"The last time we sold anything must have been about ten years ago. There's not much left."

"Do you know if Mr. Gilbert owned any other land somewhere other than in Florida?" I asked.

"I wouldn't know. As I said, we're not close. In fact, I think the last time I saw him was when we sold an orange grove left to us by our dads."

"Do you know anything about him having financial problems three or four years ago?"

"No. But I wouldn't be surprised."

"Why not?"

"Our grandfathers bought a lot of property when it was cheap. They didn't believe in selling it, so when Disney and the other attractions showed up in the area, our dads got rich selling the land. My dad was a lawyer and a member of Gilbert and Deming, but he died of a heart attack when I was in Air Force flight training. He and D. Wesley's dad were close and I saw a lot of him when we were growing up. I didn't like him very much back then. His dad got him into law school and when he graduated, he came back to the firm and did nothing. When his dad died, about two years after Wes got out of law school, Wes inherited from his dad and, unfortunately, I inherited Wes as a partner. He always seemed to spend more money than he had, and he was constantly on me to sell the property we'd inherited. He always seemed to need money. I usually refused."

"Did you ever hear anything about him having a gambling problem?" J.D. asked.

"When I was at Florida State, Wes was at the University of Florida. I heard he'd gotten into some trouble betting on horses. I think his dad bailed him out. Maybe more than once. After his dad died and Wes inherited his interest in the jointly owned property, he came to me and wanted to put the property up as collateral on a loan. Said he needed the money urgently to pay off a debt. He needed my agreement in order to sell the property and I refused."

"Did he say what the debt was all about?" J.D. asked.

"No, and I didn't ask. I wasn't going to put the property up, so it was none of my business."

"Do you know what he did about the debt? Where else he might have gotten the money he needed?"

"I have no idea."

"One more question, Mr. Deming," J.D. said, "and we'll get out of your hair. Do you think Mr. Gilbert would be capable of getting involved in a murder plot? Or maybe with gamblers or drug runners?"

"I'm sorry, Detective, but I just don't know. From what I know of him, and what I saw even in childhood, my guess would be that for the right amount of money, he'd be capable of anything. To be honest, I think he's a psychopath."

CHAPTER FORTY-ONE

MONDAY, NOVEMBER 3

KEN BROWN HAD been busy, buried in the documents Reuben Carlson had sent him that morning. At midafternoon, the documents were spread over the top of his desk, order in their apparent randomness. Ken would pull one out, discuss it, and show how it related to another document.

"I've made a cursory analysis of the documents Reuben Carlson sent me," he said, "and it looks like there was an awful lot of money going from the Fortson trusts into a lot of different accounts, mostly in the Tallahassee area."

"Did any of that money go to Wayfarer, Inc.?" I asked.

Ken thumbed through a small stack of documents. "I looked at what I've got so far, and extrapolated over the three-year period since Rachel's death that approximately ten million dollars was transferred to Wayfarer."

"That's a lot of money," J.D. said.

"Yes," Ken said, "and all the checks were for ninety-five hundred dollars."

"The feds don't get too excited unless the checks are for ten grand or more," J.D. said.

"Right," Ken said, "and these checks were sent to several different accounts that Wayfarer controls. I've listed them as Wayfarer numbers one through twelve."

"That hides the transaction even better," I said, "Were all the accounts on the same bank?"

"No. Each account was in a different bank. The banks are mostly small community banks in little towns between Pensacola and Jacksonville. And Wayfarer wasn't the only corporation where lots of money was being sent."

"How did the trusts work when it came to sending money?" I asked.

"Simple. Peter Fortson signed checks just as if they were drawn on his own account. He was the co-trustee with the bank, but he was the only one who could sign a check. Everything was run through the bank in Orlando that served as the co-trustee."

"The bank was probably co-trustee, so the trust would continue in the event of the deaths of the beneficiaries," I said. "In this case, Rachel and Peter."

"I looked at some of the corporations that were receiving the money Fortson sent," Ken said. "Most of them are like Wayfarer. We don't know who any of the board members are, or who runs them. Their offices of record seem to be for the most part just mail drops; boxes in stores where those who rent the boxes can remain anonymous. But there were some individual names that popped up who were sent large amounts, often by wire transfer. Most of them had to do with business transactions, but I think that was bogus. I couldn't find anything anywhere that would indicate that the business deals were ever consummated. No return on investment, no transfers back to the trust, nothing."

"Were you able to figure out who the recipients of that money were?" J.D. asked.

"I found out quite a bit on some of them. Several were bookies with mob associations."

"You think Fortson was involved in gambling?" J.D. asked.

"Maybe."

"Does it look like Peter was in any kind of money squeeze at the time of Rachel's murder?"

"It would appear so. The trust documents were in the stack we got from Parrish's office. The trust was set up so that Peter and Rachel's dad was the sole beneficiary, but he could also borrow from it. It looks like the grandfather was afraid that his grandchildren might be a little more profligate than his son, so the trust documents provided that upon the death of the son, that is Peter and Rachel's father, the trust would be split into two parts. There was a firewall between the two parts of the trust. Neither of the kids, Peter or Rachel, could invade the other's half. When one of them died, if he or she had no children or a spouse, the money in the decedent's trust would revert to the remaining child's trust. When Rachel was killed, Peter got everything."

"What did Peter's trust look like at the time of Rachel's murder?" I asked.

"It was almost gone. Peter had borrowed so much from it that the principal had been depleted to almost nothing. He would have been destitute within a year or so."

"Where did Peter's money go?" J.D. asked.

"I don't know. Yet. I haven't had time to go through the documents on Peter's trust that preceded the time of Rachel's death. But I can tell you that there were big checks going out of his trust to some of the same people the checks were going to just after Rachel's death. A cursory look at those documents makes me think that Peter depleted his trust funds by sending the money to some pretty bad people over a number of years."

"What happens to the money now?" J.D. asked. "Peter told me it would go to a bunch of charities, but I never saw the trust documents."

Ken said, "The trust will survive, but the money generated by it all goes to various legitimate charities. At least that's the way Grandpa Fortson set it up. But there's a hitch. Several weeks ago, Peter petitioned the probate court in Orlando to allow him to change the terms of the trust. He wanted all the money to go to one entity that appeared to be a charity, rather than the ones his grandfather had set out in the original documents. Last week the probate court issued an order refusing to change the beneficiaries. The money will go to the charities Grandpa set out."

"What was the charity Peter wanted to leave the money to?" I asked.

"It's called Ishmael's Children. He'd given a lot of money to it over the past three years or so. But there's something funny going on with it. Fortson's federal income tax returns were included in the documents on his laptop, and he never took any deductions for donations to Ishmael's Children. I checked it out. I don't think it's a charity. It's on the Department of Homeland Security's list of organizations that support al-Qaeda and other jihadist organizations. It may be a terrorist group itself. That wasn't clear, but I'd bet my last buck it isn't a charity."

CHAPTER FORTY-TWO

MONDAY, NOVEMBER 3

SKEETER EVANS SAT in the same interview room that had held Xavier Duhns several hours earlier. His right arm was shackled to the O-ring cemented into the floor. He looked like a big dumb redneck. He was wearing a sweatshirt from which the sleeves had been torn, revealing muscled arms tattooed with a mixture of prison tats and work done at a tattoo shop that catered to people who thought caricatures of naked women were fine art. His red hair hadn't been washed or combed in weeks, if ever. He sat scowling across the table at Detective Glenn Howell. J.D. and I were back in the anteroom watching through the one-way glass.

Glenn sat quietly, looking directly at Skeeter. A couple of minutes passed and then Evans opened his mouth and proved my hypothesis that he was dumber than a stump. "What the fuck you looking at, you blond motherfucker?"

The detective smiled, reached into the breast pocket of his shirt, and pulled out a small aerosol cylinder, held it near Skeeter's nose, and pressed. A quick spurt of spray, short and pungent, pushed Skeeter back in his chair. I smelled the odor of pepper spray escaping the small room. Skeeter howled and put his free hand to his face, trying desperately to make the burning go away. Glenn pushed his chair back, stood, and walked out.

"Was that pepper spray?" I asked.

"Yeah. It's kind of a sedative. It'll make him a bit more docile." He walked into the breakroom down the hall and returned with a plastic bottle of water and a washcloth. He went back into the room and handed them to Skeeter. "Here. Wash out your eyes. When you're finished, we can either have a civil conversation, or I can use up some more of that spray."

Skeeter nodded.

"Talk to me about the car you stole."

"I didn't steal no car."

"You paid Xavier Duhns two thousand bucks to steal one."

"Okay."

"Where'd you get that kind of money, Skeeter?"

"Okay. A dude gave me the money. Told me he needed a car. Xavier was like a subcontractor, you know?"

"Who's the dude who paid you?"

"Didn't get a name."

"Describe him."

"Never saw him."

"How did you set up the deal?"

"Phone."

"How did you get the money?"

"One of those messenger dudes brought it to me."

"Messenger dude?"

"You know. Those guys what drive those little cars and deliver packages and such around town."

Glenn nodded. "Okay. How much did he give you?"

"Two thousand dollars."

"Are you telling me you just handled all this, set up the car theft, and all out of the goodness of your heart?"

"The dude might have paid me for my time."

"How much?"

"A grand."

"When was this set up?"

"Last Wednesday."

"What time of day."

"I don't remember. Sometime in the morning."

"Early?"

"Yeah. Right after I got out of bed."

"What time do you get up?"

"Usually around ten."

"Who were you supposed to kill?"

Glenn leaned back in his chair, giving J.D. the signal to enter. As she walked in the door, Skeeter did a double take, recognition dawning across his face. He slumped a little in his chair, confusion replacing recognition in his facial expression.

"It's good to see you again, Skeeter," J.D. said, taking a seat next to Detective Howell. "You don't look so tough without that shotgun."

"I don't know what you're talking about," Skeeter said in a voice that carried no conviction. He was had and he knew it. He wiped at his red eyes some more with the wet washcloth.

"Skeeter," Glenn said, "I need to tell you something. Kind of in confidence, if you know what I mean."

Skeeter nodded, a bit tentatively, I thought.

"You tried to take out a cop," Howell said. "Now we just can't let that sort of thing go. I mean, can you imagine the chaos that would ensue if dumbasses like you could just kill cops when they feel like it? Why, you and your buddies would make a regular thing of it and take your chances in the system. You know how we prevent that?"

Skeeter shook his head.

"We kill you. No trial, no investigation to amount to anything, no lawyers. We just take you out in a police boat to the middle of Lake

Monroe, tie a couple of anchors around your neck and drop you overboard. You can see how that might work as a deterrent."

"I want a lawyer," Skeeter said.

J.D. leaned into the table, staring directly at Skeeter. "Man, you are dumber than a goldfish."

"I ain't dumb," he said. "A little slow, maybe."

"Then chew on this and see if it makes sense. You are not getting a lawyer. You're going to Lake Monroe as soon as it gets dark and you won't be coming back. The Seminole County sheriff will be out a couple of anchors and one very dumbass citizen. Do you get that?"

"You're going to kill me?"

"That's my preference," J.D. said, "but you have one way out. You answer our questions truthfully, and you'll be charged and go to prison, but you won't die. At least not tonight."

Skeeter looked down at the table and said in a quiet, defeated voice, "What do you want to know?"

"What else did the man who gave you the money for the car want you to do?" J.D. asked.

"Kill you."

"How was that set up?"

"He was going to send me an iPad that would track the car you were driving. I was supposed to go to Gainesville and be ready to pick up your trail when you got to the Interstate. Somebody would call me when you got within range of the iPad, and I would park in that rest stop just before you get to Paynes Prairie and wait for you to pass."

"How did you know I was going to be on the Interstate?"

"The man on the phone said he was pretty sure you would be coming that way. I asked him what would happen if you went right down Highway 19. He said he had another team on that route to take you out."

"Did he say why he wanted me dead?"

"No."

"How much did he pay you?"

"Five grand."

"A few minutes ago you said he paid you one grand. Now it's five grand."

"It was five," Skeeter said.

"Five grand? To kill a cop?"

"Well, I had to give Xavier two thousand."

"Geez," J.D. said, "I thought I'd be worth more than five grand."

"Three grand, actually," Glenn said.

"You hush."

"I'm just saying," Glenn said. "Somebody once paid a guy ten grand to take me out."

"Did you catch him?"

"Sure did. Just some sleazeball I'd sent to prison ten years before."

"What happened to him?" J.D. asked.

"He's in Lake Monroe."

"Oh," J.D. said.

She turned back to Skeeter. "What were your instructions?"

"The man told me to get the car and go to Gainesville Thursday morning. The messenger what brought the money also brought me the iPad and showed me how to use it. It didn't have nothing on it but a map. The messenger told me that I would get a call from somebody on Thursday who would tell me when to turn the pad on. He said there'd be a little dot on it that would be a moving car. There was a picture of the detective in the envelope with the money. He said the detective would be driving that car and that I was supposed to pull up beside her on I-75 when we were going over Paynes Prairie and shoot her and bring the car back to the parking lot out by the airport."

"Who was the guy in the van following me?"

"I don't know. I didn't know there was a guy in a van."

"Guy named Mabry Jackson."

"Don't know him."

"You didn't have a backup out there?"

"No."

"Somebody in a van tried to kill me after you sped on by. He wrecked and when I went to see about him, he shot at me. I had to kill him. You don't know anything about that?"

"No, ma'am. I'd surely tell you if I did."

"Does the name D. Wesley Gilbert mean anything to you?"

"Never heard of him."

"What phone did the man contact you on?"

"My cell phone. It's the only one I have."

Glenn held out his hand palm-up and wiggled his fingers in a gimme motion.

"You want my phone?" Skeeter asked.

Glenn nodded.

"If I don't give it to you are you going to spray that shit in my face again?"

"Probably," Glenn said.

Skeeter pulled out his cell phone and set it on the table.

"Let's take a break," Glenn said. "Sit tight, Skeeter. We'll be back."

As the detectives left the room, Skeeter leaned his head back and placed the washcloth over his eyes.

* * *

Glenn, J.D., and I were standing in the anteroom. "I've got a buddy at the phone company," Glenn said. "I'll get our geek to get all the numbers that came into Skeeter's phone on Wednesday morning and we can get the names of who those numbers are assigned to."

"I'm willing to bet one of those numbers will be D. Wesley Gilbert," I said.

"I can probably get the names on those phone numbers in about an hour," Howell said. "You guys want to hang around?"

"What do you think?" I asked J.D. "We could spend the night and if one of those numbers belongs to D. Wesley, we could have breakfast at the Citrus Club in the morning. Might happen to see Wes."

"Don't you have to be a member to get in there?"

"We'll be Paul Linder's guest."

"I don't even have a toothbrush with me, much less a change of clothes" J.D. said.

"We can go shopping, get some dinner, find a hotel. What do you say?"

"Okay. Glenn, can you get me the information on those phone numbers tonight?"

"I don't think that'll be a problem at all. I'll text it to you as soon as my guy at the phone company comes through."

"We might need to talk to Skeeter and Xavier again," J.D. said.

"They're not going anywhere. Let me know."

"Will you join us for dinner?" I asked.

"Sorry, Matt. I'd love to, but I've got a lot of paperwork to do on this mess. I'd best get to it."

"Don't forget to take care of those videos in the interview room," J.D. said. "I don't think they'd look too good on YouTube."

"Those?" Glenn said. "Damn cameras. They've been on the fritz all day."

* * *

We checked into the Bohemian Hotel across the street from the office building that housed the Citrus Club in downtown Orlando.

We'd had dinner in Sanford and then drove to the Altamonte Mall to do some shopping for J.D. I decided that my trousers would be good for another day, but I did buy a new polo shirt, underwear, and toiletries. We were set. I'd called Paul Linder, and he agreed to meet us for breakfast at eight the next morning. Hopefully, D. Wesley Gilbert would be enjoying the member's free breakfast at the club.

Glenn Howell texted J.D. the results of the phone search. There was only one call into Skeeter's phone on Wednesday morning. It came from a burner, one of those ubiquitous phones purchased at a Walmart that the buyer could use and throw away. No way to trace the number.

We dropped our packages in our assigned room and took the elevator back down to the ground floor lounge. We took a table in the corner and ordered our drinks. "Busy day," she said.

"Productive day," I said.

"Very much so. You want to talk about it?"

"You know, I think I'd like to just sit on it overnight. Hopefully, we'll get a shot at Gilbert in the morning and can head right back to Longboat. I'd like a fresh set of eyes on this. I want to lay out all the facts we know and see if somebody else puts it all together a different way."

She laughed. "Logan Hamilton."

"Yep. Logan's got one of the most insightful minds I've ever seen."

"I agree. Sounds like a plan."

We talked for another half-hour, finished our drinks, and called it a day.

CHAPTER FORTY-THREE

Tuesday, November 4

D. Wesley Gilbert was a tall man with gray hair and the look of a patrician about him. I knew him to be in his late sixties, but he looked a few years older. He had the face of a man who drank too much, the little thread veins around his nose were very red and looked as if they were ready to burst. He was sitting at a table by a window overlooking downtown. Paul Linder sat across the table from him. When we approached, Paul stood and introduced us to each other. If Gilbert was surprised by the presence of a woman he'd tried to kill, he didn't show it. His face remained impassive.

"I don't think we ever met, Matt, but I've certainly heard your name," Gilbert said. "You were a big-time trial guy, and I heard you'd retired and moved to the Keys."

"Not exactly. I live on Longboat Key off the coast of Sarasota. We're one of the West Coast keys."

"Of course I know Longboat Key. I've played golf there at the Longboat Key Club numerous times. Do you play?"

"No. I fish some."

"And you, Ms. Duncan?" he asked. "What do you do on Longboat Key?"

"I'm a police detective."

"Oh my," he said. "I wouldn't think there's a lot of need for your services on such a quiet island."

"More than you'd think. We just had a murder there. A man named Peter Fortson. Maybe you heard about it."

There was a slight tightening in the flesh around his eyes. A tiny, almost imperceptible indication that J.D. had hit a nerve. If I hadn't been looking for it, I would have missed it. "No, I don't think so. When did it happen?"

"Early Saturday morning. Mr. Fortson lived here. In Windermere."

"No. I'm afraid I didn't know the gentleman." He took a stab at changing the subject. "What brings you two to Orlando?"

"I'm investigating Fortson's murder," J.D. said, staying on subject. "I think it's tied to an attempt on my life that took place last week."

"Somebody tried to kill you?"

"Yes. Up near Gainesville. I think we found the man who took the shot at me. A local fuzzball named Skeeter Evans. You ever hear of him?"

"No, afraid not." It was there again. That little tic around the eyes. He was lying. "Longboat Key is starting to sound like a much more dangerous place than I would have imagined."

"Sometimes, it is."

"Well, I must be off," Gilbert said, standing. "I'm handling the negotiations on a major corporate merger, and we've got meetings all day today. Nice to have met you."

When he'd gone, Paul said, "See what I mean? Nobody in his right mind would hire that wingnut to handle a merger. He is as full of crap as a constipated elephant. Did you learn anything?"

"He knows both Fortson and Skeeter Evans," I said.

"I thought he said he didn't know either one of them," Linder said.

"Yeah, but he's lying. He has a tell, a small reaction to a lie that gives him away, sort of a tic up around the eyes."

"Can you prove he knows them?"

"Maybe," I said. "Guys like Gilbert leave a paper trail. We're looking into that."

We finished our breakfast, thanked Paul for his hospitality, and started the two-hour drive back to Longboat Key.

CHAPTER FORTY-FOUR

TUESDAY, NOVEMBER 4

J.D., LOGAN HAMILTON, and I were sitting on J.D.'s glassed-in sunporch, the remains of a take-out lunch from Harry's Deli on the table in front of us. We'd brought Logan up-to-date on our day in the Orlando area and all that we'd found out.

"Let's look at D. Wesley Gilbert," J.D. said.

"Okay," Logan said. "What are the facts that we know?"

"Not a lot," J.D. said. "He corresponded with Peter Fortson and seemed to threaten him with somebody named Wally. We think that's probably Wally Delmer, the private investigator in Tallahassee, whose one-room office is also the headquarters of Wayfarer, Inc. We know that Fortson sent a number of big checks to Wayfarer and also to a charity, which may not really be a charity, called Ishmael's Children, which is probably on the CIA's watch list for organizations that help fund jihadists. Fortson tried to amend the trust documents, so that the money in his trust would go to Ishmael's Children when he died."

"Why would he do that?"

"We think he was under some kind of pressure from the terrorists. Your money or your life. Something like that."

"Okay. What else?"

"Gilbert was emailing Fortson about a charity that doesn't exist named Abe's Kids. Keep in mind that Ishmael was the son of Abraham, and supposedly the father of the Arabs, so it's not too big a stretch to think that Abe's Kids could be a code word for Ishmael's Children. On top of that, Ken Brown says Fortson was sending some very big money to a bunch of bad guys."

"Gilbert is your hinge," Logan said. "Everything revolves around him. I think he put the hit out on J.D. and he's also somehow involved with the jihadists who're after you both."

"Lay it out for us, Logan. I've been thinking the same thing and so has J.D., but we're both so involved in this mess that we may be seeing ghosts, finding connections where there aren't any."

"Let's do a timeline," Logan said. "Rachel Fortson is murdered three years ago in her brother's beach house on Longboat. The case goes cold, but suddenly there's a break. For some reason the young man who had been hired to kill Rachel is himself murdered and makes a deathbed confession. J.D. goes to North Florida, spends three days up there and then heads home. Right so far, J.D.?"

"On the money."

"On Wednesday of last week, Skeeter Evans gets a call from an anonymous person who hires him to kill J.D. Skeeter then hires Xavier to steal a car and drive him to Gainesville. Skeeter has an iPad loaded with what sounds like a GPS receiver. The transmitter was attached to J.D.'s car.

"On the same day," Logan continued, "Charlie Bates sets sail from Carrabelle heading to Longboat Key. He's underway all day Wednesday and through the night. He docks at the Seafood Shack and spends the day hanging around the marina."

"We don't think he's involved in the attempt on J.D.'s life," I said, "but I suppose he could be the anonymous caller who hired Skeeter."

"But that seems a little far-fetched," J.D. said. "I don't see how Bates could have set up the money hand-off. Unless he'd known that Skeeter would take the job, how could he have had five thousand dollars waiting to be delivered?"

"Good points, all," Logan said. "But do you see the gap in our storyline?"

J.D. was silent for a moment. Then, "The locator device. Who put it on my car?"

"Precisely," Logan said. "Let's put that in the unanswered column for now. We'll get back to it."

"The man whose thumbprint was on the locator device was due back from his fishing trip yesterday," J.D. said. "The Franklin County sheriff was going to confront him and get back to me. I haven't heard from him. I'll follow up on that as soon as we break here."

"Okay," Logan said. "Let's look at Thursday. Somebody takes a shot at J.D. on I 75. Skeeter set up the shooting, but he professes to know nothing about the man in the van, Mabry Jackson. Since Jackson was dead, and Skeeter had already confessed to trying to kill J.D., he had nothing to gain by not acknowledging Jackson. And Skeeter's story is the same as Duhns'."

"The van driver had an iPad that was set to track the locator on my car," J.D. said.

"So both Skeeter and Jackson must have been working for the same person," Logan said.

"It sounds as if Jackson knew about Skeeter," I said, "but Skeeter didn't know about Jackson."

"I think Jackson was plan B," J.D. said. "If Skeeter didn't get me, Jackson would."

"Okay. So we have the hit on J.D. set up and in operation. What we're missing now is the answer to who hired Skeeter and who hired Jackson. I think it's probably the same person, but what was the motive?"

"The only thing I can think of," J.D. said, "is that somebody thought I was getting too close to solving Rachel's murder and decided to take me out."

"You didn't know much more after you went to Franklin County than you did before, did you?" Logan asked.

"No. But whoever put out the hit might not have known that."

"Do you think Peter Fortson was killed because they didn't get you and were afraid you were closing in on Peter and that he'd talk?"

"That's a reasonable hypothesis, I guess," J.D. said. "So far I haven't been able to come up with anything better."

"So we move on to Friday," Logan said. "You and young Carey talk to Peter Fortson. He doesn't tell you anything, but the bad guys couldn't have known that. Then that afternoon, J.D., on the spur of the moment, you and Matt go to Key West. You're out of town, and possibly out of reach of whoever's trying to kill you. That night, somebody cuts Peter's throat."

"That's about it," J.D. said.

"And the next day somebody tries to break into your condo while you're taking a nap."

"Right. A couple of my neighbors saw the man we think was trying to break in, and he matches the description Linda Jones gave of a man she saw leaving the beach shortly after Peter Fortson was killed. Both descriptions fit Charlie Bates."

"Then on Saturday night Matt has the run-in with Bates at Tiny's. Any idea what caused him to come at you like that, Matt?"

"None. Cracker mentioned to me on Thursday that a man had come into Mar Vista looking for me, and then Cracker pointed out Bates on Saturday as the one asking about me. When I introduced myself to him, he went ballistic."

"Have you seen him since?"

"No. J.D. and I saw his boat at the Seafood Shack on Sunday, but we didn't see him."

"He's still here," J.D. said. "Or at least he was yesterday. I called the

Shack's dockmaster before we left for Orlando, and he told me Bates was still hanging around."

"I think there may be more connections," I said. "It seems very coincidental that a bunch of Arab terrorists are trying to kill J.D. and me and an organization with ties to jihadists is the recipient of funds from Fortson and of obvious interest to Gilbert."

"What terrorists?" Logan asked.

"This is very sensitive stuff, Logan," I said. "It has to do with one of Jock's operations, and I can't tell you much about it, I'm afraid. What I can tell you is that we have hard evidence that because of Jock's last mission, some very bad actors from Syria, terrorists, are here trying to kill J.D. and me."

"Why?"

"They know we're Jock's family and they want to hurt him as badly as possible. They think if they kill us, it will be devastating to Jock."

"They're probably right. Is Jock dealing with it?"

"No. Jock is pretty much incapacitated. He's down in Key West with a mutual friend, hiding out. I think he's getting better, but it's kind of a roller coaster."

"How much can you tell me?"

"That's about it. The terrorists lured J.D. and me to Key West by putting Jock in the hospital with a minor gunshot wound. Six of them were down there and on Saturday I killed three of them. A fourth one is spending some quality time in isolation in the Monroe County jail."

Logan didn't seem the least bit perturbed by my admission of killing three men. "And the other two?" he asked with no more emotion that if we had been talking about pencils, instead of people.

"I don't know. I suspect they're here or on their way. If they find out that J.D. and I are back, I'm sure they'll follow us. They won't know where Jock is. He's well hidden."

"Gilbert, the hinge," Logan said. "Could he be running the Arabs?"

"I doubt it," I said. "He might be giving them some logistical support through Ishmael's Children, but that's about all. The jihadists don't trust anybody but their own people. I can't imagine they'd let Gilbert get too involved or too close to them."

"I don't understand why he would be involved at all," J.D. said.

"Neither do I, but if old D. Wesley is tied up with gamblers, or worse yet, organized crime, they might be linked in some way to the terrorist groups. Maybe they're laundering money, or just supporting them because they're being threatened. Who knows?"

"Maybe the gamblers are the terrorists or vice versa," Logan said.

"Maybe the guy at the Franklin County sheriff's office can enlighten us a bit," J.D. said. "I'm going to call the sheriff up there and find out if they have been able to get anything out of him." She went into her bedroom to make the call.

"You don't seem too concerned about the terrorists," Logan said.

"I'm very concerned. I carry a pistol with me at all times, and I'm very careful about my surroundings. I don't know what else to do."

"What about getting some of Dave Kendall's men down here?"

"I'm not sure that'd do much good. I've got to kill the terrorists before they get us. That's the only way I can start to relax a little and get back to my old life."

J.D. was back in a few minutes. "The sheriff's civilian employee, the one whose thumbprint was on the locator beacon? He didn't show up for his shift last night. They haven't been able to find him. His wife says she hasn't heard from him and the charter boat captain who was supposed to take him and his friends fishing said he never heard of the group. The sheriff says the boat never left its slip over the weekend and the captain was in Tallahassee at a Florida State football game."

"He's dead," I said.

"I agree," J.D. said.

"Whoever is in charge isn't likely to leave a guy like that alive," Logan said. "Sooner or later, drunk or sober, he'd have to tell somebody. Brag a little."

"What would make somebody get in bed with those characters?" I asked. "Money?"

"I think so," J.D. said. "The sheriff said that when they searched his house this morning they found a valise behind a stack of dirty clothes in his closet. It was stuffed with one-hundred-dollar bills. Five grand worth."

"That seems to be the standard amount these guys pay," I said. "Any prints on the valise?"

"No. It'd been wiped clean, but there was a nice piece of evidence that somebody left in the bag."

"I'm all ears," I said.

"A bank receipt showing a withdrawal of five grand."

"What bank?"

"Third National of Orlando." She had a big grin plastered across her face.

"I'm guessing there's more," I said.

"The receipt had an account number. Guess who it belonged to?"

"Peter Fortson."

"You're half right. It was a joint account."

I raised my hands. "Okay. I give up."

"The joint holder of the account is D. Wesley Gilbert."

CHAPTER FORTY-FIVE

TUESDAY, NOVEMBER 4

"WE'VE GOT TO bring Dave Kendall in on this," I said. "He'll be able to tell us a lot about Ishmael's Children. I'd sure like to know why Peter wanted to give all his money to it, and I'll bet you that a lot of those people Fortson was writing checks to are going to be associated with this so-called charity."

J.D. frowned. "I don't know. This is really just an old-fashioned murder case, so far. Will Dave think we're overstepping by asking him for information? Most of it is probably classified. I've already called Parrish. He's going to contact the Franklin County sheriff, and if everything matches up, he's going to see if he has enough to arrest Gilbert."

"I think he's got some legwork to do," I said. "Gilbert and Fortson were joint holders of the account. The deposit receipt would have a date on it, but we don't know yet what that is."

J.D. slapped her head. "I'm getting dense. I didn't even think to ask the sheriff about that."

"Don't worry about it. It could have been either one of them. The locator beacon must have been put on your car no later than Wednesday. The money to pay for it was withdrawn from the Third National in Orlando, probably on Tuesday of last week. That would give them time to get the money to Franklin County and give it to the sheriff's employee. Since Fortson was alive last Tuesday, it could have been either Gilbert or Fortson who withdrew the money."

"Maybe the bank teller will remember him," Logan said. "Or maybe there's a security tape."

"I'm betting on the tape," I said. "Let's see what Parrish comes up with."

"Do you still want to call Kendall?" J.D. asked.

"I do. If Ishmael's Children is on Homeland's terrorist list, the intelligence agencies are most likely monitoring Peter Fortson," I said. "He filed suit in the probate court to change the beneficiary of the trust. That makes for a very public paper trail. He may have been on a watch list before he filed that suit, but if not, he'll be on it now. A lot of money with his name on it went flying around the country."

"I wonder if Peter was a jihadist," Logan said.

"Good question," J.D. said. "The probable answer is that he was. Why else would he be trying to leave that much money to Ishmael's Children?"

"Another good question." I said. "He must have known that by filing the petition he was putting the whole issue in the public eye."

"The suit would certainly have put Peter on the security watch lists," J.D. said.

"I agree," I said. "Have you gotten the autopsy report on Peter?"

"Not yet. There was no hurry. We knew the cause of death, so the autopsy probably isn't going to show us anything that will be useful. I didn't see any reason to push Doc Hawkins. Why?"

"I'd be interested in whether Peter may have had some kind terminal illness. Maybe that's why he wanted to change the beneficiary of the trust."

"If that were the case," J.D. said, "why would someone kill him? Why not just let him die?"

"Peter's death would terminate the possibility that he would appeal the probate court's ruling," I said. "Maybe somebody that had an interest in the proceeds at Peter's death, like one of the charities his grandfather named, was afraid that the higher court might reverse the probate court and allow the change of beneficiaries if Peter was alive to pursue it."

"Then why not kill him when he filed in probate court?" J.D. asked.

"You got me there," I said.

"This doesn't make a lot of sense," Logan said. "The charities named by the grandfather are all old, legitimate, and well respected. I don't think they would turn into killers. We're missing something. Maybe Peter's death has nothing to do with the lawsuit or the beneficiaries."

"The timing of the two events, the appeal and the murder, might just be coincidental," I said.

"You sound skeptical," J.D. said. "I know you don't like coincidences, but sometimes they happen."

"Let's check in with the ME's office and see if they have anything," I said.

J.D. called, talked to the ME and hung up. "No disease," she said. "Other than a slit throat, Peter Fortson was in perfect health."

"Let's let Ken Brown spend more time with the documents," I said. "Maybe he'll ferret something out."

I stepped out onto the walkway that ran along the outside of J.D.'s building, and called Dave Kendall. I explained what we'd found out about the Ishmael's Children's link to Peter Fortson who was a murder victim on the key. I explained the possible connection with D. Wesley Gilbert and perhaps to some gamblers who had connections to the terrorist organizations. He said he'd have somebody who tracked the charities get back to me in about ten minutes. "Do you think this may have anything to do with Youssef and his thugs?" he asked.

"I'm beginning to think it might have. If something turns up on that front, I'll let you know. I wouldn't be surprised if there's a connection. Lots of crazies running around out there."

I stood for a while, looking out at the Gulf, visible across the tennis courts and the trees that lined Gulf of Mexico Drive between the condo property and the beach. It was getting late. My phone rang and I took the call, talked to a female analyst from Kendall's office named Paulette Brown, who sounded both sexy and brilliant, hung up, and walked back inside. "Kendall's office says one of the intelligence agencies has been on top of Ishmael's Children and on Fortson," I told J.D. and Logan. "The woman in charge will be emailing some stuff to J.D. in the next hour or so."

Logan spoke up. "I wonder about that lawyer in Orlando, D. Wesley Gilbert. He was emailing Fortson about Abe's Kids, a charity that doesn't exist, but which is probably code for Ishmael's Children."

"Ishmael's Children is not a charity," I said. "It's the name of an al-Qaeda-affiliated terrorist group that tries to act like a charity."

"You're kidding," J.D. said. "That changes the whole picture."

"It does," I said. "Somehow, Peter Fortson's death is connected to the attempts on us. Maybe only in the funding, but that's still a connection."

"Hold that thought," J.D. said. "I'm ready to call it a night. It's been a long day and it didn't start out too well. I'll call Reuben and see if he can find any more connections between Gilbert and Delmer. Maybe he can find something in that stuff Kendall is sending."

"J.D.," I said, "while you're at it, ask Reuben to send it on to Ken Brown. He may be able to find a financial connection between Gilbert and Ishmael's Children."

"I'll do it."

"I'll leave it to you guys," Logan said. "It's happy hour at Tiny's. Don't want to miss that."

"You've been a big help, Logan," J.D. said. "We'll bring you up to date when we have a little more information."

Logan left and I asked J.D., "You want to go out to eat?"

"Why don't we stay here? It's been a long day and I'm tired."

"You got anything here to cook?"

"There's breakfast stuff in the fridge. How about some bacon and eggs?"

"Sounds fine," I said. "I'll cook."

We ate on the sunporch, enjoying the rays of the setting sun that were reflected on the white clouds hanging low over the mainland. As the sun made its way into the Gulf of Mexico on the other side of the island, the colorful display began to dissipate.

"You staying here tonight?" she asked as the color disappeared from the horizon and night descended on the island.

"Is that an invitation?"

"You know you have an open invitation. Anytime."

"Then the answer is yes."

CHAPTER FORTY-SIX

WEDNESDAY, NOVEMBER 5

J.D. WAS IN the shower when Matt left her condo. He was on his way to Publix to pick up pastries for breakfast. She thought it was decadent, eating a delicious clump of sugar and fat for the first meal of the day. She was looking forward to it.

Today was one of those days she dreaded. She had been subpoenaed to give a deposition in a burglary case she'd worked a few months back. It was set for a lawyer's office in downtown Sarasota for eight thirty. She looked at the clock. It was almost seven. She'd have to leave home by seven forty-five to get there on time, giving her about thirty minutes to eat breakfast by the time Matt returned.

She had way too much to do on the Fortson cases, but she'd have to waste part of the day sitting in a conference room, enduring the defense attorney's grilling of her under oath about everything she did leading up to the arrest of his stumblebum client. The idiot always made his getaway on a bicycle he'd stolen from the home he'd just burglarized. The police officers who took the initial calls were of the opinion that the burglar picked his targets based on the type of bicycle that was on the property. Unfortunately for the thief, the value of the bike taken from one of the houses was enough to turn the case into a felony. A pocketful of crack cocaine at the time of his arrest pretty much ensured that he would do some prison time.

J.D. dressed carefully in what she always thought of as her court attire: navy suit, white blouse, and low-heeled navy pumps. She laid her suit jacket over the back of the living room sofa and went to the kitchen to get the coffee started.

She had filled the coffee maker and turned it on when there was a knock at the door. Three sharp raps. Matt forgot his key again, she thought as she walked to the door. She opened it to Charlie Bates. He was grinning broadly and holding a revolver, a thirty-eight-caliber Police Special, pointed at her. A miasma of body odor and old alcohol emanated from him like some kind of toxic cloud.

J.D. reacted immediately and tried to slam the door. Bates put a foot out and stopped it from closing. He pushed his way into the condo and closed the door behind him. "What do you want, Charlie?" J.D. asked.

He chuckled. "Didn't take you long to figure out who I am."

"Easy. You're in the system. Big time."

"Quite a resume, huh?"

"Very impressive," she said.

He kept walking toward her, pushing her farther back into the condo as she tried to avoid the stench radiating from his filthy body. Finally they were standing in the living room, J.D. with her back to the alcove that led to the master bedroom where her holstered service weapon was hanging over the back of a chair. If I can get to that, she thought, I could turn this thing around.

"What do you want, Charlie?" she asked again.

"You, babe."

"Not going to happen, Charlie."

"Oh, it's going to happen. One way or another. Take your clothes off."

"That's not going to happen, either."

He pulled a large knife from the scabbard attached to his belt. "If

I have to cut them off, I will. Might get a little flesh in the bargain, though. My hand might not be too steady. You know, the juices flowing and all."

"Charlie, the only way you're going to get my clothes off is to kill me."

"Huh. It wouldn't be the first time I fucked a dead woman. But I'd rather have you alive. We'll just have to see how it goes."

J.D. was trying to tamp down her rising panic. If she ran for her weapon, Bates would shoot her in the back. If she took off her clothes, it would only delay the inevitable. The Publix market was five miles down the island and it would take Matt fifteen minutes to get there and park, another ten minutes in the store and fifteen back. Forty minutes from the time he left the condo. He'd been gone for maybe twenty minutes, which meant he wouldn't return for close to another half hour. By then, it would all be over and she'd be dead. Maybe she could talk Bates down, slow the process. "Matt will be here in a few minutes," J.D. said.

"Bullshit. I saw him leave. I've been sitting in your parking lot for an hour waiting for him to go. I recognized his car when I drove in. I'll take care of that asshole later."

"He just ran down to the store."

"Right."

"Even if he doesn't come back, he'll know what you did and he'll track you down like a wild hog and kill you. He'll make your dying last a long time. And when you're about done, when you know you're about to draw your last breath, and you welcome it because the pain is so terrible, I want you to think about me and about this warning."

"He's a pussy lawyer," Charlie Bates said. "Nothing to worry about."

"He was Army Special Forces. You saw how he took you down Saturday night. He didn't even break a sweat."

"He sucker punched me. Caught me off guard."

J.D. forced a laugh. "Not the way I heard it. You took the first swing. With a beer bottle."

"You better start getting outta them clothes."

"I told you that's not going to happen, Charlie."

He moved toward her, the knife coming up to waist level, his pistol in the other hand and trained on her. He was interrupted by the sound of a key being inserted into the lock on her front door. It opened. Matt took two steps inside and stopped dead.

CHAPTER FORTY-SEVEN

WEDNESDAY, NOVEMBER 5

DURING THE NIGHT, a cold front had moved into Southwest Florida, making its way down from Canada, weakening as it moved south, its remnants blowing chilled air over our island. It was a little early for jackets, but sometimes the cold fronts arrive prematurely and the effects hang around for a day or two.

I'd worn a windbreaker that morning, and as I walked in the door of J.D.'s condo, I was pocketing my car keys in the right pocket where I kept my Kel-Tec PF9, a small nine-millimeter pistol that was little more than five inches long and weighed less than a pound. I didn't want to be caught unprepared if Youssef or one of his men showed up. I had a small sack of muffins in my left hand and a copy of the *Tampa Bay Times* tucked under my left arm. I took two steps inside and stopped dead, my right hand still in the pocket with my keys and my gun.

My memory of the moment when I walked in the door is of a second fixed in time, a tableau vivant, the actors still, expressions frozen on their faces, J.D. taking a step backward, Bates in mid-step toward her, a knife in one hand and a pistol in the other. His head was turned to the right, looking at me, the hand with the pistol starting to point in my direction.

J.D. was standing with her back to the alcove that led to her bedroom, Bates a couple of feet in front of her. They were maybe a dozen feet from me. Both were looking in my direction, but I was sure Bates could see J.D. in his peripheral vision.

"What're you doing, Charlie?" I asked, my voice calm.

He made that sound that may have been a laugh, or a growl. "I'm going to fuck the little lady here. Just like I promised Saturday night. I'll let you watch, and then I'm going to shoot your sorry ass."

"I don't think so." My voice was calm. I didn't want to taunt the beast.

He glared at me, and said to J.D., "Get naked, bitch, or I'm going to shoot this motherfucker. Now."

"No," J.D. said, alarm in her voice. "I'll take my clothes off." She started to unbutton her blouse, counting the buttons as she did so, trying to keep his attention, and sidestepping discreetly out of his peripheral line of sight. "Done," she said, her voice soft, sultry, inviting. She threw the blouse on the floor between Bates and me. "I'm not wearing a bra," she lied. "Take a peek and let me know what you think."

Bates turned his head to look. I raised the Kel-Tec, still in my pocket, and shot through the fabric of the jacket. The slug hit him in the neck. He dropped like a felled tree, arms akimbo, no attempt to break his fall or react in any way. My mind slowed and I saw the bullet enter the right side of his neck and exit the left, taking tissue and blood with it. Good thing J.D. has tile floors, I thought. I watched the slug fly out the open sliding glass doors, across the pool deck and disappear into the turquoise water of the bay.

I'm fully aware that I didn't really see that, and in fact the doors were closed against the Canadian air, but in the second after I pulled the trigger, my mind conjured up the results of the shot. It was like I had slipped into another dimension, and suddenly, I was back. J.D. was standing where she'd been less than a second ago, wearing her skirt and bra, a look of consternation on her face.

She walked across the room and collapsed on the sofa. She reached for her cell phone in the pocket of her suit jacket, dialed three numbers, and said, "Iva, this is J.D. I've got a dead man in my condo. Roll the guys and make sure Steve Carey is one of them. We'll need him to do the detective work on this one. Get Kevin and the crime scene people moving, too. You know my address? Thanks. Yes, I'm okay. Matt's with me."

I sat next to her. "You okay?"

"Yeah." She took a deep shuddering breath. "That was close. I was about to try to take the knife away from him when I heard your key in the door. You got back fast."

"I stopped at Harry's store for a newspaper and saw a basketful of muffins. I thought a couple of those might be a little better for us than all that sugar from Publix. I'd have been here sooner, but I ran into Mike Seamon and stopped to talk. Cyndi's volunteering full time at Mote, now that the turtles have gone to wherever they go, so he..." I stopped. My mouth was outrunning my brain, talking because I didn't know what else to do. I was shaken by J.D.'s brush with Bates. He'd have killed her just for the hell of it, and her vulnerability to such an attack had unnerved me.

I heard sirens in the distance, getting louder as they came closer. The cavalry, in LBKPD uniforms, was on the way. "You'd better put your blouse on," I said. "One guy already died today trying to get a look at those beauties. You don't want to get the reputation as a strumpet." I was trying to break the tension. I knew she was feeling a lot more than she was showing.

"Not funny. Strumpet?" she said, slapping me on the thigh as she got off the sofa, put on her blouse and went to open the door. But she smiled, and I knew she would be okay soon enough. She was a tough cookie. And she was mine. And she was alive.

CHAPTER FORTY-EIGHT

Wednesday, November 5

Steve Carey was the first cop through the door. "You okay, J.D.?"

"Yes. Matt shot the bastard."

"What happened?"

"The guy was trying to rape me."

"You did good, Matt," Steve said. "Who is he?"

"His name is Charlie Bates," I said. "Do you want me to go into detail or wait until you can take a formal statement?"

"Let's wait. Are you sure you're okay, J.D.?"

"I'm fine. He never touched me. Matt came in just in time."

Two other cops pushed through the door and in a couple of minutes the paramedics arrived. They checked the body, determined that Bates was well and truly dead, and left, telling us that the medical examiner's people were on the way.

Chief Bill Lester and Deputy Chief Martin Sharkey showed up to make sure J.D. was safe. The chief told Carey to get detailed statements while we waited for the forensics people. "That's just for show," Lester said. "Not much forensics is needed here. We know who Bates was, we know he's no longer among the living, and we know old dead-eye Royal here killed the bastard while in the act of saving the life of a Longboat Key police detective. We'll get out of your hair, J.D. Don't worry about the deposition today. I'll take care of it." He and Sharkey left.

We sat and talked to Steve Carey, who was recording our statements. The medical examiner's assistants came and took pictures and removed the body. A cleanup crew arrived to get the blood and tissue off the tile floor. Kevin, Longboat's forensic guy, came, took a look around, snapped few photographs, and left.

Some of J.D.'s neighbors had gathered in the parking lot, wondering what was going on with all the official cars and ambulances showing up with sirens blaring. The officers on the scene had assured them that everything was under control and J.D. was fine. After everybody was gone and J.D. and I were alone in her condo, she started to shake, and tears ran down her cheeks. I pulled her into my arms as we sat on the sofa. She began to sob, her breath catching as she tried to choke back the emotion. I held her tighter and said nothing. There wasn't anything to say. She needed to cry it out, and then the tough-as-nails cop would come back. Hopefully.

"I wanted him dead, Matt," she said finally. "I didn't want justice for him, I didn't want to see him in court or getting sent to jail where he'd be taken care of by the state. I didn't even want to see him executed, if it came to that. I just wanted him dead. Right there on my floor. And I wanted to do it, pull the trigger, and watch him sink into the abyss. And when you shot him, I tried to see the expression on his face. I wanted to see something, but it wasn't there. Nothing. He just closed his eyes and slumped to the floor. I was glad you killed him, but my first thought was that I wished it had been me pulling that trigger."

"I know, baby." I was still holding her, letting the anguish dissipate.

"That isn't me, Matt. I've had to kill people before. In the line of duty. But I never wanted to kill them. That guy who took the shot at me up in Gainesville last week. If I could have arrested him, I would have done so. I only shot him because I had no other choice. And I didn't feel too bad about it, like I thought I should have. But I wouldn't have shot him if I could have avoided it. Bates, I wanted to kill. And I would have killed him. Given the choice, I might have even used the knife."

"I know, baby." I didn't know what else to say. She had to talk it out.

"Have I crossed a line, Matt? Have I abandoned every belief about justice and law that I've held over a lifetime? It's dark on the other side of that line."

She talked some more and then was quiet. Her breathing evened out and she dropped off to sleep. We sat like that for a long time, her head resting on my shoulder, my arms around her, holding on to the one person who was completely indispensable to me. She'd had a close call, but she'd be okay. I'd see to that.

CHAPTER FORTY-NINE

WEDNESDAY, NOVEMBER 5

YOUSSEF AL BASHAR and Saif Jabbar were eating breakfast in a Wendy's restaurant near the intersection of Highway 64 and Interstate 75, east of Bradenton. The call had come on Sunday morning telling Youssef that Royal was back on Longboat Key. He must have driven, because he didn't go through the airport. Or at least, if he had, Saif had missed him. That wasn't likely.

The men had spent the rest of the day on Sunday trying to find some trace of their men. They had gone to the taxi company manager's house to ask about the one known as Tariq. The man knew nothing. He hadn't seen Tariq since Saturday morning. Hadn't heard from him.

Youssef shot the poor man in the head, and he and Saif drove to the marina where the ambush had been set up. No sign of either Tariq or Abdullah, or of Tariq's taxi. They called all the burner cell numbers given to the men. No answer on any of them. The phones were shut down, turned off.

Monday had been a day of frustration. They had heard nothing more from their source on Longboat Key, and when Youssef called him, the man could only assume that Royal and the woman were still on Longboat. He hadn't seen them since Saturday night. And he had not seen or heard of Jock on the island since he'd disappeared on Friday and left for Key West.

There was no word from his men. Youssef decided they were lost, either dead or in custody. The best evidence he had was that Royal and Duncan were in Longboat Key. It was time to move north.

They left Key West late Tuesday afternoon and drove to Florida City, the first town on the mainland of Florida. They checked into a small mom-and-pop motel, spent the night, and started the four-hour drive to Longboat Key at daybreak.

"What is your plan, Youssef?" Saif asked as they finished their Wendy's breakfast. "How do we find the woman and Matt Royal?"

"The American we have hired will strike this morning and kill the woman. I should have heard from him by now. Maybe he was delayed. He is not to touch Royal. They often spend the night together in Royal's house or the woman's condo. If they are together, our man is to wait until the woman is alone and then kill her. I don't trust him to take Royal alive, and we need him to tell us where Algren is.

"We'll take him alive and find out what he knows about Algren's location," Youssef continued. "Our contact told me where he lives, and what kind of car he drives. We'll strike at midnight. He'll be grieving over the death of the woman. He will not be expecting us."

"What if he resists?" Saif asked.

"He won't. You're a big man, Saif. Even if he does resist, you can take him. All you have to do is get the drug in him and he'll be unconscious."

"How are we going to take him?"

"My contact had an idea on how to do that. He will have to leave the island as soon as he has killed the woman, but he has associated another American to assist us. He'll have a place for us to hide out and even hold the prisoner if we have to. It'll all be over by tomorrow."

CHAPTER FIFTY

WEDNESDAY, NOVEMBER 5

I MUST HAVE dozed off because the ringing of J.D.'s cell phone awakened me. It was on the arm of the sofa where she'd set it down after calling in the shooting. She stirred and reached for it and turned it off without answering. I looked at my watch. It was a little after eleven. We'd been asleep for the better part of an hour.

"Are you hungry?"

"We never did eat our muffins."

"I can make ham sandwiches and we can have the muffins for dessert."

"You want to go out? We could get something at the Dry Dock."

"I don't think so," she said. "I'm sure the island telegraph has been active and I don't want to have to explain what went on here this morning."

"Ham sandwiches it is."

We ate on J.D.'s sunporch, chatting and watching the boats on the Intracoastal Waterway. "You know, we're going to have to face them sooner or later," I said.

"Who?"

"The islanders."

She chuckled. "I think I'll be better able to do that with a couple of glasses of wine. I'm surprised we haven't already had a bunch of phone calls."

"They're just giving you space. I'm surprised that we haven't heard from the local TV stations and newspapers. They're usually out right away knocking on doors and asking penetrating questions, like 'How did you feel while you were being shot?'"

"Bill Lester may not have released anything to the press yet. And besides, I doubt they could get hold of my department cell phone number. I turned my personal phone off."

"Maybe, but they monitor police radios and have all kinds of nosey people feeding them information. They'll probably be here soon enough. You want to go to my place?"

"No. They'll just show up there. Let's sit it out here. We just won't answer the door."

My cell phone interrupted us. I answered. David Parrish. "Do you know where J.D. is?" he asked as soon as I answered.

"She's sitting right across the table from me."

"I've been calling her for the past two hours. She's not answering."

"We've had a pisser of a morning." I told him what had happened.

"I'm sorry as hell, Matt. Is she all right?"

"Mostly, I think." I looked at her and grinned. "She's tough. She'll be okay. You want to talk to her?"

"I need to talk to both of you. Put me on the speaker."

I found the right button on my phone and pushed it. "You still there?"

"I'm here," Parrish said. "I wanted you to know that the FBI is going to arrest your buddy D. Wesley Gilbert late this afternoon."

"The bank had a video of the withdrawal."

"That they did. It clearly showed Gilbert withdrawing the money on Tuesday of last week. The bank account records show that was the only cash withdrawal in a couple of weeks."

"Why did they have that account?" J.D. asked.

"It was a not very slick way to move money. Fortson deposited money in varying amounts on an irregular basis. It looks like the only money going out was on checks written by Gilbert and the occasional cash withdrawals, but we don't have any way now to determine whether they were made by Gilbert or Fortson. Had to be one of them."

"Was there a lot of activity?" J.D. asked.

"A reasonable amount. The account has been open for about four years. There's been a lot of money deposited in it over the years by Fortson."

"Do you know where the money went?" J.D. asked.

"We've got people looking at that now, but it seems there were a lot of checks to something called Wayfarer, Inc. and quite a few to a Wally Delmer."

"His lawyer isn't going to let him say a word," I said.

"No, but he won't have a lawyer. We'll tell him that we picked him up on a warrant from the FISA court, the one that oversees terrorist activities. We'll use Gilbert's connections to Ishmael's Children as the wedge. We don't have to let him have a lawyer. At least not right now."

"That doesn't ring true to me, David," I said.

"That's because it's not true, Counselor. We do have some leeway in how we interrogate suspects. We might be taking a little advantage here, but I doubt this idiot will figure it out."

"What's your plan?" J.D. asked.

"We're going to let him spend the night in the federal lockup in Sanford, and one of our agents is going to talk to him at eight in the morning. I thought you might like to sit in, J.D., and maybe have some questions based on your investigation."

"I'd like that," J.D. said, "but I don't think I can get to Orlando tomorrow. We've got lots going on here with Matt having to kill the guy who was trying to kill me this morning."

"We'll do it virtually," Parrish said. "I guess that's the right term. All this newfangled technology kind of buffaloes me. Anyway, I'm told that we can somehow plug your computer into our video system, so that you can watch and hear the proceedings in real time. You won't be able to join in and ask questions, but before we cut Gilbert loose or lock him up, I'll get with you by phone and you can ask him any questions you might have."

"That sounds good," J.D. said. "How do we go about setting it up?"

"I don't have any idea. Can you get your geek in touch with our geek? They can figure it out."

"I'll have him call your guy. Give me a name and number."

J.D. hung up and said, "Have you checked on Jock today?"

"Not yet. I need to call Paul Galis."

"I need to change out of this suit." She disappeared into her bedroom, and I called Galis' cell phone.

"How's our boy doing?"

"Better, I think. He went jogging this morning for the first time since he's been here. He turned off the TV yesterday and hasn't turned it back on. I saw him reading up on back issues of newspapers on my computer last night. Said he was trying to catch up on world events."

"Booze?" I asked.

"Nothing. He hasn't had anything alcoholic since he's been here."

"How's he sound?"

"Good. I'm not sure he's ready to go back into the field, but he seems better."

"Are you with him now?"

"Yeah, but he's taking a nap. You want me to wake him up?"

"No thanks, Paul. I'll check in tomorrow. Let me know if anything changes."

J.D. came out of the bedroom wearing a pair of jeans, a golf shirt, and tennis shoes. "Is Jock okay?"

"Paul says he's doing better. He's turned off the TV and he went jogging this morning. He's even catching up on world events."

"I'm glad to hear it. Maybe he's starting to pull out of whatever kind of funk he's in."

Her phone rang. She checked the caller ID, answered, listened for a minute and said, "I'll be right there." She hung up and said, "I've got to get over to the Seafood Shack."

"What's up?"

"We've got the warrant to search Bates' boat. You want to come?"

CHAPTER FIFTY-ONE

WEDNESDAY, NOVEMBER 5

THE BOAT WAS as filthy as I had expected. I couldn't imagine how a human being could live in such conditions. The search warrant had come through at three o'clock and by four the forensics people were doing a careful search. I was standing in the cockpit, looking through the hatch and down into the salon. J.D. and Reuben were standing on the pier that jutted out from the Seafood Shack.

"I've got a laptop," one of the techs called up from the salon.

"Hand it up," I said. "I'll give it to Reuben."

Reuben Carlson took the computer, walked up the pier, and took a seat at one of the tables that served the diners who chose to sit outside on the deck overlooking the bay. J.D. and I followed him. I was getting bored standing on the boat breathing in the noxious fumes Charlie had generated in the years he'd spent aboard.

Reuben raised the umbrella that stood by the table, giving himself some shade in order to better see the laptop's screen. J.D. and I took seats at the table enjoying the view of the bay and pelicans diving for fish. One had caught his snack and was floating on the surface, the fish flapping in its throat pouch as the pelican let the water drain out. Before the bird could swallow his catch, a seagull landed on its back, waiting patiently, I guess, for some leftover morsel. After a minute or so, the gull gave up and flew away. The pelican raised its head and swallowed the fish whole. Patience truly is a virtue, I thought.

Reuben spent a few minutes fiddling with the keyboard and talking to himself. Finally, he grinned. "I'm in," he said. "What are we looking for specifically?"

"Can you run a search through all his correspondence looking for two names?" J.D. asked.

"I've got a program that'll do just that." He pulled a thumb drive from his pocket, plugged it into a USB port, hit a couple of keys and waited a few moments. "Got it. What am I looking for?"

"Try the names Wally Delmer and D. Wesley Gilbert."

Reuben tapped a few keys and sat back. In a minute or so he leaned forward and examined the screen. "I've got a number of documents with Wally's name on them. None for D. Wesley Gilbert, but there are a couple for somebody named Wesbert. That's probably the guy you're looking for. Kind of a crude attempt at deception, I'd guess."

"Charlie Bates wasn't exactly a genius. Can you get those back to the station and print them all out for me?"

"I can do better than that. I've got a portable printer in my car. I'll have them for you in a few minutes. You want all of them with both Wally's name and Wesbert's?"

"Might as well. I'll be down by the boat."

The techs were still scouring the vessel, looking for anything that might lead to answers to the many questions we had. Maybe the documents Reuben had found would lead us in a new direction.

A few minutes after we returned to the boat, Kevin Mimbs, the Longboat Key PD forensics guy, popped out of the hatch. "We're done, J.D. There's really nothing else here of any evidentiary value. We did pick up a few fingerprints that didn't seem to belong to Bates. We'll run them and let you know who they belong to."

"Thanks, Kevin. Maybe the laptop will kick out something that'll help."

"You want to come down and look the place over?"

"No thanks," J.D. said. "I can smell it from here."

J.D. and I walked back up the pier. Reuben was coming our way, stopped, and waited. He had a large manila envelope in his hand. As we approached, he held it out for J.D. "This is every one of the emails with the names you wanted on them. Most are addressed to the name or came from the name, but some just have the name in the body of the email."

"Did anything catch your eye?" J.D. asked.

"No, but I wasn't looking. The search program I was using gave me a list of the emails and I just printed them out and put them in the envelope. If you don't need me anymore, I'll head back to the station and see if I can find anything else in the laptop."

"Thanks," J.D. said. "Looks like Matt and I've got some ground to cover with all these documents."

"This is a police matter," I said to J.D. "I think I should go to Tiny's and leave you with it."

"Really? I'll remember that."

"For how long?"

"At least a month," she said. "It's hard to forget that kind of abandonment."

"I guess we better get started reviewing all that crap."

We sat at the table Reuben had vacated. The restaurant was starting to get busy, so we ordered a beer for me and a glass of wine for J.D. We divided up the stack of documents and went to work.

* * *

In the end, we found only one email exchange on each of the pages. They were short and to the point, but the point was often opaque, so it turned out not to be that much to review and even less that made any sense to us. But there was one email string that rang some bells. The smoking emails, J.D. called them.

The email string was between Charlie Bates and Wally Delmer on the previous Friday, the day after Skeeter tried to kill J.D. on I-75. It said:

Bates: "Did you hire somebody else to take out that detective?"

Delmer: "So what?"

Bates: "That's my hit, that's so what."

Delmer: "You're the backup plan."

Bates: "I'm not the second string here."

Delmer: "You were paid up front. If the idiots had got her in Gainesville, you'd have been paid for doing nothing. Now you need to get her."

Bates: "Okay. I'll do it. Fuck you."

Delmer: "I've got another job for you. I need you to take out Fortson."

Bates: "When?"

Delmer: "Tonight."

Bates: "Send my fee to the usual place."

Delmer: "Done."

"I think we solved the murder on the beach," J.D. said after reading the emails. "And I bet our friend Bates was the guy who hired the young man to kill Rachel."

J.D. called Reuben and asked him to forward the emails to Parrish and an email address that belonged to Dave Kendall and not to forget to set up the video feed for the next morning. She then called Parrish and told him about the emails between the dead Charlie Bates and Wesbert and Wally Delmer. She said she thought there might be something important in there that the FBI interrogator would like to look at before he talked to Gilbert.

I called Kendall. I wanted him to be completely informed about Delmer and Gilbert and their ties to Ishmael's Children and to Fortson's murder. I gave him a detailed report of what we knew, what we suspected, and what we speculated about. I also told him to watch for the emails Reuben was sending him.

When J.D. hung up from her call to Parrish, she said, "Well, at least we know for sure that Bates, Wally Delmer, and Gilbert are connected."

"That's something," I said. "Those sandwiches at lunch didn't go very far. You want to get something to eat?"

"What do you have in mind?"

"Let's go down to the Sandbar. It'll probably be crowded, but with all the snowbirds coming back, there's not likely to be any Longboaters there. We won't have to talk about our day."

"I have to change clothes and I want a shower," she said.

"My place?"

"Sure."

As we drove away from the Seafood Shack, we saw dark clouds moving in from the Gulf. A storm was coming, the temperature dropping precipitously as the cooler air pushed by the storm crossed the beach and engulfed the island. It was pouring by the time we reached my house, and we got soaked running from my driveway to the front door.

After we took a long hot shower together, we dressed, used umbrellas to get to the Explorer, and drove to the northern end of Anna Maria Island, sloshing through a downpour reminiscent of our daily summer rainstorms.

The Sandbar Restaurant sits right on the beach and provides a wonderful view of the white sand and the Gulf's placid water. We were a little early and the crowd had not yet gotten too big. We were seated right away at a table for four next to a window overlooking the beach, but the view was lost in the dark and the rain by the time we sat down.

The server had just gotten our drink orders when J.D.'s neighbors, Susan and Tom Mink, walked through the door, saw us, and came to our table. "Are you guys all right?" Susan asked.

"We are, thanks," I said. "Will you join us?"

"I wish we could," Tom said, "but we're meeting a couple from back home in Baltimore for dinner."

"J.D.," Susan said, "one of your policemen came by today and showed me a picture of the dead man, a mug shot I think you call it. That was the same man I saw running through our hedge yesterday."

"You're sure?" J.D. asked.

"Positive. And Marylou Webster agrees with me."

"I'm glad to know that. I don't guess he'll be bothering us again."

Susan laughed. "You guys sure bring a little excitement to the neighborhood. I know this must have been horrendous for you, J.D. I'm sorry it happened. If you need anything, let me know."

The Minks went to meet their friends. J.D. said, "They're good people. I was pretty sure Bates was the guy trying to get in my place yesterday, but it's good to have it confirmed. I'll rest easier."

We spent another hour in the restaurant, eating and talking about things not connected to either the Fortson murder or Jock's situation. It was a pleasant ending to a day that had started out so wrong.

CHAPTER FIFTY-TWO

Thursday, November 6

The hearse pulled to a stop in front of the modest house on the north side of Tallahassee. It was three o'clock in the morning. The night was clear and quiet and the tree canopy blocked what little light the stars and a half moon produced. A streetlight hung from a pole two houses down from the one in which Wally Delmer lived, providing little illumination, but enough that the neighbors, if they were awake and watching, could see the hearse.

Jim Austin walked purposely to the front door, pantomimed knocking, and quickly slipped a pick into the lock and opened it. He entered, walked toward the back of the house where he assumed the bedrooms to be, and stood quietly for a moment. He heard the sound of light snoring coming from one of the two bedrooms. He walked in, silently, and saw the lump of a man sleeping under the covers. He pulled a small instrument about the size of a cell phone from his pocket, placed it against the sleeping man's neck, and pushed a button. The Taser activated and Wally Delmer awoke, twitching and moaning, powerless. Austin turned him on his stomach, pulled his arms behind him, and handcuffed him.

The Taser charge was wearing off and Delmer was sputtering, trying to talk. Austin pulled a strip off the roll of duct tape he carried in his cargo pants pocket and slapped it over Wally's mouth. He clicked twice on a small handheld radio attached to his belt.

Moments later, Austin heard the front door open and two men came in carrying a gurney they'd found in the hearse. They moved Wally onto it and covered him with a sheet.

Austin took a few minutes to go through the house looking for computers. He found two laptops and put them on the gurney under the sheet. He motioned to his men to leave. They took the gurney containing Wally and the laptops and stashed them in the hearse. Austin took a few moments to look around for anything else he might need. Nothing. He followed the men out the door and into the hearse. They left the quiet neighborhood and drove toward the funeral home where they had appropriated the hearse a half hour earlier.

* * *

Jim Austin had been watching Thursday Night Football at his home in Northern Virginia when he got the call from his boss, Dave Kendall. "Suit up, Jim," Kendall said. "You're going to Tallahassee, Florida. There's a team and a Gulfstream waiting for you at Reagan National. A car will be in front of your house in ten minutes. Call me when you're airborne, and I'll fill you in on the mission."

"Yes, sir." The line went dead. Austin was the duty agent for the Eastern United States for the week, a job that rotated among the agents assigned to the agency's Washington, D.C. office housed in the CIA building in Langley, Virginia. That meant that when an emergency arose, he went.

Austin went to the closet in his bedroom, grabbed his ready bag packed with his toiletries, a change of clothes, and two nine-millimeter pistols. He bent over to kiss his sleeping wife.

"You got a call?"

"Yes."

"What time is it?"

"Almost eleven,"

"Who won the game?"

He chuckled. "Still going on. It's in overtime. I'll call you tomorrow. Hopefully, I'll be back before noon."

"Be safe."

"Always."

Austin left his house and walked down the sidewalk to the staff car waiting at the curb. The familiar tingle of anticipation ran up his spine, the thought of a mission into the unknown teasing his adrenal glands. Every assignment started this way. A phone call or a text message, and he was off into the nether world where he and his colleagues operated, the jungle where the predators hide and attack at will.

* * *

Austin's team consisted of two men, both of whom he knew to be agents recently out of the rigorous field training. The call to Kendall was short and devoid of much information beyond the name and address of the target.

"You're going to Tallahassee to pick up a man named Wally Delmer and bring him back to D.C. I'll have a vehicle meet you at Reagan National when you return, and we'll take him off your hands."

"I take it he's not going to come willingly," Austin said.

"I doubt it. Here's the plan. Tell me if you don't like something."

"Yes, sir."

"There'll be a car parked in the short-term parking area at the Tallahassee airport. Keys are on the front right tire." He gave the tag number. "Drive the car to a funeral home, whose address I will text you in a few minutes, and steal a hearse. They park them in the open, so you won't have to break in. Did the pilot give you a bag?"

"He did."

"You'll find a Taser, handcuffs, and keys to the hearse you're going to steal."

"No keys to the car in the bag?"

"Didn't have time for that. I called the rental car office at the airport, paid for the rental, and told them what to do with the keys. I couldn't get that done for the hearse, so we went online, got the vehicle identification numbers of all four of their hearses and got keys to all of them from our stash of standard automobile keys. You might have to try several before you get the right one."

Austin checked the bag. "Everything's here," he told Kendall.

"Get the guy and bring him home. Take the hearse back to where you got it, and hopefully no one will notice it was used."

* * *

As the hearse pulled away from Delmer's house, Austin took stock of the man he'd incapacitated. He was about six feet tall and he had that emaciated look that reminded Austin of the pictures he'd seen of the Nazi concentration survivors. Not that bad, of course, but headed there. Austin was told that the man was fifty years old, but he appeared to be in his seventies. My God, he thought, had they gotten the wrong man? It'd be kind of funny if they had grabbed the old next-door neighbor of the man they were looking for. It'd generate a few laughs around the water cooler, but he'd never live it down, and his career prospects would be greatly diminished.

The man was regaining his senses, and Austin asked his name. "Wally Delmer. Who the fuck are you?" Austin grinned and stuck a hypodermic into Wally's upper arm and, within a minute, he was still. He'd stay that way until he woke up in a safe house somewhere in Virginia.

CHAPTER FIFTY-THREE

THURSDAY, NOVEMBER 6

THE LONGBOAT KEY police station is a little over a mile south of J.D.'s condo, where we'd spent the night. As we drove to the station to watch the interrogation of D. Wesley Gilbert, I was thinking that one day we'd have to give up on this peripatetic lifestyle, moving between my cottage and her condo, never knowing from one day to the next where we'd end up spending the night. We'd talked about marriage and moving into my house, but not very seriously. She'd been married when she was a young police officer and it had turned out badly. One night, during a heated argument, her husband decided to take a swing at her. Big mistake. She kung-fued him, broke his arm, messed up his face, and the next day had her friend Deanna Bichler file for divorce.

My marriage had ended badly, but that was my fault. I drank too much, worked too hard, involved myself in all the things young lawyers do as they are trying to build a practice and a reputation. I kept putting off having children, something my wife wanted desperately. Finally, she'd had enough of me and my ego, and although she professed to still love me, she moved on. We remained friends after the divorce, and she married a good man and raised his children and then died way too early. I suspect J.D. and I were both gun-shy, but for different reasons.

At the station, we sat in a room filled with audio and video equipment. The geek's lair, it was called. One wall held a sixty-inch flat screen TV that showed a fidgety D. Wesley Gilbert sitting in a chair in front of a small table that held a bottle of water. The room he was in had bare walls and no furniture that I could see, other than the table at which he sat. We were getting the live feed from the video camera perched high on the wall of the interview room.

J.D. was on the phone with Parrish. He told her that the documents she'd had Reuben send him the afternoon before were full of good information, enough for the FBI to arrest Wally Delmer in Tallahassee at daybreak. Parrish told her they were ready to start the interview and we watched a man in a suit walk into the room and introduce himself to D. Wesley as FBI agent Sam McFarland. He sat across from Gilbert and asked some preliminary questions, such as name, age, today's date, their location. It was standard procedure designed to show that Gilbert was not mentally impaired. That he was fully capable of answering the questions put to him.

"Why am I here?" Gilbert asked, letting a little outrage build. "I want a lawyer."

McFarland said, "You're here, Mr. Gilbert, because you've been arrested on terrorism charges and you aren't entitled to a lawyer."

"That's absurd. Get my lawyer in here."

"Can they do that?" J.D. asked me. "Refuse him a lawyer?"

"No," I said. "But the courts let law enforcement officers lie and use subterfuge when dealing with suspects."

"I know that, but can they refuse him access to a lawyer when he asks for one?" J.D. asked.

"No. He's got a constitutional right to a lawyer," I said. "I don't think they'll be able to use anything they get out of this interview in a court of law."

"I guess they think they've got enough to prosecute without having to use anything they find out today," J.D. said, and turned her attention back to the TV screen.

"Ishmael's Children," McFarland was saying.

"Who?"

"The charity you're involved with."

"How does supporting a charity amount to terrorism?"

"It does when the charity isn't a charity; when it's a terrorist group."

"I'm an attorney. I know my rights. You're way off base. I want my lawyer. Now."

"I've already told you, you don't get a lawyer."

"Then I've got nothing more to say to you."

"Mr. Gilbert, let's be reasonable. I—"

Gilbert interrupted. "I'll get reasonable when I see my lawyer walk through that door."

"Okay, Mr. Gilbert, but that may take a while."

"His office is just down the street. He can be here in a few minutes."

"You don't understand," McFarland said. "We'll have to get permission from the FISA court, and that might take a while."

"How long?"

"Couple of months, maybe."

"Okay. When it's done, let me know, and my lawyer and I will come back and talk to you."

"It doesn't work that way, Mr. Gilbert. We'll house you in the federal lockup, which is part of the Seminole County jail up in Sanford. You'll be held in isolation, of course, for your own safety. If the government doesn't prevail and decides to appeal, which we will, well, that could take a couple of years."

Gilbert had that deflated look, like all the bombast and bullshit had leaked out of him. He wasn't much of a lawyer and he'd forgotten some of the most basic tenets of American constitutional law, if he'd ever learned them at all. He was lost, a man adrift in a sea of law that he could not comprehend.

Gilbert took a deep breath. "I didn't do anything," he said.

"Last Tuesday you withdrew ten thousand dollars from an account jointly held by you and Peter Fortson. Some of that money ended up in the possession of a man up in Franklin County who was hired to put a locator device on the car of a Longboat Key detective so that armed men could track her and kill her. That makes you guilty of attempted murder of a police officer."

"I thought this was about Ishmael's Children."

"We'll get to that. Let's talk about that five grand."

"I certainly didn't know that it was going to be used to kill a police officer."

"How did the money get to Franklin County?"

"FedEx."

"Who did you send it to?"

"A friend of mine."

"Who?"

"Wally Delmer."

"Why would you send Wally five grand in cash?"

"He asked me to."

"What was it for?"

"He didn't say."

"It looks like you've sent him a lot of checks over the years."

"Yeah."

"For what?"

"I never asked. It wasn't my money in the account."

"I noticed that," McFarland said. "Why was Peter Fortson putting money in that account?"

"I think I should avail myself of my constitutional right to refuse to answer that question."

"Mr. Gilbert," McFarland said in an exasperated voice, "you gave up your constitutional rights the minute you decided to engage in terrorist activities."

"Then I want to make a deal."

"A deal?"

"Yes. I'll tell you what you want to know if you'll give me immunity."

McFarland closed his file and stood up. "Nice talking to you, Mr. Gilbert."

"Where are you going?"

"We're finished here."

"What about a deal?"

"Mr. Gilbert," McFarland said, "You've been watching too much television. I've got enough to put you in a supermax prison for the rest of your life. There will be no deals. You tell me what you know and I'll let the U.S. attorney know that you cooperated. He might be able to shave some time off your sentence, maybe even get you sent to one of the country club lockups that we have for white-collar criminals. But there are no guarantees."

"Give me a minute," Gilbert said.

"I'll be back," McFarland said, and left the room.

J.D. turned to me. "He's going to let him stew for a while. Interrogation 101 at the police academy. Will that work on a psychopath?"

I smiled. "I guess we'll see in a few minutes."

Gilbert sat quietly, an aura of sadness and despair surrounding him. He was done, and the realization that he'd reached the end of life as he knew it was overwhelming. I thought he'd probably known at the time of his arrest that he was caught up in something he couldn't escape. I wondered how long he'd been involved in this mess and I actually felt a bit sorry for him.

He had been born with the proverbial silver spoon in his mouth and he must have been a great disappointment to his father. Yet, for years he'd lived a good life. Even if it was a dissolute and self-indulgent lifestyle, he had hurt no one but himself. At some point, when he'd gotten involved with some very nasty people, probably as a direct result of his gambling, his lifestyle caught up with him. He'd turned from a pitiable caricature of a successful lawyer into a contemptible bagman for the worst elements of our society. He deserved whatever was coming.

McFarland waited him out, giving him time to decide whether to continue blustering or start owning up to his misdeeds. Ten minutes went by and Gilbert sipped on his bottle of water and fidgeted some more. He looked at his wrist several times, forgetting his watch had been taken from him.

Finally, McFarland came back into the room. "Have you had enough time to decide what you want to do, Mr. Gilbert?" he asked. "If not, I can go to lunch and come back later."

Gilbert waved him into his chair, sighed and said, "It's a long story. I have an illness, an addiction to gambling. About four years ago, I lost a lot of money and became indebted to some loan sharks. I couldn't pay them back, and my life was in danger. They made me an offer. I would become what they called a financial facilitator. I would work closely with a very rich man, Peter Fortson, in delivering money to whomever they designated. In return, the sharks forgave my debt."

"Who is Wally Delmer?" McFarland asked.

"He's a private investigator in Tallahassee. I don't think he investigates anything much, but he's kind of the manager for the people who run the gambling and loan-sharking operations. He was my bookie."

"Who're the guys behind the curtain? The ones who really run things."

"I don't know. The only name I ever heard, other than Delmer, is Thomason."

"Who is he?" McFarland asked.

"I don't know. It was just a name that Delmer let slip into a conversation once."

"Did you get the impression that he was important?"

"Yes. I don't remember in what context the name came up, but for some reason I thought he was very important, maybe the top guy."

"Do you know anything else about him?"

"No. I never heard the name again."

"Your bank records show that you also sent some personal checks to Ishmael's Children."

"Yes."

"Why?"

"I was told to do it."

"By whom?"

"Wally," Gilbert said.

"Some of those checks were pretty substantial."

"Yes."

"Where did the money to cover the checks come from?"

"Gambling."

"You're still gambling?" McFarland seemed shocked.

"Well, I go to the tables in New Jersey, but I don't actually win."

"Explain that."

"I think it's part of what they call skimming. The house rigs the table so that I win, but then I have to give the money back to the people who run the casino."

"So, it comes into your account as gambling winnings and you send it out to the charity."

"Sometimes. Other times I'd just write checks to whoever Wally told me to."

"I assume the same people who control the gambling control the charity. Am I right?"

"That's the way I understand it."

"Do you pay federal income taxes on the gambling proceeds?"

"Of course. Wally insists on it. They don't want to get caught up in an IRS investigation."

"Do you deduct the charitable contributions to Ishmael's Children on your federal income tax returns?"

"No. I was told not to. Nobody wants to fool with the IRS. That's the way they got Al Capone, you know."

"Who is Thomason?"

"I told you I don't know."

"I thought you might change your mind after you'd had some time to think on it."

"If I knew, I'd tell you."

"You withdrew ten thousand dollars in cash from that account you held jointly with Fortson, right?"

"Right."

"You sent five grand to Wally Delmer?"

Gilbert nodded.

"What happened to the other five grand?"

"I was instructed to contact a man who was supposed to kill somebody and give him the other five thousand dollars."

"Skeeter Evans?"

"Yes."

"Who instructed you to get in touch with Skeeter?"

"Wally Delmer."

"How did you know Skeeter?"

"I didn't. Wally gave me a name and a phone number."

"Who was he supposed to kill?"

"Some woman. I don't know who she was."

"Mr. Gilbert, we've talked to Skeeter. He gave you up. Don't try to bullshit me."

"I don't care what he said. I didn't know her."

"But you were okay with killing her?"

"Wasn't my call. I just do what I'm told."

CHAPTER FIFTY-FOUR

THURSDAY, NOVEMBER 6

FRANK THOMASON WAS lying on a chaise lounge beside his heated pool, bundled up against the weather. He was not a big man, but he carried more weight than was healthy. He had sharp facial features softened by chubby cheeks and reddened by the wind. His head was mostly devoid of hair. He was fifty-four years old and known for his unpleasantness. It was rumored that if you got on his wrong side, your lifespan would be shortened precipitously.

He lived in a mansion crammed onto a small lot fronting the ocean a few miles south of Atlantic City, New Jersey. The pool was situated between the beach and the house, giving Thomason a spectacular view of the ocean, which on this day was gray and angry. Large waves slapped against the shore, delivering salt spray to the frozen beach. An icy wind blew across the water, carrying flurries of snow and sleet. A fog of vapor rose from the pool, the result of the cold air conflating with the heated water.

He picked up a glass cup in his gloved hand, blew across the rim, and drank the last of his hot toddy. He watched as two men, dressed much as he was, walked along the beach. They stopped in front of his house and seemed to be carrying on a heated conversation. Thomason shrugged. None of his business. He lay back on the chaise and thought some more about his problem.

It was already after ten in the morning. He had not heard from Wally Delmer who was required to check in with him no later than eight every morning. Thomason tried to phone him, but got no answer, except for a recording telling him that Delmer wasn't available and his voice mailbox was full. The lack of communication was worrisome, but not alarming. Not yet, anyway. If he had not heard from Delmer by midafternoon, it would be time to panic.

Frank Thomason walked a tightrope, always balancing his life and his lifestyle against the whims of his bosses. One misstep and he would be dead. There'd be no questions asked, no apology sought or accepted, no mercy offered. There was only death, and probably a difficult one, at the hands of a true believer, one of the young converts who would be hanging on street corners dealing drugs if not for the brainwashing they'd endured on social media sites. These youngsters were all looking for some form of salvation, and they began to believe that their own deaths, their martyrdom as they saw it, would earn them immediate entrance into heaven. This was, after all, the ultimate reward for doing the bidding of the Imams who preached hate and had nothing but disdain for Western civilization and the infidels who inhabited it. Well, that and the virgins, if there were any left, Thomason thought, a wry grin creasing his face.

The last four years had been his ruination. He'd been doing quite well, loan sharking, gambling at crooked tables, importing and wholesaling drugs, and murdering, for a price, the occasional miscreant whom the bosses decided needed killing. Then he'd fallen in love with a Syrian woman half his age, and his life went to hell, spiraling down a rathole at the speed of sound. He'd watched it happen, knew what was happening, and was powerless to stop it.

But, what the hell. He was living in an oceanfront mansion, had a chauffeur-driven Mercedes that was about a block long, a beautiful woman whenever he felt the need, a whore to be sure, but one paid by the bosses, a fringe benefit of sorts. Still, he missed the Syrian girl, who was perhaps the only person, including his parents, that he had ever loved.

Her disappearance from his life had been sudden and shocking. A little more than three years before, he had left home early one morning, leaving her in his bed snuggled under the covers. He kissed her forehead and went out the door, intent on some long-forgotten mission. He never saw her again.

Thomason had, some years before the Syrian girl's disappearance, entered into an agreement with a group of Middle Eastern thugs who were working along the entire eastern seaboard, importing cocaine from South America and heroin from South Asia. They had a well-developed and secure pipeline that Thomason could never replicate, so it seemed like good business to become the street distributor of the drugs the Arabs brought into the country.

Thomason was making a lot of money and decided to give loan sharking a try. He loaned out money at exorbitant rates to the marks who were constantly losing money in his New Jersey gambling parlor. Their addictions were played out on rigged games and tables, and they could never beat the house. Their debts mounted as their families fell apart and descended into poverty. None of this bothered Thomason. He was living the good life and raking in huge amounts of money.

Almost four years ago, he had been spending an evening in one of his small casinos when the Syrian girl appeared. She was with another woman and they took a table next to the one Thomason was occupying. He didn't pay too much attention to either of them, knowing full well that they were out of his league. He was fifty years old, and the women appeared to be in their mid-twenties. He was pudgy and balding and they were beautiful.

As the night wore on and the drinks flowed, a conversation was struck between Thomason and the women. At some point, one of the women left and the other moved to Thomason's table. Her name was Rahima and she was the American-born daughter of Syrian immigrants. Her family lived in Brooklyn, where she had been raised, and her father was a butcher in a local supermarket. She was in Atlantic City visiting a friend from college, the woman who had just left. She would get a taxi back to the friend's apartment when this wonderful evening wound down.

As it happened, and much to Thomason's surprise, she went home with him. He could never remember how that happened. Did he suggest it? Did she? It didn't matter. The fact was that she had gone home with him, made love to him, and changed his life. She moved into his house the next day and stayed for four months.

One day, two of his Middle Eastern partners came for a visit. They told him they were now going to become his partners in the gambling and loan-sharking business. Thomason laughed and told them they were full of shit.

They left. The next day, Rahima disappeared from his house. He came home at noon, and she wasn't there. At first he wasn't concerned. She had probably gone shopping. Then he received a text. The message was that the same two men he'd met with the day before would be back for a visit that afternoon. A picture was attached to the text. It showed Rahima, bound to a bed with ropes. She was stark naked. When he zoomed in on the picture, he could see tears running down her cheeks.

The two men returned that afternoon and the deal was sealed. Thomason turned over his entire operation to his new Arab "partners" and he was given the role of manager and a percentage of every dollar that found its way into the syndicate's coffers. He was never told what happened to Rahima, his questions about her were never answered, and over the years she became a dim memory and a dull ache in his heart.

Thomason continued to work for what he always thought of as the syndicate, but in reality was a jihadist group who called themselves Ishmael's Children. He had funneled money to some of its operatives who were working in the United States, and on occasion provided manpower through his underling, Wally Delmer. While he suspected what the terrorists were doing, he had no direct knowledge and therefore was able to convince himself that he was not complicit in acts that were ultimately aimed at the destruction of civilization as he knew it. Besides, it wouldn't happen in his lifetime, and he was living the good life. He didn't care what happened after he was dead.

As his mind was wandering over the bleak landscape of his life, a man wearing a ski mask, down jacket, and jeans was walking up the yard, passing close to the house, out of Thomason's line of sight. The intruder approached the pool deck soundlessly and moved closer to Thomason. When the man was a few feet from the figure on the chaise, a fracas broke out on the beach, drawing Thomason's attention. The two men he had been watching were throwing fists at each other, their voices loud and heated.

Thomason sat up on the chaise, felt a pinprick in his neck, and almost immediately experienced only darkness. The intruder called to the men on the beach, and they hurried up the steps leading to the pool deck. The three of them hoisted Thomason and quickly carried him back up the yard and to the driveway that ran along the southern side of the house, terminating in a four-car garage built under a short wing of the residence. They put the unconscious man into a work van that was backed up in front of the garage, climbed into the front seat, and drove out of town.

CHAPTER FIFTY-FIVE

THURSDAY, NOVEMBER 6

"WHAT HAPPENED?" SAIF asked Youssef. "The woman is still alive and our man is dead." They had gotten Cuban food from a take-out place in downtown Sarasota and were sitting at a picnic table in a park on the bay at the western end of Main Street.

"All I know is what I saw on television last night. There was a shooting in the home of the detective and she survived and our man did not."

"I guess that's the reason we did not hear from him yesterday."

"That's a safe assumption. Since he was dead." Youssef was getting a bit tired of the stupidity of the big man who was his companion. Maybe he'd kill him when the mission was finished. He didn't relish the thought of having to make his way back to Syria in the company of this dolt.

"What do we do now?" Saif asked.

"I guess we could call our contact and get another man, but we cannot trust the Westerners. We are going to have to take care of this on our own."

"How are we going to do that?"

"I did not trust the man to carry out my instructions. I have a backup plan. I just have to make a call and we will be able to get a boat and somebody who knows how to operate it. Our dead friend found a place we can hide out where nobody will find us. As soon as we kill the woman, we'll go to the hideout."

"Why not just go home?"

"The authorities will know that the two were killed by Arabs. They will be on the lookout for us. We need to stay out of sight for a week or two and then we have to find Algren."

"What about the man, Matt Royal?"

"We'll kill him, too."

"And Algren? Why wait to kill him?"

"We'll kill him soon. But first, I want him to know that it was I who killed his friends. I want him to grieve for a while, to know the hurt he caused my mother when he killed my father."

"What is your plan?"

"I'll tell you more about it when the time comes."

"When do we strike?"

"Tonight."

CHAPTER FIFTY-SIX

THURSDAY, NOVEMBER 6

WALLY DELMER CAME awake slowly and fitfully. He was lying on his back. He awoke and then nodded off again. He woke again with a start, his breath caught in his chest. After three or four episodes, he was awake enough to try to turn onto his side, his usual sleeping position. He couldn't. He was tied to the bed rails, or rather, as he began to discern, handcuffed to them. What the hell? Where was he? Then, as the brain fog dissipated, his memory began to gnaw at the last thing he remembered. Finally, he drew it out of the recesses of his brain, and it began to take form and shape. He remembered a man attacking him in his bed, his ride on a gurney and a sharp pain in his neck. Then nothing else. Until now. What was going on? Had he run afoul of his Arab masters in some way that he didn't understand?

He looked around the small bare room, devoid of any decoration or any sign that anybody had ever been there before he awoke. The door opened and a man walked into the room holding a bottle of water. He unhooked Wally's right hand from the bedframe and handed the bottle to him. Wally swallowed the whole thing. The man took the empty bottle and left without saying a word.

Time moved slowly, but Wally was only dimly aware of its passage. The pain had arrived and steadily worsened, but he had no access to his pills. There was nothing he could do but endure. Every so often the same man would show up, hand him a bottle of water, wait while Wally drank, and leave with the empty. Silently. No words, no gestures, nothing.

Wally Delmer thought he was going to die. He didn't know why, but he'd always known that someday, some men would come and take him away and kill him. He'd made his pact with the devil a long time ago, and he knew those deals always required a final payoff. His bill was coming due. He smiled to himself. The pain was getting to the point that death would be a relief. He could only hope that whoever was going to kill him would make it fast. Unfortunately, he understood that the men he'd been dealing with for over a decade were not much for mercy. They liked to watch people suffer. And justice? Ha. He wouldn't get his day in court. He probably wouldn't even know why he was dying. So be it. He'd made a good life for himself and he had a lot of money tucked away in offshore accounts. The banks all had specific instructions. If six months went by and they didn't hear from him, they were to assume he was dead, and they would distribute the money as he'd instructed in the many documents he signed as he set up the accounts. Millie would be a very surprised and happy woman.

He let his thoughts drift back to the early days when he was young and life was good. He had grown up in a small town on the shores of Lake Okeechobee between West Palm Beach and Ft. Myers. It had been pretty much a hand-to-mouth existence, and, as soon as he graduated from high school, he joined the Army. After three years as a military policeman, he was discharged and joined the Ft. Lauderdale police department. He was tall and in good shape and cut quite a figure in his police uniform.

After a couple of years on the force, Wally took a course to earn his Coast Guard captain's license. He knew boats. His dad had earned his living fishing in Lake Okeechobee, and Wally had spent many afternoons helping the older man run his boat and pull in the trotlines that hooked the catfish.

License in hand, Wally transferred to the Ft. Lauderdale PD marine unit. He wore shorts and a golf shirt to work every day and carried his weapons on an equipment belt just like any beat cop. And that was what he was, except his beat was the Intracoastal Waterway, the New River and its tributaries and any number of manmade canals on which very rich people lived.

One day when the sun was shining and the humidity was low and the spring breeze brought the smell of the sea wafting over the city, Wally watched as a cigarette-type speed boat came busting up the channel near Port Everglades. The boat had three men aboard and was going way too fast. Wally knew that he would endanger local boaters out enjoying the weather if he tried to pursue the boat. He sped up some, trying to see where the captain was taking the boat and hoping to be able to get him if he slowed. The boat was pulling away at a fast rate when suddenly it just disintegrated. Almost instantaneously, the sound of an explosion rolled over Wally. He turned on his emergency lights and siren and sped across the water while radioing his location and the news of the exploding boat to the department's dispatcher.

He searched the debris field until the Coast Guard and other boats from the sheriff's department and the Ft. Lauderdale PD arrived. There were no survivors, and there were no bodies. The explosion had been so intense that the men in the boat were vaporized, the medical examiner said.

Two days later, as Wally was checking over his boat and getting ready for another day patrolling the waterways, Millie showed up at the marina. She was beautiful, elegant, blond, self-contained, and dressed casually in what Wally guessed probably cost a cop's monthly salary.

"Are you the officer who saw the boat explode down by the port a couple of days ago?"

"I am. Can I help you?"

"I think a friend of mine was on that boat."

"What was his name?"

"It was a woman. Penny Parkins."

"I didn't see a woman on the boat. Only three men. We didn't recover any bodies, but I was following the boat when it exploded and I didn't see a woman aboard."

"She might have been out of sight. I think she was kidnapped."

"Tell me about it," Wally said. "We know the boat was stolen. We found enough pieces to put a registration number together. Why do you think your friend was aboard?"

"The name of the man who owned the boat was in the paper this morning. I know him. He lives near me and keeps the boat in the back of his house on a canal. I think the man who stole the boat was named Francisco Mendez. He's the son of Javier Mendez. Do you know that name?"

"Yes." Every cop in the city knew the Mendez family. They were involved in almost every illegal activity that happened in South Florida, drugs, prostitution, guns, extortion, and others. It was rumored that Francisco, the oldest son, ran the family's business branch that dealt in prostitution.

"Penny was a working girl," Millie said. "An escort. She worked for Francisco, but wanted to leave the business. Francisco told her she couldn't. She decided to leave anyway. I live in the townhouse next door to hers and two days ago, I heard a loud argument coming from Penny's place. Then she started screaming and suddenly stopped. Like somebody stopped her. I heard Francisco leave and everything was quiet."

"Did you go check on her?"

"Not right away. One of Francisco's men was hanging around in the front yard, like he was watching the place. I was afraid to go over there."

"What's your name?"

"Millie. Millie Magnus."

"Is that your birth name?"

"No, but that's all I'm going to give you." She smiled.

Wally chuckled. "Okay. Fair enough. How did you find me?"

"Your name was in the paper this morning, and I know where you guys keep the police boats."

"Did you see Penny after you heard the argument?"

"No."

"Did you report it to the police?"

"No."

"Why not?"

"I work for Francisco," Millie said. "I didn't want him coming after me."

"Are you an escort?"

"Yes."

"Why are you coming to me now?"

"Francisco's dead. He can't hurt me."

"What makes you think Penny was on the boat?"

"Our townhouses back up to the same canal where the man who owned the boat lived. A couple of hours after Francisco left Penny's place, I was taking a nap on the sofa when I was awakened by the sound of a boat coming up the canal. It stopped behind our townhouses. Because of the shrubbery, I can't see the canal from downstairs, so I went upstairs. I saw Francisco and two of his men getting into the boat. They had something heavy with them wrapped in a sheet, but they were already putting it in the boat by the time I saw them."

"Didn't that seem suspicious to you?"

"Yes. I went over to her place after Francisco and the men left in the boat. She wasn't home. I have a spare key and let myself in. The living room looked like there had been a fight, you know, lamps knocked over, a chair overturned."

"Weren't you concerned?"

"Yes, but I was about to leave for Ft. Myers with a date and I wasn't sure what was going on. I didn't get back until late last night and then I saw the paper this morning. That's the first time I heard anything about the boat explosion. There it was, spread all over the front page. I went next door and Penny was still gone. Her living room looked just like it had when I'd been in there two days before."

"Why come to me? Why didn't you just call into the station? Get the detectives out?"

"I don't want to be involved in this. Javier is still alive and would kill me if he knew I was talking to the cops. I thought you might like to take the information and maybe get credit for the break in the case."

Wally mulled this over. He was ambitious and knew this kind of break would look good on his record, maybe be worth something when he was up for a promotion, maybe to detective. "Okay, Millie," he said. "Let me think about this. Can I come see you this evening?"

"Why don't I meet you somewhere. I don't know if somebody might be watching my house. If so, I don't want them to see a cop come to my door. Even one in civilian clothes."

The affair started that night. Wally knew she was a prostitute, but he was infatuated. They spent nights at his apartment, nights when she wasn't sleeping with someone else for money. She told Wally that the others were just a way to make a living, a very good living as it was, but she was falling in love with him. He accepted that, mostly, and moved on, with Millie as the centerpiece of his life.

She was a girl from a small town in upper Wisconsin. On the day after she graduated from high school she'd fled the little town and gone to Los Angeles looking for the fame and fortune that the celebrity magazines always talked about. She knew the chances of becoming a movie star were remote, but she was a dreamer and she felt compelled to chase the dream.

The dream, though, turned sordid when she met a man who told her he was a movie producer. He had an engraved business card that said so. She was naïve and had grown up on stories of the stars who had been discovered in drugstores and hash houses. Hollywood was a magical place, but she had gotten nowhere in finding work in the movies. Then the producer showed up and on the third day offered to get her a part in a movie if she would sleep with him.

Millie thought about it for a day and talked to some of her girlfriends, aspiring actresses all, who urged her to take her shot. In the end, she went to a cheap motel with him and had sex. It was quick and unsatisfying, and she never heard from the guy again.

In the end she was used by a number of men, hucksters and cheats and lovers, and she grew jaded. The movie career was never to be. She had become accustomed to using her body to enhance her career chances and it had never worked out. One night, while waiting tables in the high-end restaurant where she worked, she was propositioned by a nice-looking middle-aged businessman in an expensive suit. He offered to pay her to spend the night with him. She agreed and found it not to be as unpleasant as she had expected. The next morning he gave her more money than she'd made in a whole week of waiting tables. From there, it was an easy transition into prostitution, and eventually the work took her to Ft. Lauderdale. She arrived in South Florida a year before she met the young policeman and settled in as a member of the stable of beautiful women that Francisco Mendez maintained. Millicent Smith, the girl from Wisconsin, became Millie Magnus.

On the day after Millie approached Wally at the marina, he arranged to meet a detective he knew, and told him that he had a confidential source that he couldn't divulge, even to another cop, and gave him the story Millie had told about Francisco Mendez.

Unbeknownst to Wally, the detective was on Javier Mendez's payroll, and before Wally slept with Millie a second time, Javier was aware that someone was talking to the cops and in the process of besmirching the good name of his dead son. He set out to discover the snitch.

A month later, Millie didn't show up for a date with Wally. He tried to call her cell, but only got voice mail. He left messages, but did not get a response. On the third day, Millie called. "I'm in the hospital," she said.

"Which one? I'm on my way."

"No, Wally. Don't come. Don't call me again. I don't want to see you. Ever."

"What's the matter?" He was talking to a dead phone.

He began calling the hospitals, starting with the largest and most likely. He told the person who answered the phone that he was a cop and gave her his badge number. He got a hit on that first call. The hospital didn't have a patient named Millie Magnus, but they did have a Millicent Smith. Wally took a shot and went to the hospital, walked into Smith's room, and saw his Millie lying in the hospital bed, her face covered in bandages.

"My God, Millie. What happened?" Wally asked.

Millie looked up. "I told you not to come."

"Yeah. What happened?"

"You happened."

"I don't understand," Wally said.

"You told somebody about me."

"Never."

"Javier told me that you talked to a detective about me."

"I talked to a detective but told him my information came from a confidential source that I couldn't and wouldn't identify."

"Somebody figured it out."

"What happened?"

She started to cry, great sobs wracking her body and tears trailing down her cheeks. "Javier cut my face. He wouldn't stop, no matter how much I begged. He just kept cutting, taking chunks out of my cheeks. He ruined me. And the surgeons can't make it better. Javier said this is what happens to whores who talk out of school. The pain was so bad I passed out. He threw water in my face and started cutting again."

"Millie, I'm so sorry. I'll handle this."

"Go away, Wally. There's nothing you can do."

"We'll see." He turned and left the room. He drove to the central police station and parked in the lot reserved for detectives and ranking officers. He was looking for the detective he'd confided in. After two hours he gave up and went home. He would be going on shift in an hour.

When he got back to the station to check in, he went to a computer and used a friend's ID and password to log into the police department's personnel files. He knew there would be an investigation and some smart cop would look at the department's servers and run a search to determine who had been looking for the detective. His friend was in Alaska on a fishing trip with three other cops. His alibi would be solid.

* * *

A week later Wally went to the hospital to help Millie check out. She wrote a check for part of the bill on a Wisconsin bank and handed the checkbook to Wally to return to her purse. He tore out a check, put it in his pocket and drove her to the airport for a flight home. She was going back to Wisconsin, to her hometown in the far north of the state. She planned to enroll in a nearby college and study to be a teacher.

Millie had come to believe that Wally had nothing to do with her being outed to Javier. He was at the hospital every day, concerned and helpful. On the day her bandages were removed, he looked at the red welts that crisscrossed her face and told her it wasn't too bad and with time it would get better. He had a plan that he did not share with her.

They stayed in touch by email and Wally thought she was feeling better about herself. Maybe being back in her old bedroom at the family home was a catalyst for good. Her parents had welcomed her with the warmth and love they'd always displayed toward their only daughter. She had talked to the college admissions people and would enroll at the beginning of the new semester that would start in a few weeks. She told her parents and her old friends that the scars on her face were the result of an automobile accident.

* * *

Two months went by before Wally put the first phase of his plan into action. He'd found the home address of the detective in the personnel files he'd broken into while Millie was in the hospital. Early one morning Wally was parked in his personal car a half block from the detective's house. He watched as the man got into his car and pulled out of his driveway. Wally followed him and when they were three or four miles from the house, he pulled up beside the detective at a stop sign, waved at him to roll down his window, and said, "I need to talk to you. I've got some good information that I don't want to be seen giving you at the office."

"Where do you want to go?"

"Let's pull into that parking lot around the corner," Wally said.

The detective followed Wally and parked right beside him. Wally got out of his car, a pistol held down beside his leg. He walked to the driver's side window and stuck the pistol in the detective's face. "Put your hands on the steering wheel," Wally said.

"Hey, man, what's going on?"

"Do it, or I'll kill you."

The detective complied. Wally handed him a pair of handcuffs. "Use your right hand and put the cuff on your left wrist."

"You are surely fucking up," the detective said.

"Do it."

The detective put the cuff around his wrist as ordered and Wally said, "Now, reverse the procedure."

The detective did so and Wally checked to make sure they were secure. "Now get out of the car and hold your arms down in front of you." The detective got out of the car. Wally looked around the lot. Nobody there this early. It had probably been a parking area for employees of the adjacent building at one time. The place may have been a factory of some sort, but it had been abandoned many years before. Grass and weeds grew through the cracks on the asphalt surface of the lot.

"Put your hands on the car," Wally said. "Assume the position. You know how to do it." The detective spread his feet and leaned into the car. Wally unlocked the cuff on the detective's right wrist, holding his pistol muzzle in the middle of the other man's back. He pulled both the man's arms behind his back, one at a time, and locked the cuffs again. He searched the detective, took his gun and his handcuffs and key. "Get in the front seat." Wally drove out of the parking lot and headed west.

"I hope the hell you know what you're doing, Officer, because your career is about to come to a screeching halt."

"You keep talking, Detective, and I'm going to shoot you in the foot."

Half an hour later, Wally turned off on a service road that ran due south into the Everglades. The road was dirt and a pall of dust billowed behind his car. He drove for five miles and came to a stop. The road had been laid on a ridge that was a foot or two above the water of the great river of grass. There was water on either side and Wally heard the occasional roar of the bull gators. They were close.

He got out of the car and sat on the trunk sipping from a bottle of water. Another fifteen minutes went by and the dust cleared. There were no cars or people in sight. Nobody would come up on him without dust being stirred up. He'd hear an airboat long before he saw it.

Wally opened the passenger side door and dragged the detective out of the car. The man fell on the road, unable to catch himself with his hands cuffed behind him. "What the fuck?" he said.

"We're going to have a little conversation," Wally said, standing over the man as he lay in the dirt.

"About what?" A hint of fear was creeping into his voice.

"About Javier Mendez."

"What about him?"

"How long have you been on his payroll?"

"I don't know what you're talking about."

"Detective, this can go easy or hard, but the end result is going to be the same. You're going to tell me what I want to know."

"And if I do, what then?"

"I'll take you in and you can give your confession all over again to the internal affairs people."

"About three years."

"What?"

"I've been on Javier's payroll for about three years."

"What do you know about Penny Parkins?"

"She was one of the whores Javier's son Francisco ran."

"What happened to her?"

"Francisco killed her. It was an accident. She wanted to leave the life and he didn't want her to. There was a fight and I guess Francisco hit her too hard. She died."

"Was her body in the boat that exploded near the port?"

"Yes. Francisco was taking her body out to sea to dump it."

"Was Francisco aboard the boat?"

"Yes."

"Do you know what caused the explosion?"

"Yes. The man who owns the boat is a drug runner. He had some cocaine stashed on the boat. He'd just made a run from Bimini bringing the stuff in. He'd off-loaded most of it, but there was some left on the boat for delivery to another dealer. That deal was supposed to go down late on the day Francisco decided to steal the boat to take Penny's body offshore. The boat owner had wired some semtex explosive to a cell phone and hid it in the boat. It could be detonated by a phone call. It was the guy's security system. If somebody stole his boat, he could dial a number, and poof, the boat and the thief would disappear."

"So, when he saw his boat was gone, he dialed the number and no more Francisco."

"Right."

"Where's the guy now?"

"Javier wrapped some anchors around his neck and dropped him in the Gulfstream."

"You're doing good. Now tell me about Millie Magnus."

"I don't know what you're talking about."

Wally shot the detective through his right foot. The man screamed.

"Want to try again, Detective?"

"Yes." He was talking through gritted teeth. "I know her. What do you want?"

"How did you figure out she was my source?"

"I staked out your house and saw her come there. I followed her home to her townhouse and got the address. I also got some pictures of her. I gave them to Javier. He knew exactly who she was."

"What happened then?"

"I don't know."

Wally aimed the pistol at the detective's left foot. "I've got lots of bullets," he said.

"No. I'd tell you if I knew. Javier paid me off and said he'd take care of her."

"What did you think he meant?"

"I figured he was going to kill her. It didn't matter. She was just a whore."

Wally shot the detective through the head. It was the first time he'd ever killed a man. He waited for the horror of his actions to overwhelm him. Nothing. Satisfaction was as close as he could come to describing the emotion that he did feel. The bastard he'd just sent on to whatever reward or punishment awaited him had sealed his fate when he fingered Millie to Javier.

Wally unlocked his handcuffs and put them in his pocket. He pulled the detective's body over to the bank and rolled it into the water. The gators would have a snack tonight.

* * *

Over the next few days, Wally heard rumors around the station that the detective was missing. The consensus was that he was dirty and had run afoul of his underworld bosses. He was probably tied to an anchor at the bottom of the Atlantic. Then, two weeks after the detective disappeared, two dour men from Internal Affairs came to visit Wally at his apartment. They had heard rumblings that the detective had been instrumental in giving Javier Mendez the identity of one of Wally's confidential sources. What could he tell them about that?

Wally shook his head. "I gave the detective some information I got from a confidential source regarding the death of Francisco Mendez, but I didn't tell him the source's name."

"What was his or her name?"

"I can't give you that."

"We can make life hard for you," the IA detective said.

"I know my rights, Detective," Wally said. "I don't have to give you a name."

"We'll be seeing you again, Officer," the IA detective said and left with his partner.

The rumors didn't stop and Wally was slowly ostracized from the police brotherhood. He couldn't be fired on what IA had, but other cops began to ignore him and go out of their way to snub him. He was never invited to the after-hours drinking parties at a local bar. He was becoming a pariah, but he didn't care.

Wally took two of his days off and drove to Tampa where he'd heard of a master forger. For three thousand dollars, he walked out with wonderfully forged ID documents including passports and active credit cards in the names of two different people.

A few weeks later, Wally used one of the fake IDs and took a flight to the Cayman Islands. He lay on a beach for five days, drinking piña coladas and enjoying the solitude. On the third day, late in the morning, he appeared at a bank in George Town that he had previously looked into and was satisfied that it would suit his needs. He opened a secret numbered account with five thousand dollars in cash and a fake ID and passport.

Two days later, Wally used the other fake ID and flew to Nassau, Bahamas. He checked into a gambling resort and stayed three days. He visited another bank and opened another numbered account with the second fake ID, using the last of his savings. Then, he went home.

* * *

Another month went by, and Wally decided it was time to strike. Time for Javier Mendez to pay for his sins. Wally knew the location of the Mendez mansion, a great pile of excess that one architectural reviewer had called a spectacle of inelegance overcome by self-indulgent profligacy.

On the night he chose to bring retribution to the Mendez household, Wally parked his personal car a block down the street from the eyesore in which Mendez lived. He had watched the place for two weeks and every evening at that time, Mendez's limousine had rolled down the driveway precisely at seven o'clock with Mendez in the back seat. He was driven to a nondescript building two miles away. Wally knew the building housed an upscale private club that was frequented by the cream of the South Florida underworld. The Mendez limousine left the club at precisely 8:50 each evening and turned into his home's driveway at exactly 9:00. It was ritualistic, Wally thought.

Wally sat and waited and when the limousine turned the corner into Mendez's street, he followed, lights out, and turned into the driveway behind the big vehicle. The driver had gotten out of the car and was moving around to the passenger side rear door to open it for Mendez when he noticed Wally's car. He stopped, and Wally shot him dead with a silenced forty-five-caliber semiautomatic pistol. He then went to the limo, opened the rear door and stuck his pistol into the side of Mendez's head.

"Get out, nice and quiet," Wally said.

"What is this?" Mendez asked.

"We need to do a little negotiation."

"My men are inside. They'll kill you on sight."

"Javier," Wally said, "you're not in any position to bargain right now. Here's what we're going to do. You call or whistle or whatever you do to contact the men inside and you tell them to come outside. Right now. All of them."

"Why would I do that?"

"Because, if you don't, I'm going to shoot you and leave your body right here in the driveway."

"I'll have to use my phone."

"Okay, but if anything looks the least little bit out of the ordinary, you die. They might get me in the end, but you'll be dead."

"I understand," Javier said, and made the call.

In less than a minute, two men came out the back door and walked down the driveway. Wally shot them both.

"Are there any more?" Wally asked.

"No. Just the two."

"Get out of the car. You're going in the trunk of your limo. I'll be back to get you in a few minutes." He handcuffed Mendez's arms behind his back and helped him into the trunk.

Wally backed his car out of the driveway, drove two blocks and parked. He'd taken the precaution of replacing his license plate with one he'd stolen earlier in the evening from a car of the same make and model as his that he found parked in the long-term parking garage at the airport. Even if the car was reported as having been seen in the neighborhood, it would not be connected to him.

He took a backpack from his car and walked back to the Mendez home. He opened the limo trunk for Javier, and said, "We're going inside. If there are any more people there, you will die immediately. Understand?"

Javier nodded. "There were only the two you killed. They were good men. Who sent you?"

"Let's go to your study. You do have one, don't you?"

Mendez led him into a richly appointed room lined with bookshelves full of books that Wally thought had never been read. Wally placed Mendez in a chair and said, "Millie Magnus sent me."

Mendez blanched, then caught himself and sputtered. "That whore."

"Yes. That whore. The one you carved up like a side of cheap beef. Time to pay up."

"What do you want?"

"I want you to wire ten million dollars into a bank account in Nassau."

"Where am I going to get ten million dollars?"

"Don't bullshit me, Javier. You've got that much in your checking account."

"The banks are closed."

"The Internet is open."

"I couldn't transfer that much even if I had it."

"Javier, you're not cooperating. That will get you killed. I know your bank. It's mobbed up to the hilt. What you're going to do is call the manager and then you're going to use your computer to get into your account and transfer the money. The manager can send a signal to the bank's computers that will approve the transfer."

"I'm not going to do that."

Wally pulled a knife out of the scabbard attached to his belt. He put the point of it against Javier's cheek and sliced downward. Blood flowed and Mendez screamed. "Does that hurt, Javier?"

Mendez nodded.

"Want another one?" Wally asked.

"No."

"Make the call."

Mendez shook his head. Wally sliced him again. Mendez screamed in pain and shuffled in his chair, trying desperately to get away from the knife.

"Make the call," Wally said.

Mendez nodded and Wally asked for the number.

"Use my cell. It's in my pocket. The bank president's name is Cal Hoover. His home number is in my phone's contact list."

Wally retrieved the number and pushed the call button and put it on speaker. "Any funny stuff, Javier, and I'll slit your throat."

Mendez nodded. A man answered the phone. "Cal, this is Javier Mendez. I have an emergency and need to transfer some money to Nassau tonight. Can you authorize an Internet transfer?"

"How much."

"Ten million dollars."

"That's a lot of money."

"I've got a lot of product coming in," Javier said.

"Okay, my friend. Give me about five minutes and I can get into the computer and set it up. I need the wiring instructions."

Wally held up a piece of paper with the routing number of the bank and his account number. Mendez repeated it into the phone.

"Give me five minutes," the banker said.

"Thanks, Cal. Talk to you later." Wally touched the off button on the phone.

"That was real good, Javier. I hope there wasn't some hidden code in there somewhere. Not if you want to live another day."

Five minutes later, Wally pulled a small notebook computer from his backpack and fired it up. Javier gave him the user ID and password to get into his bank account and another password to transfer the money. Wally had gotten a towel from and adjacent bathroom and given it to Javier to stem the bleeding from his face. He released one wrist from the handcuffs and attached the other cuff to the leg of the chair.

Wally waited for ten minutes, and then called the number the bank manager in Nassau had given him. The banker assured him the money was in his account. Wally told him to withdraw one hundred thousand dollars for his efforts and wire the rest of the money to the Cayman Island account.

"The money transferred, Javier. Thanks." Wally shot him through the head and left the house.

* * *

The next morning, Wally called the president of the bank in the little town in Wisconsin where Millie lived. "Good morning, sir," he said. "My name is Richard Wright. I'm an attorney in Ft. Lauderdale, Florida, and I've settled a personal injury case for one of your clients, Millicent Smith. I need to wire a substantial amount of money to her account and need to make sure of your routing number."

The president recited the number and then asked, "May I ask the amount of the wire?"

"Five million dollars. She had a substantial injury with a lot of facial scars."

"Yes. I've known Millicent most of her life. I'm sure she will be well taken care of. Do you need her account number?"

"Thank you. I already have it." He hung up and sent wiring instructions to the Cayman Island Bank, using Millie's account number from the check he'd pilfered from her checkbook that day in the hospital. He left his rented apartment, taking nothing with him, and never showed up at the police department again.

* * *

The man with the water came back. "You're sick," he said.

Wally nodded.

"With what?"

"Pancreatic cancer."

"How long have you got?"

"What's today?"

"Thursday, November sixth."

"I saw the doctor yesterday. He said I've got a week, maybe less."

"You in pain?"

"Yes."

"What do you take for it?"

"Morphine's the only thing that touches it."

"I'll be back."

In a few minutes the man returned with another bottle of water and a small container with two pills. Wally swallowed the pills and thanked the man, who nodded and left the room.

* * *

Wally was drifting on a cloud, his pain manageable, his thoughts scattering again. He hadn't meant to end up working for a bunch of terrorists. He'd gotten involved with Frank Thomason when he'd stumbled into Frank's out-of-the-way gambling den in Atlantic City. Wally was living on the money he'd extorted from Javier Mendez, but it was starting to run low. After a few drinks and some roundabout talk, Frank offered Wally a job, first as a bartender and later as an enforcer.

Wally had no compunctions about roughing up the deadbeats who owed Frank money. As the years went by, he also killed a few people on orders from Frank, never once considering that he had somehow crossed a line from killing a really bad cop and the man who'd cut up a nice girl just for the hell of it, to killing men with an addiction they couldn't control.

He finally tired of the routine and didn't like living in New Jersey. He moved to Tallahassee and took out a private investigator's license and settled in to live a life on the right side of the law. It didn't work, and soon he contacted Frank Thomason and went to work for him again, this time following up on the deadbeats who lived in the Southeast. Before he knew it, Frank had taken on some partners and Wally found himself working for a bunch of Arabs whom he suspected were somehow allied with the worst elements of the Islamist movement.

Not a problem, he thought. They were paying him extremely well and he was building a large nest egg. He took on more and more responsibility and became a trusted employee of the Arabs. Until now. Was it the Arabs who were holding him? If so, why give him the morphine? To keep him alive until they could saw off his head? Maybe. But then again, maybe he was in the hands of the American government. If so, it would only last for a few days and then he'd be dead. He'd handle it.

CHAPTER FIFTY-SEVEN

THURSDAY, NOVEMBER 6

J.D. AND I were having lunch at the Dry Dock Restaurant, sitting in the upstairs dining room with a view across the bay. The clouds left over from last night's storm had moved on and we were enjoying the play of the sun's rays across the green water. A small charter fishing boat had pulled into the dock at the edge of the restaurant's outside deck and the pelicans had gathered, sitting on the water waiting patiently for the scraps that would come their way as the captain cleaned the day's catch.

"That was an interesting interrogation," J.D. said. "I'm afraid your buddy D. Wesley is in for a long stay in the federal prison system."

"I think so. Somehow, I can't work up a whole lot of sympathy for him."

"I wonder what happened to turn him into a jerk. He had everything handed to him, money, a law firm, a position in the community. How could he squander that? Do you think his father expected too much from him?"

"No. I think Lloyd Deming was right. Gilbert is a psychopath. In a sense, it's not his fault. If the shrinks are right, a psychopath is born that way. I've read that a sociopath is made, that is, his behavior is learned, or at least is the result of environmental conditions, such as unfeeling parents or something that the child can't control. But a psychopath is born with some sort of brain anomaly that screws him up from birth. Neither his parents nor anybody else could have foreseen the problem or rectified it. But it'd take a psychologist or psychiatrist to sort all that out. I'm just speculating based on nothing more substantial than a little Internet research."

"If you're right, it's a shame. Maybe Gilbert had no control over his actions."

"It is a shame, but I don't think he was totally without control. The bigger shame is what psychopaths do to the people they cross paths with. They lie with impunity and without remorse. They're not even embarrassed by the lie when they're caught. On some level, D. Wesley must have known that nobody believed he was handling major legal matters, but he kept up the subterfuge. He probably couldn't help himself."

"Do you think he knew that his actions, or at least some of them, were part of an attempt to kill me?"

"I don't know. He stuck to his story that he didn't know, but psychopaths are the best liars in the world. I don't think it would have made any difference to him if he had known. Your death would have had no meaning to him. It would be just something that happened and if he were the cause of it, well, so what? He wouldn't care. He didn't know how to care. He wasn't wired for either sympathy or empathy."

"I wonder what we'll find out about Wally Delmer," J.D. said.

"I'd like to have seen that interrogation."

"I'd be more interested in seeing Frank Thomason's," J.D. said.

"If they find him."

"I've got a feeling the FBI knows exactly who he is. I guess we'll hear something from Parrish sooner or later."

Her phone rang. She looked at the caller ID, grinned, and said, "Speak of the devil."

She answered. "Hi, David. We were just talking about you." She listened for a few moments and then said, "Okay, thanks. If you hear anything, please let me know." She touched the off button.

"What's up?"

"Wally Delmer is gone."

"Gone?"

"Yes. When the FBI went to arrest him this morning, he was nowhere to be found. His bed had been slept in, but he wasn't at home. One of the neighbors said she saw a hearse pull up in front of his house at about three this morning and watched as they brought a body out. At least it looked like a body. It was on a gurney and covered with a sheet."

"And the FBI can't find a funeral home in the area that picked up the body," I said.

"That's what Parrish told me."

"I think some of his buddies decided he was becoming a liability. The body was probably real and it was Delmer."

"That's going to hurt this investigation."

"Yours is pretty much done, isn't it? Apparently it was Bates who killed Peter Fortson, and probably the one who paid the kid in the panhandle to kill Rachel."

"Yeah, but who ordered the deaths? And why?" J.D. asked.

"We may never know, but I think you can close your cold case."

"We'll see. Maybe they'll run down Thomason. I'll call Kendall and see if he's heard that Wally's missing."

I dialed Kendall's personal cell phone.

"How are things, Matt?"

"Good question. J.D. and I watched the FBI interrogation of D. Wesley Gilbert. It looks like they got most of what they need. But it turns out that Wally Delmer is missing and the FBI can't find him."

"I heard that. But I think I know where he is."

"Where?"

"In an interrogation room in the basement of an agency safe house in Northern Virginia."

"You've got him?"

"We do."

"Has he given up anything yet?"

"They're still working on him, so I don't know. We'll find out pretty soon, I think."

"That's good news. David Parrish called and wanted me to ask you if your people have any information on the whereabouts of Frank Thomason?"

"I do, as a matter of fact. He's in the back of an agency van on the way to the same safe house where Mr. Delmer is in residence."

"You and your people never fail to amaze me. But why is your agency involved in what looks like a run-of-the-mill murder that seems to have resulted from a falling out among a bunch of crooks?"

"There's more to tell on this, Matt, but the bottom line is they had a hand, perhaps unwittingly, in trying to take Jock out along with you and J.D."

"How?"

"I'll give you the details later, but they were the money men, the bagmen for some very bad jihadists, including Abu Bakr, the bomber, and his brother Youssef."

"I'll be damned," I said. "I haven't seen or heard anything from Youssef since last weekend. Do you think they've left the country?"

"I wouldn't bet on that. You're still in danger. Stay alert. I'll let you know what we find out from Thomason and Delmer."

"I take it you don't want me to report any of this to Parrish."

"No. Let's keep it quiet for now. If we get the information we need, I don't think Parrish will want to put them in front of a jury. They're connected to some very bad people and national security is always at risk from these guys. We'll go after them and take care of them as soon as we get the information we need. Sad to say, neither Thomason nor Delmer is likely to survive the exercise."

"That's pretty harsh."

"The word needs to go out again and again. You fuck with one of my agents or his family, and your death is the unavoidable consequence."

CHAPTER FIFTY-EIGHT

Thursday, November 6

Frank Thomason came awake slowly. Through the fog of his returning consciousness, he began to understand that he was bound in some way to a chair, his arms strapped to the chair arms, his ankles restrained against the chair legs. He was naked and what appeared to be electrodes were attached to his lower arms just above the wrist, to his ankles, and, most concerning, to his penis. He recognized them because they looked like the little pads they stick on your chest when they're doing an electrocardiogram at the doctor's office. Wires ran from the electrodes to a car battery sitting on the concrete floor about five feet in front of his chair. A small table and a straight-back chair were placed next to the battery and what looked like a rheostat sat on the table. There was nothing else in the room, which was about fifteen feet square, with walls of concrete block and a ceiling that consisted of beams with some kind of soundproofing tiles stretching between them. There were no windows and only one door.

Where the hell was he? Had he somehow pissed off his masters?

He was puzzling this all out when the door opened and a short man built like a refrigerator and wearing a ski mask walked in. "Good day, Mr. Thomason."

"Who are you?"

"My name is Sloane."

"Where am I?"

"In a very safe place."

"Who do you work for?"

"In the end, I work for you and all the other taxpayers. I'm from the government and I'm here to help you." Sloane let out a guttural laugh, a threatening sound that was so feral that Thomason felt his sphincters tighten.

"You're not from the government. What do you want from me? Why am I tied up in this contraption?"

"Do you recognize the gadgets attached to your body?" Sloane had moved to the table.

"They look like electrodes."

Sloane moved the dial on the rheostat and a current of electricity, a very mild shock, coursed through Thomason's body.

"What the fuck," Thomason said.

"That was just a little tingle, not enough to hurt, less electricity than the stuff the physical therapist sends to hurt muscles to help in the healing. But there's a lot more where that came from. Want to get a little taste?"

"No," Thompson said quickly.

"Good. Did you notice the little electrode attached to your dick?"

"Yes." Thompson looked down in dismay.

"I haven't turned that one on. If you give me any kind of bullshit answer to any of my questions, I'm going to fry your gonads. Understand?"

Thomason gulped. "Yes."

The door opened again. Thomason looked up and saw two burly men wearing ski masks, each holding an arm of a naked man who appeared groggy and unstable on his feet. His face was bruised, one eye closed. A trickle of blood ran from the man's hairline tracing a red line down his face. "Sorry, Sloane," one of the men said. "I didn't realize the room was in use." The door slammed shut, but not before Frank Thomason recognized Wally Delmer.

"What happened to that guy?"

"Bullshit answers, probably. They're looking for one of the rooms wired for electrical interrogation that's not in use. I thought we'd just skip all the rough stuff. My arms are kind of tired and I don't have a lot of time to waste with you. I tee off at my country club in about two hours, and I need some lunch before then. I've got to go to the bathroom. I'll be back in a minute."

Sloane was gone for fifteen minutes. Thomason sat and thought about how much information he could hold back. He didn't want to spend the rest of his life in some supermax prison, but neither did he want his head sawed off by a kid hopped up on religious fanaticism. Then the screams started. He could hear them clearly, probably from the next room. Wally? Most likely. The screams went on for five solid minutes, and then total silence. Was Wally dead or just passed out? Thomason didn't want to know.

Sloane came back into the room, carrying a plastic bottle of water. He offered it to Thomason, who nodded. Sloane held it to his lips and let him swallow as much as he wanted. When he was done, Sloane said, "Are you ready to talk?"

"What do you want to know?"

"Everything."

CHAPTER FIFTY-NINE

THURSDAY, NOVEMBER 6

DAVE KENDALL CALLED me a little after three that afternoon. "Thomason was very forthcoming."

"I guess you used a little persuasion."

"The appearance of persuasion, you might say. We hooked him up to a car battery and our interrogator might have suggested that a false answer would be a shocking event."

"Can you get enough juice out of a battery like that?"

"No. The most we could get would cause maybe a tingle in Mr. Thomason, but he didn't know that. We also had one of our staff make-up artists make our buddy Wally Delmer up to look like he'd been beaten and was about to be hooked up to a battery himself. A few screams recorded by a local community theater actor got Thomason's attention pretty quickly."

"You are truly a devious bastard, my friend."

"I am. And it worked. We got a lot of information out of him. It dovetails pretty much with stuff we already know."

"Like what?" I asked.

"Ishmael's Children is part of al-Qaeda. They're a particularly nasty little group and Abu Bakr, the bomb maker, was sort of an independent contractor on loan to it. Ishmael's Children was on our radar, but we'd never connected Abu Bakr to them. Thomason told us he was sending money to Youssef and had used Wally Delmer to provide a man to assist Youssef. That was probably Bates."

"How did Thomason get hooked up with a bunch of terrorists?" I asked.

"Not by choice. He was running a pretty small-time loan sharking and bookmaking operation in Atlantic City and had several youngsters peddling drugs for him on the streets. He also owned a casino there, one of those that's located off the beaten track and catered to people who've been banned by the big boys. Ishmael's Children was involved in running drugs from South America and Asia and wholesaling them to Thomason. Apparently, they decided they needed to move more money and launder some of it, so they moved in on Thomason's operation and took it over. They took him out of the day-to-day management and kept him as a figurehead. He performed some chores, but was for the most part just the front guy. They paid him extremely well for his services."

"How in the world did a Middle Eastern group of murderers take over a small-time New Jersey operation like Thomason's? I'm guessing they didn't buy him out."

"They kidnapped his live-in girlfriend, a Syrian woman named Rahima. They told him if he didn't cooperate, they'd kill her."

"Did he get her back?"

"No. They've still got her."

"I don't think she's coming back," I said.

"I agree, but hope springs eternal and all that."

"Is there a connection to Rachel Fortson's death?" I asked.

"Yes. Fortson was placing bets through Thomason's bookmaking operation, going through Thomason's Florida franchisee, Wally Delmer. He was losing money hand over fist and got deeper and deeper into Thomason. When the Arabs took over, they went after Fortson and told him he had to make a choice. They would make a rough example of him by killing him slowly and videoing it to use as an example to other delinquent debtors, or he could agree to kill his sister and inherit her trust and get the insurance money and pay them off."

"And Peter agreed."

"Yes. Delmer arranged for the murder, again using Bates."

"And Bates hired Jeremy Smithson, the kid in the panhandle, to actually kill Rachel," I said.

"Exactly."

"How did they keep Fortson on the hook after he paid them what he owed?"

"Old-fashioned blackmail. He had to either continue cooperating and giving them lots of money, or they'd kill him. They still had the video camera ready."

"I almost feel sorry for the bastard. He had no way out. Where does D. Wesley Gilbert come into all this?"

"He got in the same way Fortson did. He was into Thomason for a lot of money and the Arabs made him a deal that, as they say, he couldn't refuse. He was sort of a facilitator. He didn't have the money to pay them, but his status in the Orlando community, and to some extent, statewide, gave him a lot of immunity."

"Yeah," I said, "that and the fact that he was a well-known idiot who didn't have the brains to put something like that together."

"There's that. Whatever, it worked. They used him to help disguise the source of a lot of the money that Fortson was paying them."

"What do you know about Ishmael's Children?"

"Our agency wasn't really following them, but the CIA was on top of it. The man who runs the operation is a Saudi imam named Ibrahim Nazari. He and his organization were mentioned in the documents taken from bin Laden after the SEALS got him. He's a nasty one. He probably runs more suicide bombings using young girls and boys than all the others put together. His group has been more active in this country than most of them. They raise a lot of money and pass it on to the al-Qaeda nuts all over the world. It turns out that they keep some of the loot and use it to run their own ops."

"Do you have any idea about who Thomason's partners were?"

"Yes. He gave them up without a fight. We're looking for them, but it looks like they've gone to ground. We'll get them, though. Sooner or later. Ultimately, the so-called partners reported to Nazari."

"Did he give you anything on who was trying to kill J.D. up in Gainesville?"

"He did. Wally Delmer came up with the idea and Thomason agreed to it. Delmer was afraid that J.D. was making some progress on linking the murder of Rachel Fortson to Peter and then up the chain to him, Thomason, and eventually the Arab partners."

"What did Gilbert know?"

"He only knew that he was arranging for the one named Skeeter to kill somebody. He maintained that he didn't know who the target was, and he wasn't about to ask. He also sent the money to Wally to pay off the civilian worker at the sheriff's office in Franklin County."

* * *

J.D. was spending the afternoon in her office at the police station catching up on paperwork. I called her and gave her the short version of my phone conversation with Kendall. "Looks like that should wrap up both Rachel's and Peter's murder and the attempt on your life. A good way to close the cases."

"I'm glad we've got it all wrapped up, but I don't think I will be able to close the cases. The national security people aren't going to let me talk to Thomason or Delmer, so I'm not going to have the evidence I need tying Bates and Fortson and the others to Rachel's murder or to Peter's murder. I guess I can use Skeeter's confession to let the

Alachua County sheriff close that case. I don't have anything I can give the Franklin County sheriff to close the case on the Smithson murder. Dave Kendall can't turn Wally over to me, if he's still alive."

"I doubt they're finished with those guys yet."

"Maybe."

"You want to get some dinner?" I asked.

"We could meet at the Haye Loft for a quick bite. Then I'll have to get back to the office and finish up on all these cases. Have you talked to Jock today?"

"Not yet. I'll give him a call in a few minutes. You want to stay at my place tonight?"

"No, sugar. I've got to go back to the office. I'm going to have to go through all that stuff on all the cases and come up with some rational explanation as to why I want to close them. I need to compare notes with Steve Carey at some point. You go home after dinner and get a good night's sleep."

We had a quick dinner, and J.D. left to meet Steve Carey at the police station. I was still nervous about her being alone and asked, "Are you going to be okay?"

"Yeah. There's only one way into my condo and I've got a big gun. And Bates is dead. I'll be fine. I'll call you in the morning." A buss on my cheek and she was gone. I stayed for another beer and a little conversation with Sammy and Eric, the bartenders, and went home. I read for a while and turned out my light at ten. My bed felt desperately empty.

CHAPTER SIXTY

FRIDAY, NOVEMBER 7

I CAME WIDE awake suddenly, my heart racing, my brain alive and sorting through all the possibilities of what had disturbed my sleep, tuning up my reflexes, getting them ready for action. It's the way an infantry soldier wakes in the middle of the night when some little thing is out of place, maybe the sound of a broken twig, or the shifting of the desert sand, or more ominously, the tiny sound of metal on metal that a sling swivel might make on the barrel of a rifle.

I looked at the clock on my bedside table. A little after midnight. I'd only been asleep for an hour or so. I slipped out of bed and went to the windows that overlooked the backyard and bay. The moon was high, hidden by a thin layer of clouds, and shed minimal light on the area. I saw a man standing on my dock, facing my house. He stood as still as a statue. I couldn't make out his face in the dim light, or see if he held a weapon. What was he doing there? Had he come by boat? If so, the boat must be moored on the far side of my boat where it would not be visible from the house. The man seemed to be alone, but I couldn't bank on that. Terrorists tend to run in packs.

I retrieved a nine-millimeter Glock 17 from the drawer of my bedside table. I had to get into the yard and see if I could figure out what the man on the dock was doing. I went to the window again, looked out. The man hadn't moved. I quietly pulled on a pair of dark cargo shorts and a black t-shirt, and slipped my feet into an old pair of boat shoes. My cell phone was in its charger. I put it in my pocket in case I needed it to call for help, but on the off chance that somebody would call at that time of the night, I turned it off. I didn't want a ringing phone to alert anybody that I was close.

I went into the living room and moved slowly past the windows. I didn't want to show any movement that might catch the eye of someone in the front yard. I could see nothing out of the ordinary. The weak illumination from the nearby streetlight wasn't much help.

I eased the front door open, inch by inch, and slipped out, pushing the door closed behind me. I crept across the yard, bent over, and staying as close to the ground as I could while keeping my legs under me. I moved to the corner of the house on the bedroom side and peered carefully around it. I saw a slight movement. It was hard to see, but I decided it was somebody sneaking toward me, using the same technique I was. I stood stock-still and waited. More movement. It was definitely a human form, coming my way. He stopped. I didn't move a muscle, hoping to blend into the darkness. The figure waited for a minute, maybe less, and then turned and walked slowly toward the back of the house, putting one foot ahead, stopping, listening, then bringing up the other foot, another step, another stop, quietly, still bent over in an attempt to hide himself. What the hell was he doing? Where was he going? Had he seen me? Was he armed? Was it the man I'd seen on the dock? No way to tell.

I followed him, moving one careful step at a time. He turned the corner of the house and disappeared. I picked up my pace, still staying as quiet as possible. Within a minute I was at the spot where the intruder had vanished. I stuck the top of my head around the corner, just far enough to see. I peered along the back of my house. Nothing. Where had the man gone?

I caught movement out of the corner of my eye, to my left, in the direction of the bay and my boat dock. A man was walking toward me from the bay, the deep gloom enshrouding him and making him almost invisible. I turned and trained my pistol on him. "Stop," I said. "Don't move. I'll shoot you dead if you so much as twitch."

Suddenly, there was an arm around my throat, a muscled arm, tightening. I smelled the odor of old sweat and garlic breath. Before I could react, I felt a pinprick in my neck. As my eyesight dimmed, I saw the man from the dock moving closer. He appeared as a wraith floating through the fog of my diminishing consciousness. My mind flashed to the blurry photo of Youssef al Bashar and matched it to the man approaching me, his face fixed in a cruel grin, a rictus of evil. Then the blackness took me and there was nothing.

CHAPTER SIXTY-ONE

FRIDAY, NOVEMBER 7

J.D. AND STEVE Carey had made a long night of it, working on the documents sent by Parrish. She had finally given it up, left the police station, and gone home. By the time she fell into bed totally exhausted, it was a little after two in the morning. She slept fitfully, the numbers and names found in the trove of information she'd studied running through her dreams. She finally gave the night up a little before six o'clock, took a shower, dressed, made a pot of coffee, and dug into the documents again.

She couldn't concentrate. She called Matt. He was an early riser and would be awake by now. She was thinking about one of those Belgian waffles they served at the Blue Dolphin café. Breakfast with Matt would give her a chance discuss some of what she'd learned during the evening. She could use his insight.

There was no answer on Matt's house phone. It wasn't quite seven o'clock. Maybe he was already out for his daily run. She called his cell phone. It rang only once before his voice mail picked up. The phone was turned off. This wasn't right. If Matt were out of the house, he'd have his cell phone with him, and it would be turned on.

Matt's cottage was only a little over a mile from her condo. She drove there through the early morning twilight, worry tickling the edge of her thoughts. It wasn't like him to be out of communication.

It was part of the ethos of the twenty-first century. Everybody had to be in touch with everyone and available by phone, or text, or Twitter, or something, twenty-four hours a day.

J.D. turned onto Matt's street and saw that his SUV was still in his driveway. She pulled in behind the Explorer. She tried to use her key to let herself into the front door of his house. It wasn't locked. She stepped through the door and called to him. No answer. She went to his bedroom. His cell phone wasn't attached to its charger on his bedside table. The bed had been slept in, the sheets and blanket left askew. Matt always made his bed as soon as he got out of it in the morning. He ascribed that almost compulsive behavior to his Army training.

J.D. went through the rest of the house. Nobody home and no sign of Matt's cell phone. She had a thought and went back to Matt's bedroom and looked in his closet. His only pair of running shoes was there. She checked the bathroom. His toothbrush was in its holder. She touched the bristles. Dry. It had not been used that morning. Matt always brushed his teeth first thing after getting out of bed.

She checked the kitchen. The coffee pot was unused. She let herself out the back door. His boat was in its slip. She walked around the house. At one corner, she saw a rupture in the neat grass, two divots displaced. An ornamental bush was partially flattened. And beneath the bush she saw a nine-millimeter Glock 17. Matt's gun.

J.D. pulled her phone from its holster on her belt and called her chief, Bill Lester. He answered with a gruff, "I'm about to get in the shower, J.D. I hope this is good news."

"Matt's missing, Bill."

"Missing?"

"He's not at his house. His bed's been slept in, but his cell phone isn't here and he's not answering it, and I found his gun and signs of a struggle in the yard."

"I'm on my way. Call dispatch and get them to roust out Kevin and tell him to get the Manatee crime scene people moving. I'll send the patrol car closest to you on over and I'll be there in fifteen minutes. Do you have your weapon?"

"I do. I'll be all right. I'll stay in the front yard."

In less than two minutes, J.D. heard a siren coming her way and almost immediately a Longboat Key police car pulled to a stop in front of the house. A young officer got out and walked over to her. "What's going on, J.D.? I just got a radio call from the chief who told me to, and I quote, 'Get your ass to Matt Royal's house now. Siren and lights.'"

"Matt's missing, Joe. It looks like some kind of altercation took place. I think somebody kidnapped him."

"Let's hope not. The chief told me to stick with you. He's got everybody coming this way. Both shifts."

J.D. knew that the patrol shifts changed at seven every morning. The night shift would be leaving and the day shift coming on duty. There'd be a lot of cops to canvass the neighborhood, talking to the neighbors, looking for evidence, trying to get a lead on Matt's whereabouts. There'd be hell to pay if he wasn't really missing. But J.D. knew he had been taken. There was no other explanation and she realized that there was a chance she'd never see him again

She felt the tears welling, but she choked them back. She was a cop and she would act like one. Her job was to find Matt, and she knew that the best way to overcome her panic at the thought of losing him was to throw herself into the job and concentrate her mind on getting him back.

CHAPTER SIXTY-TWO

FRIDAY, NOVEMBER 7

I SLOWLY BECAME aware that I was alive. First, there was a buzzing in my ears, or maybe my brain, that diminished slowly, second by second. Then the headache hit me with the ferocity of a speeding train, the pain so severe and debilitating that I vomited, the acid burning my throat. I tried to put a hand to my mouth to wipe off the residue. I couldn't move either hand. I tugged at the right and then the left and concluded that my wrists were bound behind me and secured to the back of the chair.

I opened my eyes, expecting my head to explode. There was little light, but I could see that I was sitting in a straight-back chair, my wrists pinioned to the back of the chair by what felt like duct tape. I tried to move my lower legs. No go. I looked down. They were duct-taped to the legs of the chair. I was totally immobilized.

I looked around the room. There were windows, but drapes had been drawn, giving the room the look of twilight. I could not tell from the little bit of light what time of day it was. I just knew that it wasn't dark outside and that meant that I'd been unconscious for at least several hours, or maybe several days.

The room was bare of furniture except for the chair to which I was bound. It was quiet. I wondered if the room was soundproofed. Then I thought of the windows. If there were windows, the room couldn't be completely soundproofed. Maybe they were double-paned like the hurricane force wind-resistant windows that the newer building codes required.

My mind was wandering. What the hell did I care about building codes? I tried to concentrate, but my brain wouldn't hold still. Errant images floundered around in there and confused me. I had no concept of time, but since light was slipping through the draped windows, I deduced that it was daytime. But I'd already figured that out. Concentrate, Royal. What day? What time zone? How long had I been out?

I tried to retrieve my last conscious thoughts before waking up in this dismal room. I was at my house, in my yard, and Youssef was walking toward me. An arm was around my throat and there had been a sharp pain in the side of my neck. My last memory, but it slipped and slid through my consciousness, and I wasn't sure if it was real.

My mouth was dry, a raging thirst overtaking my senses. I croaked out a sound, a single word that I think was, "Hello." No response. I tried again. Louder. And then a third time, louder again. Nothing. I slumped back in the chair and tried to clear my mind.

The door to the room opened and a man walked in. He wore a ski mask, his face completely obscured. "You're a pig," he said in lightly accented English. "You've vomited all over yourself. It stinks in here."

"Water," I said.

"I need some information."

"I need water."

"First the information."

"First the water. I can hardly talk. Give me water and I'll tell you what you want to know."

The man left the room and returned a moment or two later with a plastic bottle of water, the kind you find at the grocery store. He unscrewed the cap and put the open end of the bottle to my mouth, tipped it up. The water came so fast I couldn't swallow it all. It flowed out of my mouth, and I began to cough. The man pulled the bottle away.

"More," I said.

"No. Now I want information."

"What do you want to know?"

"Your name."

"You already know that."

He was quick. In my addled state, I didn't see it coming. He reached out and struck me across the face with the back of his hand. I tasted blood. He hit me again, this time with the back of the other hand and across the other side of my face.

"Give me your name," he said, his voice calm.

"Matt Royal."

"You are a friend of Jock Algren?"

"Yes."

"And of the woman called J. D. Duncan?"

"Yes."

"Where are they?"

"I don't know."

He hit me again, this time with his closed fist to the right side of my face. The pain merged with the headache, and I tasted more blood. The man bent down, his face close to mine. "Don't lie to me," he said, his voice low and raspy. I used the blood in my mouth and what saliva I could generate and spit onto his face mask. I had tried for his eyes, the only part of his face that was exposed. I missed, but he apparently got the message.

He paused, drew back quickly, and hit me again in the middle of my face. I saw the punch coming, but could do nothing to deflect it. I felt the cartilage in my nose give way and felt blood running down my upper lip. The pain caused my eyes to tear. I blinked them away, tried to gather enough blood and saliva to spit again. It didn't work. My mouth was dry.

The man turned and walked out of the room. He returned a few minutes later with another man, also masked and carrying what appeared to be an AK-47 rifle. The second man stood behind me, and I could feel the rifle's muzzle against the back of my head. I thought I was about to die, and I was helpless to do anything about it. I focused on a vision of J.D. on the beach at Egmont Key. She was wearing a red bikini and looking at me with a smile that conveyed all kind of wonderful emotions, all directed at me. That was the moment when I knew without question that she loved me, the moment when my life changed forever. It was my favorite memory of her, and I wanted to leave this life with that snapshot imprinted on my brain.

Maybe two seconds had elapsed when I realized that the first man was standing in front of me with a cell phone held up and pointed directly at me. He was about to take a picture. I barely had time to smile before the flash went off.

The man with the phone stepped over to me and hit me in the stomach, a sharp, short blow that doubled me over. He stepped back and said something to the man with the rifle. I felt him grab a handful of my hair and snap my head back. The photo flash lit up the room.

CHAPTER SIXTY-THREE

FRIDAY, NOVEMBER 7

J.D. WAS STANDING in Matt's front yard as the various law enforcement people rolled in. First came Chief Bill Lester, then Officer Steve Carey, followed by a phalanx of forensic investigators. Her phone rang. She looked at the caller ID, tapped the answer button, relief flooding through her. "Matt, where are you?"

"You've got a text," a strange voice said in accented English. The phone went dead.

J.D. touched the icon for text messages. One had come in from Matt seconds before the call. She opened it and saw a picture of Matt restrained in a chair, a man wearing a ski mask standing behind him, his hand holding a clump of Matt's hair, pulling his head back at an awkward angle. He held a rifle butt under his other arm, the muzzle pointed at Matt's head. She saw blood dripping from Matt's nose and a look of pain and surprise on his face. She felt sick, swallowed hard, trying to keep the bile down. It was no good. She bent forward and vomited.

Steve Carey was coming out the front door and rushed over to J.D. "You okay?" he asked. He pulled a handkerchief from his pocket and handed it to her. "It's clean," he said.

J.D. wiped her mouth with the handkerchief. "Thanks, Steve. I'll wash it and get it back to you."

"Don't worry about the handkerchief. Are you sick?"

She handed him her phone. "Take a look."

Steve studied the picture for a moment. "Oh, shit. This is bad. I'm so sorry, J.D. Reuben is in the house. Can I give this to him? Maybe he can get something out of your phone that'll give us a lead on where the bastards are."

"Give me a minute. I'm going to need your phone while Reuben's looking at mine. Okay?"

"Not a problem." Steve pulled his phone from the holster on his equipment belt and handed it to her.

J.D. manipulated her phone, forwarded the picture to Jock's and Dave Kendall's cell phones along with a message to call her at Steve's number. She handed her phone to Carey and he disappeared into the house.

J.D. sat on the front step of the house, trying to focus, trying to think like a cop, not a woman who'd just seen her lover tied up in a room located God knows where. Steve returned, adjusted his equipment belt, and sat down beside her. He put his arm around her, tentatively, waiting for her to react. She surprised him by laying her head on his shoulder. He tightened his hold on her.

"J.D.," he said, "we're going to find Matt and we're going to bring him home. We need to talk, to get ahead of this thing. I need to know everything you know. You know how this goes. I need to know even the tiniest little bit of what you know, even if it seems irrelevant to you."

"Steve, this is really complicated. It has national security implications, and I'm not sure what I can tell you. I'll get a call in the next couple of minutes and I'll find out what I can say and what I can't."

"Jock," Steve said.

J.D. nodded. Steve's phone rang. She answered. "What the hell's going on?" Jock asked.

"It's bad, Jock. I think Youssef has Matt."

"I can see that. When did they take him?"

"We don't know. I came over to his house about twenty minutes ago and he was gone. I'll tell you more about it later, but I was pretty sure he hadn't left on his own accord. About five minutes ago I got a call from a man with an accent telling me to check my texts. I found the picture and sent it to you and Dave."

"Are you alone?"

"No. The police are here. I called them when I realized Matt was missing. Steve Carey is here with me, and I don't know how much I can tell him."

"Sit tight. I'll be there as soon as I can. I'll get Dave to send a plane for me." Jock's voice sounded businesslike, assured, focused. Like the old Jock.

"Are you okay?" J.D. asked.

"I don't know. We'll see. I've got to call Dave." He cut the connection.

Steve's phone rang immediately. J.D. clicked the answer button. It was Dave Kendall.

"I got the picture, J.D. It's got to be Youssef and his bunch. I'll call Jock as soon as we hang up. One of our jets was on its way to Miami. I just diverted it to the Naval Air Station on Boca Chica. It'll be landing in about twenty minutes. It'll take Jock to Sarasota. Can you have a patrol car pick him up there?"

"Yes. Thanks, Dave. I've got another little problem here. I need to tell my people all I know about this, but I don't know how much I can tell them."

"J.D., Matt's life is more important than any secrets we have on this. You tell them anything they need to know. Jock should be there within an hour or so."

"Thanks, Dave. Have your plane go to Dolphin Aviation at the airport. I'll have the car meet them there."

CHAPTER SIXTY-FOUR

FRIDAY, NOVEMBER 7

JOCK WAS RUMBLING around in Paul Galis' kitchen. He had awoken when he heard Paul leaving for work. There was a bag of pastries on the counter and the coffee maker was set up so that all Jock had to do was push a button to start the brewing process. He found a plate in the cabinet above the sink, placed a cinnamon bun on it and stuck it in the microwave. His cell phone dinged, the sign of an incoming text.

He looked at the message and saw that it was from J.D. A photograph was attached. He opened the picture and stared at it for a moment as the full realization of what he was seeing took hold. Matt was tied to a chair, battered and bloody, and a man in a ski mask held an AK-47 rifle pointed at Matt's head. It was a picture Jock had seen many times before. Some poor hostage taken by the sadists who believed the world should return to the seventh century, was about to be executed, or murdered, to be more exact.

But they wouldn't have sent a picture of Matt alive unless they wanted something. That gave Jock a glimmer of hope. He had to find out more and get to Longboat Key. Was he ready to take on the bastards? He didn't know. He thought he was done with that part of his life, but now the only person in the whole world that had stood with him for most of his life was in danger. Not because of anything Matt had done, but because of what he himself had done. He couldn't let this stand. He should have killed Youssef when he had the chance. His good intentions had bad consequences. He knew that possibility when he didn't kill Youssef, but it never occurred to him that his act of charity would put his only family in jeopardy.

He hadn't had a drink of alcohol since Friday. He was a little sluggish from sitting around doing nothing, but he was sober. The alcohol was out of his system. His mind was clear of the cobwebs that had infested it since he'd found the al Bashar brothers in Aleppo. His arm had healed from the grazing gunshot wound. It was a little stiff, but some vigorous exercise would limber it up enough that he wouldn't be impaired. He dialed the number J.D. had given him.

* * *

After talking to J.D., Jock called Galis. "Paul, we've got trouble in Longboat Key. I need to get there as soon as possible. I'll call and charter a plane, but I need to get to the airport now. Can you get a car out here to pick me up?"

"I stopped for breakfast, Jock. I can be at my house in five minutes."

"I'll be ready."

Jock called the charter service he'd used on Friday to get to Key West from Miami. They only had one plane in Key West and that was a small Cessna 172. It'd take a couple of hours to get to Sarasota. Jock thought it was the best he could do on short notice and told them to hold it for him. He'd be at the airport in about thirty minutes.

He hung up and was putting a couple of pistols in his carryall when his phone rang. His boss. "Jock," Kendall said, "I just talked to J.D. I've got a jet on its way to you. It's on final approach to the Naval Air Station at Boca Chica. How far are you from there?"

"About fifteen minutes, I think. I've got transportation on the way."

"We'll have you in Sarasota in about thirty minutes after takeoff. A police car will be waiting for you at the airport. Are you in a condition to handle all this?"

"I'm pretty good, Dave. No booze since Friday, and I know what I have to do. Even if I don't like it. I'll handle this."

"This isn't a suicide mission, you know."

"I know. But if it comes to that, better me dead than Matt."

"Jock?"

"Yeah?"

"Take care of yourself." The line went dead.

* * *

Jock got into Paul's car and said, "Let's go to Boca Chica. Lights and siren. I've got an agency plane waiting for me." He told Paul what he'd learned from J.D. and Dave.

"Are you okay to take this on, Jock?"

"I'm fine, Paul. Everybody keeps asking me that. Understandable, I guess, but I'm sober and in reasonably good shape. I'll be okay. I chartered a plane before I knew the agency jet was coming for me. Will you call and cancel it?"

The gate guard at the Naval Air Station waved them through, and Paul drove toward the ramp where a Gulfstream 150 idled, its stairway deployed. Paul pulled right up to the plane and stopped. Jock shook his hand and thanked him for his hospitality. He jumped out of the car, jogged to the jet, and climbed the stairs. The copilot introduced himself, raised the gangway, and locked the door. The jet started to move.

"We're cleared for immediate takeoff and ascent to twenty-one thousand feet," the copilot said. "We should be in Sarasota in less than half an hour. Buckle up. This baby climbs like a fighter."

* * *

As the jet approached Sarasota, the copilot came back to the passenger section and told Jock that a Manatee County sheriff's office helicopter would meet them and take him to Longboat Key. A detective named Duncan would meet him there.

The helicopter flight was a short hop across the bay. When it landed at Bayfront Park, J.D. was standing beside a marked Longboat Key police car, its blue lights flashing. He got out of the helicopter, waved a thank you to the pilot, and jogged over to J.D. He grabbed her in a bear hug and whispered, "We'll get him back."

She stepped back and looked closely at him. "You're really back, aren't you, Jock?"

"Partway, at least. Enough to help you bring Matt home. Tell me what you know."

J.D. motioned him into the car and they headed for Matt's house. "I don't know any more than I did an hour ago." She told him what she'd found at Matt's house. "It's been about an hour since I got the picture I forwarded to you. We haven't heard anything else, but our tech people have been trying to get some information out of the telephone company to help us find where the call came from."

"Any luck?"

"A bureaucratic clusterfuck," J.D. said.

Jock chuckled. "My, my. I've never heard you use that kind of language before."

She smiled. "Sorry. Those are Matt's words and they seemed to fit."

"Have you tried to track the phone? There are ways to do that."

"Our geek gave that a shot, but he says the phone has to be turned on in order for it to be tracked. Apparently, the man who called turned it off as soon as he finished his phone call to me. He's running a program that will tell us immediately if the phone is turned on again."

"What's going on with the phone company?"

"Nobody can give us an answer. They keep talking about warrants and all kinds of things. Bill Lester has an assistant state attorney standing by to get with a judge when he comes in at nine o'clock this morning and see about getting a warrant."

"Screw it." Jock picked up his cell phone and tapped in a number. "Dave, I'm on Longboat Key with J.D. I need to know the location of Matt's phone when the bad guys sent the text to J.D. an hour or so ago. Thanks." He recited Matt's number from memory.

He hung up and said, "We'll have it in a few minutes."

CHAPTER SIXTY-FIVE

FRIDAY, NOVEMBER 7

JACKHAMMERS WERE TRYING to bull their way out of my head, their incessant pounding bringing another wave of nausea. My nose was probably broken and it hurt like hell. I tried to concentrate on my surroundings, hoping that I could will away the pain. Somewhere in the distance I heard the rumble of marine diesel engines. They were out of sync, and I could tell that there were two of them. Probably a twin-engine boat with an inexperienced captain at the helm who hadn't synchronized the engines' rpms. I was close to the water, but I had no idea about where or even when. I had no frame of reference. I didn't know if I was still in the day of my capture, or a week later. All I knew was that I had been unconscious for an undetermined amount of time and had been taken to someplace on the water. I couldn't even guess as to what continent I was on.

I was puzzled about why they'd asked me about J.D.'s whereabouts. She was on Longboat and I was pretty sure they knew where she lived. Maybe they hadn't been able to break into her condo. Or maybe she'd scared them off with her gun. Even so, they would have known where she was.

The men left me after they took the picture. I sat for what I guessed to be thirty minutes before they came back in. They weren't wearing their masks. One of the men was Youssef al Bashar and the other was a man whose picture Dave Kendall had sent me. Saif Jabbar was young, probably no more than sixteen or seventeen, and he was big and muscular and sported a face so ugly it looked like it hurt.

The fact that the men weren't concerned about showing their faces was a bad sign. They weren't worried about me being able to identify them because they expected me to be dead. That was probably a mistake on their part. Too many people would know who they were and Jock would hunt them down and kill them. Well, the old Jock would, and I thought my death would be the catalyst that brought the newly cautious Jock back into the hunt.

I knew that as soon as I gave them what they wanted, they'd kill me. The longer I could drag this out, the more time J.D. would have to find me.

One of the terrorists, the one whom I'd identified as Youssef, smacked me in the face again, not as hard this time and with an open hand. "Good morning to you, too," I said.

"Where is the woman?"

"She's probably just outside that door with an M-4 rifle that she's about to stick up your ass and blow your dick off."

He hit me again. Harder this time. "I don't have a lot of time to play with you. Either tell me where she is or I'll kill you right now."

"Look, Youssef," I said, "if I knew where she was, I'd tell you."

"You know who I am?"

"Youssef al Bashar. And I know why you are here."

"Where is the one called Algren?"

"I don't know."

He hit me again. This time with a closed fist. On the right side of my jaw. I saw it coming and held my jaw loose and turned my head in the direction away from the blow, hoping nothing would break. It hurt like hell.

"Where is he?"

"The last I knew, he was in Key West. I think you know that. You drugged him and shot him and had a cab driver take him to the hospital. You wanted to lure Detective Duncan and me to Key West to kill us. How'd that work out for you?"

"We lost track of you." He grinned. "That problem has been remedied. Partially, anyway."

"You're a dumbass, Youssef. You didn't lose track. We outsmarted you."

He hit me again. This time in the stomach. I doubled over and retched. Nothing but a little acid came up, burning my already raw throat.

"Do you know where my men are?"

"No." This time I was lying. They were dead. Except for the cab driver, and he'd never see daylight again. I just didn't think this was a good time to bring it up. I mean, given my circumstances.

"Did you capture my men in Key West?"

"No," I answered truthfully. Well, maybe not completely truthful, since I did get Tariq. However, I could see no good reason to explain all that to Youssef. He was mean enough already.

"Where is Algren staying in Key West?"

"My best guess is that he's no longer there. As soon as he finds out that I'm missing, he's going to be after you like a cat on a rat, pardon the expression."

"Good. That is my plan. To get him here."

"Right. All you've done is piss him off. And I promise you, there's going to be hell to pay for that."

He slapped me on the side of my head. Not a hard blow, just sort of a good-bye pat. He and his buddy walked toward the door. "I need water," I said. "I'm dehydrated. And a couple of aspirin if you've got them."

Youssef looked at me and smiled. "No water for you."

"Wait," I said. "I'll trade with you. Information for water."

"What kind of information?"

"I'll tell you where the woman is." I was lying again, of course. I wasn't sure where J.D. was but I would have bet my beloved ass that she was already looking for me. I'd take the punishment for lying to them, but it'd be worth it for one swallow of water.

"You'll give up your woman?"

"Yeah. She doesn't mean that much to me. The woman for a bottle of water. Seems like a fair trade."

"Tell me where she is."

"Water first. Besides, without water, I'll probably die and be of no use whatsoever to you. Not even as bait."

Youssef said something to his buddy in Arabic and the man left the room. He returned in a couple of minutes with a bottle of water and gave it to Youssef. He came over to me, unscrewing the cap. He stood in front of me and upended the bottle, letting the water flow into my lap. Both the bastards laughed and left the room.

CHAPTER SIXTY-SIX

Friday, November 7

"They're nearby," Jock said, hanging up his cell phone. "Dave said the signal from Matt's phone bounced off a cell tower on Cortez Road."

"There's only one tower in that neighborhood, over by the fire station," J.D. said. "It covers a pretty big section. The north end of Longboat Key, parts of Anna Maria Island, and a large part of west Bradenton east of the bay. We're not going to narrow it down by much."

"It helps," Jock said. "Depending on when they got Matt, they could have been just about anywhere. Now we know that an hour and a half ago, they were still here. They have to be holed up in a house somewhere."

"We're still looking for the proverbial needle in the haystack."

They had arrived at Matt's house and were sitting in the car. "Yes, but we've narrowed down the haystacks. Has anybody made any demands?" Jock asked.

"Not yet." J.D. looked at her watch. "It's been almost two hours since they sent the picture. Maybe they just did that to let us know they have him. Maybe they'll kill him without making any demands. If they just want to hurt you."

"I don't think so. If they'd wanted to kill him, they could have done it at his house. Left his body in the yard. We'll hear from them soon.

They'll let us know what they want, and if they call again on Matt's phone, we'll have their location."

"You don't really think they'll use Matt's phone again, do you? They must know that we can track it."

"They probably do, but they don't understand how good our technology is. They know we have ways to track them, but they don't understand that we can do it almost instantaneously. They try to keep their calls short so that they can't be traced, but the second they turn that phone on, we'll have them."

"What do you think they want?"

"You, probably, and finally me. Kill Matt and you and let me live for a few days while I think about what I've caused. If we're right about what they're up to. I can't think of any other reason they'd be after you and Matt."

"Matt won't tell them where either of us is," J.D. said.

"I know. I wonder why they didn't come after you before they went for Matt?"

"Who knows?"

"Were you home last night?"

"Yes, but it was almost two o'clock before I got there. I spent most of the night in the office."

"Do we have any idea about when they took Matt?"

"No. We've got cops canvassing the neighborhood. Maybe something will turn up. Maybe somebody heard something. Or saw something."

"It might be a good idea to have them canvass your condo neighbors as well. If they came looking for you and found you weren't home, they might be waiting to try again later. Maybe they went after Matt when they couldn't find you. Maybe they're on a tight schedule."

"Did you know that Matt killed three of Youssef's men and has one sitting in the Monroe County jail?"

"I knew he killed the sniper and I met Tariq when Matt brought him to Paul's house to interrogate him, but I didn't know about the other two. What happened?"

J.D. told him about Matt's run-ins with the man in the bartender's house and the one in the car. "Both of them tried to kill Matt, so it was self-defense, but he told me he would have killed them in cold blood if necessary. He told me they were vermin who needed to be eliminated to protect ourselves."

"He's right."

"Do you still believe that?"

"I do. I just don't want to be the one doing the killing anymore."

Steve Carey approached the car. Jock rolled down the passenger side window. "Man, am I ever glad to see you, Jock," Steve said. "Come on in. We've got coffee and donuts inside."

"Steve," J.D. said. "Can you get some people over to my condo and talk to the neighbors? Will Glade, the property manager, should be there by now and he can tell them who's in residence. There're only thirty-eight units and a lot of them are still empty, waiting for their snowbird owners. It shouldn't take you long."

"What'll they be looking for?"

"Jock thinks the bad guys might have come for me before they came to Matt's house. Maybe somebody saw something."

"Good idea. We'll get right on it."

CHAPTER SIXTY-SEVEN

FRIDAY, NOVEMBER 7

DIANA WIPPERFURTH WAS in her eighties and still a glamorous woman. She carried herself with a self-assurance that beautiful women often have, a sense of confidence and composure they seem to acquire as small children. By the time they start school, that aura of confidence brightens any room they enter, and it stays with them for a lifetime. She and her husband Bill had been winter residents of Longboat Key for more than thirty-five years.

"Come in, Officer," Diana said.

"Thank you. I'm Officer Steve Carey, Mrs. Wipperfurth."

Only ten of the units in J.D.'s condo complex were occupied, not counting the one J.D. owned and lived in. The three-story building that housed the units fronted the bay. Each unit had a deeded boat slip and shared a dock with the owner of the slip on the other side. The docks lined the edge of a channel that ran off the Intracoastal and along the perimeter of the condo property. Steve and another officer had divided the units and he was on his last one. None of the others had seen anything out of the ordinary.

"Can I get you a cup of coffee, Officer?" Diana asked.

"I could sure use one, ma'am."

Diana brought the coffee back and sat down. "So I hear you're looking for somebody who may have been here last night."

Steve laughed. "Word travels fast around here."

"I saw you at Marylou Webster's door and I wanted to make sure she wasn't under arrest or something. So I called her." She smiled.

"Miss Webster's clean. I don't think she's a threat to the neighborhood."

Diana chuckled. "I'm relieved to hear that. I did see something kind of strange last night. Well, maybe not too strange, but at least out of the ordinary."

"Tell me about it."

"I was up late reading, sitting out on the sunporch. It was probably about eleven thirty when I heard a boat coming up the channel. It didn't have any lights showing and that seemed a bit odd."

"Could you see the boat well enough to give me a description?"

"No. It was too dark, but it was powered by an outboard. I could tell by the sound."

"Single or twin?"

"Single, I think."

"Could you tell how many people were aboard?"

"Three, maybe. But I'm not sure. It was overcast last night, and dark."

"You're doing good, ma'am. Did you see where they went?"

"Are you familiar with the layout of this property?"

"Pretty much. I've been here a number of times and have come into the marina area with the police boat."

"Well, you know how the channel curves around and passes in front of the condos next door?"

"Yes."

"I lost sight of the boat when it went around that curve. I thought it was probably somebody from the other condos coming home late, but a few minutes later, I heard a noise from the parking lot. A sneeze, I think, or maybe a cough. It sounded like he tried to suppress it. I looked out the back bedroom window and saw two men walking across the lot. They were coming from the direction the boat had gone. I think they may have been the ones on the boat."

"Did you see where they went?"

"That's the funny thing. They walked all through the parking lot, like they were looking for cars, one car, maybe. At first, I thought they might be trying to steal one, but they never did anything other than look."

"Did you see them leave?"

"They left the parking lot and then I heard the elevator. It only worked long enough for someone to get to the second floor."

"Do you think they were trying to break in?"

"If they were, they were in for a surprise. The only way into the units on the second and third floors is through the front doors and those doors are break-in proof. I guess if one were not too concerned about a lot of noise, one might get in, but not otherwise."

"Did you see them again?"

"Yes. I heard the elevator come back down to the first floor and saw the two men walking back across the parking lot. A few minutes later, I saw the boat going back up the channel. I watched until it got to the Intracoastal, and then he turned on his running lights and headed north."

"Did your husband see anything?"

"Bill? He was sleeping like a log."

"Can you describe the men you saw in the parking lot?"

"No. It was too dark."

"What about their clothes? Could you see what they were wearing?"

"Not really. It looked like they were wearing t-shirts and long pants, maybe jeans, but I couldn't swear to that."

Steve stood. "Thank you for the coffee, Mrs. Wipperfurth. You've been very helpful."

"I'll show you out, Officer."

Carey met the other cop in the parking lot. He had nothing to report. None of the people he talked to had seen or heard anything. Steve told him about the boat and the men walking around the parking lot late at night.

"You know," the cop said, "somebody called the station this morning and reported a boat had been stolen."

"I hadn't heard that. Can you get me the report?"

"Sure. I'll run by the station and get a printout. I'll see you back at Matt's house."

CHAPTER SIXTY-EIGHT

FRIDAY, NOVEMBER 7

"THE BOAT WAS stolen sometime last night from a dock at Cannons Marina," Steve Carey told Jock and J.D. "She's a thirty-foot Grady-White center console that was at Cannons for its annual maintenance."

"The way that place is lit up at night, I'm surprised anybody could get in to steal it," J.D. said. "You know David Miller's people wouldn't leave the keys in the boat."

"If Youssef stole the boat, he had to have had help," Jock said. "He wouldn't know anything about boats, much less how to hotwire one, if that's what they did. And he sure as hell couldn't navigate one."

"You know the canal that goes up to Cannons is just around the corner from my place," J.D. said, "and the men Diana saw sneaking around the parking lot could very well have been the terrorists. Maybe they had somebody who knows how to steal boats to help them and they came directly to my place from Cannons."

"Why go to all that trouble?" Steve asked. "If they were looking for you why not just come by car?"

"Because," said Jock, "they're holed up somewhere accessible only by water."

"Good call, Jock," Steve said. "I'll get our marine unit to look for the stolen boat and ask Manatee County for help. They've got several boats at Coquina Beach. We can probably get the Longboat Fire Department's boat as well."

"Tell them about the cell phone call that bounced off the tower at the Cortez Road fire station," J.D. said. "That narrows down the scope of the search."

"Don't use the radio," Jock said. "They could be monitoring it."

Steve held up his cell phone and walked off. He was back in a minute. "The deputy chief is calling in favors from the Manatee sheriff and the fire department. What do you think the bad guys were doing, Jock?"

"I think they planned to come in and take J.D., then go to Matt's place, get him, and head for wherever they're hiding out. They were in the parking lot looking for J.D.'s car to make sure she was at home. Maybe they went upstairs to see if they could break into her unit and discovered they couldn't do that without a lot of noise. If she wasn't home, she'd probably be at Matt's. At least they'd know they had to be ready to handle two dangerous people at Matt's. They couldn't have known that J.D. was working late at the station."

"Even if I had been home," J.D. said, "how would they have gotten me out of my condo without making a lot of noise?"

"Maybe that wasn't the plan," Jock said. "Maybe they were going to put a bomb in your car and then kill Matt at his house. That would have accomplished their plan. Both of you dead and me left to mourn and blame myself. They leave in the boat and the police would be looking for a car. But who knows what those idiots were thinking?"

"Then why take Matt alive?" Steve asked.

"They don't know what kind of man he is," J.D. said. "They probably thought they could get to me through him. That he'd tell them how. Or maybe they thought I'd come to his rescue and they'd have me."

"They wouldn't expect you to come to the rescue," Jock said. "In their culture, women cook, clean, and raise children. They don't drive cars and rescue lovers. They're betting Matt will put you in their sights. When they figure out he won't, they'll kill him."

* * *

A lot had happened in a short time, but now it was nearing nine thirty in the morning and it seemed as if everything had come to a dead stop. J.D. was antsy, her nerves frayed from worry about what was happening to Matt. She knew that time was short. If they didn't find him soon they would be looking for his body. It'd be what the Coast Guard called a recovery operation rather than a search for survivors.

She was sitting on the living room sofa, thinking about how many nights she and Matt had spent snuggling there, talking about their days, sharing a bottle of wine or a pizza or a real meal, watching the night descend. Happy evenings. Were they over?

Steve Carey interrupted her reverie. "J.D., we may have found the boat."

"That was quick."

"If it's the right boat. It's docked at Jewfish Key."

"You said if."

"The registration numbers are different, but they could have been altered. Our marine guy saw the numbers, but he didn't get a close enough look to tell if they had been changed. He didn't want to pay too much attention in case somebody was watching. But the description fits the stolen boat."

"Is the boat at the common dock?"

"Yeah. But I don't think any of the residents are on the island. They usually let us know when they show up, and we haven't heard from any of them."

"They must be in one of the houses. They're six of them out there.

We can't go storming all six. We've got to sneak up on them or they'll kill Matt."

"The sheriff's helicopters have thermal imaging capabilities," Steve said. "We could have them do a flyover and find out if any of the houses have people in them."

"That'll work. There's enough helicopter activity in this area that the bad guys won't think anything about another one flying over."

"I'll get the sheriff's people moving."

CHAPTER SIXTY-NINE

FRIDAY, NOVEMBER 7

I HAD NO concept of time. I didn't know how long I'd been tied to the chair, but logic told me it was still the same day that I'd been kidnapped. I was not particularly hungry when I regained consciousness, and if I'd been out long enough to have traveled a long distance, I'd most likely have been hungry. I'd heard the diesel boat earlier and over the next couple of hours I'd heard the occasional outboard engine running at high speed. Gulls cried in the distance, their squawking music to my ears. All of the signs meant that I was probably still in Florida. Maybe close to home.

I had no idea what time it was. I knew I'd been awake for at least a few hours, but I hadn't been able to keep up with how much time had actually elapsed. My headache had eased some and was now more of a dull pain than the pulsing, raging agony it had been when I first awoke. My shoulders were cramping from the way they were bound around the back of the chair. I was dehydrated and my body was demanding fluids. I called out to my captors. "Are you guys out there?"

Saif opened the door. "What do you want?" His English was heavily accented.

"Water."

"No." He started to close the door.

"Saif," I said.

He came back into the room. "How do you know my name?"

"Saif Jabbar."

"How do you know that?"

"Saif, I know your name and I know you have a family." I was taking a shot in the dark on this one. If he had a family, maybe I could gain some leverage. If he didn't, he'd just laugh at me and walk out. I had nothing to lose."

"You know nothing about my family," he said. "You're lying."

"I didn't say I knew anything about your family. I just know that you have one."

"Everybody has a family."

"I don't. Jock Algren doesn't. Youssef doesn't."

"If you don't know anything about my family, why should I care?"

"Because some very bad men who work for my government know all about your family. Right now, they're probably moving in to capture them, maybe kill them. They know who you are and where your family lives."

"You Americans would never be able to get to them."

"That's what bin Laden thought. If you kill me, our intelligence agencies will track you to the end of the earth and kill you."

"Then I'll be a martyr and go straight to paradise."

"Your family will be dead by tomorrow if I'm not released. Do you want that?"

"My brothers and sisters are very young. Even you Americans would not kill them just because we kill you."

"Did you ever see the results of a drone strike, Saif? It's nasty and indiscriminate. It'll kill anybody nearby. Including women and small children. They're in our sights and if you try to call them on one of your cheap cell phones our National Security Agency will be all over you. Your family will be dead before they can move."

Saif stood for a moment, as if pondering the information I'd just given him. Then he turned toward the door.

"One more thing, Saif," I said. "You bring me some water and when I'm out of here and you're dead or in prison, I'll make sure that nobody bothers your family."

"You have that power?"

"If I wasn't important to our government, do you think Youssef would have gone to all this trouble to kill me and J. D. Duncan?"

Saif left the room and quickly returned with a bottle of water. He put it to my mouth and turned it up. I don't think I'd ever tasted anything so delicious. I got two or three swallows before he snatched it away. He put the cap back on and slugged me in the face with his fist. Hard. I felt my broken nose flatten some more and the pain was so intense I wanted to scream. Not a chance. Never let the bastards see your pain. Blood started to flow from my nose again, running down my chin and onto my chest. I had no way to stop it. I bowed my head and let it flow. Saif left the room without another word. A small victory, nonetheless. I got my water and Saif was rattled.

As he left the room, I heard a helicopter overhead. Probably the Coast Guard.

CHAPTER SEVENTY

Friday, November 7

"I think we've got them," Steve Carey said, putting his phone back in his pocket. "Only one of the houses has a heat signature. It shows three people in the one on the northwest tip of the island."

"That's right next to the sandbar, right?" J.D. asked.

"Yeah. The one with all the rowdy folks on weekends."

"There're usually boats out there during the week, too," Jock said.

"Any day that the weather's decent," Carey said.

"We've got to take the chance," Jock said. "Go in now."

The Longboat Key deputy chief of police, Martin Sharkey, had joined the little group in Matt's living room. "I'll alert the Manatee County SWAT team," he said.

"I don't think that'll work, Martin," Jock said. "I know the SWAT guys are good, but we've got to surprise the terrorists. I doubt more than two men are involved. Matt killed the rest of Youssef's team, and they haven't had time to bring in any replacements. I don't think they'll be watching the island, but they'll be on alert in the house. I just need one more man. The two of us ought to be able to handle it."

"One more woman," J.D. said. "I'm going, Jock."

Jock smiled. "That's what I meant. J.D. and I can handle it."

* * *

Jewfish Key is a thirty-eight acre island that hunkers near the northern end of Sarasota Bay and is accessible only by boat. There are six widely spaced waterfront houses surrounding a seventeen-acre preserve that has been left in its natural state. The island is bordered on the north by Longboat Pass and on the east by the Intracoastal Waterway. Longboat Key lies a few hundred yards to the west across a channel of open water. Some of the houses have their own docks and there is a larger common dock at mid-key on the eastern side. In early November, the owners of the homes are still somewhere up north, waiting out the holidays before flying south.

Jock and J.D. borrowed a boat from one of Matt's neighbors, a twenty-four foot Sailfish center console. They boarded it with a cooler and a beach bag full of towels and pistols. They were dressed in shorts, t-shirts, and athletic shoes. Jock had a ball cap pulled low on his forehead, hiding his baldpate. Dark sunglasses hid part of his face. J.D. wore a large straw hat with a wide brim and big sunglasses. Her hair was tucked up under the hat. If they were spotted, they'd just be another couple out for a day on the water.

A boat from the Longboat Key Fire Department, manned by firefighter/paramedics, was stationed at Moore's Stone Crab restaurant just across the lagoon from Jewfish Key, but not in sight of the house. It shared a dock with boats from the Longboat Key police department and the Manatee County sheriff's office. Both of the law enforcement vessels had a contingent of SWAT team members aboard. A Longboat Key fire department ambulance was parked in Moore's lot. Everybody was at the ready, awaiting a radio call from Jewfish.

The neighbor they borrowed the boat from lived on a bayou a block down the street from Matt's house. His boat was moored to a dock behind his house. Jock and J.D. clambered aboard and idled down the bayou until they reached the bay. Even if one of the terrorists was smart enough to keep an eye on Matt's house, he would not have seen the boat leave from there.

When they reached the bay, J.D. put the boat on plane and headed south. She rounded the southern tip of Jewfish and moved into the Intracoastal, running north. When she came to the intersection of the Waterway and the Longboat Pass channel, she turned westward and ran for the drawbridge before changing course back around to the south. She idled onto the sandbar, and dropped anchor just out of sight of the house that was their target.

During the summer, J.D. and Matt had visited Jewfish with Sammy Lastinger and a young woman whose father had rented one of the houses for a month. The man had been a gracious host and showed them around the island. J.D. remembered a path that ran through the scrub and approached the house in question from the south. The path ended at a small outbuilding built of coquina rock that sat at the edge of the property only a few feet from the house. J.D. told Jock that the local lore was that the man who built the house had lived in the coquina hut during his home's construction. It would provide good cover, and J.D. was pretty sure they could sneak in that far without being seen.

They climbed out of the boat and waded across the sandbar until they reached the shore, holding their weapons above their heads. Each had a belt and holster containing a nine-millimeter semiautomatic pistol. Jock carried an old mint-condition M-1 military rifle that he'd found in Matt's closet and J.D. had Matt's twelve-gauge shotgun. Loaded for bear, she thought.

They came ashore on a small grass beach that was crowded at the landward edge by Australian pine trees, a non-native species that the locals loved and the environmentalists hated because they thought the pines were crowding out the local flora. As they walked the path, Jock and J.D. were shaded by the overhanging trees. The path was brown with fallen pine needles, and wide enough for the golf carts that were the only vehicles allowed on the island. The quiet was broken by the calls of birds and the almost silent crunch of their shoes on the trail.

They walked carefully, quietly, and at a fast pace. As they neared the coquina outbuilding, they heard what sounded like a man moaning. Jock eased toward the door, which for some reason faced the path rather than the house. He put his ear to the door and listened for a couple of moments. He walked back to J.D. and whispered, "Somebody's in there and he's crying or moanng, like he's in distress. It doesn't sound like a child. I don't know if the door is locked, but I'm going to try to open it. You cover me with the shotgun. If it's one of the terrorists, don't hesitate. Blow his ass away."

She nodded and they moved next to the door. Jock put his finger on the latch, looked at J.D. She nodded again. She was ready. Jock pulled on the latch and pushed the door open, stepping back out of J.D.'s line of fire. Nothing. Jock looked into the one room hut and saw a young redheaded man lying on a single bed, his arms bound to the bedrails. A piece of gray duct tape covered his mouth. His cheeks were wet with tears. He was looking at them, his eyes wide in horror, the moaning starting again.

"I know you," J.D. said. "You work on the fuel dock at Cannons."

The man nodded.

J.D. moved toward him, stood over him. "I'm a police officer. I'm going to remove the tape on your mouth, but if you make any noise whatsoever, my friend here is going to gut you with his big knife. Do you understand me?"

The man nodded and J.D. jerked the tape from his mouth. He took a couple of deep breaths and said, "They're going to kill me."

"Who?" J.D. asked.

"The men in the house."

"How many are there?"

"Only two that I know of."

"How did you get here?"

"Am I going to be in trouble?"

"It depends."

"I was paid to borrow a boat and bring them out here."

"Who paid you?"

"A man named Charlie."

"Charlie who?"

"I don't know his last name. He was on a sailboat moored over at the Seafood Shack."

"A smelly guy with a beard and dirty clothes?"

"You know him?"

"In passing. Was he the one who paid you?"

"Yes."

"When?"

"Tuesday."

"How much?"

"Two hundred bucks."

"How did you meet Charlie?"

"I clean boats when I'm not working at the fuel dock. I was in the Seafood Shack marina working on one and he came over to talk to me."

"And he paid you to borrow a boat and bring these guys out to Jewfish?"

"Yes. Well, he told me these guys might need to get to Jewfish and he was leaving town."

"Charlie said he was leaving town?"

"Yeah. He paid me and gave me a cell phone. Damn thing wouldn't work like a regular one, but he told me to hang on to it and if the guys who needed to get to Jewfish needed me, they'd call."

"What if they didn't call?"

"Then I'd get to keep the two hundred bucks. Charlie said I could throw the phone away."

"Where did you borrow the boat?"

"From Cannons."

"David Miller let you have it?"

"No. I just borrowed it. Didn't ask anybody."

"You stole it."

"No. I was going to bring it back. That's borrowing, not stealing."

"Where were you supposed to pick up the men?"

"They went with me."

"Where did you meet them?"

"At the Seafood Shack."

"How did you get to Cannons?"

"In my car."

"Where's your car?"

"I left it in the chapel's parking lot, just down the street from Cannons."

"Did you come straight here?"

"No. It was crazy. First we went to the condos that are around the corner from the marina. They got off the boat and walked around and came back. They were speaking some kind of foreign language, so I don't know what they were saying."

"Then what?"

"We went to Mr. Royal's house, and they brought him to the boat. He was out like a light. I didn't know what they were doing."

"You recognized Mr. Royal?"

"Sure. He's a good tipper. He brings his boat in to fuel up and he's a friend of the boss, Mr. Miller."

"Weren't you curious about what they were doing?"

"Yeah, but they told me to shut up and do what I was told."

"What did you do after you got Matt into the boat?"

"We came here. To Jewfish. They had a map and one of them disappeared for about twenty minutes. The other one stayed with me and Mr. Royal. He had a gun. Then the other guy came back driving a golf cart. They put Mr. Royal in it and we drove to a house. Then they put me in here and tied me up. They said they'd need me to drive the boat back to Longboat, but they'd kill me and drive themselves if I caused any trouble. But they were going to kill me anyway, weren't they?"

"I'm sure that was their plan. I'm going to put this tape back on your mouth, but we'll be back to get you in a few minutes."

"Okay. Do you think Mr. Miller will fire me because of this? I just borrowed the boat. I didn't mean no harm."

"What's your name?"

"Buddy. Buddy Murphy."

"I don't think you'll have to worry about your job for several years, at least."

"That's a relief."

J.D. looked at Jock, who'd been standing quietly in the corner of the room as she interrogated Buddy. He nodded and J.D. put the tape back in place.

CHAPTER SEVENTY-ONE

FRIDAY, NOVEMBER 7

J.D. AND JOCK had looked at the house on Google Earth. There were no ground-level pictures, but they could see the layout of the surrounding area and the roof of the house. The trees were too thick to give them any sense of what the area surrounding the house looked like. They'd had a pretty good view of the house as they idled onto the sandbar and knew it was, like most waterfront houses built in the past thirty or forty years, on stilts. The first floor of the house was eight to ten feet off the ground.

They stood behind the coquina hut and Jock peeked around the corner. There was a sweeping stairway, positioned on the east side of the building and leading up to the long veranda that ran the width of the house. The front door opened off the veranda at the top of the stairs. That was going to make it difficult to get inside without being seen.

Large picture windows fronted on the two sides of the house that overlooked the bay. There was a smaller window that overlooked the little hut. Maybe a kitchen window, Jock thought. Still, if anybody were looking out of it, they'd have a good chance of spotting him and J.D.

"We need to make a run for it," Jock said. "We need to get under the house. They won't be able to see us there."

"Got any ideas on how to get up those stairs without being seen?"

"Not yet. You go first. I'll cover you."

J.D. ran across the twenty feet or so that separated the hut from the house. Nobody seemed to notice. As soon as she got under the house, Jock followed.

"What now?" J.D. asked.

Jock pointed to a ladder affixed to the underside of the first story of the house. "What's that?"

"Let's go see."

The ladder stood straight and had the look of a built-in feature. There was what appeared to be a trapdoor at the top of the ladder. Did that open onto the veranda near the front door, or were they standing directly under the living room, or whatever was just inside the front door? Jock walked off the distance between the foot of the ladder and the edge of the house. He didn't know how wide the veranda was so his calculations could be off by several feet.

"I'm going to climb up there," Jock said. "See if I hear anything. If anybody opens that trapdoor, shoot him."

"Gotcha."

Jock climbed to the top, stood there for a minute, listening, trying to discern any voices or household noises. A TV was on, the volume turned low, some sort of daytime talk show. He climbed back down. "Somebody's watching TV, or at least it's on. I felt cool air coming from around the trapdoor. That means it opens to the inside of the house. It's still warm outside and that veranda sits right in the late morning sun."

"What do you want to do?"

"I think we might want to go in that way. I'm going back up. I wish I knew the layout of the house. That trap door might have a table or a sofa sitting on it. If it's in a hallway or the foyer, it might open. I'm going to try it. If I start shooting, you put some lead through the floorboards."

Jock climbed back up and put a hand up to push on the trapdoor. It moved easily. He inched it up until he could see through the crack between the door and the floor. He balanced on the ladder and put his other hand into the crack and pushed something aside. He let the trapdoor down quietly and climbed back down the ladder.

"It opens into the living room," he said. "The man who built this place may have put it in as a fire escape. If his front steps were in flames, this would be the only way out. There's a rug on top of the trapdoor. I had to push it aside, but I saw one man sitting on a sofa watching TV. There's a closed door just to the right of the opening of the trapdoor and the kitchen is to the left and a little behind. I can see a staircase all the way over on the far side of the living room. I'm thinking the closed door might be the master bedroom. Maybe that's where they've got Matt."

"This may be the best way in," J.D. said, "but there's no way to set up covering fire. There's not enough room."

"Precisely. The stairway outside is plenty wide enough for both you and me to go up side by side. If we make it to the front door, we'll at least be able to cover each other. With one of the guys distracted by the TV, we might have a chance."

"We've got to get in there quick before they can kill Matt," J.D. said. "If they haven't already."

"He's alive, J.D. I can feel it. Let's go."

And that's what they did. J.D. hugged the right railing of the stairway, and Jock stayed on the far left. They moved as fast as they could without making enough noise to warn the men in the house. Jock counted twenty-three steps, and they made it in less than ten seconds.

When they got to the veranda, each took up a position on either side of the door. They could hear nothing but the TV. The plan was for J.D. to go in first, with Jock guarding her. J.D. would take care of the man in the living room while Jock forced the door to the right of the trapdoor. Hopefully, that's where they held Matt.

Jock was on the side of the door nearest the handle. He pushed down on it. Not locked. He looked at J.D. She nodded. Jock threw open the door and J.D. rushed in, Jock right behind her. J.D. had the shotgun at the ready. Jock was holding his pistol, the M-1 slung over his back.

The man on the sofa stood quickly and turned toward J.D. She didn't hesitate. The shotgun blast pushed the man backward into the picture windows overlooking the bay. Blood splattered and started running down the inside of the window. J.D. was aware of the large hole in the man's torso, and she was also aware that he was very young. And very ugly.

She turned quickly as Jock pushed open the door. She followed him into the room, her shotgun ready for action. Her gaze slipped around the room and rested on Matt, sitting in a chair, his arms and legs taped to it. He had bled a lot. His t-shirt was soaked with it. His nose appeared to be broken. His upper lip was split and there was fresh blood on his teeth. An enormous bruise was spreading across his left cheek, reaching toward his forehead. A man was standing behind the chair, a large hunting knife at Matt's throat.

Matt's grin was lopsided, as if the left side of his face hurt too much to look happy. "Glad you guys could make it," he said. "About damn time."

CHAPTER SEVENTY-TWO

FRIDAY, NOVEMBER 7

YOUSSEF CAME INTO the room holding a large knife. I could hear a TV on the other side of the door. Saif soaking up a little Western culture, I thought. Youssef stood close, staring at me, taking my measure perhaps, as if I could do anything while bound up like some poorly wrapped Christmas present.

"I've got to pee," I said. "Do you want to cut me loose and let me use the toilet or do you want to hold my dick and let me piss in a jar?"

He slapped me. It wasn't unexpected, but it still hurt. The bastard had no sense of humor. He was pretty much just bruising the bruises. I hadn't seen a mirror, but I was guessing my face looked like Mike Tyson had worked me over.

"I'm going to cut off your finger and send it to your woman. I want her to know we've got you. She can run the fingerprint." He laughed, sounding a little bit like a hyena. He was losing control. No telling what he had in store for me.

Oh well, just roll with the punches, Royal. They can't stay here forever, wherever we are, and when they get tired of abusing me, or decide they have to leave this place, they'll kill me. It'll all be over. I thought I could take a couple of days of their crap, and then just float off into whatever comes next. Death isn't something to be afraid of. It's something to regret, I guess. At least when you're on the side of the divide where you're still breathing. I had always believed that one of two things will happen when you're dead. If there's no afterlife, there's just oblivion, and I won't know anything. If there is another life out there waiting for me, it'll be a place of pleasure, of renewal, a time to be with those I've loved the most. Jock and J.D. My grandmother. My parents. A few others. The real test is getting from here to the other side. At least, that's a problem when you're at the mercy of a bunch of nutcases who think death is about getting laid by a bunch of celestial virgins.

"You know, Youssef, this isn't going to happen without a fight."

"I don't think that'll be much of a fight. Not with you tied to that chair." He laughed again, that high-pitched yelp that really got on my nerves.

"Try me," I said. And I heard a shotgun blast.

The door to the room flew open and Jock rushed in, pistol in hand. J.D. was right behind him, the shotgun stock under her arm, her finger on the trigger, the barrel pointing right at me. Youssef moved quickly behind me, squatted a bit, using me for a shield and making himself as small a target as possible. I felt the knifepoint dig into the right side of my throat. I said something, but I don't remember what it was. I was very happy that my friends were there. I was thinking that the shotgun had probably taken out Saif and wondering a little crazily if J.D. had read him his rights before she sent him to wherever he was going. Hell, I supposed, if there was such a place.

"Give it up, Youssef," Jock said. "I don't want to kill you."

"Your friend will be dead before I am," Youssef said.

"But you'll still be dead. Think about it. You can live even if it's in prison, or you can die here. Today. I'd rather you live."

"You killed my entire family, you bastard. Why do you care if I live or die?"

Jock's voice was cold, like a wind blowing from a grave. "I guess

I don't, Youssef. But I'm giving you a chance. Take it or leave it. It makes no difference to me."

"If you kill me, I'll die a martyr. I'll go directly to heaven. I'll sleep with Allah and the virgins."

Jock still held his pistol pointed at Youssef. I could feel the pressure of the knife increasing. I could feel blood starting to drip down my neck. He'd punctured the skin. He was about to kill me.

I jerked my head to the left and Jock shot Youssef through his forehead. "Go fuck yourself to death, you witless bastard," Jock said. "Tell the virgins I'm sorry I missed them."

* * *

"Where are we?" I asked, as Jock was cutting away the tape. J.D. had hugged me and didn't seem to want to let go. She finally stepped back so Jock could get to the restraints.

"Jewfish Key," she said.

"You're kidding me," I said. "I could've swum home."

"I don't think so," Jock said. "Not with that chair taped to your ass."

"Man, am I ever glad to see you two. How did you find me?"

"Let's talk about that later," J.D. said. "I've got to call the paramedics."

Within about five minutes the place was swarming with people; paramedics, cops, forensics techs, medical examiner's assistants. The paramedics took a quick look at me, listened to my chest, felt around on my abdomen, gingerly touched my nose and cheeks, and grunted to each other. "You're going to be fine, Matt," their lieutenant, Pete Collandra, said. "Now get your ass on the gurney."

"I'm fine, Pete. I don't need no stinking gurney."

"Did anybody ever tell you that your impersonations stink?"

"Yeah. All the time. I think you're all just jealous of my talent."

"Right," said Pete. "Now get on the gurney."

"I'll walk, Pete. You guys will probably lose me on those steps."

"You've got a point. You can lean on me."

"I've always known that, Pete." And I was afraid I was going to cry. Most everybody in that room was a friend and some of them were close friends. They'd put on a big operation to find and free me. I think I'd silently said good-bye to each one of them when I thought I was close to checking out for good. Sometimes, a little self-pity is called for.

Jock had been talking to the deputy chief, telling him what had happened. He walked over to me and said, "Glad you're okay, podna, but you're sure one big pain in the ass. Don't get lost again."

So much for self-pity, I thought. I might as well enjoy it because I sure wasn't going to get any from my friends. And I appreciated that.

CHAPTER SEVENTY-THREE

Friday, November 7

We were clear of Jewfish by noon, and I didn't think I'd ever want to see the place again, maybe not even a glance from my boat going by. Given that I could see the place from my house, I'd just have to get over that.

Buddy Murphy, the young man Jock and J.D. found in the coquina hut had been looked over by the paramedics and taken to jail. It was a pretty good bet that he'd be there for a few years. I didn't think he'd be charged with kidnapping, but he did steal a boat and that would probably get him some prison time.

Jock was at the Longboat police station giving a statement. There was a lot he wouldn't tell them, but nobody was going to push too hard. Since Jewfish Key is part of the Town of Longboat Key, Chief Bill Lester was in charge of the investigation and he knew about Jock's ties to the intelligence community.

The ambulance had taken me to Blake Hospital and after more poking and prodding and a few needle sticks and a nose splint, J.D. drove me home. She hadn't said much since my rescue. "You want to talk about it?" I asked.

"Not yet. Let's get home and open a bottle of wine and talk this out. I was so afraid I'd lost you. And now, I'm just so happy that you're here. I want to hug you and I'm afraid I'll hurt you. It's like I've felt about brand-new babies my friends have had. They're so fragile, and yet, I wanted to hug them and squeeze them."

"Hey, sweetie. I'm not going to break. How do you feel about the man you blasted with the shotgun in the living room?"

"Not good. We need to talk about that, too."

"If it's any consolation, that guy was the worst of the two. He was a sadist and seemed to live to cause me agony." It wasn't true, of course, although Saif had done his share of the beatings, but sometimes you have to lie to the ones you love to spare them pain. I was pretty sure this was one of those times.

By the time we got back to my house, the police presence had cleared out. We'd stopped by Jose's for a couple of Cuban sandwiches and ate on the patio overlooking the bay. The weather was cool and the relative absence of humidity made for a pleasant day. I was hurting from all the punishment I'd taken, but felt nothing but relief that the danger we'd been facing for a week was over. I could actually feel myself slipping back into island mode. No worries. That was the island creed, and I had subscribed to it without reservation. It was time to get back to normal.

Jock called and said he was going to have lunch with Chief Lester and Deputy Chief Sharkey and would stop by later. He'd checked in with Dave Kendall who insisted that he take some time off before coming back to work. I asked if he wanted to stick around on Longboat for a time and he said we'd talk about it.

"How is this whole thing going to affect you, Matt?" J.D. asked, her voice tinged with concern.

"I don't know, but I think I'll be okay. I've had worse days."

"I can't believe anything can be worse that what you went through."

"Combat is worse. People shooting at you, mortar and artillery shells coming into your position, watching the teenaged soldiers who looked to me for leadership die before they'd really had time to live.

Getting a gut full of shrapnel and thinking I was about to check out. All that in a single day. That's worse than what I went through today. Today, I knew that you and Jock would come to the rescue, but if you didn't, I'd die and find out what's on the other side. I'd come to terms with that. In the minutes when I thought death was inevitable, I focused on you sitting on the beach at Egmont Key, looking at me, somehow silently letting me know that you loved me. That was the vision I wanted to go out with."

She hugged me, not tightly, but just enough to satisfy my need without adding more pain to my beat-up body. "I love you," she said, and held on some more.

She sat back and looked at me, her green eyes unwavering. It was like she was trying to memorize my face. It unsettled me. "Are you all right?" I asked.

"I don't know, Matt. This last week has changed me in ways that I don't think I like."

"How so?"

"I've always believed in the law, the procedures that hold it all together, the nobility of it. I grew up with a dad who was an honest cop, who taught me to live by a code that encompassed all those beliefs. This past week showed me a side of myself that I didn't know existed. I would have gladly killed Charlie Bates, gutted him with that big knife of his. Today, I used a shotgun to kill a man. I didn't give him a chance to surrender. He wasn't armed. He was just standing there by the sofa, probably trying to figure out what was going on. I hated his guts. He was one of the men holding you, threatening to kill you, and there was no question in my mind that he would have gladly cut off your head. And at that point, I hadn't even seen what they'd actually done to you. I killed the rat bastard in cold blood, and I don't even feel bad about it. Have I become one of them?"

"No, sweetie, you're still you. You were put into a position today that you could not have foreseen. It's different when your loved ones are in danger. You react differently. You weren't there today as a cop, you were there as a woman trying to save someone she loved, and not at all sure he wasn't already dead. You're human and you reacted like most every human being would have under the same circumstances."

"That's not quite true," she said. "I knew there were two men in that house with you. I had time to see that Saif wasn't armed. I knew that you were probably in the room where we found you. I killed Saif because I wanted to. I wanted the people who would take you away from me to die. And I made sure that happened."

"You did what had to be done," I said.

"Maybe," she said.

"You made sure that Saif would never harm another innocent person," I said. "Come here."

And she did, enfolding me in her arms and holding me as tight as she dared. There'd be more talking, more analyzing, more second thoughts, more hugging, and just plain old more living. I was satisfied with that. I was alive and wrapped in the arms of the woman I loved. Everything was going to be okay.

EPILOGUE

Saturday, December 20

The island fairly jingled with Christmas spirit, a unique joie de vivre that seemed to infect everybody. Visitors from the north basked in seventy-degree weather and took pictures to text back to their snowbound friends who spent the holidays in more frigid climes.

It was a nice counterpoint to the November week that began with Skeeter trying to kill J.D. and ended with my capture and rescue. That terrible week was a time of cognitive dissonance for us, a time when our little world went cockeyed, as if the earth was wobbling on its axis and creating a strange universe in which we could not find our place.

I had recovered from what J.D. insisted on calling my recent unpleasantness, but there were some lingering memories that showed up occasionally in my nightmares. The bad dreams were getting fewer and farther between, and I didn't think J.D. needed to know about them. Maybe I was just afraid of appearing a wimp in her eyes. After all, macho men should not be having nightmares about a few unpleasant hours spent in the presence of idiots, even murderous ones.

Jock was still with us, enjoying his time in the sun, but after New Year's Day he'd be going back to the agency and the wars he fought in the shadows. Dave Kendall had sent an agency psychologist down to spend some time with him, and it seemed to be working. The first two weeks were intensive, sessions every day, some lasting two or three hours. From then on, the shrink flew down once a week to meet with him and they talked regularly by phone. Slowly the old Jock, a man full of confidence and resolution and courage, began to emerge from the husk of himself that he had inhabited during those terrible late autumn days.

Dave Kendall and his wife Peggy had flown down to spend the holidays on Longboat Key and to bring us current with the end game, as he called it, the final chapter of our story. Jock, J.D., the Kendalls, and I were having lunch under the trees at Mar Vista, enjoying the warmth of the December day and the view of the boats cruising over the flat bay. I could see Jewfish Key from our table and it didn't bring on a shudder. Progress, I guess.

Dave was running through the *dramatis personae* that comprised the end of our sordid tale. None of the actors in the final scene ended up well, although their fates were deserved.

D. Wesley Gilbert had stared into his future and made the best deal he could under the circumstances. He pleaded guilty to aiding and abetting terrorism and was sentenced to fifteen years in a federal prison located in Coleman, Florida, about forty miles northwest of Orlando. It beat the hell out of a supermax lockup in Colorado. Given his age, it was a pretty sure bet that he'd never see freedom again.

Skeeter Evans was back at the Glades Correctional Unit serving a twenty-five year sentence for the attempted murder of a law enforcement officer. He thought that was a better result than a one-way trip to the middle of Lake Monroe.

Xavier Duhns was still in the Seminole County jail awaiting transport to a state prison, where he would spend the next five years. After having ascertained to his satisfaction that Xavier was plain stupid, the prosecutor had decided that the idiot had not intended for the car he stole to be used in the murder of a police officer.

Shaheed Mustafa, also known as Tariq Gajani, was interrogated at length and Jock's agency was able to roll up a growing conspiracy to blow up the Sun Life Stadium in Miami Gardens during the Orange Bowl game on New Year's Day. Shaheed and his friends disappeared into a supermax federal prison and will never be heard from again.

Buddy Murphy, the young man who stole the boat from Cannons Marina, pleaded no contest to the boat theft. Since he had no prior criminal record of any kind, the judge withheld adjudication, meaning that he would do no jail time, and if he satisfactorily completed three years of probation, he would have no felony record.

"In many ways," Dave said, "Wally Delmer was the most knowledgeable of those we interviewed. He was dying of cancer and told us everything he knew, including some things we didn't know enough about even to ask the questions."

"Was he the one who set up J.D. for the murder attempt?" I asked.

"Yes," Dave said. "Wally had taken on a lot of things that normally would have been controlled by Frank Thomason. He was in direct contact with his Arab masters and was being placed in a position to take over the entire operation in case of Thomason's death."

"I take it Thomason's death was fairly imminent," J.D. said.

"Very much so."

"And that didn't seem to bother Wally?" I asked. "Taking his friend out?"

"I don't think Wally even thought about it," Dave said. "He'd started out on the right path. He was a Ft. Lauderdale cop, but a corrupt cop, and some very bad mob guys sidetracked all his good intentions. I think those events stole his humanity. By his own admission, he killed with impunity, without compassion or remorse."

"What happened to him?" I asked.

"The cancer killed Wally three days after we picked him up, but he spent the entire time sucking up morphine for the pain and talking a blue streak. He told us all about Nazari and that was worth the cost of the morphine we provided."

Ibrahim Nazari, the man who ran Ishmael's Children, ordered his men in America back to Syria because he was afraid that after the disappearance of Thomason and Delmer, the CIA or FBI or somebody was closing in. Rahima, the Syrian-American butcher's daughter from Brooklyn who had lived for a time with Frank Thomason, had become one of Nazari's lovers and was living with him in his home, which Wally described as a small palace, in a quiet corner of Syria. Nazari was pretty sure that nobody in the American intelligence agencies knew much about him and were ignorant of the location of his house. He called his entire team to his home for a conference. They needed to regroup and reconstruct their American operations.

"Wally had visited Nazari a month before I sent Jock to Aleppo," Dave said. "He used a false passport and other IDs, so our intelligence agencies weren't aware that he'd left the country. He spent a week there and was briefed on the American operation. Nazari was preparing him to take over."

As it turned out, Rahima had been an unwilling participant in turning Thomason into a recalcitrant partner of Ishmael's Children. She did what she'd been hired to do, seduced the man and made him fall in love with her. Much to her surprise, she fell in love with Frank, and was shattered by the necessity of leaving him. She knew if she didn't, both she and Frank would be killed. So Rahima left America and moved into what she thought of as Nazari's harem. She could never go back to the United States or any other place in the world for that matter. If she left him, she would be hunted down and killed. Her death would be messy and painful.

While Wally was at Nazari's home, Rahima approached him and asked if there was any way to get her back to America when he took over the operation. She told him that she'd truly loved Thomason, but she wouldn't try to contact him if she returned. She just wanted to go home.

"Wally told us where Nazari lived and that Rahima wasn't happy and wanted to leave," Dave said. "We inserted an agent into the area and he contacted Rahima one day when she was in the market in the little village near Nazari's home. She was willing to help. She also told us about the upcoming conference with Nazari's top people."

Over the next few days, the agent determined the exact GPS coordinates for Nazari's house, and then arranged for Rahima to meet him in the market. He had a new passport for her and a new identity. He also had a Land Rover ready to leave the area. At the appointed time an American drone appeared and, using a laser-guided bomb, obliterated the Nazari home and all who were in it. The agent and Rahima left the area.

"Where is Rahima now?" J.D. asked.

"She's in a safe house giving us everything she knows about the Ishmael's Children's operation," Dave said. "We think we've got that bunch completely neutralized, but the information will help us with some of the others we're looking at."

"And Frank Thomason?" J.D. asked.

"Unfortunately," Dave said with a grin, "Frank completely disappeared from the face of the earth. I'm pretty sure he won't be seen again. There are consequences when one messes with one of my agents."

"Okay," Peggy Kendall said. "That's enough shop talk. How're you doing, Jock?"

Jock had sat quietly during our entire conversation, listening, but not engaging. Now he smiled. "I'm fine, Peggy. I know I was doing my job when I killed al Bashar, and it wasn't my fault that I was pointed at the wrong guy. I've come to terms with that. Still, those little boys are going to haunt me for the rest of my life. I'm not sorry I killed the men they became, but I'll never erase the mental image of them standing there pleading for me not to kill their father."

The conversation turned to more pleasant subjects and we finished our meal and climbed aboard my boat for a cruise on the bay. It was a salubrious day, a time of renewal, of putting horror and death behind us, of looking forward to the days to come when life would once again be good.

The world wobbled no more. It had settled on its axis and brought a measure of equanimity to our island, reaffirming our place on the sun-washed speck of land surrounded by a turquoise sea. My best friend, with a little help from the agency shrink, had restored himself and rejoined reality. The wondrous Jennifer Diane Duncan truly loved me and made my life bright with anticipation of the years that would define our lives. As that old lawyer David Parrish once said in his measured Georgia drawl, "It just don't get no better than this."